T5-COB-536

A MILLION WORDS AWAY
12 BOOKS VS. 1 BRAIN TUMOR ™

This book is a work of fiction. Names, characters, places, & incidents belong solely to the author's imagination &/or are employed fictitiously. Any resemblance to actual persons, living or dead, or in between; events; or locales is entirely coincidental.

Copyright 2020 by Ian Blake Newhem. A former incarnation of "Losers Weepers" appeared in *North Dakota Quarterly*, Winter/Spring 2005, Vol. 72 Nos. 1 & 2: 104. Print, under the name "Ian Blake Newman."

All rights reserved, including the right of reproduction in whole or in part, in any form. Published in the USA by A Million Words Away, a division of The Ghost of the Future, LLC.

AMillionWordsAway.com

TheGhostoftheFuture.com

This novel was created in 30 days for National Novel Writing Month (#nanowrimo). Please support that cool 501(c)(3).

Please purchase only authorized copies, & do not participate in electronic piracy of copyrighted material, which is punishable by law, & generally uncool.

Cover design and internal art © 2019 Norman T. Mallard.
Author photo © 2019 Dov Smile Photography.
Logo design © Rahul Panchal Studios.
Printed in the USA by Allura Printing, Costa Mesa, Calif.

Two Spirits

The Kittakwa Tales

Eight Novellas by

Ian Blake Newhem

For my mythic Ángel

& for Bernardo Atxaga

Contents

Altogether Elsewhere, Vast 1
  —Consider the myths— 30
  —Influencer Talbot— 34
The Twin Eater 41
  —With your dead white friend and all— 65
  — It's all fun & games until someone loses an I— 70
Ground Rules 75
  —Winter gives you a boner— 126
  —You just touched me— 129
Mission 133
  —Wrong— 165
  —... like the ditch at Wounded Knee, & the origin of Augie's middle name— 168
Can't Hold a Candle 173
  —Gimme 10 inches and make it hurt— 214
  —Said no one ever— 217
Losers Weepers 223
  —The missing letter— 247
  —We cowed him— 249
Looking Backward To Seeing You 253
  —A turd-eating grin— 299
  —Cultural appropriation— 306
Two Spirits 309
Author's Note: Who – and *Why* – are the Kittakwa? 345
Acknowledgments 347
  —Norman Mallard: A wee bit about the arteest— 349

While Anglos pronounce the tribe Kit-tAH'-kwah, the natives pronounce it Kit'-taw-kway

Altogether Elsewhere, Vast

Altogether Elsewhere, Vast

For Bart Weinberg

> *... they are marvelously stricken with love and friendliness and desire, and cannot be separated from one another for even a little time. These are the ones who spend their whole lives together ...*
>
> —Plato, *Symposium 189C-191D*, 370 BCE
> (translation by Will Roscoe 1995)

They came, they always came, with the promise of civilization. But civility was last on their lips, last on their list. They had come to the South and to the North for centuries, the Vikings and Spanish, Portuguese and English. They snatched up tens of thousands of natives for their trade. They hauled them off to Europe and the Caribbean. They chained them on their plantations even as they griped about their own lack of liberty under European overlords. It took them longer to come for the Kittakwa people. But come they did. And when they did, they'd honed their skills at coming, and hardened their hearts for a long while to the taking away.

They hunted the "Forest Kits" for sport. Slaughtered them to feed their dogs. Scooped them from the woods and from the river. Exploited them as servants of tea and ale, scrubbers of their underwear, and planters in their fields and gardens. And used them as purchase for their planting.

When they came, they took the maize, beans, and squash, the "Three Sisters," to make them fat and build the populations of their "Old World." In return, they left their daughter, Smallpox, for the Kittakwa and their cohorts, compliments of their fatherlands. Sometimes they left her accidentally. Other times they spread her on the blankets they handed out to the Indians as gifts. Then north and south and there in the middle of the Kittakwa territory, that dreadful daughter held the natives' hands. She dragged them by the millions to the underground.

Finally, they came for Akt'adia. The year of their Lord, 1777. She was barely eight, and would celebrate her first haircut soon. They planned to sell that hair. They meant to use every fiber of her. They intended her to be everything for them—yet she was nothing to them. It did not strike them that within this girl dwelt a soul just like the one that rode within themselves, that they so cherished. Even in their lapdogs over which they cooed. And fed goose liver. And memorialized in poetry after they died. They saw their dogs run in their sleep, watched their eyelids flutter. They said, "Look, he's dreaming."

But it never struck them that an Indian could dream. That a girl with that heart, that brain, those eyes, could dream at night of chimeras, horned rabbits, and a panoply of fantastical animals. They never considered whether she could, when that day came, feel any dumbfounding crush in her heart. Whether when she watched her brother's friend (drawing back an arrow with the forefinger of his pulling hand under his chin, the string touching his nose and lips, his long black hair blowing in the wind) she could swoon. It did not occur to them that although their ways were different, their way was just the same.

When they came for Akt'adia, her brother and his beautiful friend fought them. The boy who could trounce the girl's heart with a glance got his own heart trodden by an English boot. They mishandled her as they held her brother back. They killed his friend in front of them both. Three of them together with the butts of their rifles bashed his face into obscurity. They laughed at his eye popping out. These are the things that made their people laugh. Then they threw her down. They tossed her to the ground like leavings, like offal. Was she so worthless that they didn't even want her for a slave?

But they wanted her brother. She never saw Lix'eyo – "Streaking Comet" – again.

They took him south, a sack on his head the whole way. To one of their holdings on a river that looked the same as the Kittatinn River – which they rechristened the Christos Creek – but wasn't the same. It was warmer, wider, brown. They sent him to pick tobacco on that shore. But first they stripped him, chopped off his hair. They stood him naked in front of strangers, men, women, and kids. More people than he'd ever seen in his entire life, all white. People lifted up his scrotum, looked in his rear end, then put their fingers in his mouth. They were tabulating teeth. They slapped his stomach where his hawk totem had been branded. They squeezed the muscles of his calves and thighs. Then one of them bid on him. Paid for him. "Handsomely," the man was wont to remind his new property. They'd traded coin for his body and soul. He belonged to someone now. Astounding. The rusty shackle on his foot, ever chained to a post, helped him appreciate his new condition.

For a boy whose people had never seen a tobacco plant, they said, he proved industrious and strong. They said they were proud of him, and smiled when they saw him. Once they gave him bread and jam and let him rest on a river stone. He closed his eyes and thought of home, Akt'adia and the sword fighting with sticks. They said he was prospering there as he never would have with the savages from whom they had freed him. Ignoble lot. They called him Prosper. He had 11 years. But in his 12th, he and his master did not see eye to eye on a certain matter. Said master set overseers against him. They ensured he would never talk back again.

Soon after, in the night, he escaped with another captive, an African who had not yet picked up even slave patois. They had to take a life – an overseer – to steal the key to their manacles. While crossing a marsh on their way back north, an animal that neither of them recognized mauled Prosper's friend to death. It was sleek and black and growly, and might have been a panther. *Better an African should die by wild beast than a white man's whip*, he thought. He removed his friend's heart with a stolen knife. He tried to take a big bite as he'd seen the warriors do, but the heart was too tough for his 12-year-old teeth. He set it down for the animals – he couldn't risk a fire – and moved on. He stuck to the timberland, drank from its rivers, hunted its game. Like that black panther, he traveled at night.

Months like that passed. He overshot the Kittakwa claim by a few weeks' walk, attempting to skirt some American encampments. And he couldn't double back, as the British had advanced into the land now south of him. So he passed into that country over the border to the north. He thought that there, at least, he'd be free. He was, and then again, he wasn't.

For a long time he hid in the forest and caves and holes and empty barns, yearning for the sanctuary of Shelter Rock, the sacred boulder at the center of Kit land and lore. He watched and learned as best he could. He ate little and grew lean. He never made a sound. And then the winter came.

He'd taken up on a deserted deer blind outside Drumhill, a little village north of the border. The ladder up to the planks had long ago rotted. From there, for weeks, he watched the boy called Declan – "Laddie Declan" – a bonesetter's grandson. When the lad set off with his granpa to do some healing, Prosper followed, out of sight. Laddie Declan traipsed through the chest-high snowdrifts of Drumhill. He usually lugged books strapped on his back, else his granpa's healing tools. Prosper spied him one day on the homestead of McGregor King, a bootlegger who'd lately cracked his clavicle sailing backwards off his horse outrunning a constable. And he knew that something of his purpose lay there, with that boy, Laddie Declan. Forces had conspired to lead him exactly there, exactly then. They hardly mirrored each other in aspect, ancestry, or attitude, but somehow he knew that boy was his twin.

He watched Laddie find his granpa, Ridley "Fix" Glover, up to his elbows in the washtub outside with a moaning patient, King. The bootlegger's bloody shoulder jutted from the steam. It looked just like a chunk of ice after someone cut salmon on it. Fix wrestled the bones while intoning a queer incantation.

Fix Glover was blind as a mole, so Prosper could sneak up increasingly close. Laddie Declan had long before espied the boy, and smiled in his direction. So far, the elder seemed none the wiser.

Maybe he'd lost his sense of smell, too, in the same blunderbuss misblast in the Seven Years' War that took his sight—or so it was said.

They fed McGregor King whiskey, but the patient couldn't catch his breath for the pain. So Fix offered Laddie a dram to stave off the chill, with a *don't-tell-your-grandmother* look. Then they carried King, passed out, naked, to some blankets bundled by the outside fire, as if he were a bitch whose water had broken. Fix assembled a thumb and finger on either side of the man's Adam's apple, and said, like a mother, "You hush," to cease the writhing. Then he took his grandson's hand, spreading Laddie's fingers over King's breastbone. He held the hand down with his own in the steam. "That tickles," said King, half-conscious with his pain and drink.

"Tickles me, too," said Laddie, smiling all the while at Prosper, who'd crept up now to within pissing distance, and hid behind a snowbank.

"Aha. So you feel it?" said Fix. "Now shut your eyes, Laddie. Listen." All four of them attended. The heart. It must have spoken because the boy translated: The heart, it shouted, "Let me fly out of this cage."

"Not yet," said Fix.

Laddie Declan shot his granpa a grave look, and sucked his teeth. Because he could see how King would die. In the imminent. He saw it as clearly as he could see his own cock. Laddie assumed Prosper didn't know yet what he saw—not specifically. But on their way home, the grandfather would interpret for his grandson (and Prosper following behind) the images that had popped up and rolled through the boy's open mind. Yes, he had the power to see a person's impending death. Yes, it was a family trait. "No, it ain't at all a blessing, but it pays the rent," said Fix.

"Does he know he's ganna die?"

"Only we do. And Him above. Thereabout eleven months I figure," Fix told Laddie, as they struggled through the snow toward home before their Sabbath started.

"Seven," Declan said, correcting him. "Seven months. McGregor King's ganna leave us then."

Two Spirits

Bonesetting school in the afternoon. Laddie Declan let Prosper in the way you'd allow a stray dog to warm his hide by the fire. Only he mustn't make a peep, mustn't move a muscle, lest Fix get wise and boot him out. No problem on the not making a sound front. Prosper hadn't spoken in five months.

So both boys benefitted from Fix's lessons. Sinew separates from bone with a rip-crack that sounds like his grandparents' wedding quilt, said Declan. As on that grim day when his Nana tore it off its dowel, and damned her husband for taking a jam jar from some young woman's "bankrupt bed." He made Laddie Declan, with a blindfold and bare hands, bury its pink passenger beneath the arbor. Later, Nana dragged them both to the gravesite to pray. She made the sign of the cross for the youth that would never be, the husband, the father. During their subsequent exile to the "Heathen Landing" (the back barn and its abattoir), Laddie Declan brought his granpa strong tea and honey scones, purloined from Nana's racks. Nana said, "For every babe you bury in a cave before its natural time, you're ganna pay the piper twice over."

There in the abattoir Laddie Declan (and the silent but attentive Prosper) studied the secrets of the bonesetter's trade. Laddie Declan learned with his hands the anatomy of a living hog: the atlas bone, the ulna, the tarsus of the hock—and then a dead hog. Everything inside, all strung together, every bit. Inquiring hands. Hungry hands. And every minute movement Laddie Declan's hands made, Prosper, close behind, a shadow, mimicked. When circumstances called for close-up work, Laddie Declan performed the maneuvers in the air, so Prosper could follow. If Granpa Fix caught a whiff, put his finger to his lips and cocked his head, Prosper dropped like a spider until Fix said, "Never mind—sometimes the old ones linger and visit. Sometimes those hundred-and-thirty boys and girls of Hamelin come out and dance." Then he moved on to the next lesson.

There in the abattoir Laddie Declan reckoned the magic of his hands. His granpa's granpa had christened it, "the *Puissance*"—the power. It had passed down from the procession of his pedigree back in the Grampian highlands of Scotland. Somehow that faculty had hightailed it out of the sheepfolds there. It sailed over a million mutinous whitecaps, and all across those Indian lands like a falcon starved. It finally found wee Laddie Declan Glover, and it touched him. But how – and more importantly, why – had it clasped the Glover men as it had those Great Physicians of history? Those healers who'd embraced a thousand mostly ungrateful lepers, and mended them all on a hundred good, red roads like that one by Galilee? "Ours ain't to wonder why. Ours is to mend the men, and hie."

"What the Glovers ever done to deserve the *Puissance*, Granpa? Was it the same curse that took your eyes with that gun?"

"What we done? What ain't we done? I figure now we're making up for at least eleven generations of skullduggery."

At the follow-up examination, on which date Fix had been firm, Laddie Declan's hands told him McGregor King would live through spring. Three months or four now, but with a limp and his left arm still slung. He should get his affairs in order. Before infection conquered his province. King would afterward insist the whisper of the kid's first handprint on his ribs remained there still. Prosper had heard him tell anyone who would listen. That space still crackling like the barley after lightning. The boy's hand that seemed the only thing keeping the man's heart in its net now like a twitchy salmon. Or a monarch moth enfolding a chestnut as you sometimes see in summer. A hand to hold as King limped in June across the Veil. Early July, the latest.

Neither would the bison on the plain survive. Meaning no meat for the Glover clan. No one could stem the herd's oozing sores, nor keep the scraggiest standing upright. The sickest of them fell into a madness. They raged, and savaged each other, mounted children, gnawed off the heads of their young. Nana said it was a sign. It was written, this thing, and everyone should settle their accounts before buying their ticket to enter the Veil.

Prosper knew not what these whites were going on about—but it set his heart to thumping nonetheless. Especially what they said about the nearby Indian tribe. The Yellowfoot clan wouldn't live through another Starvation Winter, they said. When their deputation came to the Glover cabin to commiserate with Fix, sick with the pox. They came to behold Laddie Declan, too, as they knew he was heir apparent to the Glover *Puissance*. And to show their amulets of timber wolves and Cooper's hawks nesting in hickory sticks. They came, as well, to trade decoctions with the blind old goat one last time. They even asked about the Indian boy who hid in the woods. Fix frightened them by saying that was only Laddie's shadow, long out ranging, looking for its master.

They were right, Nana and the Yellowfoot medicine men. There was something in the air. Whatever the old man said, some of the Drumhill townsfolk had actually seen that devil himself in the woods outside the village. Else it was the person of an itinerate Indian, a stalking horse for the devil if ever there was one. Prosper could hear them whispering everywhere.

When he passed his granpa Fix rocking an ankle one afternoon late June, Laddie Declan grabbed it. And the curtain between the two worlds opened up before the boy. He saw a great and terrible monster crouched in burning sulfur, roaring and licking its chops as it unfurled its wings. And he knew: *A month*. Why must he go there, his granpa, so good a man? Why must he of all people descend?

"Oh, Aye," said Fix with a lick of his lips. "My Laddie." He coughed. "Come here, Boyo. You're too good at this. Don't tell your Nana what you seen across the Veil. If you're ganna know, you ought hear from me. It was a whore. In Glasgow. I didn't mean to do it. I think I even loved her. So lovely, she was. Her name was Rosemarie. This is how I think I lost my eyes. No blunderbuss. No gun. But shot through by Rosemarie."

Prosper, sitting under a window outside, knew he meant from syphilis. But Laddie Declan was thinking it an omen.

Two and a half months passed. McGregor King passed, right on schedule. And long after Reverend wound down the hill from Umber Grove that August, Laddie Declan still knelt in the graveyard. He pressed his handprint in the soil, turned it. "The once and future

King," he said. Meantime, Prosper sat with his back against a nearby tombstone, then disappeared. Into the hills? Where did he go?

Later, Laddie Declan squatted in a tadpole maw of the Yellow Deer Kill. Below the snow-capped backbone of the Earth the Yellowfoot claimed the Devil Whites would snap sometime with their wickedness. Soon. He was alone. But not alone. He knew that Prosper, lurking still in those caves above the house, was watching him, tirelessly, subsisting on some bounty of nature. Prosper, too, knew Laddie Declan's heart, though nary a word had passed between them. Laddie didn't know yet that the boy was called Prosper, no less Lix'eyo, his Kittakwa name. But he had come to know the boy. To trust him.

Soon his granpa, too, came to rest in the Grove, fell into the presence of those burning wings. That was terrible. Too soon. Declan wondered at night whether Ridley Glover's commiserating with Rosemarie down there would constitute adultery.

Declan, no longer Laddie, had become the Drumhill bonesetter now. Declan held the skulls and sacra, listened with his hands that were susceptible as swallowtail wings. He felt every vibration, an energy that flowed inside a living body like so many rivers surging from a single source. How fast they coursed, how blocked where the beavers of disease and infirmity dammed the way. And with his hands, he could manipulate that charge. And heal the ailments of the body, mind, and soul. Sometimes. But all the while the *Puissance* showed him where that energy would stream once the body passed away. Into what abysmal gorge the soul would seep, or through what aperture in the clouds it would uprush in a flash and sizzle. He saw it all. He didn't always wish to see it.

Prosper had taken up with the Yellowfoot by then. They didn't seem to regard him as a threat after all. At least not more than the whites. And he spoke English like the English – well, didn't speak, *per se*, but wrote and read it and translated after a manner – which they figured might come in handy in their trading. They crossed the Yellow Deer with beaver meat and a cache of pelts to where the Drumhill whites resided. Too, they carried bundles of salmonberry, which their people called *quamash*. A young squaw holding hands with Prosper smiled at the white lad, who could tell his face was deadly serious. Declan raised the hand, which heard from somewhere close at hand, yet far beyond, where all of them were headed. And when. "Heard." *Detected* from some indescribable, electrical pulsation over the Veil was more like it. Their agony. The weariness in their arms and legs. The months for some. The weeks.

But he could not foretell the future of the red boy he didn't yet know had come from down America-ways. The Kit boy who had been spying. The shadow he'd let stay in the corners of the Heathen Landing's abattoir to learn the Glover trade in secret. Declan couldn't see this boy's end. Of that end, he saw only bits and pieces, each hurled away before he could mark it, from a swirling center that could not hold. His past was like a cauldron with a baby in it, boiling.

Mid-autumn, Declan healed a prominent personage's horse. When he touched its shivering withers, he heard its mother whinny from the other world. The grandee paid well for the privilege of the *Puissance*, enough to get Declan through another winter. In an aspen grove alone that October, he lay on a blanket of needles and leaves. He placed his palm on his heart, his lungs, his liver, in order to listen. His loins.

In late November, he found himself dispatched to the farm of a deacon, Elder Daniel Robinette. Elder had severed his little toe with a scythe. And there he met for the first time, properly, the one they called Prosper. He was an escaped slave, they told. He'd fled from some tobacco parish in the scrotum of the American South. "I've heard of the kid," he said. "Seen him, too. Well. He seen me." They nodded to each other.

Reverend called him "a saber, a perilous one toward the sinners of Britain. A Formidable Nigger Indian of Yahweh come at last to cleanse our sanctuary. Verily."

As his Granpa Fix had, Declan found Reverend comical, a jester. The boy was well read – much better than most – yet still had no idea what Reverend was ever on about.

As the deacon Elder's daughters peeped on from beyond a door – twin specters with hollow eyes – Prosper laid hands and took away the man's pain. And Elder declared him a nigger witch for it. What was a nigger? Anything that didn't look as though he ought to be sympathizing with a Scots sheep? Or just someone – some *thing* – you simply couldn't let slip by without insulting it—something like a cockroach, hornet, or a trickster fox?

On the way back over the ice, Reverend said, "Thank ye, Boys. Elder has apparently lost his manners along with his daughters' vigor. And forgotten the utility of men in attendance to do a man's work. His nephew Christian had abided with him, but the boy was sent away once the girls were old enough to … Well, when they got old enough. *Christian*—Never a less apt appellation for a lad."

Reverend always preached a Great Doom would end the settlers in the Canadian dominion. Brimstone, inferno, and all the attendant fright of both Testaments. "Verily." Maybe it was true what Nana, destined one of the December dead, had said. That the armies of the apocalypse had arrived already, amassing in North America for the final battle on Earth, the Armageddon. Deploying north already. The Americans would retreat up here to lick their wounds from seven years of beatings, and meantime rape the lasses. The British had already come to take back what they felt was theirs, which was all of it. The French—well everyone knew what the French were capable of. His Granpa Fix had been in the habit of recalling this, mysteriously, apparently ever since he fought in the North American theater of the worldwide Seven Years' War, during the time Drumhill was still considered part of New France. The Germans, too, and the other metropole nations. And then the Indians. Everyone would arrive, all intending to settle old scores.

"Then many an imperfect one of us shall decamp downward," Reverend insisted. But the bonesetter boys must never stoop to heal their burns—not those burns. Ever. Some should burn, to learn, for an eternity.

Declan understood that whole scenario could not be true. A Father in the sky who would torture his own children everlastingly?

Two Spirits

To what end? "Laddie, if it don't make immediate sense to the senses, ain't no sense forthcoming," Fix used to say.

Now the boys worked as a team. Prosper walked down the pass behind Declan in homemade shoes. He was mute. Some do-goods down south somewhere had lopped out his tongue and fed it to a bluetick hound. It was all Declan could do to keep his fingers out of that Indian's mouth. Maybe his healing hands could actuate a voice again inside the slave. For him to tell of his people, his sister, his birthright as a future Great Warrior of the Kittakwa clan. Whose people, all counted, numbered six times the population of wee Drumhill.

Reverend, well behind, said something about how children ought to suffer, verily. And Declan looked behind at Prosper. Both of them smirked. One step through the terraced meadow seemed to require a season of effort, like trying to push through hip-high honey. The next dozen steps whipped squirrel-fast as though their limbs were spindly and paper-light. It was like a dream after eating the Yellowfoot bark. It was always like this when he journeyed with Prosper. He, too, worked his own kind of *Puissance*. And it thrilled and terrified Declan what they might accomplish now they'd combined their forces. But it didn't thrill any Drumhillian. It made them narrow their eyes and slink back when they passed.

They passed beneath a canopy of bowed spruce and birch. Prosper brushed Declan's back with his finger tips, to stall him when an adder crossed their path ahead. But as the white boy turned around to mouth a *thank-you*, he found the silent nigger Indian a long way behind. Too far to have touched him with any appendage attached to his material body.

Then Nana died on Christmas Eve. And in Umber Grove again, the former Laddie Declan, now the man of an empty house, knew that Prosper must come live with him instead of outside in the snow caves. Or with the Yellowfoot, who, if truth be told, treated him from the beginning like an underling. So – verily – Prosper would no longer have to live in anyone's shadow.

"'*One in five children died by fire,*'" Declan read, "'*between Athenian times and ours.*'" Prosper stretched himself by the hearth. It reminded him of his family, of Akt'adia toasting corn cobs there, their father holding the stick for her so she wouldn't burn herself. "Imagine all them skulls stacked like some kinda puzzle to the past, uncovered by antiquarians with horsehair brushes and whatnot. But I don't believe it," Declan declared, slamming his granpa's book shut. "It's just a terror tale to remind us to put out the light."

But Prosper nodded, all the way low so his chin hit his chest, and then high, like a horse annoyed. His hair, like all the boys' in the village, had been shorn against the lice that were annexing Drumhill. He tapped the chalk slate hanging from his neck. Declan had procured it on a run for salt and sugar.

He clicked his lips.

THAT TRUE

he wrote, and rapped again, and underlined. Two times.

Was it Reverend who'd taught him his alphabet, or his master prior? They had all taught him a great many useful things. And now, said some of the townsfolk of Drumhill, he's a very clever nigger Indian, ain't he? And what the hell good ever came of that?

Prosper knew lots of old Indian lore, which tonight required a titillating hour after midnight for him to recount on the tiny chalk board. He wrote in block letters with broken chalk. Every night there was a new tale, a fresh fib for Declan to think on. This one concerned seven young Kittakwa little chiefs, in charge of the outposts of their people.

They were fleeing a presumably excruciating death at the teeth of the people's Great Stone Foe. If he ate your heart, he would grow stronger by degrees. And he'd continue to consume the hearts of the Kits until his own heartbeat was so overwhelming that the Father fist shook and loosed the Mother stone from his grip. And all the people slipped off the world as it rolled into oblivion.

"But why?"

Because he didn't take kindly to all the noise of enterprise, of love, of warring with the other tribes. Of the pride of humanity, to put the Bard's spin on things. He was a jealous enemy. So when all those sounds of life echoed up to his crag, he writhed and moaned and suffered on that mountain. He had to stuff boulders in his ears so he didn't have to hear them below. But he still heard them.

Grt. Ston Fo loves me

The tiniest chirp of delight from the serenest babe could crack a stone in the Great Foe's ear a year after it ushers out the mouth of the child.

"Why?"

Because he had once been one of the people.

Human Born

And though he'd been transformed into this mountain monster, deep within him still beat the heart of a man. If he could only focus on his one, original heartbeat, he could increase its reverberation, just the right resonance to shatter the rocky crust and release the man he once was, the man trapped. Painful, yes, painful. But—

"But then he would feel more than only pain again?"

Prosper nodded.

As he scrawled the story on the slate, the side of his hand went white from erasing between each sentence. He also pantomimed some parts. His shirt was drying on Nana's rack. Declan's heart set to beating fast as he watched the muscles dance on the red-skinned chest, brow up and neck tendons tensing. On Prosper's abdomen, the falcon in flight, its black eye corresponding with the boy's navel. On his back, a hundred scars christcrossed like the currents of sand at the bottom of the mouth of the Yellow Deer Kill. The sight of those marrings occasioned a gurgle in Declan's bowels. Every time.

They were residing together in the Glover cabin, weren't they? Like man and wife? Not quite. Because who'd be man? Who, wife? Surely they were both en route to manhood, and neither toward any kind of wifedom. Or?

… So these seven little chiefs and the Great Warrior at the Kittakwa home camp made their hearts so big that the Great Stone Enemy could never gobble them. If he tried, he would choke and have to spit them out. With just a narrow little fissure for a mouth, like the opening of an animal warren—

"How they ganna make their hearts so big?"

Good question. Two ways.

FIRST—LOV

"Love?"

Yes, by loving as much as they could, and as many people as they could. By caring so much about the people that their own needs became but secondary. And feeling big feelings that might have scared off a lesser people. Heartache and sorrow, regret and great gladness. Fellow-feeling for the whole clan.

"Empathy."

& 2ᴺᴰ … BY EATING EACH OTHER'S 🖤

"You mean—?"

Sure. The white people call it cannibalism. But just the heart. Just a bite and a shot of blood. That's all you need to take another being's heart into your own, and enlarge it. Of course you wait—you don't hasten the other person's death just to eat his heart. Unless you're already at war with—let's not worry about all the rules.

He didn't remember exactly anyway.

Oh, and you burn the rest of the heart once you're done with it, else you leave it for the animals if no fire can be made.

Two Spirits

It must have been a terrible burden to walk around with hearts so large, Declan thought, hearts the little chiefs had to carry for all of us.

As Prosper slept that night, Declan flipped through one of his granpa's favorite medical books. The North American Indian race. The high brow and wide nose. The long bone of the shin. The "lazy way it all hung," Fix would have said, and that'd be about right. But when Declan explored the sleeping boy's face, he saw no sign of the *"prognathous jaw of the ape-like Man"* depicted in *The Forms of Human Intellect by the Races as Evinced in the Anatomy & Physiology of the Cranium* by Gardner Ward. Fix had sworn by that tome, dog-eared and worn out over the decades. Declan read the first sentence under the diagram of the savage's head—and threw the book into the fire.

He brushed the boy's red belly with the back of his hand, back and forth. "I must get the comb," he said, and Prosper scratched, opened one eye, stretched, and yawned exaggeratedly. The stump of his tongue an unpleasant sight, so Declan looked away. "I see you're toting some wee companions still, my brother."

And so they slept for several months of winter.

When they emerged, Drumhill had turned green and leafy. No Great Stone Foe had descended from the wooded pass to eat their hearts, as prophesied in Prosper's tale.

In April, they were summoned again to the Robinette farm, a gloomy backwater a mile outside of Cunny's Gulch. Elder Robinette, he of the nine toes, met them at the dilapidated, rabbit-addled gate. His twin daughters had succumbed to the pox, he said, matter of fact. But his wife could not wrap her head around the fact. He'd left the bodies in the barn.

"Your lasses find themselves alive in the Higher Mind," Declan said later, as he meted out the Sleep to Elder, one tablet at a time.

His wife wouldn't take the Sleep. She said she'd stay awake forever now. She shaped dough. She nodded. She rocked. She smiled like an idiot child. "We look forward to the coming rebirth," she said, crust at the corners of her mouth. And she said it again, or variations on that theme.

"She means the Resurrection," Elder slurred.

"Oh, Aye."

But it didn't sound to either boy like she believed it.

The Robinettes kept the girls' cousin, Christian, from the wake room, despite his pleas and weeping.

The lads plodded over a greening plain on Messenger, his one half-bitten ear twitching at the horseflies. Prosper's grip slackened around Declan's waist, and a wet cheek pressed his shoulder. The whiter latter knew the redder former had fallen asleep behind him in the saddle. On a rope behind them, Messenger's mother, Old Volunteer, huffed and lumbered. She lugged the Robinette twins pitched over the curve of her back, tied up in sacks. She looked in Declan's eyes with one glaucous eye when he turned around to check on her and Prosper. "Do you prosper back there, Brother? Or are you expired?"

Yes, and no. Then the bonesetter boy, the new Man Declan Glover, closed his eyes to find the horses' harmony. Clop and rock, a head and rump, and the Kit boy's breathing. Just like the rhythm of the daughterless mother's kneading.

The nags moved them on toward the Heathen Landing.

Back at the Glover manse, Reverend stood under a water-gall from the gutters he feared "prophetic for its imperfection. Verily." Prosper chalked a question mark on his board and flashed it at Declan. Declan shrugged his shoulders, shook his head.

Reverend trudged inside with a bucket of oats in one hand, and in the other a jar of elderberry jam tied with lemon yellow ribbon. The oats he proudly worked with his own hands, he said. Hands too delicate for the blast in the vast chasm, he worried. Verily. And the jam, his wife, Amy, had crushed in her claws between a cheesecloth of silk she'd inherited from her mother. She'd refused to let Declan or the "Devil's Savage Hammer" manipulate her knuckles and knots. "These are for shaking when I wake," she said. All that Resurrection twaddle again—or was it? Would Granpa Ridley Glover, "Fix," come back again, this time all his imperfections fixed?

Would the twins return with or without the buboes on their groins? The starving scarecrow skin? The bleeding eyes?" Would Granpa Fix re-entertain his eyes?

The boys plied Reverend with biscuits and ripe Glover Cheddar, which made him smack his lips not unlike Prosper's main means of "verbal" communication.

They could tell Reverend wanted to remain with them. He kept finding buttons that needed a mend. He stroked their worn pajamas on the line, looking for frayed seams to bring back to Amy. "She needs the plain work. Aye." And he kept eyeing the Glover marriage bed, but found no blanket on the floor, no civil cot for the savage. He muttered and rubbed the stubble on his underchin. "Those busybodies under Elder's spell across the prairies would intervene here. Verily. Especially now he has no children of his own to rear."

Prosper looked at Declan.

Then Reverend stood from the table and paced, creaking over floor boards. He gazed out the window. "Do you know when It will come, lads? How soon will It come for us? For me? They say—I've heard you may know. Verily."

A spider climbed over Reverend's left hand from the windowsill. He snuffed out its life with the right. The boys didn't answer him. Then he crossed and peered at a tiny, faded watercolor of Fix and Nana Glover when they were young. "Somewhere in the hill country? Yes? Before infection took her eye – one eye for the two of them – and all her kindness."

Before or after Rosemarie, the whore of Glasgow?

"Your granma was of the … other persuasion? A Papist?"

"Aye, Sir. Roman Catholic, I'm afraid."

He nodded, eyes narrowed, as if Declan had just publicly declared his grandmother a vampire.

"Mind if I perambulate some?" The boys studied his ramble through the cabin. He tinkled the instruments of the Glover art, hung on hooks: The forceps, catheters, and saws. He stopped to examine the long, slender, rusty rectal probang that swung whenever the door closed or opened.

Then Reverend sat back at the head of the table. He pressed his thumb on some syrup, and licked it off. "We cannot ignore the unsympathetic stuff Elder's preaching about you two. 'You separate the sheep from the God damned goats,' he insists. And like that."

"Aye. We heard him."

"Well, mark that Elder well, Laddie. Man. After all. And my Sanguine Saber of Yahweh. He's dangerous like a—"

"We been to see him. His Missus called us. Ganna go again. He's under."

"Under."

"Fever and ague, yes."

"Shame, it is. A worthy servant in the day. Verily."

Prosper scratched onto the board:

& FOR A TRAD?

"Why, my Scarlet Anvil of Jehovah, that man was a horseknocker. Best of the best. He trained your granpa, Laddie, in yonder abattoir out back."

Prosper took Declan's hand in front of Reverend, which Declan knew was custom for the Kits. He doubted Reverend knew this, and yet he didn't care. Prosper rubbed the tops of Declan's fingers with his thumb as he had his friend's back home. It pained him to remember Rhash'eyo, the boy who'd died protecting his sister. *Oh, Akt'adia!* He could barely stand to think of what must have become of her.

Outside Messenger neighed.

Behind the house in the Heathen Landing where Fix had set up his dead house far from Nana's sense of smell, Declan plied his Granpa's trade. It was situated a distance from all the prying eyes, especially on Sabbath. Hunched over the crude examining table, he dissected two pairs of browning kidneys, compliments of the Robinette twins. Prosper laid hands on *materia medica*, one tied bundle at a time. The bonesetter, feverfew, and stinging nettle hung on drying hooks. Many and various vessels and crocks of all manner of as-yet undiscovered natural abundance. Prosper kicked through heaps of sawdust sopping blood from the floor beams. He raised the trapdoor on the barn cellar. Down below a wide vat of old spirit of boxwood entertained those daughters of Elder, along with a bighorn sheep, lately to his sleep.

Tomorrow a doctor from the Company would come up from London Town to fetch them. He'd give Declan his 11 shillings—five, five, and one for the sheep. His idea was to confer on Prosper all that money and then some. And enough supplies to take the Yellowfoot squaw down south back to his land, his people. Where maybe things would make more sense—at least to him. She'd never survive another winter across the kill with the remnants of the Yellowfoot tribe. A murder had already orphaned her. The culprit was a surly 24-year-old, Christian Robinette, the oldest son of Elder's brother. He claimed vengeance for his father, killed randomly by a Frenchman expelled from Acadia by the British governor in the run up to the Seven-Year troubles, and tormented as an exile in Drumhill since he was a pup. Robinette ravished her repeatedly on the steeple stairs, then passed her body off to some choirboys. As blood feuds go, that ended it.

Back in New York, Prosper could rule his clan with the biggest heart of all of them. With his new queen, he could keep that Great Stone Foe's fangs off his people. Maybe the Yellowfoot and the Kittakwa could join to become one giant tribe. It's not that he fancied the idea of Prosper shifting out of his compass. In fact, the thought of losing him shriveled his organ meat. It was just the right thing to do. As his granpa would say, "When you know there is a right thing, and you ken that right thing, you ganna have to do it. Or else."

But Elder Robinette was suffering some sores on his behind. And he'd grinded his teeth to nubs since his measly daughters went off through the Veil on Old Volunteer's back. So the boys were called again. The boys were always called. Even by their detractors. Because months before, Drumhill's only proper physician had begun to practice in an office well beyond the Veil, compliments of the pox.

Declan took the rear. Elder allowed Prosper access to the jaw, non-prognathous. Elder even, albeit reluctantly, thanked the kid. But he looked sidelong at the squaw the whole time. And she looked likewise back—he looked just like an older version of his nephew, who'd dishonored her.

Afterward, Elder invited the bonesetter boys and the Indian girl to the river. His horse twice ventured on a donkey-mount, and everyone laughed but he. He led his little flock to a sliver of killshore, and Reverend limped behind. He couldn't go into the water for suppurating sores on his feet, "as though I've already walked the coals," he said.

The whole of the Yellow Deer Kill was cold—it was only April. The churning eddy under a canopy of lupine and tamarac disgorged a frozen juvenile thrice a year. They called it "the Plunge," "which pool endows," preached Reverend, reverentially from shore, "first through the instruments of generation, an Athabaskan cold." That meant it shrunk up your ballocks. "Verily."

The Glover bookcases, which included two thick volumes of Mr. Shakespeare, were arguably the most extensive in the Drumhill environs. Yet Declan seldom gleaned Reverend's meaning. Verily.

The scrotum-shriveling Plunge is where Elder chose to hold the urchin Yellowfoot squaw underwater with both his hands. And where Prosper snatched for his black board, and Declan tried to stay his hand. "Nobody sings for the dip anymore," Elder yelled above her thrashing, "and God Damn they should. Sing us a bloody barbarian tune."

PUL HER OUT

Prosper pointed, tapped, tapped, as the ice water agitated over the squaw.

Two Spirits

Still Elder kept the girl down under, flailing. So Prosper hiked into the river, tossed. He jerked her from the cleric's grip. She gasped like a walleye, and he held her to his breast. "I said go ahead and *sing*, you Nigger MacCrimmon Indian! Go drum a calfskin fiddle and fucking sing!"

From whence does such a sudden fury spring? That old grudge begot by French and British colonists ought to have died when no brother of the squaw came forward to relieve a Robinette of his tonsure after they left her bleeding at the steps of the steeple, as her future husband should have done.

Prosper leaned low while still holding her, then stood and conversed with Elder—by flinging a wad of mud that slapped the man dead in his aforementioned jaw.

And the three of them ran. Declan yelled between quick breaths, "Go back. Back down to your people in New York. Find out if your sister lives. Go, take the girl, before the British land up here again and ganna—before it's all gone. Go."

Then Elder yelled, "Why do my daughters rot, and this nigger Indian lives to sing or not to sing?" Upon which, he collapsed to his knees in the water, wiped the sludge from his visage. And whimpered into both hands.

"Run, Prosper. Keep up, Girl."

Run before he rounds up enough of his coterie to build that Great Foe of yours out of crosses and the stony hearts of brethren. Run.

But you can't run from this.

Declan returned to the cabin alone. Once, he felt that ghostly whisper of a hand on the middle of his back, and turned, and found no body there. The second time he felt it, he didn't bother turning. He just said hallo. He shut his eyes and filled his heart. Then he realized he ought to reach out in the same manner to Prosper. He did just that. Sure enough, he sensed the boy right in front of him, felt the heat coming off his skin. When he opened his eyes, yes, Prosper was there—a kind of Prosper, shimmering crimson ghost.

A few moons later, mid-June. Lonely without his shadow for company. Declan went to see about a sprained neck. On the way back, he found Reverend sitting on a stone above the Plunge. He wept. He was Weeping itself. He was Lear on a wet stone promontory over the Yellow Deer Kill. His hands and shirt were covered in blood. "They got him," Reverend sniveled. "Christian's armed band captured them up in yonder caves. They cut the squaw's ear off. They did worse to our Anvil. Oh, I can't say it, Laddie. Here …"

Declan held Prosper's hand.

For he to-day that sheds his blood with me
Shall be my brother …

He underwent a fragmentary flash he hadn't ever felt when that hand had been fed by the boy's blood course. Not that other world beyond the Veil. This world, but the worst of it. America. The past:

Before he'd come up over the border, Prosper had been whipped. By a plantation overseer with a cypress switch, and another man, the overseer's lackey, with long leather straps. His sin? Tearing tobacco leaves before they'd dried. Hence that map of America lashed on his back.

Reverend had discovered the red hand – the right one – in an ash grove, green, he said. The Robinette men had orphaned it and every other part from the host. Declan kissed it above the clotted arteries, the carpals snapped and dangling. He placed it face up in the grass on the west side of the kill. He remembered the Kit custom Prosper had explained. When a warrior dies a dishonorable death, such as when he's netted by an enemy and misused, he must be returned to the Great Mother in a certain configuration. Prosper had drawn it on his black board.

So a long way away, a long walk from Reverend, he marked the parallel and equidistant point on the left bank. There, he rested the left hand, palm up, on soil in a glade. He interleaved his fingers in the stiffened digits momentarily. He hoped he'd been a friend still worthy of sharing that custom. Nearby, a toad first croaked, then hopped, and that seemed right. There can be a cataclysm, and the toads croak on.

Nothing could be more disrespectful to a Kittakwa Indian than enemy dismemberment. Declan would set it right.

Down south when he was 9, they'd hacked Prosper's tongue out with a dandelion weeder.

Two white brutes held him down, two great sons of Virginia.

He had blessed his master under the switch, back when he'd had the wherewithal to bless. They tried to take his boyhood, too. Declan had seen the wound sometime on the river, and when they bathed in the kitchen tub. Prosper thought the scars had rendered him undeserving of the Yellowfoot squaw. He said – he wrote – he was,

½ A MAN

Declan told him he was twice the man of any man in all the provinces. More man that he, Declan R. Glover, would ever be. "Does it still—does it work?"

O IT WOK

They made him pretend to swim in the blood. They said, "Nigger Indian, swim. You can make it across the James. Then the Potomac. You can be home in time to bugger your sweet sister for her birthday."

So one of those slavers failed to wake up the next day. The other wished he hadn't.

One of their hearts made Prosper's all the grander.

Granpa Fix had insisted human intestines stretched to 30 feet. Difficult to fathom such a distance when they're all coiled hot inside us. When they're doing their business as intended. Fix had gawked at them hung, he'd said, strung around a lecture hall at the Medical College on the banks of the Rideau Canal in Ottawa. Now Prosper's bowels dangled from stabbing candelabra of red maple branches. Declan could not disentangle them without tearing the flesh apart.

Soon all his fingers were enmeshed in the sticky skin. He pictured Christian Robinette unspooling them like ribbon from Prosper's belly.

He followed with his eyes: Over a boulder, they draped. Meandered through the marsh grass. Happy as a clam, a little cheeper pecked at capillaries. Then they extended past Reverend, still sitting, shining purplish-grey like some magnificent and tired snake. And from where he stood, Declan could not determine their genesis, nor the terminus into which they wended. But this felt right—Prosper was a Kit. Now he was everywhere, and nowhere all at once. As far as the rites were concerned, the bowels would not require any reassemblage.

Declan once wondered aloud whether after the world was hung and let spin, did Whosoever did the hanging get so bored so fast He turned to some other, more pressing affairs elsewhere? Like a preacher who falls for a harlot in some other parish, and neglects his own flock, as Elder's brother, Christian's father, supposedly had before the governor banished him?

Prosper insisted in chalk:

AIN'T LIK THAT

Mother fits perfectly into Father's palm. Father keeps a firm grip on Mother. Declan preferred that model for a metaphor. On balance, it struck him as more hospitable than all that flood-and-fire, smiting shite.

Prosper also told him how the entire equilibrium of the world depends sometime on the resolve of the individual human heart. If that's true, God—our species better worry.

The Yellowfoot squaw, sans right ear, carried Prosper's heart, washed clean by river water. She held it out to Declan in both hands. She offered some half-remembered prayer in her tongue. Why had he never learned her name? He knew the approximate date and manner of her impending death, yet never even knew what to call her besides "squaw." A word which seemed to him base and offensive, though he couldn't say why. The bonesetter boy took the heart. Her hands flew away from her breast like birds, the fingers dancing. As if spinning threads into every direction, or indicating some outburst of butterflies or moths. He saw for the first time she was beautiful—a haunting, wraithlike beauty, despite the recent marring. Her eyes told him they had relished their marriage up in that cave, she tending house, him hunting for their supper. And her eyes told him, too, she didn't understand why they'd let her live. Except perhaps that she could tell of the justice they'd exacted. He imagined they took her ear as she tried to cover it against her lover's screaming.

He took her hand to walk with him into the water. Together they carried Prosper's heart, released of its yoke. They mounted it on a boulder in the center of the kill. Perfectly still, exactly between the upturned hands on either shore. Declan well remembered the image Prosper had rendered of the heart in the middle and the hands out on either side. He'd drawn a straight line through them, and an intersecting vertical line also crossing through the heart-center, the legs laid out on either side in the bottom quadrants.

He doubted Prosper's tormentors had known the Kittakwa custom that called for the severance of the heart, and its consumption. He knew now the origin and rationale behind the rite. It seemed now no more or less ridiculous and grotesque than the ritual beliefs with which he'd grown up in his granma's house. But he questioned whether he'd be able to bring himself to go through with this one. In principle, it had socked his conscience as romantic, gallant. Maybe even primal and imperative. Now faced with the prospect of carrying out the ghoulish tradition – actually biting the organ – he retched.

But why? What had he learned in the years he'd apprenticed as a bonesetter if not the inseparable connections of body, mind, and spirit? Of each to each. Of this world and the next. It was as if the universe, with Prosper's parts strewn throughout, was telling him,

Prove it, Laddie! Prove you really see your face in all that moonshine in the water.

He was just about to conclude, *I don't. I most certainly don't.* But with one hand on the bloody boulder, and another firmly placed on Prosper's heart, the thought of a moment washed over him. Solaced him. It was not the future but the past. His own. A memory arriving on the wings of the *Puissance*, gift of the Glover tribe. First the words came. In the voice of his Nana – a buzzard of a woman, frankly – they came. But the words were feather-soft. Then the image of her, soft, too, fuzzy, even kind. Her eyes looked kind. Her face. She was reaching toward his mouth with a white wafer of bread. Golden sunshine behind her. He was young, so young. The whole moment unfolded for him now:

Reverend was down with the pox at the time. Everyone thought he would die. Elder and the other deacons all cowered under clouds of contagion they imagined gripped the meetinghouse. They all stayed home, the cravens. "Cocks that will not fight," Granma Glover called them. "Cocks afeard of the pox," said Fix. Christian Robinette was going around town with a rag wrapped around his mouth insisting sick children be burned alive in a barrel. As Drumhill awaited another minister from somewhere, the womenfolk, with Nana Glover at the helm, took over all religious education in the village.

His tongue was out and with the wafer came her words, "This is my body." He took the bread into his mouth, where it began to melt. Then Nana held up to his lips a goblet of wine and said, "This is my blood." This prospect stunned him. Drinking heartblood was the province of a savage, a monster, a demon, no?

He saw now it was the same as the Kit's ritual. Exactly the same.

Of course the Protestants, when they snatched back control from the mad Catholic woman, protested. You weren't supposed to take it quite so literally. "They're ganna burn your hide at the stake, Missus," offered her husband, Ridley, helpfully.

Two Spirits

Declan found himself now some distance from Prosper's heart while he remembered this with a smile the color of blood. He swallowed. He wiped his mouth with his sleeve. Eventually, he found the feet, clumsily chopped off. He placed them in their proper alignment a seven-minute walk below the hands. He and the squaw laid the long bones out between. They situated the pelvis and the hips on the river bottom near the Plunge downstream from the boulder heart. Where the mystic Indian had acted her knight in armor. The hips reminded him Prosper came from horse people, and didn't his granpa tell him real horsemen embodied righteousness? "All of them ganna be upraised in a glorious and blinding beam, all them warriors atop their mounts, imagine."

Did he believe it? Did Prosper's sister, Akt'adia, right now, when she placed a hand in her river, know what had become of her brother in this one? Weren't all rivers, ultimately, united? Just as sure as all points in the circulatory system of the human body connect.

On the slate in a gorse bush he found his red brother's last words, lines and curls in chalk that Declan wanted desperately to stand as signs for deeper meaning. Passwords to the time to come. For entry into somewhere better. More than the words, though, the body parts were signs now, his signature writ large across the Drumhill wood. Or notes on a page that stood for some epic choral opus.

Reverend, shock-eyed, mum, reeled the viscera like rope. He set them to floating from the center rock like letting out a line to a ship adrift. He washed his hands in the kill, and stood. And with only Declan, the Yellowfoot lass, and all the walleye in the congregation, he began his Sabbath sermon. But it was only words. They meant nothing. Yes, it was an excellent story, rife with might and magic. But it wasn't true. Not true like the twice-abused squaw with her hand now trilling on the surface of the swirling water. Smiling faintly because her Prosper's cells were skipping by on their way back down to his people. *Go, go, back to your sister. And though it might take a long time, when you get there, rise again. Embrace her. Tell her, though you still might be speechless, tell Akt'adia not everyone as white owns so black a heart.*

Yes, the bonesetter boy felt Prosper's presence humming in his femur now, and his opposing humerus. His nose bone. He'd sensed something similarly special in the other's carved-up corpus still. He hadn't ever touched another who gave him the vision not only of the future on the ground – meaning *under*ground – then past transparent muslin palls of the Veil beyond. But here again—*back here again to ride*. Or still at riding. Resurrection after all. The same substantial soul still riding strong on this plane somehow. In a different body, a rebuilt one. This, despite Drumhill's theological and medical experts attesting to the permanency of parting.

When he touched the ground now. When he lay a hand on the water. When he reached up to the sky. Even when he touched his own chest and felt the heart beat beneath, that's what he saw: Prosper riding home. Bolting home. Charging home. Dust rising. Mud flying off hooves. A dawn journeyer. A midnight rider. His brother. His shadow. His twin.

On the bridge up-river were the lips upon a skull someone clever had tried to scalp. Lips above the neck cut clean by a Robinette cleaver. In the stubbly hair, still there because the skull would not give up its people's power, his Kittakwa *Puissance*, there were the lice still dancing. Dancing at Declan's decision to ensure Elder and his nephew would get their due reward. He'd bide his time. Keep serving the citizens of Drumhill. And someday soon they'd call him for another of Elder's complaints. That would be the end of him.

Later that afternoon in a hidden glade, behind a house-sized stone, the dregs of a fire smoldered. At its core the breeze of the nearby Plunge whipped into the air wisps of orange-grey coal dust. They had once comprised the carved out, drunk-from, bitten-through heart of a Great Warrior. That boy would yet ride into battle under colors of peace. And Declan decided there under the pinking sky that when his business with every last Robinette was done, when he was sure the squaw was safe, he would someday, someway, find her. Akt'adia Kit. And in her, find their brother.

—Consider the myths—

Monday Sept. 10: Day 7 of the Two Spirits *film shoot.*

Somewhere remote in New Mexico

TWO SPIRITS

A Screenplay

By Augusten B. Talbot

FADE IN:

EXT. KITTAKWA RESERVATION, UPSTATE N.Y. DUSK (PRESENT DAY)

SUPERIMPOSE: CHICORY: JAUNDICE, RHEUMATISM

MAX LIGHTNING, 73, a Kittakwa Native American, raggedy leather jacket, shotgun slung around his shoulder, chews chicory root in the woods. Squatting, he looks over his shoulder when a SHOT rings out in the distance. He puts the chicory in his shirt pocket and addresses someone O.S.

                    MAX
         Consider the myths, Bon. The Thunderer.
         The False Faces. You heard of them?

                    PD (O.S.)
         What are you doing out here, Grandpa?

On Max's rugged face. Graham Greene after 10 years in SuperMax, and no dentist for twice that.

                    MAX
         The Lightning land. My land. Yours.
         Here to take a stand.

BOOMING in the BG, STRAFING, a child's faraway SCREAM. During lulls, the PEEPERS start up, abruptly quitting whenever the "war" resumes.

                    MAX (CONT'D)
         I'm thinking of Francis Scott Key.
         Thinking about all the ways our white
         Uncle sent our people packing up the
         road a piece. And the road was all
         blood, shit, and weeping sores. Caves.
         Gullies. Bars.

                    PD (O.S.)
         You remember you took me to that bar in
         Arctadia? Kidnapped me, basically. I
         was five. Torn red bar stools.

CU on Max's face.

                    PD (O.S.) (CONT'D)
         Smelled like scrambled eggs and poison.
         You scared me.

                    MAX
         I meant <u>behind</u> bars, not in 'em. But
         you make a point.

Two Spirits

Max surveys the landscape of the Lightning ancestral land. Upstate New York in all its "gorge-ous" glory.

                    MAX (CONT'D)
          We got boxed in here, Boyo. We used to
          roam all the way from Canada to Staten
          Fuckin' Island. Balls out, blood-
          painted, proud. Killers, we were.

He adjusts his shoulder. He stares at—

PD LIGHTNING ("BON"), 15. Short hair, a small scar over one eye, and the eye blind as though by acid. He's on his knees in the mud by a lakeside dock. He looks down at something big in his lap. He wears an "AFD Junior Fire Frog" T-shirt, torn at the collar.

                    MAX (CONT'D)
          It don't matter shit. No more. But, Bon
          ... some things do matter. My Papa,
          your great-grandpa Leonard - not worth
          half a twat, that one, and perpetually
          soused - he talked a storm 'bout the
          Great Spirit. If there is a Great
          Spirit - and mind you, I ain't seen
          fuck all of no Great Spirt in 73-odd
          years - that shit matters. Even if
          spirit and matter seem, what's the
          word? "At odds?"

                    PD
          Incompatible?

                    MAX
          Incomfuckingpatible.

                    PD
          I'm sorry, Grandpa.

                    MAX
          Goddammit, Bon. I'm so sick of our peo-
          ple saying we're sorry.

                    PD
          My Mam?

                    MAX
          Sure. There was the queen of sorry-ass
          girls.

PD looks lovingly down at the thing in his lap, still O.S. He caresses it, smiles. He looks up at Max.

                    PD

32   *Two Spirits*

                    Why won't anyone tell me about my
                    father?
                              MAX
                    Shame.
                              PD
                    Not from me.
                              MAX
                    'Cause you don't know your own dick
                    from a bottle of Sioux City Sarsapa-
                    rilla.
                              PD
                    Know you're ashamed of me.
                              MAX
                    Oh, you're proud of your grandpop all
                    of a sudden?
                              PD
                    So, it's mutual.
                              MAX
                    'Course.

Max shuffles the thing off his lap – it seems like it might be
big as a body – and stands.
                              MAX (CONT'D)
                    It's a family. The Lightning legacy.
                    Fuck it.

Max looks out to the four directions. A battle rages somewhere
far too close, and closing in. SIRENS. BULLHORNS. Rat-a-tat-tat
of semi-automatic RIFLE FIRE. Then he turns his attention to
his grandson.
                              MAX (CONT'D)
                    So, Bon. Who's the dead white
                    boy?

OK. Hold. Hooold. *All righty. Cut! Let's wrap Dead White Boy. Wardrobe, get his ass dressed. Kid's about to freeze ... Sully doesn't look so hot, either. I need Script and, let's see, Art, in my trailer in five.*

—*Influencer Talbot*—

Tuesday Sept. 18. Day 2 of the trial.

Way out where Jesus lost his BVDs, New Mexico

In his eyes. His eyes. That's how I knew. I knew. I knew he would never be the same again. He was gone. He was not him anymore. Not Sully. Gone. Not anyone. You know. You did this. You know. You put a—you people fucking know. How could you? I keep—I'm sorry, I—I don't know another way.

Go on.

Ya. Go on, you say. But look at him. Look at me. How do I go on?

You just do. You go. On. You must.

So, like, one day at a time, you're saying?

If that peppers your radish. If that butters your scone. If that pops your—

You're deliberately—the food references? Where do I start?

Begin with your name, if you would.

Everybody knows me. I assumed this was a kidna—Oh—you mean for the record. Right? Ya. The record? My name is Augusten Bon Talbot. Augie. Is that good?

For the record. Profession?

Job. Influencer. I'm an influencer.

What do you influence? The moon? The tides? How?

No. Ya. Opinions? I guess? Fashion. Can you loosen these? No? Politics, a little. Gossip, really. Like—it's pretty flimsy, truth be told. A social media influencer. I have 42 million followers, though. My vlog. Followers? Adherents? I do fan fiction, and I just wrote a—Do you guys even have—? No.

Disciples?

I suppose.

Disciples require discipline.

Yes. So, no. Not disciples, *per se*. Followers. We call them followers.

Were you influencing on that mountain pass where we found you? Influencing the other boy?

His name is Sullivan Winter. Sully. Umm. No. I was – we were – making a movie. My first big—I wrote it. They asked me to write— He's starring, kinda. He's a—We got lost. That snow. This. We— spent the weekend together. We were going to go skiing, But the storm—we got lost when the pass closed. It's a major—a movie? Fuck. We were "influencing" each other. No one was—They knew me from online. They asked me to write a movie about the Rez. I'm from—we both, we're from—

We know where you're from. We know who you are. But do you?

Umm. So. Ya. I was making a movie. A big one. Gosh, these are so tight. Can I please have some water? Can I—God, it's cold. It's so cold. Why did you do it? Why?

We will ask the questions, Influencer Talbot.

Augie. Rhymes with "doggie." Heh. This leash … I'm named for my—never mind. What—what more do you—?

Tell us everything, from the beginning.

I don't understand.

"Tell:" explain. "Us:" we assembled. "Everything:" all the—

No, I know what the—I just don't understand why. You were there. You were—you did those things. All of you. You just said you—all of you turned him—you—Look what you fucking—

We will need you to use complete sentences, please.

Fuck you.

—For the record.

Fuck you, complete sentences. You! You're fucking—what? Barbarians, is what you are.

Middle English (as an adjective used in a derogatory way to denote a person with only different speech and customs): They were said to

Two Spirits 35

sound like, "Bar bar bar ..." Do you think we sound like that, Influencer Talbot? Bar bar bar ...

I think you're sub—you're animals. Monsters. You. And you, you fucking—Why am I—?

Hungry? We have not fed you for – what is it now – two, three days? This makes one hungry. We will not feed you unless you earn it. Until. A big if.

Why am I—?

Naked? Because naked, you are cold. Are you not cold? And you are vulnerable. If we – any of us 12 – want to harm you, it is easier this way. You understand. We are a practical people. The tender parts. Shall we demonstrate your vulnerability as we did with your friend?

Why am I here? Who are you people? Who are you? Please. What do you want? Please. Is Sully—I want to go home. I want to go home.

Home? And where's that? Now stop shivering. Stop. We will ask the questions. You may ask only of yourself. You are here, on trial here. For manifold crimes against your ancestry. Your people. The codes. You are on trial for your life. I am Kenneth.

Kenneth?

You were expecting "Avenging Owl" or maybe "Anvil-of-the-Heavens?"

Kenneth.

I am Kenneth, and we 11 are the Shards. We have reassembled from far and wide like yonder pottery. Like these pieces I work on here from up on the mesa. Some hundreds, some thousands of years scattered. But once whole. Now re-collected. Soon whole again.

Fuck.

This is our wee home camp. We face a fire, surrounded by fire towers. We are the Shards. We can give—and we can take. We are the Shards and we will be the final arbiters of your life.

Ya, fuck.

We wish you to join us. Be our twelfth. We are from 11 tribes, far and wide. And we have but one thing in common. We think you might know what. Be the last Shard that seals the Whole. Prove you are worthy. Tell us of your people and prove your worth. Tell us of your Two Spirits. Answer eight questions. You answered the first already: "Why don't the people complain." Because of Prosper's tongue.

Now seven more.

No way.

Answer the next question: "Where do the people come from?" Join us or die.

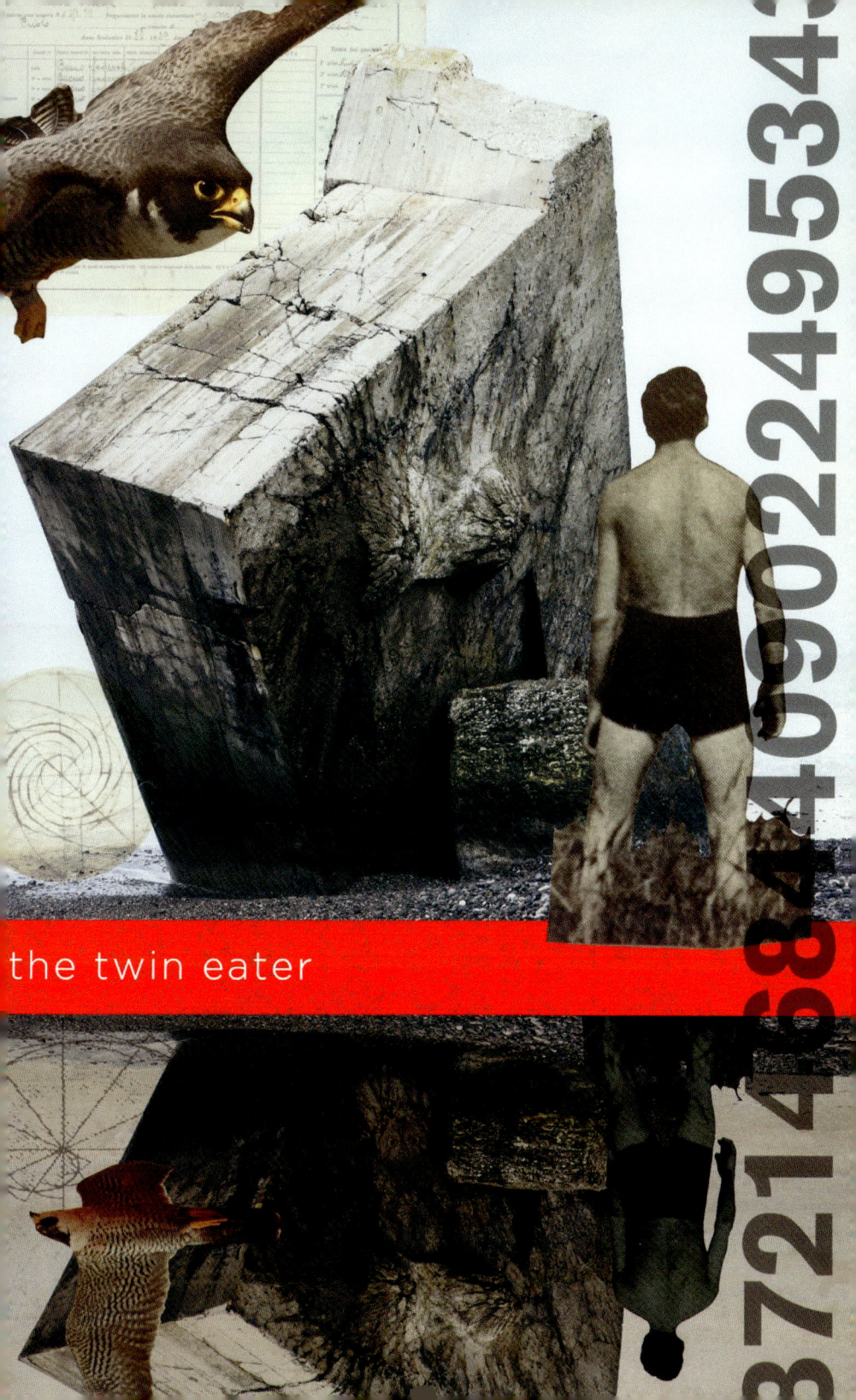

the twin eater

The Twin Eater

For Etgar Keret

And I say also unto thee, that thou art Peter, a small rock, and upon this large rock I will build my Church of those called, and all the forces of Hades shall not prevail against it.

—Matthew 16:18

There's a flat top mesa not far from my Kenyan stake; you can see it for a hundred miles. And although it bears no particular resemblance to that seminal outgrowth of my youth in upstate New York, I find it reminiscent. If that's why I settled here, it's not the best escape. I drive a big old Nissan 4x4 whose flanks are scratched beyond cosmetic surgery by brush. And every time I climb aboard to drive somewhere, I know I will see that stony table in the distance.

A mesa should not be confused with a butte, which is smaller. A mesa's a high rocky tableland or plateau; specifically, a flat-topped, sawed-off hill of rock possessing one or more steep sides, typically rising abruptly from a surrounding plain, and common in the arid and semi-arid areas of Africa, as in the North and South Americas. Ours has an unpronounceable name. But, to translate (and here I rely on my Collins—not a Collins English Dictionary, but the person, Collins Wangari, font of local lore) from the nearby tribal tongue, it's called the "Twin Eater."

They believe, as I understand it, that every soul arrives in this universe twinned. Two parts of a whole. Two personalities. Two potentialities, as in physics. But insubstantial, not yet formed into compacted bodies as we know them. Together, hand-in-hand, they glide – or however they might locomote – over grassland tips, and undertake to wind their way up the switchback path to the tabletop. One helps the other if his brother flags. One shows his twin whatever hatchlings, cubs, flowers, or morning stars appear along their way. They talk of their Father who delivered these gifts, every one with its sister, every being beside its brother. Until only one of each pair after time becomes manifest as He commanded, and the other—*well*—

Once they reach the top, they know that only one of them will descend in the end. It ain't the hill that will judge them, Collins says. They work it out together. They dialog their philosophies of an imagined life ahead, their loyalties, their fears, what they hope to accomplish in the stony land, the land where when you knock, you know what you are made of. And jointly they decide which one of them should find a solid future as an entity, a being, a penguin or hippo, seahorse, a bamboo stalk, or human in the womb of a woman they will also choose together. As Collins says he chose his mother, the big, laughing woman called Mercy Faith Wangari, my third mother on Earth.

They swear an oath. So only one comes down alone to find his mother, the Mother. The other falls deflated as the sun goes down and the moon comes over, then, no longer floating, lies on the rock. Then turns the correspondent of its face down to the stone, the equivalent of eyes onto the hinder plain below and skyblack jacket overhead, and humbly waits for elements of Earth at length to eat him. The solid world absorbs her, bloats upon his body, this soul nutrition, and then transforms him or her back into the rudiments, the fundaments, the weather. The fog. It lives. It lives there still and always.

This is how the Twin Eater steadily accreted mass, how it grew its height, and earned its breadth, say the tribesmen, at least according to Collins, albeit educated in Mombasa choked with truck exhaust, and late back to our haboob-scoured bush. When the initial twins met for the first creation summit, they assembled on flat ground, at the level of the sea that Collins says he can smell on me—though we're supposed to smell like sour milk to the blacks. You might assume, rightly, that geophysical features erode in time and climate;

not so the Twin Eater, which, in fact, increases. It grows. Like the lumps in me that swell for him; like my love for him. Like cancer.

★★★

When I was growing up, we all called it "Shelter Rock," though it has many names. Some shelter. A boulder, building-big, a "glacial erratic," they call it, probably picked up remotely by the onslaught of a crawling frozen wall a mile high, and then disgorged longwindedly in the course of its retreat in the mid-Jurassic, when it likely measured three times higher than today, which is hard to imagine.

Yet, my nemesis, my anchor stone, dumped by destiny as much as cold advancement in the center of a dense, dark hemlock forest at a juncture that would become North Kittatinn County, New York, 120-odd miles northwest of the great slab that houses The New Colossus. I, too, found a home there, 100 million years post-settlement of that gigantic immigrant among my people. In the land of my fathers. The Kittakwas considered it a holy site; they worshipped there. They banged and sang. They slaughtered the first bighorn bucks of the season there. Ate of their hearts and made offerings of viscera. It has been a womb, an incubator.

And a cenotaph, a sepulcher—"tomb stone," one Lincoln Christmas, honorary Kit elder, christened it, and more on that later. It would have been a shrine, by Teddy's "aught-six" proclamation, as 22 national monuments relate to Native America, and one is Kittakwa. But that boulder did not rest on federal territory—not yet. They tried to wrest it. Tried all the time. Tried all their tricks. And wouldn't succeed until that affair with the Divine Twins, PD and Noah, which would come. It would come one generation.

But back then it nested on what was a sizeable – extensive – private plot. It belonged, along with the surrounding 41,011.7 acres, to a well-heeled Colonial family of Scottish origins—the Christmases. Not exactly my ancestors, but the forebears of those who took me in, the benefactors of the boulder. Family legend held they'd "bought" it from the (assumedly reluctant) Kittakwas in 1791 or thereabouts. The details of that contract, like the rock itself to the Kits, forever lost to the slaughters of antiquity/modernity, the *Lix'eyo Páæhgwa-ken* (The "comet's path," meaning the coerced Indian slave diaspora), but nonetheless still a sore spot centuries on.

My name is Conner Christmas, but I wasn't born a Christmas. Nor a Conner. I took the names of he who took me in, and he who "found" my family. Today, 1968, technically, legally, (whether properly, justly, depends on the skin of the queried), Shelter Rock – the second largest freestanding boulder in North America – belongs to me. But really, I, despite 8,000 miles of apartheid, belong to it. Shelter Rock returned to the proud protectorate of a Kittakwa, notwithstanding the fact that I bolted from the Rez. More shame on me then for absconding, for fleeing farther than (as a child staring at the stars) I could imagine. For finding hot charred corncobs cooked on every corner, and baboons gorging in the larder, a thousand dialects constructed on analogy, not unlike the ancient idioms of my Kit County antecedents. For finding my great love, my mirror dark, my "Uncle Tom" Collins W. (I say in necessary jest). My African twin.

Can a man ever break away from the spell of so immense an entity? The gravity of Io daily pulls on Alpha Centauri Bb, Earth's farflung exoplanetary doppelgänger, if ever so faintly, the way an animal's eye locked on mine many years ago must still exert an influence on how I peel an orange, tie my laces, kiss my shadow in the morning before he heads off to his ugly war against the Other (who looks to me just like him).

***

Its footprint spans some 5,300 square feet. It is six and a half stories high, the first often shrouded in whirling fog. Its volume is somewhere near 38,000 cubic feet, though much debate haunts that figure among SUNY scientists and nerdlings at the USGS station in Barbaravale. No one has ventured an estimate of its weight, though they push against it isometrically, try to fathom its mass and magnitude. I recall my second mother (elderly, adoptive), Mrs. Condolcezza Christmas, inciting me – with sweetness, until the end of time –with the logically fallacious paradox of omnipotence, viz: If the Lord can make anything, then can He make a stone so dense that even He can't lift it? Well, this conundrum kept me staring at the ceiling many nights in my own room, in my own house, cradled now beside the Christmas kid who'd bequeathed this castle of our conquerors, whose stocking was filled with every rock and gem from my abundant land. My brother. My second brother of three.

As I matured enough to snoop and wonder, I learned that Shelter Rock makes cameos in a couple of key Kit County surveys of yesteryear, major regional guidebooks, notes of a bellicose Patriot's journal, and at least one geological textbook from every generation since the turn of the 19th Century. Until the 1940s, the Christmas clan, under the eventual aegis of the patriarch, Jackson Christmas, my grandfather (adopted), had granted occasional – and often costly – access into the ambit of the whopping stone to various geologists, historians, archeological seekers, and the scant quotidian gawker. And those couples hunting rustic backdrops for nuptial snaps, who couldn't afford the trek to Niagara—whenever the bride was worth peeping through a spyglass from the balustrades of Christmas House.

In the days of Jackson's grandfather, Jared – the Golden Age of Alpinism – Jared Christmas had proposed a world bouldering tourney to pit the best mountaineers of England, France, Austria, and Germany against each other in a competition to the top without the benefit of ropes, harnesses, or crampons. The granite fascia features protracted cracks and slabs for toe-, heel-, and finger holds. At our local library, I found old photographs of one of the earliest of these autumn fêtes. They made me wear white cotton gloves to handle the images in that box. One portrays four old fashioned gentlemen in three-piece suits and bowlers – possibly Christmas cousins – standing folded-armed in front of the boulder wall, which consumes the entire frame. In another, you can see the unease on the face of the man identified by a red-penned circle and arrow as my (adopted) great-great granddad, Jared Christmas. Notes on this event describe the pioneer climber to summit – a mutton-chopped Swiss behemoth who'd conquered the 10 highest unclimbed (but entitled) peaks in Europe, and surrendered half a foot in a couloir on *Kaisersgebirge* – turning to gloat downward for the maximum annoyance of all opponents, and, catching his boot toe on a burr occasioned by ice damming, bouncing his face to the detriment of the squamous curve of his frontal bone just above the orbitals. There was nothing for the big man but an extra-wide pine coffin and a couple of hasty words about his foothold on the paramount of his heavenly arcana. Fog turns the red a pleasant magenta.

Surely our Jacksons and Jareds had entertained the legend—the portent. For thousands of years, the Kittakwas knew not to attempt to climb Shelter Rock. *For whosoever stood upon its top would die forthwith* (Chief Kittadoga qtd., ceremoniously, betwixt feathery asterisks, in the diary of Phoebe Christmas, 1852). The Christmases had at first considered the concept quaint. Yet three-quarters of a century before the smugness of that mountaineer induced the crude rivening of the skull his mother made for him –just a generation after acquisitioning the monster – they strung rope ladders, and Jackson's great-grandfather's brother, Enoch, 12, the eldest son, inherited the honor. At the zenith – none could see him way up on the top – he called, "Papa!" then squealed, uncharacteristically effete, and failed to answer upon their request for confirmation of a boyish, beating heart. So a deputation of Christmases and assorted Kittatinn landsmen scrambled up reluctantly to discover what fate had befallen the blond, handsome lad who had been so apt to sing "Yankee Doodle" that they'd dubbed him "Macaroni," however disinclined our summiteer had ever been to foppishness.

They did not find Master Enoch "Macaroni" Christmas on the top of Shelter Rock. None of the rescue party placed more than 10 fingers on the topside, but they all gave a good look. Can't be too careful when it comes to old Indian curses. Had young Master Christmas mystically departed? A rapture of adolescents underway outside of Arctadia? Nothing so Romantic. Enoch had simply tripped, it would appear, and tumbled some 49 feet over the aft side, and, landing backward in the loam, broke his neck. He died, head bent grotesquely, those aquamarine eyes and pink mouth gaping like a bass at the bottom of a boat. That slender neck adorned with a string necklace of painted acorns that made his mother uneasy, according to her diary, given its genesis, endowment of the boy's best friend, a reedy, green-irised half breed Kittakwa, grandson of some warrior and a white woman that the more talkative in town alleged had kipped among them, of late dispossessed of his home in the shelter of the rock to a camp of ramshackle cabins on the Christos.

A council of senior Christmases banned expressly any further expeditions, each father insisting to all his sons that they must never violate this edict, on the pain of certain death. A Kittakwa maxim: *Doom shall fall upon the father of the sons who are foolish enough to forget the saga of their lot.* Or something like that. I don't remember much of my native lexicon.

Forget we do. Yankee Dandies accidentally find their way to barbed entanglements and swollen horses of the Somme, and then all tragedies of past appear to pale. In '25 or '26, an associate professor of archeology from NYU convinced one Flora Christmas, Condolcezza's sister and my adoptive aunt, then custodian of Shelter Rock, her husband having left his head in a rush on that Frankish watercourse, to grant the professor a looksee, under the unambiguous restriction that neither he nor any of his party of graduate assistants could traverse the boulder's terrace, *per se*. They could make sketches, take ample photographs, and narrate for notes any relevant topographical/phrenological features as they might detect from a safe perch of scaffolding. But not a boot could touch the stone up top. They needn't be banned should they break this promise. But of course the instructions, sworn to in the newly expanded kitchen of Castle Christmas, went entirely unheeded once the expedition, from the loamy ground, eyed its kill for the first time.

The library microfiche. The tutor's foot found its way inexplicably – inextricably – into a fissure occasioned by two million years of expansion and contraction of that brittle and translucent, crystalline solid that our Maker made more potent than His Adam's Ale—the same brew that brought Shelter Rock to the Kittakwas before we were a people. This mishap occurred less than one meter onto the upside of the stone. Remarkably, the rescuers determined that the safest, wisest course hinged on removing the encumbered limb between ankle and knee with an ad hoc bone saw passed up on a half hitch knot. Two weeks later, the young instructor succumbed to gangrene, a screaming, stinking sponge of a man, in a Bay Ridge, Brooklyn bedsit. The bones in the boot, they were married to the boulder.

And all before I was born.

★★★

Fast forward a further 15ish years. The new World War. Flora's sister, Condolcezza's son, Kendall Christmas – "Dall," as we called him – became our best friend when we were all 10 and 11. We met at the swap meet in Arctadia, which we kids relished because of Skeet, the ice cream man who parked his stand on the outskirts, and wore a conical cap with a big white wig, facsimile of a vanilla scoop, or butter pecan. Dall's father, Lincoln Jr., put Dall and his sisters to work hawking handmade birdhouses. I sold rabbits. The sign I posted in front of the chicken wire pen read in red: *We Are Not for Meat.* An albino man once told me, "Sonny Jim, look here: A man buys himself a rabbit, he gets to do whatever the shit he wants to do with it."

"You got that right. And a boy selling rabbits got the right not to sell you a goddamn rabbit, Sir." *He who consumes an innocent soul without necessity and apology will find himself in talons soon.* Or something like that.

Whitey left, harrumphing. This is how you handle bullies. With balls and declarations—not with brawn. Thus spake Lincoln Christmas Jr., the man who would become my father.

A long time ago, when no one was looking, longhouses morphed into doublewides. The scant few hundred Kittakwas who'd survived into the mid-1900s, almost as one, turned their faces from their fire circles toward a row of ugly, parti-colored propane tanks. Even fewer now, or more diluted, you might say. Into such a vanishing milieu my brother Spence and I were born. Early on, some older boy with a wispy mustache and fake ID had schooled us in the lore of Shelter Rock. At some point, we'd even looked for it in aerial photographs at the library. Impossibly gigantic. Spence swore he could see something indistinct, on the top – the whole thing was blurry, the closer you got – and he declared it the restless ghost of some brave massacred by Forbes. For generations, kids had tried to see the giant stone with their own eyes—it was a rite of passage in Kit County for whites and Indians alike, like swinging on the rope attached to the girders below the High Damien, the skyscraping railroad viaduct, improbably high above the Christos, chaste of trains since 1931.

Not surprisingly, a century ago, hired hands spent three seasons one year, enclosing the Christmas claim with an elevated, inbent electric fence featuring yellow diamond signs hooked through with twist-ties every 10 feet, depicting the icon of a stick figure man hurling backward in great shock and agony. *Beware! Danger! Warning! No Ingress.* Peligro! There was only one gate, at the entrance to the mile-long, pine-lined driveway. And the gate, adorned with the stylized Christmas tree crest that has become renowned thanks to its ubiquitous attachment to all Christmas commerce, from canned spiced apple concerns, to high-macro-mineral-content cat food production, from bagged cement to scaffolding, the icon wound from ground to pinnacles with angry-looking, rolled barbed wire, all painted black and red-speckled, as if in metal elegy for the brothers and cousins caught up in the Great Shaping of the 20th Century.

★★★

The word derives from *boulder stone*, from the Middle English *bulderston*. This specimen comprises something like 88 percent pregmatite granite containing raspberry pink and mint green tourmaline, about 10 percent by volume there. Assorted other rare earth elements, including an unidentified and dense lavender mineral prone to obscure cleavage, make up the remainder. This became evident when I was 15, on July 5, 1948, sometime between midnight and 1 a.m., when at a previously plotted plane, a massive splinter cracked and slid off the main body of the rock, overturning on its back like a giant clumsy tortoise, during which occasion the resident Christmases woke to the sound of a rocky Apocalypse in their back woods. This large slab they dubbed "the Orphan" on the spot, and that name stuck. They let the newspapers come and take shots from every angle. The scarce remaining natives took it as a sign: Shelter Rock was attempting an escape back to more hospitable ground. It might take it a million years to migrate, but what's that in Kittakwa time?

Not incidentally, the calving of Shelter Rock uncovered a—something. An opening. A passage …

For the record, we Kit Indians, like many other Natives from the ocean to Ohio, have employed pink, green, and purple tourmaline as a funeral gift for centuries. It's still worth a pretty penny; hence one pragmatic rationale for the grand security circumference around Christmas Isle. But, said Lincoln Christmas to his sons, myself included, on a snowy afternoon that revealed two pair of footprints that strode up to the stone – and only one pair hastily retreating – one must also endeavor to protect oneself against frivolous claims brought by the parents of foolhardy braves. And finally, mustn't one also conserve one's natural resources, no matter how duplicitous or even dangerous they might become, even in one's own hands? This ethos we redmen share unabashedly with the white man, the black man, the yellow man.

Safe bouldering requires keen analysis of the gross and minute characteristics of a particular rock's "problems" before a climber can painstakingly execute a survivable ascent. The paths outlined – the "solutions" – depend largely on the species of stone one wishes to mount and dismount intact. It also helps to study all previous catastrophes that have befallen one's progenitors. But of course such preparation is never foolproof. In the icy shade of certain summits, still uncorrupted corpuses of failed climbers sit erect in their boots, looking stunned or serene for a season or a century to bring this point home back to Davenport and Denver. They say to their wives back in Dallas or Davos, *So sorry, Dear. So right you were. And so, I should have listened.* And so it was for our father. Our first father. Mine and Spence's.

Kittori, named for the spirit of the owl who screeched in the beech tree outside the building of the birthing. Kittori Wayne, a borrowed name, who never took a drop in his life. Who refused to ever use an adverb when the accurate verb would do. Kittori, whose intoxicant was neither alcoholic nor adverbial: It was pride. I wish I had been there. I wish it had been me and not our father and my brother—my twin, my shadow and crux, my Spence. My family, "missing" way too long until a superannuated student pilot, the nature writer Connor X. Mayne, in the dead of leafless winter eyed their bodies on the top of Shelter Rock, and made another pass, and thus confirmed it. So the Kit County Sheriff and scores of other first responders soon assembled in a tent they built beside the boulder to hatch a plan to scale it and retrieve the remains. It was not lost on anyone in that grim party that the stories they'd grown up with – or, in rare cases, learned upon arrival as adults from other parts – were evidently true. These firefighters, rescue climbers, EMTs, and boys in blue, all trained to operate in uncongenial environs, drew straws to determine who'd scale Shelter Rock to bring down two long-dead Indians. Two fucking stupid Kits.

I say *pride*. A roof rack of luggage there that's unintended. I don't mean he was prideful. I mean *proud*. He was proud to represent a dying breed, he said. He was proud to have produced his twofold heirs to carry on their scratching at our vanishing tradition. The ghost dance in figure-eights around the fire pit. The cubes of meat cooked in cauldrons whenever anybody died. Spuds, squash, and onions—the triplet sisters that sustained us for millennia. Our mother had not been nearly so gratified by the accident of her ancestry, particularly on the afternoon she turned the stove up to high, blew out the blue flame, waited 45 minutes, then struck a barbeque lighter in our poky kitchen. Our home, our mother, our hope, all borne in a micro-moment to our Maker. Our mother, the target of barbs from babyhood because of her wide nose, her coal-black hair they called "the witch's wig" or "the devil's do," and the accent she inherited from her maternal grandmother, who'd reared her after her own mother swung over turbid Christos waters from the High Damien.

Our father climbed Shelter Rock perhaps because it had never belonged to the Christmases – he called them "*X*-mases" – whose Arctadia cement factory, egg-processing plant, and over-tapped maple acres, employed the vast majority of the tiny minority of relatively able-bodied Kits left in the county. Of late, their outsized , shimmering truck dealership, GMC pickups by the hundreds just off the Arctadia Highway, put Kittori himself to work after a stint of unemployability, brushing snow off windshields every morning, or buffing the residue of raindrops from Dover White, Canyon Blue, and Omaha Orange vehicles he couldn't afford even to hope to ever own. He climbed Shelter Rock because there was a reason it got dropped on the property we'd occupied for a thousand years or 10 depending on the branch of Kit History you wore. Because it was ours.

Spence, because Spence dedicated hours to asking our father about our people; the old times; his grandfather who was a horse-knocker and healer; how he met our mother at the burial of some baby run over by a snowplow in the arms of her mother. Not I, who was more inclined to studying the body of my brother as he snored beside me on the cot we shared in the kitchen, attempting to reckon myself and discern the bottomless depth of my desire. I, who looked in library books for my history, rather than to my own father, who fucking lived it. I, whose name at the time was not yet Conner Christmas, who would become another kid, the terrible twin of a better, but deader, boy.

***

The bodies of a pair of Kits at rest. The writer in the Piper Cub saw only their bottom halves—a somewhat comic spectacle, it must have seemed. It would appear that at the top of Shelter Rock, a sharp, black crevasse opened up and appeared to go deep, deep down into the stone, maybe even down into the Earth below, some said, though that always seemed to me geologically improbable, given that the Earth itself predates the rock – right? – at least in its present form. But this explains the hollow constitution of the dark haze that Spence detected on the satellite image of the stone. Picture their hands and forearms reaching down into that dark, buried up to their waists, their hearts and minds lost in the void, Spence behind our father, two sets of legs still sticking out like discarded dummies. I was way too young to have even considered the idea of reading the coroner's report, but it must have remarked on the pooling of blood. It would not have told why they had been trying to climb down that chasm. Why? Even a cursory inspection of the narrowness of that crack would lead anyone with intact faculties to understand that getting jammed in there was inevitable. What were they looking for in that mist-emitting cleft? Regardless, it ended as it had for the academician's ankle of yore: There was no extracting the cadavers without the sharp, gas-propelled implements of the Arctadia FD. And some of my brother and father would have to remain forever on the rock, in that rock. Of that rock. Apropos, some of the more culturally considerate argued, or so I've heard—just.

Oh, and by the way, some said – many believed – the stone itself was the source of our famous mist. "Boulder Fog," they call it in the ancient language of the Kits. The stone said to have fallen out of the ear of a monster known as the Great Stone Foe of the People, dislodged by the sound of a joyous babe at play—anathema to the brute.

★★★

Rising 2,380 feet above this expanse of otherwise unbroken East African lowland, The Twin Eater's wide side shows the unmistakable face of a man the tribe believes is the likeness of the first surviving twin, the Ur-Twin, the boy who, having won the privilege by unanimous acclamation between himself and his brother, came before us all; delivering us blood and memory. Somewhere on the other side of the planet (a long-haul trucker at a roadside haunt regales me many years after I made a colony of Kenya), another monolith portrays a related face, the simulacrum of that soul who was that first day laid waste in favor of his brother. Sublimated through the stone into the soil, and seeped all the way past the middle of the Earth where our Maker molds our souls, where his Father re-formed him, offered him reign over all twins extant in this Middle Forge, and those to come, as recompense for surrendering the birthright to his sibling sans storm. So all twinned things – all things – exist in the Top World, but all those rejected doubles that climbed up the switchback trail together and were subsequently sent back down now made their own world in the Middle Forge—a world so much like our own that we'd scarcely recognize the difference. Except for the light, the man at the public house announced. The only visible difference in Middle Forge was its perpetual dimness, the absence of enlightenment. Its inhabitants, rabbits to rabbis, could recollect a sense of it, but only obscurely, inscrutably, from their single morning's sojourn in the light before their plunge. Most soon adjusted to the indistinctness, murk; they soon forgot entirely the bright flipside of their settlement. Once in a long while, though, one of these precluded twins, either wise or wishful, would stand alone and look up at the pitch black sky to find its single star, The Glimmerer, unambiguously billions of light years out there, and fix oversize eyes upon it, and propose that this flickering marvel constituted the perforation letting this world out to an Upworld, dazzling and vivid beyond imagination.

   And there in the in-between the banished Ur-Twin reigned, judging all made things by their worthiness; he, the sole arbiter, lest any errors made at any of our untold geneses persevere, to the peril of those in both worlds. And because of this he was empowered to occasionally propel one of the rebuffed cousins up through that bright white aperture. And that is what he did, said the man, after a fourth cold Tusker beer. And that amazed me, chilled me, thrilled me so I broke my beer glass in my hand by over-gripping. Because I am one of some familiar with that other side, the egress of that skylight. I lived beside it for the first nearly 17 years of my life. I have seen that face. I have heard the voices in the fog.

So both brother souls share dominion. One here in the sunshine and sky full of stars, and one upon some nether stone in the hot bowels of the Earth where the only star's a portal to the world we take for granted. And thus sometimes our Upworld evinces true twins—twin kookaburras, toads, twin human hearts, whose quest it is after crawling up into the supershine to seek its sister, discover its brother, one way or another.

Shattered into shards, I was, a Lego block figurine that had existed interlocked to make a model of a man that all collapsed into a fragmented heap. How to reconstruct myself? I had seen that other face. I had seen that face but had not marked it so, not a mile from my birthplace. Represented in a grey and ghostly discoloration, lichen on the south face of my childhood companion, my totem, Shelter Rock. An Ur-Twin—he who ruled that hell of not knowing, not seeing, unbathed in the sun. The place some of our people called "the Under." I had seen that face since The Orphan found itself divorced from its mother. That face whose higher eye forever called one, beckoned, "Come."

★★★

None of its facets met the ground at a right angle. Shelter Rock was rounded at the bottom, as though long submerged in a swirling pool, so that ledges hung around its whole perimeter, between about nine and 15 feet up off the forest floor, which feature created a deep, dark channel, like a mote, cool and shaded, kissed by swirling mist, and bereft of vegetation but for moss and mushrooms and two varietals of a silvery creeper vine locked in lethal combat for possession of the underhang. Hence the name, Shelter Rock. It was 10 or

20 degrees colder in that hollow. We learned at suppertime stories, at Indian School (after regular school) that Kittakwas had sheltered beneath this canopy for hundreds of generations, hundreds at a time, divided by lattices hung with groundhog pelts and branches of birchwood and aspen.

In fact, I'd lost my entire family in that forest, amid Kittatinn trees.

Most people think I was named for the author and philosopher Connor Mayne. Not so. No. Rather, it happened this way: When Lincoln Christmas first beheld me, bedraggled and bony at the funeral he financed for my father and brother lost and found on his boulder, his jaw fell open so that I could see his missing molars, silver fillings, and the jagged angle of his tongue, half-lopped off by shrapnel in a firefight with some European horde. He seemed an old man already then, as his wife was an old woman. He penetrated me with tight and teary, blue-grey eyes, eyes a color no Kit had ever generated absent his parents straying from the Rez with their organs of procreation. And he planted himself in front of me in his white wool suit, and knelt on one knee in front of me, nerve-clangingly close, nearby the two closed caskets that contained the bagged remnants of Kittori, my father, and Spence, my twin, and I could smell tobacco on his breath, which reminded me of my father there behind me. And he pulled the fabric of my shirt at the shoulder, the only unstained button-down I could borrow from my mother's brother, and the old man said, "This is swimming on you. We'll get you some new clothes in town, Boy."

And I said, "I have lots of clothes. This is my favorite shirt—my uncle said it was my father's once, a hand-me-down."

And he said, "Well. I see. Then this paternal hand-me-down you shall wear to your heart's content. No one will ever take this shirt from you. It shall become, as they say, inextricable from your person."

He said all this the way one with a tongue root intact but gnarled tongue body would say it.

And I said, "Sir, does your son ever wear a shirt of yours?"

And he said, "You know Dall, Boy?"

And I told him I knew Dall from selling rabbits at the outdoor flea market close to his birdhouse concern, and Dall had always been kind to me and my brother; Dall had laughed with us at stupid, fat white folks and the terrible jokes the skywriters made with grey smoke in the blue on behalf of some of the more established vendors: *Russian nesting dolls—they're so full of themselves.* We were always looking up. Or gorging on ice cream, which I managed never to pay for because I played the Poor Indian Case, and procured enough frozen provisions for me and my brother, sometimes from Dall, which I knew was probably financed with his father's money. And Dall said I was a master at the con. And so it was Dall who christened me, "Conner."

And my future father said, "Kendall's not a wears-his-father's-shirt type kid. Kendall's – well, I guess Dall's his own man, isn't he?"

Then a woman I didn't know, a white woman from the big white County building in Arctadia, took my hand in her moist hand, and I yanked it back because I was 12, but then she steered me by the shoulders out into the parking lot. And I climbed into her yellow van with the logo of a happy cartoon boy in big boy pants and girl in a hoopy skirt holding hands below a rainbow. "Climbed aboard without a question," my new father would later lament, half-teasingly, and half to reiterate a lesson about a necessary element for the free-flowing outlet of the *Lix'eyo Páæhgwa-ken*. Before the kidnapper got around the front of the van, I saw Mr. Lincoln Christmas, a little out of breath, stopping her bodily in front of the ticking hood. And they talked, exchanging animated gestures, but I couldn't hear what they were saying because someone – in fact, a Kittakwa named Maurice, who'd once broken into Kitskill Caritas Hospital – a wing long disused – to steal pain killers for his wife – was blowing leaves with the big cylindrical machine strapped to his back. "Beasts of burden," my father, my birth father, always said at such a sight. Look what these people have done to our people, Bat (He called me "Bat" since I made clear my wont for screeching as a baby, and because "Owl" was already claimed by an anomalous uncle of his). I know: Bat Wayne. Superhero's first appearance: 1939 vs. my origin in '33.

Two Spirits　　　　　　　　　　　　　　　　　　　　　　　　　　57

And a week later, I was in my own room next to Dall's, and Mrs. Christmas ordered all my old clothes burned outside, excepting my interment shirt, and bought me all new ones in town, and somehow knew my exact size—even my shoes. And gave me a hundred dollars (!) and let me pick out all my own pajamas, underwear, and socks at the flea market, as, she said, "A man procures his own undergarments." And there was a maid and some kind of social secretary for Mrs. Christmas, and a cook, and Maurice, a gardener for my new father – all four Kittakwa – and all four of them looked at me in a manner that made me squirm like my father and brother trapped and trying to pull themselves up out of that lemon-squeezing split in the top of the rock.

***

Dall and I explored. Every teeming acre, every limb and hollow, every season. The vast bed of crunchy mica shards. The oval of burned dirt, like some saucer once touched down to celebrate the advent of a Christmas. The crisscrossing Christos Creek, all its little cataracts and eddies full of smooth stone and tadpoles. Kittatinn Pond, its raft and swing. The High Damien and the stone bridge below, said to have been the place both Chief Kittadoga rejected the Iroquois Confederacy, and Akt'adia Kit, our first female warrior, and young, performed the rites that brought the mist-borne Ghosh'eyo into the Kittakwa fold. And other expanses. BVDs and PJ flies. All the crooks and valleys. The plain of abdomen and twin-mounded back garden with its unlocked gate to promises once undelivered by and to my brother, now living in the Under, unless this was the Under, and he was in the Upworld. One could never tell.

***

But I was not the born son of a Christmas. I spent as much time in Dall's company as was humanly possible and still moderately seemly. One morning a few months after my adoption, in a cold midwinter that had dumped four feet of snow already, I sat on my haunches in a blue snowsuit, watching Shelter Rock, looking like the back of some bearlike beast dozing curled up faced away from me—sleeping after eating all the men of my clan. Dall shadowed his father at the bureau office in Albany – I was not invited – so I went to the woods to commune with my brother, mostly. In the echo of the mote, I could hear him answer me back when I called. But this day, we both said "Look" at the same time, as I spotted a deer – a five-point buck – muzzling down through the snow to graze; then bolt, darting serpentine before running headlong into the wedge below the rock, where he jammed his antlers, and seemed to twist his neck. His hooves kicked out, and he emitted an otherworldly wail, ferocious like a wolf's. And I felt all the chambers of my heart blow up, detonate like the mine Lincoln Christmas would soon step on at a godforsaken jungle deerpath crossing littered with dead child soldiers, half of them girls—or the black powder blast that would later bring the ceiling of the Christmas Crystal Mine down on the lighted helmets of a hundred men, half black, half Kit, a dozen stoic cousins of my mother among them.

But what could I do? A boy. A former Wayne (Bat Wayne) fresh off the Rez. I couldn't help a giant, wild thing survive. But nor could I sit still, a lump inanimate as a petrified tuber. So I got up and clambered through the drifts over which that nimble buck had bounded on his kamikaze mission. And I found a spot to kneel behind his heaving back where he couldn't kick me to oblivion, though not for want of trying. His body was rank, steaming. Some tiny, black somethings crawled crazily over each other under the matted, ice-clotted fur of his belly. I spoke to him. I insisted that he stop his caterwauling, stop his struggling. I told him to let go all his pain, all his fear of the future. It was a better place, our future, Mrs. Christmas always said, and it's just around the corner. And when I touched his hock, his skin flinched for several seconds, then all his muscles seemed to slacken, and he heaved, and then was still. The snow around the Rock was considerably shallower—its bulk prevented mass accumulation. But I was no less cold there with my new friend in my arms.

I scooted into the cave hollow, where I at once felt warmer, and I put my hand on the animal's head, spread out my fingers between the antlers, right in the middle of a white spot the same shape as the hourglass that Mrs. Christmas used to time her biscuits in the oven and her sons in the bath. His skull was so solid, so—something. And I said, "See my brother." And Shelter Rock said back to me, "*See my brother,*" and a surge of warmth then swam all through my groin and hips and legs and chest and belly, tingled my scalp. And the animal's white eye turned, and I was sick on the snow.

The voice inside the boulder was my Spence's.

***

I never envisioned I'd come to Kenya for love, no less *the* love. *Love chases the unwary traveler,* some old Kittakwa aphorism says. Or something along those lines. I met Collins when I went running after some stray, seriously wounded dog in a Nairobi neighborhood I had no business being in. He ducked out deftly from a doorway and snatched my quarry with one hand by the scruff of its neck. "I've been after this one and his friend for a week already," he said. "Ate one of my chickens, I think."

"Friend?"

"This is the first time I've seen this one alone. His mate met a lorry, I assume."

Or maybe some kid took him home?"

"You must be American. Where all boys rescue puppies under cotton candy clouds."

"Unicorns." He didn't know the word. I made like I was neighing, galloping with my hands turned under, and then I indicated the conical horn. "Never mind. Look, I'm a doctor. Not a vet—a people doctor. But I was thinking stitches, antibiotics. I've got some here. I think I can manage that."

"So our conquering hero shall save this hound. This way, Doctor Welby. Through there—the canteen. We have the perfect table for an operation."

The building from which Collins had emerged showed absolutely no sign, literal or figurative, that those within desired company or commerce. In fact, I saw weapons, munitions, maps staked everywhere, on open display. Three men playing cards at a shitty little table. One young man in the corner cleaning what I'm pretty sure was an AK-47. "Let's ... Perhaps ..."

"No, don't worry, Marcus. White American medics who chase after broken-down strays are not the target of this particular revolution."

"Good to know."

Good-natured smiles all around. "But how about you don't ask me who's the target."

"I will not." And up onto the operating table went our quickly diminishing patient.

"Marcus Welby never loses a patient."

"That's a fiction."

"We shall see."

Then one month later, Collins and I sat at another table in the far more palatable Karen district. Sometime after the main course and prior to coffee, our fingers intertwined beneath the tablecloth, and I realized when I looked into his eyes, his open smile, that I loved him. Not since Dall arranged to break the stone of my heart into rubble had I felt this way. Dall returned as Daddy had, in a flag-draped wooden coffin with a medal and a hundred soldier's signatures, gems of the jungle.

***

Long before modern gerontological studies acknowledged the fact, Kittakwa medicine held that humans, like other biological organisms, recycle their entire organic systems – including every single heart and brain cell – almost exactly every seven years. So I say that I was literally a different person at 16, a month before I left for greener grasses, when I came upon the brother of the buck I'd urged to die when I was 12: I am hunting hunters, who cut holes in our fences as they know we boast an abundance of prey on our default reserve. They come onto our land with bow and arrow – iron-age irony – so we won't hear them. I'm tucked into a high blind built up in an elm when I hear him (first) then see him vaulting over baby boulders with a bead on Shelter Rock. Two men's voices, maybe three, not far off, poachers instructing each other urgently about the course of their hard-earned buck.

He stops and huffs just underneath me, and nearly topples over, falling on one knee. I did not anticipate that he'd been shot once already. The tell-tale quiver. He lows – I have only heard an animal emit this sound now twice in my lifetime – and blood is pouring from his nose. "*Oh—*," I say, and he looks up at me, directly—right into my eyes. The eyes. And as if the configuration of those antlers were not exact enough, I spot the patch, the hourglass white on his forelock. Then he looks down, raises his bulk off that bent leg, and trots forward, head held high. He disappears into the cavity of Shelter Rock in the distance. Was this, impossibly, the same big buck that I held onto into death? But surely he'd have shed those branches? And anyway, there's no way he could have extracted and righted himself that day years ago, disencumbered himself from that gap under Shelter Rock. Plus his neck was broken! Breath stopped. I look up out into the slate sky through the manifold branches, looking for the everyday, the truth, the answers. And when I look back down, the two killers, only boys, are standing right below me. One says to the other – they're obviously brothers – "We gotta finish that fast fucker off. Can't leave him wounded like that. I told you—don't shoot until I say. You hear? *I* say."

It does not occur to me until three decades later, one night under the zoophilic constellations, I and Collins, that the animal I saw that day was not a ghost, but my buck's brother. Twins.

What if a place where sacrifices happen someday gets a taste? What if a mass, a body, a thing, wishes never to erode, but grow. What if it organizes augmentation along some moral code—say, consuming only one of each pair, so the other can go on. Broken, yes, rent from its other self, and forever after looking—but still a one?

What if that dog hadn't crossed in front of me on the Nairobi road, black and bleeding?

What if I'd been in bed with my brother the day my father came for a son to explore Shelter Rock and plant a flag—in bed with my brother instead of curled up in a white man's smokehouse with a white man's son, a lantern, and a sleeping bag?

Can one person ripple the world's cold pond with the puny skipping stones of his best efforts? What can I do? In my thirties. Here where they call the elephant an enemy, and hack its tusks off with the cheeks while he bleats and begs for his mother, our Maker, for mercy. Here where some same-looking-black folks from the neighbor nation took over a farmers' market and went person to person demanding that mothers and children recite a certain verse, and when they couldn't, shot them all twice in the face. Here where every railroad bed's a graveyard.

Paradox: The diatoms at last revealed by the cleavage beneath the boulder, evidence of a prehistoric seabed, are defined both by their hollowness and jagged frames. Together these diametric features make them whole, form and function cocreated. They animated the Christmas Crystal Mine, for decades, my people employing my people, one breathing the others' dust. Both choking. Until it all collapsed.

Ask the boy: Above that, Shelter Rock's as solid as—

But ask the man. We know it's not. It is a kind of chaos, only partially, magically under the appearance of control. Inside that stone, electrons orbit the nuclei of their atoms at seven thousand million times per millionth of a second. The least substantial, least unanimous things in the universe. How do you measure their speed? How does the Rock escape a quadrillion constant, terrible collisions, total instability—how is it that it doesn't fly apart to find its Maker? Instead it seems as semi-permanent as our planet itself. And what of us? Can we even argue we're not all connected? That the spooky distant action of our brother does not motivate our atoms?

Two Spirits

***

How to stay still. How to countermand the drawing? The Twin Eater drew me. I could've settled anywhere. I could ply my trade – a doctor without borders – anywhere that certain maladies now take babies and the wives of the long-haul truckers who fuck their favorite boys at the crossroads, boys who pull their pants down only for lack of water in their *banda*, lack of a globe and chalk and abacus at the shack they call a school. Here where a good man like Collins Wangari finds himself cast out of his boyhood home by his own mother for the way his Maker made him come to such a trucker, who hugged him as his father never had, who let him listen to the radio, and talk to other truckers on the citizen's band, men as far away as Durban, who once took him to meet the drivers at the rally in Dakar, and they slept on the seventh floor of a hotel and wore white terrycloth robes on the balcony.

Why here and now? I came here, I stayed here, because looming over the even, ochre ground, I found the Twin Eater, and it wasn't going anywhere. Because I might not have seen the face of the child in the rock façade until my barmate outlined it with a gnarled finger for me that dawn—but it had marked me. And it said: *Stay*. In the voice of Spence, it said *stay*. *Come into my shade*, said Collins. There is a war inside, but also me. Stay and be my brother.

And then one day I climbed it. One day I set out to see the top, to tread upon it, to look down at the bottom where I lived, looking up here to this cloudland. And after hours climbing, struggling, dragging, carrying my weight first on two legs, then two hands, then one, I reached the top, and marveled. And walked obliquely to what appeared its geographical center; and there I saw a hole, a mouth, a maw, that seemed to have no bottom. And there I squatted in the manner of the tribesmen I had come to know, my forearms on my knees. And when at last I called into that chasm, when I yelled, "Hey—is anybody there?" it answered the very next second. It said, "Yes, you are here—and you're still there at once."

—With your dead white friend and all—

Wednesday Sept. 12. Day 9 of the shoot.

New Mexico mountains

EXT. KITTAKWA RESERVATION, UPSTATE NY. DOCK. NIGHT

SUPERIMPOSE: ROSE LEAVES: BEE STINGS, IMPOTENCE

In a shady glen, birds slalom-race for their insect midnight snack.

In PD's lap, a long-haired white boy, NOAH, 16. A large flap containing the boy's ear is folded halfway over bloodless lips, which PD brushes with his thumb. PD folds the skin back up, pats it. Noah's blue eyes are wide open. Body limp. At peace.

A long-in-the-tooth Shepherd, MEAT PUPPET, licks Noah's face. She loved him, too.

>   PD
> Noah.

>   MAX
>   (laughing)
> Ain't he supposed to survive the flood?

>   PD
> Supposed to, yeah.

>   MAX
> Ridden hard and put away wet. He one of them?

Max gestures to the unseen enemy closing in.

Meat Puppet roots in the loam beside Noah.

>   MAX (CONT'D)
> He one of them, Bon? I'm askin'. Cause if you killed one of them, Well, goody goody gumdrops for you.

>   PD
> Not this one. He's one of us. They ran over him with one of their quads.

Two Spirits   65

                    MAX
              Seen that before.

                    PD
              In the war?

Max lights a hand-rolled cigarette. Takes a deep drag.

                    MAX
              In all of 'em.

PD tears off the scraps of Noah's blood-soaked Dirty Jew concert tour T-shirt, and begins to unbutton the boy's 501 Blues.

                    MAX
              Well, now.

                    PD
              Will you help me?

                    MAX
              He a Jew? Don't look it.

Max swigs from a canteen. Spits on his cigarette. Limps over.

The two Lightnings pull off Noah's bloody Levi's. PD looks over the body in pale blue underwear.

                    PD
              Just a band. A musician.

                    MAX
              Kids today.

A sliver of lilac-tinged organ meat peeps from a gash beside Noah's navel. One of his hips is dislocated, grotesque. The long bones that run parallel up his leg diverge abruptly now below the knee, thrusting out either side, snapped like celery stalks. His torn face looks like a loose Halloween mask.

                    PD
              This one's different.

Max surveys the boy's long hair, his delicate features.

                    MAX
              You said it. I seen them "different"
              sorts before.

                    PD
              Behind bars—or in 'em?

                    MAX
              Good one.

PD starts pulling Noah farther down the dock. Max watches, then stoops, reluctantly helps.

                    MAX (CONT'D)
          There was this one—He weren't much
          older than you. They swarmed him. Took
          him. Well, you know what they do to
          their young in a joint like that.
                         PD
               I don't know.

Max stops, and Noah plops to the dock. The Old Man chews his
soaked cigarette and looks off into the distance.

                         MAX
          Oh, they tattooed him. On his ass, you
          know. Right about here, where you got
          that rash when ...

He toes Noah's left buttock.

                    MAX (CONT'D)
          They wrote, "BITCH." About yea big.
          That's some shit. Permanent record.
                         PD
               He was your friend?
                         MAX
               Well, now.

The SHOTS intensify. Whistling of ROCKETS. A distant HELICOP-
TER. They start dragging the body again.

                         PD
               You saved him?
                         MAX
          None of that. He would read, that one.
          Long hair like this one here. He'd read
          a lot. Like you. At the little library
          they had up there. Whipsmart. I asked
          him a question one day. A test. I said,
          "Why did the Kittawkwa give up the Rock
          so easy in 1791?" He said, "They did-
          n't. The British dishonored them."
                         PD
               Did he pass the test?
                         MAX
          Goddammit. You don't know? See, he did-
          n't spout off, "They tricked 'em." They
          never sold our fuckin' rock. He said
          "dishonored." Sittin' there shittin'
          blood. Sittin' on "BITCH" and all, but
          he said the right thing. We lost our

Two Spirits   67

                    Shelter 'cause we got our asses
                    tricked.

PD looks down at Noah's face.

                              PD
                    What was that boy's name?

                              MAX
                    Told you. His name was "BITCH."

PD nods.

                              MAX (CONT'D)
                    So, what are you proposin' to do with
                    this "different" one now? Now you've
                    uncovered yer Noah's nakedness?

PD looks over the still, dark lake like black glass: Kittatinn Pond.

                              PD
                    We're going Under. Away from all this.

Now it's Max's turn to nod.

                              MAX
                    Under. Well, now.

Max removes the wet cigarette in his mouth, contemplates what to say next.

The fighting gets closer. A CHOPPER passes over, its searchlight almost catching them. More SHOTS. A war?

PD takes Noah's headphones from the boy's backpack, and carefully puts them over Noah's ears. The kid's head flops like a well-used Teddy. He forwards the iPod to Noah's favorite song, Dirty Jew's "Boys Say Golem."

                              MAX (CONT'D)
                    Goddammit. What say you wait maybe half
                    an hour.

                              PD
                    What happens in half an hour?

                              MAX
                    Well. I got every swingin' dick still
                    kickin' with every shotgun and pistola
                    on the Rez up on the ridgeline, all on
                    the High Damien, and they all made
                    peace with their mams and wives. Second
                    wave. We're gonna take back our land.

                              PD
                    Going Under. Told ya.

                    MAX
          I know you got a very modern way of—
          with yer dead white friend and all,
          Bon, but I hope you understand our
          fuckin' leaf - none of our plants or
          trees or roots or critters of any sort
          - not a fuckin' one, I tell you - be-
          longs to these pale cunt overlords.
          Second wave. We take it all back. You
          with me?

That's all so interesting, Influencer Talbot. Your take on that seminal event. Your interpretation. The realism. The grit. True grit. Let's call this an adequate answer to the question. But I wonder. A lot, actually. We wonder. Why does – forgive me – did – the grandfather just allow his grandson to – what? – essentially kill himself, right? I mean. "Under." That means the bottom of the lake. The pond. Whatever. But under *it. So the next question has to do with the interaction of the generations: What protections do – and don't – young people require from the old? Go. Godspeed and go.*

— It's all fun & games until someone loses an I—

Thursday Sept. 13. Day 10 of shoot

New Mexican mountains

[FLASHBACK]

EXT. KITTAKWA REZ - DUSK (2 WEEKS BEFORE)

Noah lies on the loamy ground, blindfolded with his own cornflower blue boxer briefs. He covers his nakedness with a pair of over-ear headphones. He's lithe like a pale jungle cat, almost pretty with his long hair.

                   PD
          You ready?

At the sound of PD's voice, Noah cocks his head. But PD moves, breaking a stick on Noah's other side. Noah quickly shifts his head in that direction. He's half-smiling, half biting his bottom lip. PD waits behind a sugar maple, barely breathing.

                   PD (CONT'D)
         Are you ready?

                   NOAH
         No.

PD creeps up noiselessly, passes a fat leaf over Noah's lips. Noah sniffs.

Meat Puppet WOOFS.

                   PD
         Taste.

Noah opens his lips.

                   NOAH
         Like gum. Peppermint?

                   PD
         Boy wins a cigar. That was an easy one,
         though. Wait.

A wild blueberry's next.

                    PD (CONT'D)
          Can you smell?

                    NOAH
          Nada.

                    PD
          Stick out your tongue.

                    NOAH
          I'm trusting you.

                    PD
          Of course.

Noah rolls the berry around, squishes it with his tongue against the roof of his mouth.

                    PD (CONT'D)
          Huckleberry.

                    NOAH
          Bullshit.

                    PD
          Legit huckleberry. Last month, they were
          still amazing. OK, ready for the next
          one?

The fluffy white ball of a dandelion, over Noah's neck, behind his ear. He flinches, then leans into it.

                    PD (CONT'D)
          If you have a liver or kidney problem,
          or indigestion ... plus, it makes you
          pee.

                    NOAH
          No clue.

                    PD
          Come on. It looks like a flower but
          it's really a cluster of tiny flowers
          packed together, and each of the seeds
          has, like, a fuzzy thread the air
          catches like a parachute ...

                    NOAH
          Charlotte's babies?

                    PD
          Ha. Just like that. But I wouldn't put
          a spider on you while you can't see.
          You trust me. Give up?

                    NOAH
          Ah, a dandelion. *En français: Dent-de-
          Lion.* Tooth of the—
                    PD
          I never realized that.
                    NOAH
          I'm a font of information.

PD sits back on his haunches. Pulls his shirt off.

                    PD
          You're a font, all right ...
                    NOAH
          I want ...

He squirms a bit, shifts, lifts his headphones from his lap. He knows PD's been eyeing him everywhere.

                    PD
          What do you want?
                    NOAH
          This is no fair. I wanna ...
               (whispers)
          I wanna ... see you, too.

PD pulls Noah's underwear blindfold down until it's around the boy's neck.

                    NOAH (CONT'D)
          I like looking in your eyes.
                    PD
          Eye.
                    NOAH
          No. Both of 'em.

[END FLASHBACK]

Cut. Right, Boys. Wardrobe. Cover him, please. Tell me again whose idea it was to shoot New Mexico for New York? And September for summer? Tax rebates, aside, baaad *idea. Can we have our* enfant terrible, *the screenwriter, Master Augusten B. Talbot, fetched from his cozy trailer, please? I have a coupla story questions here that didn't come up in our readthrough. Then you guys can go on your little "skiing" trip. That's right. Your director knows all. He knows more than you will ever know.*

ground rules

Ground Rules

For Dennis Cooper

*You don't save a pitcher for tomorrow.
Tomorrow it may rain.*

—Leo Durocher, *New York Times*, 1965

Nothing beats Kids League Baseball for tear-jerking drama or good-looking boys. This afternoon these twin glories remind me of a former Kids League champ named Bo Silver and our days, bygone. Today my Podunk New York – technically, Kittakwa Indian – town is hosting the tie-breaking seventh game in the 1997 World Series of KLB. The man on Cable SportsCenter says it's the focus of sports fans everywhere. Never mind that our brand new stadium – pride of the "New Kittakwa" – is a stone's throw away, or that my business card proclaims I'm a sports photographer—As ever, I have to stay home to attend to the unpleasant business upstairs.

Tonight, a congenial interlude, I hope. Then, tomorrow morning, it all ends. Everything ends by a special undertaking. Through the business of terminating my irksome consciousness with a bunch of ecru tablets, and shutting off some red switches upstairs in service of perhaps reanimating another's consciousness, though on some other plane. Either way, no more artificial life support for either of us two.

Meanwhile, the whole Rez is going apeshit. Along the half dilapidated Main Street, welcome banners are waving in English, Kit, and "Spanglish." In cul-de-sacs and sandlots, boys are smacking balls around. Few, of course, will ever fulfill a swing worthy of escaping this forsaken burg. I've passed those boys in the Jeep Bo used to hoard for himself and the Arctadia High School baseball team he coached. I still feel guilty driving the Jeep. Guilty and a little weird, too, considering what Bo last used it for. I still carefully remove my Wrigley's wrappers and pistachio shells, and brush the floor mats of gravel and grime whenever I get out. No use losing all respect for precedent, all honor for my spouse.

★★★

The Mission Viejo, California boys arrived over the weekend at Stewart Airport. A convoy of Kit coaches picked them up. They've been kipping at the New Yorker Hotel on Route 30, the one that reeks of chlorine. Tonight, their last night here, the players are scheduled to split up among local host families, which is where I come in, though not every native might consider ours a family in the strictest, census-taker's interpretation of the word.

Their challengers, representing Tepic, Mexico, came in a ramshackle, three-tone brown diesel bus with little by way of a muffler. Have they been grateful for the inhospitable Kit Community Center / Cultural Hall with the marquee outside boasting *"Indoor Heated Poo–"*? They can race the darkened hallways at night, sliding in their socks. Is the Rez, with its half-dead outlet mall, disused concrete concern, mega box stores, and firetruck factory – elders' attempts at relevance – some kind of paradise to them? My own reaction was more subdued the day in 1968 my mother moved us up to my father's birthplace, Kittatinn County, from Staten Island. I was 10, and not a champion at anything. We crossed the Verrazano Narrows Bridge, the longest suspension bridge in the world at the time, and I remembered what an uncle had told me, that I was the man of the house now my papa was dead (and that three-out-of-four steel workers on bridge jobs were Indians, because they have no fear of heights).

I kept my rabbit, Honey Dijon, in a box in my lap for the entire three hour drive, rubbed her hot cheeks, and made her epic promises, but she would not survive our first winter upstate. My mother would blame it on "psychic trauma." And what about me? Could I survive?

The first Indian I ever saw (besides my father, kind of) was a young hitchhiker hotfooting it off the Rez with a sign outside the pharmacy that said, improbably, "Africa or Bust."

When the young athletes poured into town last week, I was at that pharmacy on Main Street waiting for a new prescription of Sieract. I was plotting on a lawn chair beside the candy counter when the bell above the door roused me. A clean-cut boy, about 13, strode down the aisle toward the back of the store. His eyes were in shadow under his cap as he walked by me. He peeled some change out of tight, white baseball pants. He turned toward the soda machine. This was the same soda machine from which Bo and I bought bottled Cokes when we were this boy's age. It was ancient and complicated, even back then.

With a cleat, he scratched his calf where the trouser leg tucked into a blue stocking. I looked away from the curved straps of his jock beneath his pinstripes. Prominent calves. Wide-set stripes. I looked away.

The kid reviewed the directions stenciled on the contraption, and dropped three quarters in its slot. When the coins plunked into the change bin below, he tried again. Just the slightest shuffle of his feet and cock of his head gave his agitation away, but he maintained an even keel, a champ's persistence. He seemed a no-nonsense boy, one who expected a pop when he was thirsty. In this sense, he again reminded me of Bo at 13.

"Excuse me," the boy said – past me – to Hazel, the fat old owl behind the drug counter. "Is this machine alive?"

"That machine works nicely," she said. With a lit cigarette, she pointed to a hand-written sign taped to an upper corner, which, indeed, proclaimed as much:

> THIS MACHINE WORKS NICELY
> FOLLOW DIRECTIONS
> AND DON'T ASK FOR HELP

The kid chewed his bottom lip. This time he leaned in, and read through the steps, following with his finger, moving his lips. He dropped in his coins for the third time, and once more they fell through without capture. The fat slag sighed, and dragged her carcass from behind the counter with a jumble of skeleton keys. Without apologizing for her cunty doubt, she opened the behemoth while her cigarette bobbed between her lipstick-smeared teeth.

"Flavor?"

"Grape."

The boy, Number 8, didn't thank her, didn't look at her. *Good for him*, I thought.

"Brownie," Hazel said to me, "Got that Sieract Five-Hundred. Wowza. One a day max, you got it? Or it's goodnight, Irene. Sign the doohickey."

Number 8 held open the door for me, must have walked that aisle awful slow to find himself still there when I arrived. He picked a ball and mitt off the storefront bricks, and slid off south toward the Common, offering me a goodbye with his chin in the manner of boys these days.

Yesterday there was an Independence Day parade with a special welcome to the champs, both teams, who were tied thus far in this most contested Series in Kids League history. I watched on local access as the whole town marched down Main and Grady. The California team was near the end of the parade, between the county children's theater float ("Annie"), and a huge green military Humvee, the need for which in exurban Kit County was a mystery to me. The Mission Viejo Mounties filled a slow-moving flatbed trailer advertising Lou's Books. I looked for Number 8, but he didn't stand out.

Last night I called Lou, who'd taken the coaching reins from Bo. The *Kit Banner* said he was responsible for coordinating host accommodations for the players.

"Number Eight," I said.

"Gray Cooper? Story there, for sure. See, he's—"

"He's eighteen. I mean eight."

"Oh. The pitcher? Gavin Bledsoe? Any special reason?"

"I need one?"

"No. Anything for … I'll shift some stuff around. Say, Brownie," he said, "How's, uh … tricks out there?"

"Living hell. You? The wife OK?"

"Same vag, different day. So I'll see you later? Wish us luck."

★★★

Gavin Bledsoe. He's on TV now, so I sit up, my neck tensing as though it's my boy stamping his feet in the batter's box. It's 3-1 Cali already, bottom of the fourth. A capacity crowd chants *"U-S-A! U-S-A!"* Ironic, given we're technically a sovereign nation. In the stands some of the players' mothers have painted American flags and their sons' numbers on their faces. I think of my own mother, and I know this will be the closest any of these women come to greatness. They exist in a world where their adolescent boys have already eclipsed their achievements – probably even their potential – and they're bat-shit happy for it, having made this deal somewhere along the line as most mothers must.

The CSC sportscaster says offhandedly that Gavin Bledsoe is the best friend of the coach's son, the Mounties' catcher, name of Danny. I wonder why he was alone then at the drugstore last weekend. The announcers make vague references to Gavin's triumph-over-tragedy. I want to know his story. I see Gavin's silky blond sideburns, shaved close, beneath his cap and blue batter's helmet. A thin line of sweat has streaked down to his ear, and black grease paint is smudged under his blue eyes—surely an adult athlete's affectation, and unnecessary on an overcast afternoon. It makes me smile. Gavin pulls his batting gloves from his back pocket, and puts them on.

"Two ducks on the pond," says the announcer in that half-whispering way of announcers, as if the players can hear him. "Bledsoe. The pitcher. His stance open, as always. He's looking for a base hit, move his men …"

The dusty face of Mexico's ace pitcher – as though reanimated from Aztec DNA – is stern as he surveys the bases. The Tepic boys are striking specimens, but somehow looking more like small adults than their all-American opponents. Our boys look like they still have years left in clean-handed boyhood. I've tried to nab this—what Bo used to call "the Norm*al* Rockwell thing" whenever I photographed his boys playing ball, which was often. I'm pretty sure I'm trying to recapture Bo as I first saw him when we were 11, chewing Juicy Fruit and punching his mitt in center field. I wanted him to yearn for me as intensely as he desired the ball to smack that leather. When he was a Kids Leaguer, I had him look right into the lens when I shot him with my old Brownie—so he'd be looking at me when the picture came out. It's so fucking obvious. So cliché. But what are you gonna do?

"Lopez's stretch, and … it's his bread and butter pitch, no surprise," says the announcer, whose name we come to know is Reg. "Outta the strike zone."

Ball one.

Gavin spits, something black and sticky. I see above his mesh V-neck jersey he wears a reddish black leather choker with some kind of charm—possibly a shell or a stone. It must be salty in all that sweat.

"Murphy and Delfinio both leading quite a bit. Bledsoe's thirteen years old, ninety-seven pounds. You remember those days, Chuck? Ninety-seven pounds?"

"I sure don't, Reg."

"And I bet the wife doesn't remember, either."

"Easy, Reg."

"I meant you at ninety-seven pounds, Chuck. I wouldn't go there, believe me."

Gay banter, Bo used to call it, ironically.

"Ball two. Lopez's all over the plate today."

"Hog wild," says Chuck.

The third pitch brushes Gavin's back, which spooks him, though he tries to stay cool, it seems.

"That's revenge for Bledsoe's knockdown pitch to Lopez Thursday?"

"Or sloppy pitching—either one."

Lopez tries to mix up his pitches, I think. Gavin strikes out once. The next two pitches are out of the zone again. Gavin walks. He's dragging his feet now, not the confident, grape Crush-chasing boy from the pharmacy.

Then a time out offers the director a chance to cut to a wide shot of Christmas Memorial Stadium, taken from CSC's signature blimp. Squat, ugly Arctadia pales beside the wide Christos Creek and the Kitskills, in which I live remotely in the house Bo built us with his bare fucking hands while I was on a series of assignments: Tanzania. Argentina. The Pike Forest Fire, where 17 hotshots died. There's the main shaft of the Christmas Mine, collapsed after consuming a contingent of Kits and poor blacks from the adjacent Slope.

They run Gavin's sepia-toned bio. I don't know much about the fine points of athletics, despite my peripheral involvement. But I love it when sports shows produce these segments. It really makes me feel like I'm invested in the outcome of the game when I know the players' dramatic narratives. The background music is Beethoven's "Ode to Joy." We see Gavin in jeans and a sweatshirt, walking on the beach and skimming rocks in a calm cove of the Pacific. Gavin lacing up his cleats, and Gavin wailing a ball in slo-mo toward the camera, his form near perfect, if I recall correctly what Bo always said about the hip bone flailing out and the wrist loose. There's Gavin shirtless and shoeless with a black lab at his side, and it is a white clamshell around his neck on the leather strap, flying. It's always Gavin alone, pensive, and never boisterous with friends. Where's Danny, the coach's son?

Cut to the smoldering wreckage of a jumbo jet in some jungle, shot from a shaky chopper. I sit up.

Just a tender 12 years old, Gavin Kiefer Bledsoe suffered the unendurable. To celebrate his '95 Series showing in Brasilia, the Bledsoe family was flying to Caracas, Venezuela. They planned to tour the rainforest, and experience Angel Falls and the majestic Orinoco River. But they would never take that tour. An hour after takeoff and hundreds of miles from civilization, their 727 crashed into a remote mountaintop. There were 135 people killed that day and, amazingly, Bledsoe was among only three survivors. The rest of his family perished. Suffering broken legs – and surely a broken heart – Gavin Bledsoe persevered nearly seven days until rescuers arrived through the fierce fog and the heartless, Amazonian terrain. This boy's bravery is indescribable. His maturity, unquestionable. The spirit is unquenchable and the heart of a giant in this small package; the heart of a hero.

Bledsoe recovered at the home of his coach and godfather, Derek Hartman, and his son, Danny, Gavin's best friend. This courageous champion defied doctors by walking in a mere three months. He withstood intense physical therapy at the Children's Hospital in Santa Gardena for three more, and pitched again just eight months after the terrible crash. "Bones heal," he told Sports Illustrated for Kids *last month*. But the 5'5" athlete's injuries did damage deeper than bone. He'd lost not only his parents, but his beloved older brother – his hero – Andy, just sixteen when he died. Andy Bledsoe, a former pitcher himself who took Mission Viejo to the Kids League Series four years ago, was on the fast track to the Major Leagues, with colleges from coast to coast vying for the power-lefty.

As for young Gavin, despite the enormous efforts that got him here today, he says he doesn't covet professional baseball. This boy says he doesn't know where he'll be when he becomes a man, but it won't be in the Majors. Wherever you go, Gavin Bledsoe, we think you're special. We stand in awe. You're a man in our eyes, and you are our hero. Back to you, Reg.

Fade out.
Jesus.
I'm stirred beyond swallowing my mouthful of Corona Light. I'm filled with melancholy awe and sadness for Gavin, but I'm also trying to quash a certain embarrassment for all the pissing and moaning in which I've wallowed these past months. It's like that first night at

the Kitskill Caritas Hospital when I wept for what happened to Bo, wondering what I'd do without him. I looked up from my hands and saw a nurse wheel a bald little kid down the hallway toward some unimaginable butchery. He wasn't crying. He was playing himself on a magnetic travel chess set.

Over the years, many models of similar courage came to stay with us in a guest room after various life catastrophes, sometimes overnight, and sometimes for a summer or a year. They played videogames and baseball, and mowed the lawn, and got better, then moved on. Some of them have written or called me, and one or two have come to see Bo—but only once. They don't ever come back.

Realizing we TV-land pansies would be depressed after Gavin's story, the director calls for a lighthearted shot. The competition on the field is so awful that the only time the boys look and act like boys is in the dugout. Two American teammates are spitting for distance through the chain link fence, unaware of the camera, and one behind them is snoozing under his cap. There is a merry squealing, a good-natured ribbing in the dugout. The second baseman's mitt is on his head so he looks like George Washington or Barbara Bush. Two boys from the crowd are facing away from the camera, peeing on a chain link fence. Of course, it's right beneath the Great Seal of the Kittakwa Nation. The camera quickly cuts away.

I'm taking deep, meditative breaths like Bo taught me when we were kids, to keep the world from squeezing the life out of me like a sponge.

On the field, though, they are as men, sometimes emulating their favorite athletes (listed in their stats at the corner of the screen), but more often just genuinely aged by the enormity of this experience.

"You look at those faces, Chuck. I'm talking about the Murphys, the Bledsoes, the Coopers, the Juan Diazes of this Series, and you see boys tilting over the edge into manhood," says Reg. I agree emphatically. Times like these call for clichés.

"From obscurity, to local celebrity, to worldwide renown," says Chuck. "Sometimes in one short year."

"You could say the same for this amazing stadium, eh, Reg? I mean. Wow. The tribal elders here could have built a casino, but objected on moral grounds. Good for them."

"Well, now."

"Decided instead to throw their hats in the sports ring. And boy howdy, they built a great one, winning this KLB contract by a landslide. Proud to show it off."

"Indian pride."

"Native American pride, Reg."

Do they know the stadium never would have been built had the mine not collapsed? It is a memorial stadium after all.

I know for certain those boys have savored what I never even tasted at their age. I never approached importance, honor, or any victory worth noting. My father had cooked in Napalm when I was two, leaving me crates of photographic equipment, but no memory of him besides what my mother gave up sparingly after glasses of May wine. She sensed that I was less hawkish than the man she'd met when he took her picture for a nudie magazine before the war. She had no idea how to deal with me, a guy who cried and wanted to cuddle. Whatever I most feared or longed for, whatever I couldn't hope to understand, I took a picture of, and developed it in the dark room my mother allowed me to build in the former laundry cupboard. Then I would make a careful study over hours and days in my hot attic room, while hornets buzzed and bounced along the nail-studded ceiling like knockers at heaven's gate.

I was otherwise alone.

At first I wasn't as aggressive a cameraman as my dad had been. I never actually felt like I was in the middle of any action, as he often described in postcards to my mother from Asia (once noting that many more war photographers – and far more American Indians – than Generals had been killed over there). As a young snapper, I thought of myself as entrenched behind sandbags, faraway and still pissing my khakis. My mother, who addressed all mail to her husband as "Dear Heart," nicknamed me "The Eyeball," as if I hadn't a heart to hurt, nor a brain to process what I saw through the lens.

Only Bo ever knew the real Brownie Ransom, the boy who loved him more than 30 years, and damn good thing for him.

It would be a few years of taking pictures until I comprehended that particular banality my father had scrawled on his last postcard, smudged with dirt—that his lens was a shield behind which he was invisible and immune. But on every gory field of battle that a soldier fought in Vietnam, he had a weapon and a fighting chance. My father had none.

★★★

Bo was my grammar school principal's son. I met him on the diamond during gym the first Fall after we moved back to Arctadia. Bo Silver was always picked first for teams, always glad-handed by parents, always forgiven for his "impish" antics. He even got away with wisecracking to teachers, who considered him a good spirit and sophisticated comic (it helped that his father made it clear that he thought so). He was taller than I, handsomer, better-built, with bright blue eyes and a messy, golden mop of hair. That's right. Golden. He'd come with his white family from South Carolina, because back in those days we couldn't muster a qualified high school principal from inside the tribe.

Bo had what he proudly referred to as a "snaggletooth," which, when flashed, seemed directly connected to my deepest and most secret self. There were freckles sprayed across the back of his long neck and shoulders. His feet were huge, like a golden retriever's.

Bo was a skinny-dipper. He stripped and swung on a rope into the Christos, into Kit Pond, in front of girls, boys, grownups, ghosts, whoever. He had no shame, and rightly so. He looked so pure and perfect naked. Just an all-American boy you'd expect to be good at baseball and fishing and maybe a quirky hobby such as agate collecting and polishing.

Bo had rescued from beneath a waterfall a battered and bedraggled basset hound named Lurlene, his best buddy. She swam with him, loped ungainly beside his bike, played catch and attempted to play

Two Spirits

Frisbee with him, and every night slept nestled in the angle of his open legs. Until I came along and banished her to the foot of the bed. The only time I ever saw Bo cry was when Lurlene lost most of an ear to a nesting jay.

I, on the other hand, was prone to jags of weeping. Bo made me cry in front of our math class in late October the first year we met. He hadn't meant to. He was just jumping on the bandwagon driven by a kid named Stevo Elk who was always calling me a war orphan, even though my mother was alive and working in the school library. On this occasion, Stevo said my father probably hadn't been the victim of friendly fire after all, but was likely shacked up with a "slanty yellow cooter." Stevo said you had to fuck them sideways over there, then Bo chimed in that, in fact, you could buy a cheap adapter at the airport nowadays. They found it funny. So funny. I was lost.

I couldn't blame Bo. We didn't really know each other yet. I'd been to his house once (his father and my mother might have been "dating") but he hadn't yet been to mine. I accidentally stomped on Lurlene's tail, and she yipped. My stomach dropped, but in two seconds, Lurlene started nuzzling my leg and wagging. "She's letting you know she forgives you," Bo said.

So while they were making fun of me in school, I looked straight into Bo's eyes until he stopped laughing. Then I applied Lurlene's principle, and wrote Bo a note, asking him whether he was going on the haunted hayride that weekend. He wrote back sloppily, right away, inviting me to come with him. "*Will Stevo be there?*" I wrote, and slipped it across his desk. "*Allergic to hay,*" Bo wrote back, "*Makes his balls all itchy.*"

Laughing at Stevo's expense, not to mention sharing a secret about another boy's balls, began our bond. I couldn't sleep that night. The only thing that calmed me was taking pictures of a spider on my footboard.

All the kids including Stevo called Bo "Bandit" – a nickname he earned after a bean ball pegged him in the eye and blackened it – but he signed all his notes to me as "Bo," short for his Christian name. In our three decades together I never called him anything but, and I never disposed of a single piece of paper – be it a birthday card or a list of errands – on which he'd written both our names.

The haunted hayride wasn't especially haunted. A dozen teenagers imported from Scotland for the season leaped out moaning from behind hay bales whenever the tractor-pulled wagons full of kids ambled by. They sported fake head lacerations, fake drop foot, fake fangs. One kid had a fake scar drawn from his chin down, disappearing into his pants. Afterward, we drank hot apple cider, and then got hammered on something Bo brought in a copper flask he'd hid down his pants. I held the flask, hot from his skin, smelling the metal whenever I drank, and burning inside.

Bo was the only kid who ever asked to see my pictures. I showed him hundreds on the floor of the stifling attic/studio. He held each print and scrutinized the images just as I had when I captured them. I watched his pupils shrink to pinpricks or burst out in flowers at the "beautiful" or "terrible" things I'd found in my year alone on the Rez: a honeycomb, frozen. Hornets fucking midair. A rusty Volkswagen Beetle upside down, with the tires half sheared off by a guardrail—someone died in it. Every kind of gorgeous, impossible Hudson River Valley bird. Several – OK, many – of Bo's fellow athletes making their physical magic. I distinctly saw him caress one (picture). Finally, the famous Wayne fire, the house blown up by the mother with her in it. Back in the day. Now rekindled by kids. Junior Fire Frogs blurry in the background, and in the fore in perfect focus, a fireman's helmet atop a Halligan bar driven into the ground—my favorite photo, and his.

Bo reacted with audible whoops or sustained silences, and even grabbed my arm a few times when most impressed. He played a game with me, in which he never used the same adjective twice to respond to a picture. If one was "awesome," the next had to be "grim," and the following, "intense." After an hour, it was taking forever to summon up vocab from the cobwebbed corners of his frontal lobe, and we laughed.

He was surprised how many shots of him I'd taken (though I'd only shown him the tiniest fraction). He was also flattered, I could tell from his face. He asked for one of me, of which there were none, until I showed him how to use the old Brownie. We tried a few early one morning on the upstairs porch, overlooking the river. Later, of course, he'd take more – thousands – but I remember best that first morning I lived in his lens like a spider on the footboard, entirely in his frame. "Now off with the shirt," he said. "Let's do a David Cassidy. Make *looove* to the camera, Brownie. That's right …"

Within a month, with the most popular kid's endorsement, I got tapped as photographer for the *Bon Voyager*, the brand new school yearbook and, more importantly, for Arctadia's Kids League Arrowstars, whose captain and star was my patron, the blond bandit, Beauregard Silver.

★★★

Propped up on pillows and under a quilt, I'm mesmerized as inning after inning America maintains its wide lead over Mexico. But despite my intrigue for one Gavin Bledsoe, around the bottom of the sixth, as the stoic Tepic boys try their damnedest to ignore the home field crowd's attempt to shout them down, I start to root for them. I'm remembering an assignment I once had in Mexico, how Bo and I watched boys of only six or seven do the proverbial work of men in an open-pit mine (after winning some prizes for my pictures of Christmas miners, I traveled to nine countries' mines to photograph men, children, asses, collapses).

Of course I'm proud of the California kids, but it's clear the Latin American team has had to conquer obstacles far graver to get here to the Land of Milk and Twinkies. Or is that just a dick thing to say? Racist, or whatever?

If our guys lose, they'll have lots of other opportunities to live the American Dream. A few will become proper heroes, surely. Most will make money. They will survive the loss, and they will be allowed to revert to childhood once the game is over (When the National Anthems come to a close, they say "Play ball!" after all, not

"Work ball!" somebody famous once said—no doubt Yogi Bera, who said all that type of shit).

The American boys – with names like Gavin Bledsoe, Chad Murphy, and Duke and Scotty Swanson – might even need to lose, let's say, and learn from losing. Right? That's what Bo would have said, at least. Look how perfect their teeth are, how snazzy their uniforms. Look how easy they have *everyfuckingthing*. It's the reason Bo chose to come back to the Rez to coach, why he turned down offers at numerous other schools.

I don't know. Maybe it is racist. To assume the poor kids won't recover as easily. That's the definition of racism, isn't it? But then again, what's ever wrong with rooting for the underdog?

It's more complicated, anyway. The sportscasters tell the story of one of the Mission Viejo kids, Gray Cooper—and how he got that Anglo name despite his clearly Latino features. He'd been abandoned – literally abandoned – as a child. Rescued, "like a puppy," by some white tourists when he was a baby.

The Mounties are leading by two at the top of the seventh. A few of the boys' girlfriends – or are they just groupies from town? – are giggling in the stands, leaning forward on their knees, dramatically reacting, gossiping, yearning, occasionally screaming in that way only preteen girls can scream. I get it.

At the moment, Gavin is the center of their attention. Equal power and finesse, the boy is hurling bullets at a steady 69-mile-an-hour-clip, about 10 percent faster than most other boys his age, barring one Japanese prodigy who regularly wails past 80, according to Reg and Chuck. On his twelfth pitch of the inning, he beans a skittish outfielder named Pedro Marquette, square on the collarbone, and Marquette spins backward into the catcher, Danny Hartman, his face kissing Hartman's chest pad. He grimaces on the ground, rubbing his clavicle, shaking his leg, but gets up without a fuss as the Tepic coach stands up to come forward, then waddles back over to the dugout bench. Danny helps brush the boy off—a tiny, probably unconscious gesture with a world of class and good breeding behind it. Bo would be proud.

A close up on Gavin's face. He squints, bites his lip, but doesn't seem shaken.

"He's got a gun-shy batter already, and now he's an easy out," Reg says. But the next pitch is a cookie, and Marquette gets a piece of the ball and a ticket to first.

Gavin kicks dirt on the mound.

Reg says, "Two men on. It's a calculated risk. Coach Hartman's chewing it over; there's eye-contact there. Can he afford to put Nevo back in with that bad elbow?"

Chuck says, "He believes in Bledsoe, Reg. Kid's usually a closer."

"Yeah, but we're not seeing that stamina or consistency here today."

"He may know it, Reg. Look at that face. This game's gone well beyond, 'Just-have- a-good-time-out-there, boys.'"

"Sure as shoot, Chuck."

Hartman nods to Gavin, sitting in the dugout as though he hasn't a care in the world. But he's chewing his gum real quick on that porch. That's his tell. His insides are likely agitating worse than a Maytag.

A shot of Tepic's fat coach, chomping a cigar and glaring hopefully between the mound and home plate. His red belt unbuckled like Santa on the 26th.

"Here's Aguillar looking menacing."

"Does he have any other look?"

Marquette and the Mexican kid on second are sidestepping leads, their legs spread improbably apart.

Gavin's chin is up, but he seems to be gnawing his tongue. He winds up, breaks with the rubber, kicks, and lets it rip. His eyes close even before the release, and he's already collapsing in on the follow-through. The Mexican left fielder swings and gets wood. The collision seems to split the air like a rifle report. Gavin hits the deck as the ball whizzes one inch over his head. A sloppy error by the center fielder, and Gavin has allowed a homer the Mounties can't afford. The score is now 4 to 2, *Gringolandia*. A small contingent of Mexico fans erupts in a dance near the top of the bleachers. *"Hey-hey. Ho-ho. Something-something-Me-he-co!"*

The blimp glints in the distance behind them. The clouds are dispersing.

Reg and Chuck give credit where credit is due.

Like the announcers, I'm waiting for Hartman to pull Gavin, but he just crosses his arms and nods in the kid's direction. Between his cupped hands, he shouts something encouraging, which I can't make out. The next two pitches, one attempted change-up and one curve ball, amble toward the batter, and it's only by some bizarre baseball voodoo that the boy strikes at one and is frozen by the other. But a third Mexican connects with the next pitch and helps bring home a *compadre*.

Danny pulls up his face mask and so does the umpire, looking to Coach Hartman.

Time out.

Hartman, a rangy, soldierly looking son of a bitch, summons his son and his "adopted" son to his post near the dugout. The Mounties all skulk, holding their belt loops and spitting. The camera zooms on Gavin, who drags his feet over the turf toward Coach Doom. It isn't fair. I sit up and feel for the Jeep keys in my pocket. I could be there in seven minutes if I can find parking. Bless the handicapped plates—thank you, Bo.

Then an amazing thing happens. CSC has mic'd the conference – probably the coach himself – so the TV audience can experience with clarity the exchange. Gavin's cleats scuff the turf, and he pulls his cap down closer to his eyes as the sun brightens.

"The hell is going on out there, G.?"

"Just ... I'm letting the whole team down."

I'm surprised his voice cracks, and he gulps air to keep from crying.

"Shame on you."

—"Oh—that hurts," whispers Reg to the TV audience.

"So you lose your focus? You're tellin' me you're through? 'Cause I'll yank your behind right now. I'll put Cooper or Nevo in, and you can go home and watch MTV."

Two Spirits 91

Gavin tugs at his choker, touches the white shell. "No. I'm in."

"That's better. Then throw the ball, G., and focus. Let's see those speedballs out there. Let's see eighty-two."

Gavin nods, fakes a smile behind his lips.

"You're a stone cold killer, G. You show these boys what you've got."

"Can you even imagine," Reg intones, as Gavin heads back to the mound, "hearing 'Shame on you' come from that hulk?"

"I cannot."

"Well it's got to be devastating, Chuck."

"No bout a doubt it."

Danny runs up, pats Gavin on the butt, and says, "You got this, man. Hang in there."

I could die.

★★★

Bo's dad, Principal Silver, had to quit one afternoon and go away for a while back to Charleston. Whatever the reason, neither my mother nor the school board took it with anything less than Trang Bang stride. Bo came to stay with me in the attic. We had our own bar fridge where we kept Cokes, and a couple of cans of Pabst Blue Ribbon hidden in an Entenmann's all butter loaf cake box. We had a black and white TV with two sets of headphones. We watched *Mannix* and *Kung Fu* and *Barnaby Jones*, and when we rolled up a towel and stuffed it in the crack under the door, there was no way my mother could tell that we were up so late watching Johnny Carson. She was not keen on hiking up the long creaky staircase anyway – not to mention after Bo's father went away, she fell into a languor almost worse than after that visit from the Army with a flag – so life in the attic was private and sweet, albeit almost unendurably steamy in every season.

Years later, throughout the '80s, Bo liked to reminisce of these days to any new gay couple we met, usually while traveling: Our first time. Because he was never reluctant to get naked in front of me when we were young, he chided me for my bashfulness, and one day in the attic after swimming, he actually started to rip off my shorts and T-shirt when I told him I wasn't too crazy about my scrawny bod. This turned into an all-out Greco-Roman mêlée with laughing and heavy breathing and such, and when he finally did get me out of my skivvies, my feelings about the affair where amply evident. He stared a long time at this perfect cliché, catching his breath, his freckled shoulders rising and falling, his smile fading. Finally, he reached out and brushed my rib, then cupped his hands over my hip bones, pulling me close to him. We ran the first three bases that night.

He was almost home before I tagged him out.

***

Seventh inning stretch. The children of the Kittakwa Reservation put on a genial, godawful show of New York Native American dance. Chuck and Reg do their best to review our history, conflating all sorts of Senecan, Mohawk, and Onondagan stuff. It's a socio-historical shitshow.

I fold the blanket. Recycle the empties. Shower. First time in a few days.

I clean up, check the cupboards.

Generally I don't leave the house unless the visiting nurse, named for a month, is upstairs. It's too late to make arrangements, though. What's the worst that can happen? In the Jeep on the way to the stadium, I hear on the radio Gavin strike out the last mad Mexican hitter, and the ninth inning start. The three miles to Christmas Memorial are snarled with traffic, a rarity on the Rez except for leaf-peeping season. Mission Viejo's two power sluggers, Kyle Delfinio and Duke Swanson, arrive on bases only to be sent back to the dugout. I get to the parking lot just in time to hear a geezer of a guard tell me Mexico has tied the game in the top of the ninth with a Chinese home run that just barely plonked over the fence. "That kid in the pasture by the name of Murphy gave it a go, though," the old bird says, clacking his teeth.

America rallies, and an extra inning is underway when I step through the gate, squinting at bright sunlight.

An agonizing half hour.

Lopez is up again. He and Gavin have been slugging it out all week. I look up at the scoreboard. We're fucked. Gavin's crippled—something Bo taught me on one of my thousand nights serving his boys orange slices and Gatorade between snaps. The pitch has a count of three balls and one strike. So Gavin's got no choice but to try to pitch over the plate for a strike (and the cripple shooter, Lopez, knows it).

The crowd grows still.

The pitch. The swing.

The fat part of the bat smacks the cowhide. I hear Reg's tinny voice coming from someone's transistor radio. "Oh my God. It looks like Doctor Longball, Chuck. Up, up and away." Mounties herding the outfield. "*Wait … Wait.*" It could drop straight down. "Swanson calls it. Yes. Number Nine, the rookie Scotty Swanson's glove is up and Oh my God, Chuck—he dropped it! He dropped the ball! Tepic's making the rounds now, folks, and this game is dead over, a stunner, a …"

"I don't know what to say, Reg. Heartbreak here in Arctadia for our boys and our country. Bury our hearts here, bury us well. Christmas Memorial indeed."

Scotty Swanson, a towheaded slip of a boy, burrows his head into his arms on the artificial turf—his life is ruined. It's a long time before a teammate (not his brother, Duke, but the Mexican-American, Gray Cooper, with what looks like a little notebook in his back pocket) finally tries to rouse him from his woe. Their faces. They are eating themselves up from the inside.

Tepic throbs in a heap in center field, leaping on each other like pack dogs. Their teeth are so white in contrast to their skin—I can see them on the Jumbotron by the scoreboard. Aguillar is handing

Two Spirits

out stogies. The news crews seem to be wrapping up coverage already, bundling cables even before the Mounties assemble their souls into a line to slap the dark hands of their victors. *O, Dios Mío*. Why am I so focused on the fucking contrast between their skin and their teeth? Is it only because I'm a visual artist?

Tony Squash's "rez-taurant" has been reserved for the celebration, but the boys decide they'd rather debrief in the locker room, shower, and split up with their host families instead. I shake Coach Hartman's hand and say I'm sorry. He's got a brave face on, smiles wide.

"I love these fucking guys," he says, rubbing his star hitter's head. The boy is crying.

I wait on the bench with Coach Lou and his hangdog assistant coach, Adam. A few of his Arrowstars surround him, just as they used to orbit Bo. Lou's supposed to take home Scotty Swanson. "Oh, God," he says. "Christ Jesus. Fucking vanquished in the ninth by one run. Van. Quished."

"That kid ain't gonna eat much tonight," I say.

"I mean, shit. His heart."

***

In the Jeep, after politely responding to my small talk and faking a few smiles, Gavin stares out the side window and watches Arctadia's few non-baseball oriented residents in lawn chairs, or mowing their Kentucky blue grass, half-supervising their kids in turtle pools. He was out of the locker room in five minutes, still in his uniform, asking if he could shower at my place.

"Sure. Got all your stuff?"

"Right here in the blivit. That's ten pounds of shit in a five pound bag."

"Your dad teach you that?"

"Coach. Learned it in the Army."

I'm creeping up the long Kittatin Hill road wondering why this kid was available for hosting at all. Shouldn't Lou have made special arrangements for a boy who just lost his entire family in a fucking plane crash? Or is that the "stuff" he had to "shift around" for me? Are they just going out of their way to treat him like everyone else? How did Bo do this? Maybe this is why …

"Gonna be OK there, *Numero Ocho*?"

He nods slowly. "Yup." Clears his throat. "I can handle it. This and more."

I turn onto our private road, then get out and put the chains up. I note that Gavin watches me out the back window. I drive a while uphill through the dense, bug-infested woods. Our mist has arisen since I left. They say it comes from somewhere deep under Shelter Rock. They say a lot of things.

"Thing is, you don't have to handle everything, you know. There's no rule that says you have to, I mean. You can fall to pieces if you want. I don't care."

He looks at me, a penetrating gaze. "Are we talking about the game, Mister Ransom?"

"Brownie. I don't know—are we? I'm just saying you should think of this as a safe space, you know, to be yourself."

"Oh, yeah? Who am I? Tell me." Incessant cicadas. They come with the mist. "I never knew anyone named 'Brownie' before. Are you a chocolate brownie or a nut brownie? Or are you a pot brownie? And, also, doesn't 'brownie' mean—?"

"Yes. It's a nickname I got when I was your age, because of my camera, which is called a Brownie. My real name's Barney."

"So … you're wondering if I'm gonna, like, burn your place down or something? Blow my head off in your barn?" He picks at the simulated wood of the dashboard. "Nah. I already dealt with that shit last year. Coach makes me go to a cognitive behavioral therapist—didn't they tell you?"

"Nope."

"You didn't get, like, a binder? A file folder or some shit? *'Here's your mission should you choose to accept it …'*"

"Nothing. Is there a whole folder?"

"I'm assuming. But I'm fine."

"Well. I bet you're not exactly 'fine.' Who is? By the way, you should just tell me to shut up if you want."

"OK. Shut up, Brownie."

After a quarter a mile, we turn to each other, and we're both smirking. The entire outside is shrouded in fog, like a movie scene from the Midnight Picture Show. "Starved?"

"I can eat a horse between two mattresses," he says.

"Well, I can eat a nun through the convent gate," I say.

"But that's what I had for lunch." He somehow manages this with the straightest of faces.

***

The house is quiet and dark, and I shut my eyes a moment. I can hear the machines upstairs. Since Bo's surprise, I don't go in much for TV (I even had to dust off the screen before watching the KLB Series). Neither are houseguests high on my agenda. Usually, I just take care of business upstairs, then read downstairs, one of Bo's hundreds of pocket-sized books – Damon Runyon, dog stories, Steinbeck, and that sort of thing – and fall asleep on the couch.

Forty-two minutes later, Gavin stands beside me running cold water over a colander of elbow macaroni. I am stirring marinara sauce. Although he's showered, his hair lies flattened against his head from his cap, which he's taken off again. He'd replaced his cleats with sneakers so as not to scuff the oak floors, but now he's kicked off his sneakers, too. He's tucked them neatly on the mat in front of the dishwasher, where we used to keep the dog bowls. Gavin stands in bleached white socks on the tile. Picture perfect. It does not escape me that he smells like strawberry Fluff. I suffer about 11 seconds during which I think I might have a panic attack. I breathe in the steam of the sauce.

If you're getting uncomfortable, welcome to my world. Get to know me.

I reach around to help Gavin pour the heaps of pasta into a big blue serving bowl, a gift of Bo's ex best friend, Max. I remember first smelling Bo. A combination of No More Tears shampoo (which I still use on him), bubble gum, and that sweet perspiration elicited by the two too-hot showers he liked to take daily when he was a kid—not hot enough unless his balls turned red. Now under the chemical berry scent of Master Bledsoe, I think I might even be able to smell his leather necklace, still wet. Bo never mentioned any effect this smell might have had on him every day coaching his boys, mentoring them in the locker room, a towel-slap or whistle-blow away from where they lathered, rinsed, told secrets. He must have noticed it. How much it reminded him of his own boyhood, of different days, of possibilities and impossibilities. Or maybe it never occurred to him at all. Gotta be a small fraction of fudge factory workers who're there because they can't get enough of the odor of fudge. More likely, just the opposite. Right? Surely many a non-perverted fellow finds himself spending all his days among children?

This is all about – all about – nostalgia tinged with paternal instinct. All about that. All.

The kid is behaving responsibly beyond his years. He doesn't need to be told to get milk glasses from the cupboard—he just intuits their location and fetches them. He doesn't need to be told twice to help himself to anything. He opens the fridge and roots around for a can of soda he likes (diet cream, the least likely kid drink therein), then chooses one for me, a diet orange.

What's your story, Gavin Bledsoe? Just what happened to you on that mountain in the Andes? He says, "If I can balance these cans on my head all the way to the table, will you let me stay up as late as I want?"

"Come again?"

"It's a game we used to play in my family."

"All right. You're on."

He stacks one Stewart's can atop the other on his head, and glides to the table effortlessly with his arms at four and eight o'clock, like a debutante in a posture class. Then he tips his head and catches one can in each hand.

"Well, I guess you got a deal, Young Man," I say.

"I never make a bet I can't win," he says.

"Cocky."

He smirks.

While I'm slicing the Italian bread, he looks at the few photographs that over the years I've deemed worthy of kitchen display. There's two of a nearby river island in mist. "Huck Finn," he says. I only nod. Of course I want to interview him formally, endlessly, hear a nonstop disquisition on my pictures. But I only nod. One of Bo and the Arrowstars doing a high-ropes challenge in the woods, shot from far down below. One boy's leg has slipped from where it had been wrapped around a rope, and he seems about to plummet. Bo's arms with his tattoos are plunging out of the mist to grab him. Gavin studies that one a long time, his head cocked, before moving on.

"Whoa," he says. It's an Adirondack Trail long distance runner, getting up close and personal with the railroad ties on the High Damien trestle. That one made page A1 of the *Times*. An even greater coup is hung just above, framed in blue. A cover photo for a *National Geographic* feature on the KLB league. Gavin says he knows the kid on the mound in my picture.

"I know. Gray Cooper. Saw him today. He's good, right?"

"'The Gray Lady,' they call him. He's a hustler," Gavin says. "Wicked curveball."

"Yours is better."

"Well, yeah. So, you ever get in *SI*?"

"Maybe every other issue for a few years, but not this year. See the cover with the Tar Heels in '95? I did that. In fact, I got a ball signed somewhere if you want it."

"Nah. Not my team. But that's cool."

Gavin doesn't ask for seconds. He just helps himself to another heaping plate. He takes big bites—as a 13-year-old should. He chews thoroughly before swallowing. It might be a healthy lifestyle thing, a religion/philosophy, or it might be a consequence of his time in the jungle.

Already I'm scheming subtle ways to ask if I can take his picture.

"Gimme a number from one to twenty-six," he says, mouth full of macaroni.

"What's your number again?"

"As if you don't know."

"OK then. Eight."

He counts off on his fingers, "Eight. So that's A, B, C, D, E, F, G, and *H* is eight. Whoever spots something in the room starting with H gets the last piece of garlic bread. Deal?"

"*Homo Sapien*," I say, pointing at him. "*Hungry homo sapien.*" He can't disguise his disappointment.

"Oh, I'm the homo?"

Interesting.

"I'll split it with you," I say.

"No, a deal's a deal."

With his mouth stuffed, he looks over at the pictures on the breakfront. It doesn't take him long to spot Bo. It's an ancient shot of Bo as a boy in Kit Pond. He'd just swung in on the rope and broken the surface. I caught the splash perfectly, and Bo's sheer joy. He's naked under the water, though there's no way to tell that unless you assume—or hope.

"Who is it? Not you. Blond."

"That's Beauregard Silver – Bo – the old coach of the Arctadia Arrowstars. Before Lou. A long time ago when he was about your age. He built this house, you know."

"No shit? Is he a relative?"

"Sort of. Like my big brother, I guess. Like Danny is to you. But … Well, more than that, I suppose. I know. Or?" My fumfering is not lost on Gavin, who's one smart cookie, as my mother would have said. "Bo was always looking out for me, teaching me things. He was a special friend."

Gavin's eyebrows go up, and he gapes at me.

"You know what that means out in California? 'Special friend.'"

I nod. "Yup. It means the same thing here."

He seems unfazed, resumes chewing. I cut the last piece of garlic bread and give him a hunk twice the size of mine.

"So did you and the coach get a divorce or something? My parents were getting divorced, I think."

"Divorced? No."

"Then why isn't he still around?"

I wipe my mouth, put the napkin back in my lap. "He is still around. Sor of. I can show you if you like. It's a little weird, though. You up for weird?"

"Me? Even in California they call me weird."

"Bo used to say California's like a bowl of cereal. If you're not a fruit or a nut—"

"You're a flake, yeah, yeah," he says.

"All right, smartass, come on, then."

He places his fork and knife upside down at the edge of his plate, something I imagine Mrs. Hartman taught him. Where the dining room meets the hall, I reach behind me just to guide him around the little telephone table with picture frames on it—It's easy to knock them over. He takes my hand! My heart throbs in my uvula. He squeezes my hand deliberately, one step behind me on the long dark staircase lined with photographs of Bo and me through the years. I have to pull my hand away it's so ... It's like—

It's like. Suddenly I have a son. Suddenly somebody loves me; someone demonstrative. Just for a moment. Only a moment, but one that might last a lifetime. Or—

It's like I'm 13 again. Thirteen and not alone.

At the top of the stairs, I turn to Gavin and say, "Besides the nurses – a coupla local gals called the 'Medicine Sisters,' you're the first one to come up here in ... forever." I have no idea what to say about the hand.

We pad down the hallway with the soft carpet, and I see my Nikon on the chair under the window. This kid cannot leave until I take his picture. I push open the door to Bo's room, the former "trophy" room (those are in the garage now), and usher Gavin in. He walks across the green carpet unceremoniously to our most expensive piece of furniture.

"Hi," he says to Bo.

Inhale, Bo responds.

"Hey," he tries again.

Exhale, Bo retorts.

"He won't answer. He can't. He probably doesn't even know you're talking right now, I don't think. But maybe. I just gave him his medicine before you came. That's why I was in the—you remember."

"I remember."

Gavin kneels unflinching beside Bo's hospital bed, studies the various gadgets and medications all around him.

"Fuck. What happened to this poor guy?"

"You know what a euphemism is?"

"Like a stroke?"

"No, that's an embolism. A euphemism."

He thinks. "Oh, right. Like 'special friend'?"

I laugh out loud. "Right. Well, you want the euphemistic answer, or the truth?"

"What do you think?"

"He tried to kill himself."

Gavin turns back toward Bo. "Buzz crusher. Divorce would be better."

"Yeah, on the one hand."

"I can touch him?"

I don't answer.

He presses an open hand, fingers fanned out, on Bo's chest. "Hella-warm."

"Of course."

"Why of course?"

"He's alive so—"

"Is he, though?"

"Yeah, that's the sixty-four-thousand-dollar question."

The boy moves his hand up toward Bo's neck, touches below the breathing tube.

"Andy was cold. My brother."

"You touched him?"

"Andes Andy."

Now he stares into Bo's face, his fingertips back in the xiphoid. "Of course. He was naked, you know."

"Your brother? What do you mean? Why?"

"A lot of them were. Their clothes got ripped off in the crash somehow. It happens a lot, I read. So when I found him, he was—There was this lady next to him. Maybe a stewardess. Right? She was naked, too. He would have been psyched. All his douchebag buddies would have been proud. But she was—her—was—not pretty."

"Shit."

"Uh-huh. But this necklace was still on him. He made it himself at baseball camp, and I got it. After. I took it, I mean. See, inside the shell, he painted this sunrise over the ocean."

He turns back to Bo, lifts his hand, puts it down. "He wasn't so bloody. Weird. Just a little. The first night, I slept next to him. That's what you guys did, right? Special friends?" He turns his face toward me. "You guys slept naked together. In the big room we passed down the hall."

When I don't answer right away, he turns back and pats Bo's head. "Yeah, that's what you did. But not anymore, right?"

"Right," I whisper.

"But that's not why you tried to kill yourself," says Gavin to Bo. "You didn't mind being special friends."

"No, he didn't mind," I say, clearing my throat. "I don't know why he did it. Why does anyone do it?"

"Duh. You get too sad."

I walk over and kneel on the other side of the bed, across from Gavin. "I wish I knew exactly, though. He was the last guy in the world you'd think would get too sad."

"That's what they always say," Gavin says. "Would you think I was the type?"

"I hope not."

"Well, I am," he says, looking right at me over Bo's rising chest. "And I bet you are, too. And I bet this guy was not the last guy you'd think would do it. I bet he was probably the first guy."

Falling.

"This isn't like talking to a regular kid," I say.

"It's not like talking to a regular grownup, either. What color are his eyes?"

Rising.

"Blue. Ice-blue. Whattya mean I'm the type?"

"Never mind."

"Umm—no. I won't 'never mind.'"

"All right. It's like this," he says, facing me. "You're living here in this big house all alone, pretty much. This guy you live with since you were kids tries to off himself and now you have to see him every single day and be reminded that he wasn't thinking about you when he did it, right? Or—he was. Plus, you're giving away your autographed baseballs and you're not even thinking straight enough to know that if I told anyone you wanted to hold my hand, they'd put you away and some dude named Bubba would murdalize you with extreme … whatever because some perv – some shopping mall Santa or whatever – did that shit to him when he was a kid. Not that I'm gonna tell because I don't give a fuck, either."

"Ice cream?"

"Only if it's chocolate."

"What do you take me for?"

"Dunno. Could easily be vanilla."

He has no idea.

He eats two scoops from the silver cup at the kitchen table before he says another word.

"See, I made this decision earlier, Brownie. An important decision. Guess the color I'm thinking of and I'll tell you."

"Blue."

"Ice-blue. Huh. All right. I decided if we won the game, I'd do it tonight. And if we lost, I'd wait till tomorrow."

"Do what?"

"You know."

"Those are the options? Why would … Why for—after winning the Kids League World Series?"

"That doesn't mean anything, duh. Nothing does. I'm, like, dead already, Brownie."

I give him the look I used to give Bo. "I don't get it. Gavin—you're not dead. You just have to give yourself some time to feel stuff again and to hope—"

"No, not that kind of dead. Not, like spiritually dead or whatever. I mean really dead. Look, there were these research guys from some engineering college, right, and they did a study with computers and they studied the plane crash, right? Like an aeronautical university or whatever. Matter of fact, they looked at hundreds of wrecks. They created this computer whattyacallit, with math and statistics and predictions and shit—"

"An algorithm."

"Right. They said there's no way I could have survived. You can look it up, serious, they wrote an article and everything in some scientific journal thing. Based on, like, physics and whatnot—I died there in Brazil. Everybody around me, even my own seat got, like, shredded up and torched and crushed."

"But you did survive."

"Like, obliterated."

"You beat the odds. And weren't there others, too?"

"One lady's a vegetable, worse than him upstairs, Mr. Beauregard. Another one's got no legs now and shit, and her husband left her. The guy from *SI Kids* told me all this. The other guy who survived wound up dying about three months later. And one guy whose kids got their heads chopped off in front of him? Well, he conveniently 'fell' onto some subway tracks – '*Woops!*' Right? – a while back, around about the time a train happened to be coming into the station."

"Survivor's guilt, they call it."

"Hey, you could charge the Hartmans a hundred-something bucks an hour to talk like that, you know."

"Don't you think it's possible that God spared you because he has some plan? God, or you know, whatever—something greater than the laws of physics?"

"Duh. Yeah, there's a plan. The plan is for me to live here miserable for as long as I live—so I say, not so long, fuck you very much."

"The thing with your hand, Gavin, on the stairs. You—"

"'S'cool. It's more than cool. I won't tell about that, and you won't tell on me."

***

I say Bo was the last person, but that's bullshit. Gavin's right. It wasn't even the first time. Back in college. Bo played baseball at Albany, and I went to Vaughn, a little liberal arts place just outside the Rez, to do photography. We saw each other every weekend when he wasn't playing away, thanks to an old Volvo station wagon he'd inherited from his father's probation officer. But one weekend, he just never showed up. I had rice boiling and wine poured. I had an ABBA tape queued up. I had tickets to see a play co-starring my old freshman roommate, who had promised me numerous nude scenes.

My English Professor, Dr. Richter, kept me calm, and drank the wine. I couldn't get an answer all Friday night. None of his housemates were home that weekend. I called his father at the halfway house, with whom Bo was semi-estranged; he told me Bo was probably out "hound-dogging." I drove out on Saturday, and knew he was home because I saw the Volvo, the bumper stitched on with wire hangers. I climbed the stairs and let myself in, wandered from room to room, searching like Colombo for some kind of clue.

He was semi-conscious in a cold bath, a radio underwater in his lap. His eyes were open and his body was blue and quaking from the cold. Incredibly stiff. Everyone assumed it was an accident—the star hitter was in a popular frat, got straight A's, and wrote a sports column for the alternative paper. He'd even been "out" to his frat brothers for a year, and seemed to maintain their respect and friendship to a man, which I attributed to his genuine kindness and character, not to mention his unquestionable masculinity. His teammates, friends, and brothers all could speak to Bo in a way they couldn't to anyone else. They all knew me, of course, and tended to treat me like Bo's geeky kid brother, tousling my hair, making fun of my lack of sports knowledge, generally looking after me while trying not to seem too attentive, and constantly commissioned me to take their pictures, you know, for their girlfriends ...

Bo and I slept in the same bed at the off-campus house owned by his frat, and frequently endured ribbing in the mornings for having gotten laid.

Bo was studying Sports Medicine and minoring in Economics. He knew by then he'd never make the majors. I took artsy pictures of tombstones and parking meters, abandoned churches, warehouse docks, dirty miners, and tribal elders in full regalia and out, and published them in the *Kit Banner*, the Vaughn *Guard* lit mag, and some other local artsy poetry journals. Once or twice I even got paid. I took pictures of Dr. Richter and his wife, Hilde, stooped and smiling, during their daily intimacies and ablutions.

I knew it wasn't an accident, because Bo never took baths. He also hated the sound of music echoing on tiles, and never listened to the radio – only albums and my homemade mixes – because he despised the commercials.

He couldn't finish out the season. He came back to Arctadia for that second semester of our junior year, and I came home to be with him in the attic every weekend. He pretended to my mother that his lethargy and antisocial tendencies were a product of the accidental jolt in the tub. But I knew he was depressed—clinically so. His mother had remarried (his father's probation goon) a few years after Principal Silver was sent away, and lived in Newburgh now with her new husband. I assumed she believed him implicitly when he told her it was a teeny mishap, and he was fine. All he had now was me and my mother.

Yet for a few weeks, he didn't want me to sleep with him in the old bed we'd shared since childhood. He said his skin hurt when I touched him. I knew after so many years that he wasn't suddenly turning straight, and I knew him too well to get insecure about the bigger picture. I was not a flavor his palate could come to do without.

He cried.

He stopped wanting to shower.

But by July 4th, he was getting back to his old self. He and my mother played lots of Scrabble, and watched baseball games together during the day while I took a summer semester because of all the time I'd missed at Vaughn. Dr. Richter even came to the attic to tutor me in Milton and Chaucer, Blake and Wordsworth.

Two or three times I gently broached the subject of Bo getting professional help.

"It ain't goin' down again, Brownie."

"How do you know?"

"I know."

"But how do I know?"

★★★

"You think he's ever coming out of it?"

I shake my head no.

Gavin says, "That's, like, the official diagnosis? And you don't think he even knows you're still there, like, giving a shit and telling kids how you were special friends?"

I don't.

"So you have to give him baths and stuff? With a sponge?"

"A nurse comes in, like I said. I read to him sometimes, though. They say it's good for him. I don't know. What do you think? I read to him from this guy who wrote about elephants."

"Can I?"

Two minutes later, Gavin is nestled in the rocker with the last of his Ben & Jerry's, and reading to Bo animatedly from a baseball mag.

He disagrees with much of what the writer has to say, and tells Bo as much. I go downstairs to do the dishes. I reach down and lift Gavin's sneakers between my thumb and fingers. They are worn and soft inside, and shockingly light. It's all I can do not to sniff inside their darkness.

Upstairs again half an hour later, I sit in the hallway chair with the Nikon in my lap, turning the lens far wide, then back in tight. I can't see in, but Bo's room is silent a long time, then, finally, barely, I hear the boy talking. To Bo.

"So I told her about sleeping next to Andy, right? She's got, like, five hundred degrees on her wall, and she wanted to know whether that was something I'd always wanted to do." I could hear him opening the bedside drawers – bandages, salves, replacement tubing – then shutting them, still talking: "I said, 'Duh. No,' but then, why did I do it again the second night, right? That's the sixty-four million dollar question. Why do I dream about it all the time? Still."

"So you're serious about this suicide plan?" I interrupt, breezing in.

"The thing is, when I do it, I won't fuck it up like this schmuck did," Gavin says, turning to look at Bo's face. He stands and surveys the devices on the steel rack beside the bed. "Was it pills? Was it not enough, or did they pump 'em out before they did the trick?"

"It was carbon monoxide."

He's not satisfied.

I stare out the window, down at Shelter Rock, far below, like a raft int the dissipating mist.

"One day after work, he just left the Jeep running in the garage. I found him, still alive, but he never really came out of the coma. Know what, though? He killed Therman. That was our beagle. We always had beagles. It all seeped in through the pet door from the kitchen. Therman always went nutso when Bo got home. He'd be destroyed if he knew. But I don't think he knows anything. He looks happy, though, doesn't he? Content."

"His brain is fried. So it worked."

"For him, I guess it did."

"But he should have gone way out in the woods or someplace where no one would find him for a long time. Or you could burn the whole place down, too, right, while you're in it, and then you get the insurance money. Or if you do the pills, you have to 'stagger' them, they call it. You take just enough to make yourself really dopey. Then just before you go to LaLa Land, then you take the mondo dosage. That way you don't puke 'em up. Or you have to take them with bread or chips or something."

"Not that you've thought this all out then, huh?"

"I swore I'm not gonna rat you out for coming onto me, so …"

"I—Let's get something straight. You took my—I've got zero—you're a fucking—child."

"Whatever. Dude."

"Gavin. I'm just trying to be your friend."

"My special friend?"

"*Aaand* … I also … understand, like you said. What's going on in your head, I mean. As a matter of fact, smarty-pants, I've also been planning, was thinking tomorrow morning … Well, until this afternoon, that is."

He lifts up the blanket to see Bo's feet, but finds the tight sheets block his view. "So what happened this afternoon?"

"I reconsidered."

"Because?"

"…"

"Well?"

I walk toward him. "Well, because I met you." I clear my throat.

He slaps his thighs. "I fucking knew it."

"It's not like that. I told you. It's just, I saw your face. I thought about that mountain, and I …" I reach out toward his ear, run my thumb down his sideburn. He doesn't shy away, but leans right into it, Lurlene-like, Thermanesque, closes his eyes.

"So in the drugstore last weekend?" he says.

I nod.

"You were getting pills, but—not for him?"

"For us."

Two Spirits

"Oh. Right."

"You saw me?"

"You saw me, too? You scoped me out? Checked out my ass while I got a pop?"

"It wasn't like that."

"You noticed me?"

"Yeah, I noticed you, Gavin. You. How could anyone not notice you?"

"You wanted me?"

"Wanted to know you, sure. I wanted you to stay here. I asked for you. Asked Lou, you know."

He smiles, closes his eyes again, and turns his face – his nose, his lips – into my palm, so I have to pull it away.

"I've got some baby Xanax in my bag" says Gavin. "You're supposed to take one a day. I took two before dinner and they're kicking in. Feels like sweet air at the dentist. I've got twenty-four left. So what's your plan?"

"*The best laid plans* ... Look what happened to *his* grand plan."

"Tell me, Brownie."

"All right. Bo here goes sleepy-bye with a bunch of crushed up Sieract in his IV; enough to stop his heart, but just in case, I shut off the breathing machine here, and unhook the feeding tube – that's this one – and call the day nurse, and cancel her. I get real mellow with just a few pills myself, then carry him downstairs once he—you know. He's really light now—he used to be built. Like, solid."

"Like Andy."

"Then I take the Jeep off the edge of a dirt road maybe a mile from here – he fucking loves that Jeep – into an old quarry lake – on the other side of the Christos dam – that's a couple of hundred feet deep. *Glub glub.*"

"Dang," he says. "Good one. Mystery and no mess. But not the easiest getting this one down there and buckled up and all. Could use an extra pair of hands."

"Speaking hypothetically," I say, to try to snap the wobble off this über-surreal exchange. "I told you. I had a change of heart."

Two Spirits 111

"That's right. You met a lovely lad, and now your life's worth living."

★★★

The grand tour. Barefoot behind me through the den and home office, Gavin doesn't make a sound. He insists I open every door; he inspects all the spaces, all the objects hidden away. He touches everything. In the pantry he fingers the soup and cereal labels, appreciates the clean lines of the stacks on the cedar shelves. I spend a lot of time in here, too, marking time by expiration dates. I shop at the savings clubs still, dragging a U-boat of family-sized portions behind me. Then I live night to night, only to cycle through a regimen of dry and canned goods as though compelled by some cruel inevitability. Thursday: Chickarina, Wheat Thins, pack of Devil Dogs. Friday: mac and cheese, dill pickle, fat free pudding cup. This week: no green bananas.

I didn't balk at introducing Gavin into Bo's room, but here with him looking at the stocks, the bulk, the SS-level order of the pantry, is like exposing my anus to a stranger with a stick. "Creepy," he says. "You ever read Stephen King?" Because he can't detect the chinks in the logic, the duplicate freestone peaches in light syrup that prove I'm not obsessive. I shut the light on him, disappear.

We both laugh nervously in the garage, go figure. Where we used to park the Jeep is now piled with cartons—Bo's belongings from his office at the school, packed sedately by confused, loving students, and delivered via U-Haul with a Hallmark card signed by the team and the faculty. In the other spot is Bo's tricked-out gunmetal '71 Mustang convertible, his other high school sweetheart. "'Stang" was a gift from me after I sold my first book of photos. At some point, a family of raccoons – "trash pandas" – took residence inside, and we never drove the car again.

Back in the kitchen, we each grab some Fig Newtons, and I lead Gavin outside, down the deck stairs, into the foggy, buggy black sea of our backyard. By the edge of the fern-choked woods that stretch down to the river, Bo built me a studio with a darkroom, a desk, bookcases, and endless storage for photo boxes and albums. There's even a bed on a loft, where guests who could brook the rusticity used to stay. This is now Gavin's favorite place in the Milky Way, he declares.

He is digging through albums, searching for shots of Bo.

"That picture of him in the river that's in the kitchen? That was around here?"

"Close by."

"Are there more from that day?"

"God, I wouldn't know where to look."

"Try."

While I'm searching, I hear him say, "I mean before he jumped in. You know what I mean."

"Oh. Well, that's a whole other variety of photography, Mister Bledsoe."

"No duh. Lemme' see 'em."

"I don't know."

"I seen 'em before, that kind of thing."

"You have?"

"Yeah, Andy had magazines with all that kind of stuff."

"With boys?"

"Whatever. Boys."

He starts thumbing through albums on the shelves. "So if I was a secret album of pictures of … where would I be hiding?" he says.

I stand still and say nothing. Then he comes over, lifts my hand and presses it to his ear. "You want to touch this here?"

"Gavin, you know I don't go around just doing this sort of …"

"Come on. Lemme' see 'em." It's the whine of a toddler now, extremely effective.

"Up there," I motion with my chin. "In the loft."

"Up here?"

He's climbing the wooden ladder as though his Christmas presents are hidden at the top.

With every step I am thinking I get closer to the hell I deserve. *I will be punished. This is not right. I can stop it. Now.* "In the bookcase beside the bed. It's dark red and old-looking."

Here's my logic, probably twisted, possibly psychotic: If he procures the pictures by himself, I'm not corrupting him *per se*. I'm just not obstructing nature from taking its course. But there's more to my motivation, a percolating urge under my consciousness, too weird to articulate. He is so much like Bo had been at that age. Take-charge. Daring. Brutally honest. Beautiful and dangerous. "Sexy," I'm afraid I have to say of a 13-year-old boy, though it's more complicated than that. I wouldn't actually—couldn't anyway. Full stop. My body would never—and yet I feel something with him. Safe somehow, protected. As though despite his youth, he'll look after me, make sure nothing awful happens while we're together. And that silky blond hair that hugs his temples—can't say enough about that. And those ears, that clean and naked throat and that pendant del mar. Maybe I'm just confusing him with—maybe. Maybe.

Naturally, I am not a pedophile—of course. Not *per se*. It's just that since the accident, I've been more aware of boys. I notice them, three-on-a-bike, at the King Kone ice cream stand. Smacking red fire-buttons and twisting joysticks with whole body English at the mall arcade. Fishing off the Arctadia Ambit Bridge and the High Damien trestle, threading hooks through folded worms. They wear overalls without shirts, with one buckle undone, hanging over their hips. They ride skateboards down stairs. They wear sleek, modern, two-tone sneakers with no laces, which simply slip over their bare feet, leaving their ankles exposed. And they're all over the TV. Forward boys with backward caps, as a poet that Bo used to like recently wrote.

When I register their presence, I regress, inhabit happier, more hopeful times. They aren't strange boys, not other mothers' sons. They are merely Bo and I, me and Bo, carefree at the Tony Squash's rez-taurant, ordering cookies and cream with rainbow sprinkles. I have suffered. Bo suffered. It follows I don't want to suffer anymore—nor would I allow them to suffer under my thumb or any other man's anything.

I am not a—I am not. Right? Right.

"You coming up or what?" he calls. "You know you wanna look with me."

I climb the ladder and see him patting the mattress on the loft. I sit, hunched beside him on the quilt my dead sister made, our thighs touching, our feet touching. The Itty Bitty Booklight clipped to the headboard casts a cozy yellow light into Gavin's lap where he holds the album. He takes a breath, opens the cover to the first page.

Populated by old neighbors who posed for me. Ambie and Landon. Setting traps. Raking. Picking onions. Picking radishes. Hugging. Swimming. Smiling. Getting undressed for bed.

Then Gavin turns the page. He falls into that image of Bo as though nothing else around us even exists. "Holy cannoli," he says.

I die. That picture. That day. Bo languishing on the lakeside, Lurlene's sopping fur against his back. That satisfying zip of focus, click of shutter, pond drops caught in light forever, revisited now by him. By Bo. Up here with me, come to life again, the way I remember him. Hot and unpredictable.

"He looks so much like me," Gavin says. "'S'weird."

He traces the outline of Bo with his finger. "This is like me. And that. I don't have that yet, but maybe I will. How old?"

"I think ... fourteen and a half."

He turns the page. "And a half—" Bo as Dracula—a shot out-of-sequence. He wears an open cape and cowl, pinned at his neck, plastic fangs and nothing else. His hair greased back with gobs of Vaseline, and he's posing. He was doing the Count from *Sesame Street*, I remember so well. "*Vun. Vun Vunderful ball*," he was saying. "*Ha ha ha! Two! ...*"

Then Bo sunning his back on the beach, his rear end glistening, legs mostly closed, but still a glimpse between of darkness, of wonder.

Two Spirits

I know, goddammit, that I'm discussing here a child in a semi-sexual way. It's not like that. *I* was a child. I was a child. We were children together, and children whose bond, whose whole—

"Oh, this is my fucking favorite," says Gavin. "Oh, holy—"

"Mystery and no mess."

He laughs. First time.

It's all OK. It's fine. You're saving him. You're saving each other. Nothing untoward is gonna happen here. Nothing's gonna go down.

He says, "OK, Brownie, if on the next page Bo's facing forward, I'm taking my clothes off."

"The hell you are."

Flip.

Aha. Here's Bo bare and straining, eyes squeezed shut and slender neck stretched back on the bamboo papasan chair on the attic patio, actually jacking off in the morning. There are several of these on succeeding pages, including Bo climaxing onto his stomach and then laughing open-mouthed afterward, as he often did, uncontrollably. Bo with a sheepish smile, saying something obnoxious to me, which I can't remember. Then Bo curling up to sleep protected, filtered, soft, and slightly blurry.

Gavin says nothing of these, just gazes intently, and turns the pages slowly back and forth. He sighs, not like a child.

"OK? You said you've seen this sort of stuff before …"

"Oh, I lied about that shit," he says, just audibly, never raising his eyes off the page. "It was all twats and nipples in Andy's stash."

"Not for you?"

"I don't know. But this …"

It does not escape me that I have just shared child porn … with a child. So wrong. So wrong. No matter how you slice it, right, no matter how you parse it? Wrong.

I try to pull the album away. He resists like I'm yanking his spleen out.

He takes a few big, deep breaths, and his head lolls a bit. It's late. Big day. He's on Xanax, paradoxically aroused, having just lost the Kids League World Series of Baseball. But this wakes him up: On the next page, a big surprise. Yours truly. Thirteen. I'd forgotten all about it. Reading in bed, half-hugging a pillow, oblivious to the camera. I can see in the picture the indentation that Bo had just left beside me when he snatched the Brownie off the night table.

"Fuckin' A," says Gavin. "Wow wow wow." He cocks his head and studies the nude boy. He turns to me and lifts my shirt to look at my stomach, presumably to check for the appendectomy scar. I pull down my waistband an inch to confirm his hunch. "Yup," I say. "In the flesh."

"You can tell. You can tell he …"

"What?"

"You can tell he loves you."

"What do you mean?"

"Duh. By the way he took this picture. The way he just had to, because of how good you looked right then."

Unexpectedly, this insight makes me want to weep.

"Like brothers," he says.

"But different. But better."

"Special friends."

He turns the page again, and there's the only nude photograph of Bo and me together as kids. It wasn't easy to stage, and I scrapped about 42 shots before I knew I'd hit the jackpot. I'm so busy staring at the picture that it takes me a while to notice that Gavin's hand is on mine. Again with the hand. "Take a picture of me," he says.

"Oh—Bad idea."

"No, and give it to me. You can develop it here, can't you? We'll look at it, and get rid of it together. I mean if you don't keep it, there's nothing bad about it, right?"

"Gavin, I don't know. No. No way."

"I look at least as good as you guys do," he says. "Did. Don't I?"

"Oh, you have no idea. But that's not the point." He unties his sweats and makes to pull them down in one fell swoop with his underwear.

I fling myself out of the bed, nearly plunge eight feet off the loft onto my light tables below. I cling to the ladder railing.

"Relax," he says.

"Gavin. Whatever you do."

He squirms in the bed. "All right, I got it," he says. He covers his lap with his hands. "Tell you what. If it was an even-numbered year when that picture was taken, you have to take my picture. Odd, you don't. But don't lie. Cause I'll know. So what year was it?"

"Gavin. Just. No."

"What fucking year?"

"Flip it over."

He opens the plastic sheet and peels the picture out. It's difficult. "Sticky. Lessee'… Seventy-four. Oh, yeah, baby, that. Shit. Is. Even. So get the camera. Take my picture like his. I'll do anything you like."

There is always a loaded camera nearby.

"You'll show me how to do it?"

"What?"

"What Bo was doing in that chair. And Andy did all the time. I walked in on him once."

"No."

"I love the feeling of the air on me."

"Yeah. But no."

"What if we didn't kill ourselves, Brownie? What if the Jeep just disappears like you were scheming, in the quarry water? And we just like, vanish completely. But not die. Tomorrow morning. They expect me back at the airport and I'm not there, and you're not here. And you leave the machines on and call the nurse—or maybe not. But no one we know ever sees us again. And we can even make it look like we got kidnapped, so they don't think you're a pervert or something. Or torch the place. You can cut my hair and dye it black and you grow a mustache and get a tattoo of a bald eagle on your back, and we can get a motorcycle and ride to North Dakota, stay at truck stop motels along the way."

I'm cleaving halfway up the ladder again, Nikon in hand. I don't want to stare, but I don't want to miss this face, either. The eyes. I'm looking at them through the lens now. There's a faint fuzz on his cheek, which I notice only because it catches the unseemly glare from the booklight, and reflects it pure.

"South America's a good place," he continues. "Yeah, bet you're surprised to hear me say that shit. Some villages, it takes a week to get there, and you have to go in a canoe with headshrinker cannibals. No one would ever in a million years find us there. No one would miss me anyway. My whole family's, whatever, dead. We can be our own family. We can say you're my father. You're old enough?"

He cups himself under his sweats, stretches, bends himself (I can tell), moans a little, smiles. Shameless, just as Bo had been. When he cranes his neck back, the scallop shell charm on the choker covers the hollow of his neck.

This has to stop. This has to stop.

But I don't want to invite shame into his chamber. But. "Yeah, I'm old enough," I say. "Too old. And you, my friend, are way too young. You need to be with the Danny's of the world. The Pedros."

"Or we could be brothers. Cooper's got a pen pal right around here. They send each other ... I think they're—"

"Gavin. We can't do any of that stuff." Click. Advance.

"*Hmm* ... What to do, what to do," Gavin mocks in a grownup voice. "You want to, though, right?"

"No."

"I know you do."

"I don't. I have less than zero interest in you—in that way, I mean."

He flips onto his belly and slides back toward me, his face now close to mine. "Brownie?"

I let out all my air. I do look down. Just to the edge of his rump. I look at that ridgeline, and back up to his neck. "Gavin. Part of me does. Yes. A little part. God. But not like that. Just to. Hold you. Sleep, maybe. But we can't. We absolutely cannot. Not. No. None of it."

I protest too loudly?

"That's only if I don't want to. Aren't those the rules?"

Two Spirits

He thrusts forward slightly and gives me a peck.

"There are a lot of rules. Good rules. Wise." I can see over his shoulder now and down into my past.

"I don't look as good as him?" he says.

"Gavin. You're perfect. You're—That's not the point. The thing is, you should—I'm going to look after you. So not me—and not your brother. But someone who's, you know, your equal."

"You and Bo were ever equals? Bull fucking shit."

"What the hell is that supposed to mean?"

"Please don't be mad."

I can't restrain myself from holding his ears, kissing him quickly on the lips. "You're impossible. You don't know it yet, but this is like one of those letters that men write into—"

"So we're not gonna do it?" His face is sulky. I see goose bumps over his flesh.

"No, we're not gonna do it. Not that. You're not—ever. Not with a—but I'll tell you what, though, Number Eight with a bullet. If you can get dressed in the time it takes me to put this camera down and get to that door over there, I will disappear with you tomorrow morning—*poof!* Like you want. Deal?"

★★★

Days before the missionaries who came before the first wave of rescue workers, the Indians from a village downriver discovered the wreckage. Matriarchal, covered with spiderdye tattoos, they lived in mud tunnels and had managed little contact with the outside world. They were frightened of the blackened boy who screamed like a monkey, and clung to one of the corpses. The boy was naked, wild-eyed, and bones protruded from his shins. Compassion and instinct compelled them to help, but there was something less than innocent about that child, something more than victim.

Some of his tribe had come before with medicines and their storybook, but once, one had come to stay a long time and took a special child with him – a flamingo boy – when he left. That one and others had taught the metal birds were not the devil's chariot. Just giant boats in the sky, to take people from big village to big village. But still. Some thought the boy must not have been a boy at all, but a gremlin that brought the metal bird down to the earth. Some thought he was their missing boy, the flamingo boy, returned, a wicked changeling.

Most did not believe this. They named him. *Monkey Surprised to Find His Vine Didn't Reach His Destination Tree.*

Only the women who were mothers saw the scene for what it was. The bodies were the little boy's tribe, and the one he clung to, his young Chief. So they wrapped his ravaged legs in wet banana leaves, and cleaned around his eyes with their saliva. They cooed like pigeons to make him sleep. They aimed at his mouth with their milk. Finally, the missionaries of his tribe visited, and they brought all the noise – but no storybook this time – and a fleet of the devil's chariots descended, chopping leaves and chasing fish away. The first ones that came, they said it is written in the storybook that a village should treat a stranger as if he might be the Biggest Chief. But when they had gone, a medicine man later explained to the villagers that it was only human nature to desire for such a boy as they found, to be dead and to be quiet with his tribe in the Other World.

★★★

Back downstairs, I crack open some RC Colas that were under my cutting table, and we suck the foam off the lids. Gavin wears one of Bo's jerseys.

"It's a good way to live, I'll give you that," I say. "As though every day were your last. It's good to ask yourself, if I were going to buy it tomorrow for sure, would I be happy to be doing what I'm doing today, right now?" He looks at me. "You know. Like an anvil could drop out of the sky at any second, so—"

"Or an airplane."

"Yeah."

"So are you happy, Brownie? I mean, here you were planning a whole … you know."

"Happy? Well, I don't do a lot of new things around here."

"No shit."

"Even before. It used to drive Bo crazy, I was so predictable. Not spontaneous, he used to say. 'Routine and mechanical.' You know, like when we took a trip, I never liked getting off the highway like he always wanted, to go 'exploring.' And even—never mind."

"Sex. Tell me," he says against a backdrop of photos of Bo on the corkboard wall. "It's a big night, remember? Don't hold anything back."

"Your coach probably tells you that there are consequences to risks. All the time, I mean. Actions have consequences. One unsafe move, one slip-up, you know, it's curtains."

"So tell me. What would you do?" he asks, "if tonight was it. The anvil is way up there, by the moon, but it's on its way. Falling. There's an 'X' in Magic Marker on the top of your head."

"Take pictures."

"Cool. You?"

"Play baseball."

"No shit?"

"Right?"

We stare at each other a moment, heady with warm soda. Then I snag my new Canon and we break for outside. The grass is dewy in the yard, and a light mist is traveling off the river. Weird sounds – as always – usher out of Shelter Rock. The wind? Water somewhere? All the mica?

"Where's a ball and bat?" he asks.

I throw him a few balls from a plastic hamper that Bo keeps under the deck. Then I shoot a few pictures of him tossing balls in the air and whacking them toward the water. The flash splits the night, and afterward fireflies blink like crazy.

"I'll pitch you some," he says.

"I stink."

"Just rusty, I bet."

"But I thought baseball didn't matter anymore, huh, Gav? You were just going through the motions like the living dead you are."

"Well, it was getting a little ... 'routine and mechanical,' yeah, but it's different tonight. You know. It's my last night on Earth."

"Would you please stop saying that? I've got enough problems. And you don't know all the amazing things you have ahead of you."

"Yeah, how's that working out for you, Brownie? When was the last amazing thing that happened?"

"I told you."

He motions to toss the ball up to himself, but doesn't let it go. He takes a practice swing, readies the ball, but again doesn't release it. Then he drops both ball and bat, and runs over to me, hugs me hard. He's crying now. I wipe his eyes with my thumbs. "It's OK, Number Eight."

"It's so not fucking OK."

"Hey, over on that mound," I say, "I buried Therman. Seemed appropriate. And Bo's dog, Lurlene, she's over there. Some other dogs gone by in between."

He starts to laugh. I laugh.

"I'm sorry."

He can't catch his breath.

I kneel down in front of him as I've seen Bo do a thousand times. I hold his hips and look him in the eyes.

"Why wouldn't you—you know?"

"Because I care about you, Kid."

"I don't get it."

"I know. Now teach me some baseball."

He pulls himself together, poises himself to pitch. I walk a distance. I swing and miss time and again, despite his gentle chatter of encouragement. Finally, on a sweet, slow cookie I hear *CRACK!* as the ball wails off the bat five times faster than it came in. We watch it soar into a pitch black sky a moment before it descends in a beautiful arc and smashes through the window of my studio, thudding onto the loft mattress where only an hour before, I nearly shattered both our worlds.

***

Was Bo so lucky? He spent an enormous amount of time and energy trying to catch his boys in the rye. "Blood, sweat, and tears," he used to say nearly every night when he doffed his clothes to shower. He held their esteem sacred, and he pushed them to the outer limits of themselves without ever knocking them over the edge. He spoke of the downtrodden, awkward ones with more reverence than the Arctadia Arrow-"stars." And they worshipped him. They fucking worshipped him.

Relevant: There were places that Bo didn't like to be touched. You couldn't go near his neck, for instance. He couldn't even wear his whistle around his neck, but clipped it to his collar instead. We joked about that a lot, but it's really not funny.

***

Overlooking the quarry lake and the High Damien railroad trestle, with the soft top off and the engine purring, just after dawn. The tires only inches from the edge. I'm thinking this is how the Jeep must have sounded to Bo as he fell slowly, pleasantly to sleep, maybe or maybe not thinking of me, and us as children, running our bases—or maybe of his father. Gavin and I unhook our seatbelts – *seatbelts!* – and breathe in the cool, predawn August air. The fog is just starting to form.

At home, upstairs, on those machines, the lighted switches, and on the night table, the bottle of Sieract, and the day nurse's number.

Silence. The bottom of the quarry is seething with fog. If the dirt crumbles in front of us, we'll surely tumble down. Frogs suggest ideas from far below.

"You sorry you lost the game, Number Eight?"

"That was yesterday. But I guess so. For Danny and Coach Hartman. So, Brownie …? Do you know where I think Bo is right now?"

I glance at the dashboard clock. "No."

"I think he's in the lake. What's it called?"

"Kittatinn Pond."

"Kittatinn. Yeah. That day. When he swung out, you know, without—and you took his picture."

"That's a lovely idea." I look at the car phone. It rings.

He looks at it, too. "And you know what else? I think he's waiting for you. His special friend."

"You think Andy's waiting for you somewhere, too, don't you, Kid?" On some celestial baseball diamond somewhere.

He doesn't answer. Then he smiles, turns to me as the phone keeps ringing. California number. "So which direction are we facing?" he says.

"I have no idea. East? We have to wait for the sun, just a minute."

"All right then. If the sun comes up over there," he points forward, "you put the pedal to the metal as soon as you see it. And I fly again, OK?"

Ring. Ring.

"And if it comes up over there?"

"Then you back up and we drive south—way south like I said. Deal?"

—*Winter gives you a boner*—

Friday Sept. 14. Night. En route to "ski trip."

Literally fucking nowhere, New Mexico

I hate snow.
 Snows a shit-ton on the Rez, though, right?
 Yeah, like, a lot.
 Remember our moms used to put Baggies on our feet so they'd come out of our boots all quick? But this is ridic. How much, you think? I love snow.
 You love fires now, Sully. Fires in the snow.
 How'd you know?
 Saw you at every one back home. Ya. Every wildland. Every old coot's cabin in winter. We were <u>both</u> Junior Fire Frogs, remember? Just because I wasn't all badass like you doesn't mean I wasn't there. Somewhere. Be it in the deep background …
 Watching. Waiting. Secretly writing your movie, right?
 Studying. All that training in the bitter fucking cold. Ya. I think winter gives you a boner.
 Name's Winter. So Winter gives <u>you</u> a boner, Augie.
 Right.
 But I never saw this much snow back home. Not anywhere around in Kit County.
 Ya. No. It doesn't snow quite like this in upstate New York, I guess.
 It does. It just didn't in the, whatever, 12 years we were conscious. But this is, like, three feet? Overnight. Jesus. So much for—
 —Who never knew an inch of snow. Desert guy, our Lord was.
 Your lord. It doesn't snow in the high mountains of Israel or wherever? It must.

It does not.

Another fail for American Geography classes.

On and off the Rez. Jesus. And health class.

You didn't bring any condoms?

Mel carries them for me. How about one of those Baggies our moms used to pack our feet in?

Mel's the personal assistant—or the Tesla driver? How many are in your fucking whatycallit? Train?

Mel's a production assistant. An intern. They call them PA's.

Right. But what's that word? "Retinue," right?

I know the one. You mean the "entourage."

Yes. The entourage. How many?

Who are we counting? Like, hair and makeup, too? All the wardrobe chicks? Script supervisor dorks? Catering. Fuck, it's cold. Anyway, I'm just the writer—with the little cameo, of course. Ya.

Of course.

You're the star.

Heater's no bueno since we ran out of gas an hour ago. When you have to ask who's included, you have an official entourage and must be put down.

When I'm representing gay Native American youth everywhere, and not only do I have to get the Kit shit right – it's <u>Akt'adia</u>, not <u>Arctadia</u> – but everyone's shit. Every fucking tribe from—Not to mention be everything to all gays, say everything for all gay boys.

And girls.

Shit. <u>Now</u> put me down. But what about you? How many thousands of fangirls does your 'gram have? Of both genders and the one in the fucking middle, speaking of our ancestors. Why don't you and your sweet little honey bum have a coupla dozen of those rubber puppies in your wallet? Figure you'd have—you know. Because of the thing.

The thing? You mean my kid? My son? So much to unpack there, Augie. I don't carry condoms – which are latex, BTW – cuz it just seems, I don't know, presumptuous? We were going skiing. Right?

Ya. But. No.

Two Spirits

No? What's on the roof rack that took us a fucking—

Everyone knows skiing means getting busy by the fireplace after hot cocoa.

Oh, everybody knows that? Guess neither of us was a Boy Scout.

4H all the way.

"I pledge my hands to greater service …"

All right. The hands have it.

They'll have to do …

Mmm. Hot cocoa.

Speaking of catering.

Speaking of cold hands.

—You just touched me—

The prior year.

Arctadia, New York

We could call him "Bon."
  Oy. Join the bandwagon why doncha?
  It's not a bandwagon. It's to honor the guy—You of all people, I thought would—
  I know who PD Lightning was. But you know what we have to call him.
  I know. Diablo. Diablo Sullivan. Take off your turnout gear. I'll wash the socks if I can waddle over there.
  That kid Augie washed 'em already. Got no socks on under here.
  Sully … But we can call him "Bon" or "Noah" for a middle name, no? Or how about both?
  Veronica. Whatever you like. I'm sorry, this is soaking wet. The rehab … He was writing his movie, and not giving much of a shit about the rehab. I'll make that venison we got hanging. With mushrooms maybe.
  Are you, like, freaked out?
  Hell yes, I'm fucking freaked out. Aren't you? We're 18 – you're fucking 17 – and we're gonna have a goddamn baby tomorrow.
  Don't say "goddamn baby," please. Glorious baby. Gorgeous baby. God—
  Diablo. Leave that Flying Buffalo-Meat Monster out of this. You sound like Augie.
  Augie Lightning or Augie, Diablo's brother?
  Augie Talbot, of course. Choirboy Augie. Nerdling Augie. Writing the Great American Movie still. Forever.
  How is he? Can you imagine? Your best friend but <u>his</u> brother.

His twin. Don't forget. You don't get over that shit. How is he. Shit. This gear smells like who-knows-what kinda cancer-causing chemical whatnot. I'm gonna hang it outside.

Please don't go out there naked. It's—

Who knew you could cum without a proper woody?

Sully!

I'm sorry. I—you just touched me. You know. We never talked about this. It wasn't working. Hold on a sec ... Was it? It wasn't working and I—you tried to—and all of a sudden ... How did we never talk about this?

Sullivan Winter. You had just lost your best friend. You looked at me. We've known each other since—You looked at me. Don't look at me that way. Put this on. It's not like I, you know—stop looking at me like that. Ooh, I don't like that look.

I was lost. I lost him, Vero. And I was lost.

I know. But I found you. We're found. Let me hug you now. Let me. Open up. Don't go away. Don't disappear into your—Little Diablo's gonna find you tomorrow at Kitskill. This was meant to be. Please tell me you know that. I don't think I could deal with—

I know. But who knew? I wasn't even—

You believe it, right? You believe in destiny? In fate? In predit— We're going to be a family.

Are we?

What makes a family? What? Is it only love? Or something more? What are the imperative constituents? Get this right and go on. Get it wrong, and maybe members of your own family face a wee little challenge or three in the upcoming weeks ...

MISSION

Mission

For Kyle

We must be willing to let go of the life we have planned, so as to have the life that is waiting for us.

—E.M. Forster, *A Room with a View*, 1908

What makes a family? We never swam nude in a Greek lagoon. We never celebrated a "holy union," heard our best friends toast us, sing. We never hired a band—not for anything. We never protested, and certainly never fought in a war. What exactly were we waiting for all those years we were busy waiting? This hurts to reckon, more than a bullet blowing out a lung.

What we did do, though, we did really fucking well. We did the "kids," Kit and Silas. Like Michelangelo, we did them.

★★★

"It's perfect," says Jonah. He nods as though he belongs among all the elegant oak, the antique dust, and diffuse light of the gallery on the plaza in up-and-coming Cutchin, near our new home on the (can't believe I'm saying this) Rez. "This, Rory. This is the ideal dining room set."

Well, why the fuck not? After all we've been through. It's three month's baker's wages for him, a month of my pay in a good year. It's a third of the price of my parents' first house on the Rez, where I was born and grew to fathom (alone between the stucco and a dense yew bush where daily I bided) that when the far-off millennium finally arrived, I'd witness it with a mate like my mother had in my father, and not vice-versa. There was a way his T-shirt fit around his arms and shoulders, a way he held his Thermos of tomato soup, and cast a fly in waders up to his waist on the banks of the Christos. A thousand times, I followed his boots with the big-looped laces up the grassy, granite slope behind our house. I listened to him coo and nuzzle Alaska, the mutt he loved when he didn't know I was at the top of the stairs—mornings I heard him say things to my mother I shouldn't have heard. I closed my eyes while he squeezed the back of my neck sometimes as I sat at the table reading Spiderman comics on the sticky tablecloth. *With great power comes great responsibility.* That cheap house burned down when they played hooky from work one day I was at school learning lies; they lit a bunch of candles and lined the stairs, then fell asleep on a blanket in the hall. Not even Alaska made it out alive.

Hit the button on the View-Master. Flash forward. Blur. One moment you're inhaling oil fumes, your pants around your ankles with a pal in the boiler room at The Aric Hatch Grammar School in Arctadia, New York. Blink. You're back. Improbably back. You're co-signing a short-term mortgage and replacing the gutters with your long-term partner, all loose and shabby around the joints like the Velveteen Rabbit.

Back on Kittakwa land. Where once were only woods and maple syrup vendors now stands a nascent antiques district, several "Ye Old"-type "Shoppes," a gourmet ice cream parlor, a fudge and candy store. All for the tourists. More to come—and not only in fall. All part of the alleged, oft-romanticized, and overly hyped "New Kit County." What's new?

I nudge Jonah away from earshot of the salesman, a smartly dressed, ethnically-mingled young man named Silas. He cannot be more than 18. I don't want him to know how much we love the table, how we would literally choke a puppy to procure it for our new dining room. "Would you *shush*?" I whisper to Jonah.

This is my role. To sermonize. To codify. To urge. And it hasn't gone unnoticed. Owing to my propensity to lecture – not to mention my profession as an architect, my paternal efficacy, and my predilection for men's men – Jonah has dubbed me "Mike," after Mike Brady of television family fame.

He pecks my lips and pats my behind surreptitiously. "Oh, Mike …" Has Silas seen? As usual, Jonah is drunk with avarice, like Babar coveting spats and a derby hat on his first day out of the jungle. Our relatively recent tragedy has necessitated us giving the heave-ho to the old clunky dining room table I insisted we move from our last home outside America's second favorite Southwest city. A modest settlement with the gun manufacturer, once it paid all the hospital bills and set up the college account, allowed us to buy a two-year-old black Impala with a spoiler and tinted windows – the one with the big, big engine – for Jonah, my gearhead. And now we intended to redecorate the whole (small) homestead outside Arctadia in mission style. "*Welcome to Our Humble A*dobe" reads the copper address plate beside the door, but nearly no one notices the "typoglycemic" joke.

I'm suddenly aware that Kit is missing. The kid doesn't usually stray from his "neighbor-dad-thingies," as he calls me and Jonah. Too far away and he quickly becomes anxious, which manifests, for reasons Dr. Mahler has explained, in great, disproportional confusion—*disorientation* is a more apt account. Soon, some helpful cunt will come along, advocating on his behalf, insisting floorwalkers make announcements. And Kit will cling to our thighs, but suddenly, inconveniently, forget who he is (!), or transpose the letters in his name. "*Tik?! Did you say 'Tik,' Son? Who names their kid 'Tik?*" Then a security goon will insist on "sorting this out," awkward phone calls will ensue, and nervous adumbrations of ties that sound suspect, even to the tellers. Then we are only reluctantly allowed to slink away peaceably in the black Impala, which suddenly takes on the exact specifications of a dime store novel-getaway car. This is because it is clear what's going on here (roofies, brainwashing). Or maybe we kidnapped this adorable (surely semi-retarded) boy from a fun fair somewhere, dyed his hair, and burned off one of

Two Spirits

his ears with a sizzling iron (Yes, Kit has only one ear; "Kit-The-Earless- *Wunderkind*," we call him. [More on that later]).

"He's fine," says Jonah. "Cut it out. He's playing with some other kids."

"Don't tell me to—"

"Relax."

"Joney," I say in retribution, because he despises when I call him Joney in front of strangers – especially such fine young specimens as Silas the Sexy Salesman – "Can you just go check on him, please, and while you're doing that, I'll fill out the paperwork, and we'll buy this ideal dining room set, OK?"

"The whole shebang? Serious?"

"The table, the sideboard, the hutch, the whatever-it's-called."

"The *credenza*," Silas suggests from where he's hovering a safe distance from the connubial wrangling, yet near enough to close the deal at the perfect time.

Jonah smiles.

I sit at the head of the huge table – too big for our new dining room, truly – smelling some expensive, citrus-scented polish. Surely Silas will try to sell us something, the furniture equivalent of undercoating. This was my grandfather's seat (stroke, caused by alcoholism), my stepfather's seat (pulmonary embolism; alcohol), and now that I have a son – kind of/sort of – it makes sense that it's my seat now (not a gunshot wound, but not for lack of trying).

It makes sense, but not the kind of sense a level makes on a railing when one gets a contract to design and build a baseball stadium on a lesser known Native American reservation in upstate New York.

Two years ago, at Jonah's cousin's wedding, on the grounds of an old pine chateau past the railroad bridge, decorated year-round for Christmas, on said Rez. When we first heard their plans to build the stadium instead of a casino. When the elders first approached me, "proud (not) Kittakwa (kinda) son." A symphony played Vivaldi. Jonah guided me out of the crowd, past the Viennese table, through French doors and into a wing long fallen into desuetude, where we slumped on a settee in what had been some Christmas baron's (Jackson's? Jared's? Farther back?) ante-parlor. A balcony built around the massive boulder, Shelter Rock, outside. Campari and soda, and not a little codeine.

I said, "Does it bother you that when we're dead, that's it—show's over?"

"No," he said. "Does it bug you that when you get bellybutton lint, it's always a different color from the shirt you're wearing?"

"No."

Our rooms in the inn abutting the mansion were furnished in mission style, and that's when we decided how we'd do the new little house we'd pledged to buy for the duration of the contract, to rescue ourselves from a rut. Notwithstanding the substantial take from the Christmas Memorial Stadium job, we had accrued lots of debt, and accreted expenses – major expenses – related to the failed adoption, and lawsuits there appertaining.

In the gallery where I see New York City people, Connecticut people, Westchester crème de la crème, I click the pen – open, closed, open – and spread my palms on the hewn-oak tabletop.

"OK, Sir?" says Silas. "It really is an excellent investment, I think."

"Oh, you think? How old are you? I'm sorry. It's just. Are you really impressed by a dining room set, or is this all a *shtick* for commission?"

"Not sure how to answer that, Sir."

"Don't worry—we're buying. Seriously, though. What are you? Nine?"

"Something along those lines, Sir."

"Mmm-hmm. What are you doing here? I mean, shouldn't you be, I don't know, like, out dancing on a speaker with your shirt off at some club somewhere?"

You couldn't call it a blush, exactly, but some element under his yellow/brown skin blazes for a second. Shafts of light from high arched windows crisscross all around him, each revealing galaxies of dust. He adjusts his designer glasses. He caresses the knot of his tie, a subtle blue and gold.

"It's my father's gallery."

"Ah."

"But I like to be around these things. So no, it's not a '*shtick*.'"

He crosses his legs, not a typical teenage maneuver. Bespoke shoes: An easy eight hundred. The affectation has aged him several years.

"Tell me what you love about it here," I ask.

His eyes lock on mine.

"All right. Well, first off, I don't love the Rez. Obviously. But I love coming in here in the morning. When I open up. I love the way the roof creaks. And at night, too, when all the customers have gone." Now he is blushing. "Sorry. I didn't mean—"

"Go on."

"Well, when I'm all alone with all these things, it's kind of a magic place. I mean, it would be magic to travel back in time, wouldn't it?" An animated boy in there, dying to scrabble out. He catches himself. "I once had a dream where it was … This'll sound ridiculous …"

"Tell me."

"… Where it was … revealed to me …" He squints toward me to gauge my reaction. My face seems to have passed some test. He looks around us – for his father? For my partner? – and puts both shoes on the floor, pulls the chair in closer. "Well, somehow it was revealed to me that there are six great tragedies in being human, and I woke up and I felt … well, I guess … enlightened, for a while, and I suppose just more OK with the world."

"As you would."

"And one of the tragedies is that we can't travel back in time. We literally can't escape the nineties. Not backwards, at least, and the other way goes so slow."

"Right." I nodded soberly. "That is tragic, isn't it?"

His smile tells me I've been inadvertently patronizing. So I lean back and commit to really taking it in, this boy's real tragedy.

"It feels like we can, though," I say after a moment. "Travel back in time. Like if you really spend a lot of time thinking about the past, some pasture somewhere on the outskirts of …"

"Munich."

"I was going to say—but Munich, sure. Or even your own childhood—that's the past, too, isn't it? If you dwell on it, you kind of dwell in it, you know?"

"Yes, but only kind of, as you say. It only feels like you can because you so wish you can, but of course everyone knows you can't. So the thing is, I like it here because …" His eyes are chocolate colored, almond shaped. "Well, put it like this: First of all, it isn't full of hokey 'Indian' gewgaws for the leaf-peepers. And these antiques are hundreds of years old, right?" His skin, as though forged in a caramel mold. "There's a hall back there, see? With doors, all doors from villas and castles and mansions, and some are almost a thousand years old. Which is just insane when you think about it. I mean, the dirt on them is that dirt from our old München orchard. And spiders made webs in the crevasses when …"

"When Marco Polo pissed his pants."

"When Hector was a pup," he says. "When the Divine Triad beat back the British. And doors and gates are symbolic, too, don't forget," he says.

"You can't help but think who went through those doors."

"Maybe Akt'adia. Aric Hatch."

"In and out."

"Ghosh'eyo himself."

"Or what they kept hidden. Or who. It's nice to meet you, Mike."

"Rory Dane." I say, outstretching my hand.

"I'm sorry. I thought—"

"It's a long story, but it's not 'Mike.'" If his hand is warm, I think, I will know him still on the day I die. "It's good to meet you, Silas."

I motion to the lapel of his suit.

"Oh, I hate this thing. I told my father it was low class, you know, very flea market furniture outlet."

"No, I like a nametag," I say, wanting to touch it, all those curves and lines etched in plastic. "I think we all should wear one."

"Whoa, that would really … That would change the world, wouldn't it, Sir?"

Two Spirits 139

"Rory."

"Mister Dane."

Maybe it's always the simplest stuff that changes the world. Like love. A hot hand. Or a 12-gauge shotgun shell.

★★★

I watch Jonah spotting Kit and a little fat girl jumping from part of an ancient staircase onto a lime green davenport. They are shouting, "Dive-bomb!" "Kamikaze!" "Cannonball!" I love being right.

Silas is back to business when my *de facto* family returns. He's smoothing the crease on the credit app.

"What do I put for 'relationship,' Sir?"

"What do you put for 'relationship,' Silas?"

"On the form, he means," says Jonah.

Yes, Jonah, Sheesh. It's called flirting. Deal with it.

"Umm ... *Domestic partners*, I think, is the legal designation, ain't it, Joney?"

"'Cellmates,' I'd say," he puts it. Very *Who's Afraid of Virginia Woolf*.

"I'll leave it blank. If you'll give me just a moment."

Kit and the fat girl conspire under the table. The rails at either end make a nifty jail.

"Lemme' out! I didn't do it!" he shouts. Shades of his "sperm dad," his real father.

Kit's completing sentences again. This is good—he's pushing 10. Dr. Mahler tells us it's "palpable progress." She tells us we shouldn't finish his thoughts for him, though, however frustrated he gets from the aphasia. I had thought that rule applied to stutterers only, but here, as elsewhere when it comes to the rearing of other people's children, I'm out of my depth. It's almost always something exogenous (to use the doctor's designation for the world around our Kit) that triggers the aforementioned disorientation. Which implies – to me, at least – that something from without, such as my words or presence, a certain touch, can trigger an equal orientation. But then again, the likes of Dr. Mahler warn one not to wake our wee sleepwalker, even with the most comforting embrace, or someone might lose an ear, or face.

Triggers. They trigger an action, Mahler says, some mechanism of operation, the endogenous analog – re-action – ostensibly more complex to anatomize, but infinitely simpler and more obvious. There's break-action. Pump-action. Bolt-action. And Kit's stock in trade: semi-automatic. Lock and load.

★★★

I feel only the stream of heat I've heard described by various victims on reality TV. Like a jet of hot water passing through my neck. Friends had often wondered aloud what would happen if Kit one day inadvertently (or advertently) worded something to his sperm dad that would come off as "fishy" to a bigoted galoot. We got lots of counsel in those days. We should see at least a tribal lawyer, visit Kit's therapist, make sure he knows our intentions are strictly paternal. As opposed to—? Our friends loved to intone the term "strictly paternal" in front of us at the New Yorker motel pool or one of Main Street's two "rez-taurants," or on the hiking trails around Kit County. We should get stuff in writing, on file, on the record. We need to hightail it to Canada with the kid. We ought to at least send an e-mail to his father with elaborate and detailed instructions on how to parent a human child: *#437: Ensure boy changes socks daily to hedge against foot odor.* One might send such a manual anonymously, or deliver it with the forged imprimatur of some plausible and officious agency.

We got most of it right, and we got cocky. We joked that perhaps we should roll into careers as itinerant parenting counselors, traveling from hamlet to dale proffering relief with the wee ones, and maybe occasional decorating advice to boot: *It's classic Electra issues with Claire, so be sensitive to the emergence of latent hostility. And, oh, a nice sponging effect would work wonders on those foyer walls* ...

Jonah reminded me constantly that we ought to treat Kit as any other niece or nephew we knew and, yes, loved, and that included affection manifested in the form of kisses and hugs and hours-long, house-wide, knock-down, drag-out kick-fights and other "happy horseshit" as my father used to call it, of which Jonah and Kit never seemed to tire, but which made me an anxious wreck for fear it might someday, somehow find itself misconstrued by predisposed extremists (so much for it being "paranoia," Joney). *If it please the Tribal Court, we submit there is a marked difference between tickling and molesting, which surely Your Honor (and any eight-year-old child, INCLUDING the fucking RETARDED) can detect without special training and a naked rag doll.*

We never did discern the exact words Kit used, the inflammatory narrative he must have shared with his father, because the subsequent "action" precipitated in Kit a total loss of memory going back about six weeks. But I suspect it's no coincidence that his father chose to shoot us all only two days after Jonah had to spend the night in the big chair next to Kit's bed at our place, first reading at the kid's most urgent application that awesome, fearsome children's version of *Paradise Lost* we found at the reservation's annual firehouse bookfair (local author, Professor Richter of Vaughn U.), then later trying in vain to soothe him after a nightmare of epic *Sturm und Drang*, a sea of writhing snakes with the tiny, twisted faces of the fallen, rebel angels.

★★★

Except for his job – fashioning firetruck parts on the night shift at the factory on the actual other side of the tracks – Kit's father didn't fit the description of the stereotypical abusive parent, never mind attempted murderer/infanticidal maniac. He was neither heathen nor fundamentalist. He didn't drink cheap beer as far as we knew, preferring a crisp Chardonnay with dinner when appropriate. And not even out of a box.

He kept a small, clean house at the end of the street where our first little "temporary" house was, the one the Council rented to us. We saw him once scrubbing their yellow toilet, Navy-style, all effort and humility, with powder blue rubber gloves. He seemed interested in Kit's schooling and his 4H troupe that for some reason specialized in carving wooden ducks, which they sold at church fairs and farmer's markets (They carved a shit-ton of ducks. We have a flock of them in our house – the strange and silent children of our association – and we've heaped dozens of ducks on all friends and relations for every holiday imaginable, and several occasions we had to invent to cull the wooden herd).

Kit and his father shared a passion for toy ballooning, too. They built miniature aircraft to scale, then launched them, often with a couple of hapless wooden ducks aboard à la Laika). They pinned to the ducks a Post-It note with Kit's father's address, requesting a response from the finder. We discovered one such wreck soon after we moved in, and offered asylum to the downed fowl pilots. The note inside had been scrawled in poor English and even more tortured Spanish. Instead of going down the street to deliver the refugees and their crumpled craft, we wrote a letter as requested. Two days later, Kit's father took him on an excursion up the block, and knocked on our door. It was obvious to us that he immediately cottoned on to our "domestic arrangement," as he called it, and appeared relatively unperturbed.

A week later, Kit passed out after "huffing" (we thought it was Testors paint or modeling glue, but later determined it was the dark, heady duck stain). In any case, the man hightailed it to our house – and not to the hospital – with a limp Kit in his arms. A wicked migraine, and his head hung low during our triple-team lecture. Then Kit fell asleep quickly, hugging his stuffed javelina, "Javier," and the rest of us three guys stayed up late, sprawled on the floor over a bottle of Pinot Noir, reminiscing about our teenage years, and touching on articles of correspondence as the mist crawled in through the open windows. Yes, our worlds were not so different, and the inklings of a potential bond leapt about the room like the static electricity that issued off Javier after his spin in the dryer.

Over the next few weeks, Kit's father was quick to assist us with assembling our new chiminea, welding our faucet, and schooling us in the reservation's knotty water restrictions. He helped us put up a birdhouse and stayed to watch an Eastern Towhee stop for a home-made peanut-butter-and-agave snack of Jonah's devising. A specialist in lamb and ham, Kit's father invited us over for dinner twice, hoping to impress the "chef," and accepted our mealtime hospitality in return, coming four times for dinner and twice for lunch over a period of six months, as the foundations were dug and the frame of the stadium went up. With every visit came another carved duck or 11. We traded recipes for skin-on chocolate pudding. We all went for haircuts together once, a few months in. Almost imperceptibly, we began to like the man, more or less. We even started to ask for more wooden ducks, to fill a corner cabinet I built into the den with his help. Those fucking ducks.

We learned that Kit's father never finished high school at AHS, having had to take care of his "ailing" mother after his father's early departure into permanent inebriation. We discovered he didn't know how to properly use the term *"per se,"* nor the term, "quote, unquote." Although any intimation of gay sex left him positively nonplussed, he was not averse to our "lifestyle" as he called it, and seemed to accept my suggestion that he begin to think about us in more three-dimensional terms. "Lifestyles" as such don't bleed when you bash them with a baseball bat, I can even recall saying, in reference to a recent attack outside a bar/Chinese joint on Main Street. Ha!

"Per se," he began, "I'm not saying you gays are quote-unquote 'asking for it,' quote-unquote, but maybe if you kept it in the sex clubs …"

He first "dropped off" Kit with us when he went fishing with a "gal" from work, a former machine mechanic of some sort who had been promoted to bookkeeper at the firetruck factory. He was taking her to his cabin in the mountains, left to him by his brother, Kit's uncle, who'd killed himself building a bomb to blow up a train depot. He asked us whether we thought it would be better for Kit to see them together in the morning right away, or whether he should "ease on into it, *per se*."

"It'll drive you batty," he said, sighing. "Being a dad."

We nodded gravely.

As the courting between Kit's father and the gal progressed, we began to see more of the boy. At some point, his father stopped dropping him off, and the kid just showed up at our door with his sleeping bag and Javier. Quickly, he made us privy in a boyish way, through mopes and jokes, to the secrets of his life down the block, and the thorny texture of his internal life. Some of those details we found disconcerting at best. Not to say his father ever abused him (*per se*). He simply wasn't present much of the time, even when he was there. Days went by when his father didn't make a meal or wash the clothes. Sometimes, according to the kid, his father sat in a chair for hours, smoking, not even watching TV. No communication, no communion. So Kit, too, sat on the floor and zoned out, maybe hoping to meet his father somewhere on the plains of catatonia. Oh, and—for some reason his dad liked the feeling of balancing stuff on his head. Remotes. Cellphones. Cassette tapes. Etc. So sitting perfectly still with something on his skull.

★★★

It's only half in jest we say now it's the scars we share that make us a family. I'm as proud of mine as my mother had been of her cesarean scar. I got mine through the neck. I was more astonished than anything.

I've been shot, but I'm still standing. I can breathe, sort of.

You'd think the neck would be a sensitive area. We have defenses, though. A body can take a beating as it holds onto its ghost. Somehow Kit's father had learned that lesson himself, long ago. At least that's what we've come to believe, evidence *per se* remaining elusive.

Two Spirits 145

He shoved me out of the way. They asked us in court about this: He never used any epithets, didn't threaten us, didn't talk at all, as a matter of fact. Eerie. I remember thinking he must be in one of those "states" Kit had told us about. *Zombie Hours*, as we had come to think of them. He went after the sound of Jonah shouting, scrabbling up the hall. In his underwear, Jonah saw me behind Kit's dad, and tried to stop, sliding in his socks on the hardwood floor like Tom Cruise in *Risky Business*.

Here was my dialogue, by way of explaining the morning's events to my partner of 11 years: "He's killing us." But it was all a grotesque gurgle of blood and carbon dioxide.

I watched Jonah take one in the ribs. He spun nearly all the way around, smacking a tin and tile mirror we'd bought on an extremely hot day in Mexico, after some teenagers offered to sell us steroids in the street. He fell like a postal sack. The horror in his eyes was all for me, he later said.

"You were not a pretty girl."

"Please. You could have fallen with a little grace."

Up till then it made a sort of sense. Not the sense of a stadium's steel skeleton in an architectural diagram, but some sort of misplaced, quasi-honorable sense. You will lie in bed a long time. Then later, you will sit around a lot of waiting rooms and depositions, eating packets of food from vending machines. And you will ask a lot of questions of yourself and each other. Was he straight-up deranged? Did he believe on some level, even in – or because of – his altered state, that he was protecting his son? Avenging him? Was he competing with us for the kid's affections? Is there anything we could have done differently? Why did he go after the boy? Did any of this have anything to do with his weird predilection for balancing random objects on his head?

I staggered around blubbering, trying to get to Kit's room. What we called "Kit's room" was really a guest bedroom that his stuff and his powerful presence had slowly commandeered. His stuff consisted of an IKEA dresser of clean clothes, about 80 percent of which we'd bought him; a poster of some new pony car he and Jonah slavered over; a collection of *Captain Underpants* books, the *Paradise Lost* reanimation, and *Mad Libs*; a 10-gallon tank and its occupant, a brown tarantula named "Decepticon;" and his most prized possession, Javier the stuffed peccary, a gift of his father.

The first bullet exploded one of Kit's little lungs. The second took his ear apart like the skin of an orange. Both shots went straight through him and out. He was totally still when the paramedics got there. The quietest I'd seen him in days. The only sign of life was a bloom of tiny bubbles in the blood pooled on his chest. Having dragged my body over like a slug, I held Kit's hand as they tried to help us. I assumed Jonah was dead, because the cops and medics around him evinced no urgency. A Zen-like, meditative calm overtook the room.

★★★

You get a certain number of therapy sessions for your insurance dime. No mistake, I chose Dr. Mahler. We go back—way back. To when I was a boy Kit's age. Luc was older, tougher, and infinitely cooler than I. Our janitor's son. He came from one of the Southern Canada tribes—maybe Ontario, I can't remember. He went to another school, off the Rez – maybe Drummond? – but had to wait for his dad at Hatch for an hour after his day ended. I had to wait, too, because my foster parents worked in the City and couldn't pick me up until late. The secretaries in the office let us have the run of the school.

One day Luc took my hand in the art supply closet where we were cleaning up after all the other kids went home. He took my hand and put it to his belly. He said it was growling, and asked me if I could feel it. I told him I could, and looked up into his eyes. He smiled down at me. He ate a piece of melted Marathon bar some kid had left, and he gave me a piece. It got all over our hands. He asked if he could feel my tummy, too. I said mine was quiet. He said, "Let me see anyway," and slid his hand up under my shirt. I could smell the chocolate on his breath. I could feel it smearing around my skin.

Over the course of that year, we migrated from the art supply closet to the boiler room, and from the belly to parts south.

They said he did terrible things to me. They said he hurt me. But nothing Luc did hurt me. They took him away, and his father, too. They said I was a victim, a broken boy. I was. I was broken because I lost Luc. Because they got punished, because I loved him. In my foster parents' house, I tried to hurt myself for the first time. They sent me to Dr. Mahler. She was kind.

★★★

No one ever promised you'd get easy answers. There's no logically decoding guys like Kit's dad. After we recovered, after the police had thoroughly searched Kit's house and sealed it up, we went over several times with the key his dad had given us, to comb through every cranny. We even shook out all the books as they do on British mystery TV. We turned over all the wooden ducks. We looked for a lock box of depraved Polaroids, donkeys and carrots, thousand-pound, armless women in lingerie. *Nada*. We hunted for a cache of creepy souvenirs, totems of some pathology, perhaps a Baggie full of cigarette butts with lipstick stains, or a shoebox chock-a-block with his mother's yellowing Lee Press on Nails. No such luck. No Rosetta Stone, no chocolate handprint on the abdomen. We knew it was connected to his mother, though. Kit had never met his grandmother. She was "institutionalized" at Sculton, just north of the Rez. Where Mahler worked. You gotta believe there's a story there somewhere, some chain of causality.

But Kit's dad wouldn't talk. All through the trial, he just sat there, immovable, untouchable, like some mustachioed Pacific idol. He kept trying to balance pens, packages of Chuckles, binder clips, on his head. And something about the mouth, the slightest smile, made me believe he was romping in some oblivion somewhere full of puppy dogs and rainbows, perfectly content and not on trial. They ruled him insane – no thanks to a good "Jew lawyer" the gal had enlisted – and sent him to a recently reanimated asylum in Cornwall, near West Point, where he remains, his only visitor said gal and the fellow zombies of his mind's eye.

We searched our memories for signs. We used metal-detectors, Geiger counters, feather brushes, Q-Tips, electron microscopy. We'd all gone walking once in the High Kitskills, and a long time passed without words. Then Jonah tossed a grape, Kit caught it in his mouth, and I thought I saw something odd flash across his father's face—then it was gone.

The shooting nearly broke us up. But that's ABC Afterschool Special shit, and we're more dignified and novel than that cliché.

A triple shooting'll cost you. The media were birds of prey. The social service people swarmed. The authorities didn't trust us for foster parents. Nurses wiped our asses. We did, in fact, suffer the third degree about all manner of personal quirks and belongings the cops had unearthed in our environs. Our e-mails to each other were read by strangers and interpreted to fit unfortunate bills. Our videotapes were collected and cataloged by clerks, fast-searched in case we'd cleverly sandwiched our kiddie snuff porn between old episodes of *Alf*, Jonah's favorite show, or *This Old House*, mine. Lawyers, Jewish and Gentile, fucked the boy in ways that we, of course, never dreamed of.

People who didn't know us thought it apropos to write to the local rag, the *Kit Banner*, opining on aspects of the case as varied as the origins of pedophilia, and the vengeance of the Lord. *60 Minutes* did that "neutral" profile on us. Had we ever been good fake parents? Did Kit's father perhaps deserve some mercy? After all, he was unwell—not evil *per se*. But I had been re-broken. Not by the bullets, and not even by watching Kit and Jonah suffer. No, this time, and irreparably, by the false accusation, even the whiff of a heinous misdeed. I had been raped.

Jonah was first out of danger, so he spent the most time with Kit in his recovery. Kit was comatose for a few days, then thrashing in various agonies for several more. "Combative," they called it. Insane, it looked to me. Dying. When they first wheeled me in to see him, I would have shot him again if I'd had a gun. I would have smothered him with Javier.

He suffered brain damage, they told us, the stuff of cheesy TV. Some "diminished mental capacity," which, frankly, was the last thing the kid could afford. Twitching and numbness in sundry parts. Missing his mouth with spoons of applesauce. Terrible, shredding frustration at trying to make himself understood. Tying his shoes was out of his ken, and sitting on the toilet, a Sisyphean hurdle. For months on the parallel bars, he sputtered along like Pinocchio. And of course, there was the wrecked left ear. At first, I couldn't bear to see him. I made up excuses to stay alone in private abject misery. Jonah snapped me out of it, cruelly but necessarily. Then the only way I could engage with Kit was to dull my love with a lovely drug called Vicoprofen.

Time and physical therapy smoothed out about 80 percent of the awkward gait. A titanic Kit speech therapist, cousin of the locally-famous Medicine Sisters, worked to undo the advent of logaphasia. They had to crack open his chest, twice, "stem to stern," as my foster father had been fond of proclaiming after his own open-heart procedure. The second time, they had to leave the wound open, so we could literally see the interplay of his organs, different from the fluffy white inside of Javier uncovered by one of our dogs. And now the beautiful boy was short one apricot ear. That would take half a dozen operations to repair, which would start next year, after a tutor helped him make up what he'd lost of the fourth grade.

Dr. Mahler said with time, he'd start to remember, and that's when the real trauma would begin. For now, he had no recollection of his father at all. Blessedly, he remembered us, his neighbor-dad-thingies, for the most part. Some nights he regressed developmentally to an alarming degree. He held my hand and sucked his thumb and stared into my eyes as he had when I cradled him on the floor that day he lay bleeding out on our wide-plank floors.

Two or three times, Jonah and I parked by Hatch Grammar's playground and watched him gamboling around, showing off where his ear used to be, as though it were a badge of honor. Some kids seemed to gravitate around him—others openly shunned him and mocked. The things you see when you don't have a shotgun of your own. Girls in particular liked to baby him, and he seemed to acquiesce. "Chicks dig scars," Jonah told him.

It took me six months to get back to my job site, which progressed steadily without me—a mixed blessing. The less said about what my neck looked like, the better. I coughed and cleared my throat a lot, and even had to spit in a hanky a few times an hour, none of which is endearing to well-wishers or clients. Sometimes I hacked so much that I wrenched my back. Jonah had no choice but to insist he sleep downstairs in the chair beside Kit's bed.

Little known fact: The cops and rescue folks don't clean up your place after a multiple shooting. They give you a 3x5 index card with a list of names, then you have to hire a firm that specializes in such an operation. It isn't easy to get gore out of grout, to restore a wood floor slaked in half a gallon of blood. And it ain't cheap, either. They had to go so far as to replace the plaster. They removed the dining room table, permanently stained, and drove it away in a truck that looked like a Dumpster on wheels.

"It's like that clean-up machine in *The Cat in the Hat*," said Jonah. Still, the house was no good to us now. We'd have to move.

After the chaos and retrenchment, we were three wounded men eating lots of mint chocolate chip ice cream, watching too many *Oprah* reruns and a shitload of *Nick at Nite*. During the former, Kit pointed to the TV and said only "fat" or "skinny" according to the diet era when each episode had been taped.

Only slowly, we emerged back into the humidity and heat of Kit County in midsummer. To face the faces at the knockoff Blockbuster and the Indian version of the IGA. First, we had to abandon the house. Buy a new one. Then consider filling the rooms with things, as that mission had been put on hold. The cool, dark Cutchin

Two Spirits

Village gallery we'd come upon now seemed so full of promise, a gateway to a peaceful, productive, and fully-furnished future.

"Your credit is sterling," says Silas, as he emerges from the business office up a flight of dark stairs. Then, sheepishly, he says, "If someone were to want to dance shirtless on a speaker at a club, exactly where would he go? The City, right?"

"Right."

★★★

Jonah posits the pee stains, not the nightmare of *Paradise Lost*, were the impetus for the shooting. A week or so before, Jonah was folding the laundry and commented to me about the pee stains common in Kit's underwear.

"No one's ever taught him he should wipe it after peeing; that's all," I suggested.

"Or shake it at least."

"A little piece of toilet paper does the trick."

"Oh, sure."

So we told him, matter-of-fact, while he was watching some inane Korean robot cartoon. He nodded, agreed, and didn't seem disturbed at all. Had he related this conversation to his father? And how? We'd never know.

The gal from the firetruck factory comes to see us once. She wants to meet Kit officially (the Judge had ordered everyone to steer clear of him during the trial). She tells us that since the shooting, she's been grinding her teeth at night, and that has knocked her jaws out of whack, causing severe tension headaches. Jonah offers her some of our "Vikes," and I shoot him a look. The gal is trashy, but funny, too, with a mouth like a trucker. Under different circumstances she would have made a good bowling friend, or maybe we might have gone to see some go-go-boys dancing on speakers in the City.

We've written to Kit's dad twice. We sent pictures of Kit, and we didn't mention that he lives in a world, for now, in which his father never existed. A night nurse at his new home, too young and sweet to know better, told us some particulars of Kit's dad's evening routine. He doesn't do anything outwardly crazy, besides not speaking, as some of the patients do (wearing only one shoe, searching fruitlessly under cushions for phantom objects, hiding chicken bones in the rectum). He plays a lot of cards with other inmates. Crazy Eights. Hearts. UNO. A fast-paced, rollicking game called 99. He reads, too, she tells us. Mostly about violins. At first, we thought she'd said, "violence," but it was just her accent. Eventually, we find out that Kit's father has begun to speak again. He takes over teaching the woodshop class, and finishes a correspondence course on building stringed instruments. The gal orders the raw materials for him, and brings him a carton with every visit. He asks about Kit all the time, she says. We don't know whether to believe her.

Jonah and I have agreed not to bring Kit to see him, and Dr. Mahler concurs. Not till he's older.

Loving Kit as I do – and not hating his father *per se* – makes me feel closer to God than I ever thought possible. One night I go downstairs, and when I open the door to Kit's bedroom, the dogs, surrounding him in his bed, all look up, growling. What fresh hell? Jonah is asleep in the chair with an entire, encyclopedic tome about mousse in his lap. I rouse him and lead him upstairs.

***

After Silas's 20th birthday bash, we sit dozily around the great mission table he sold us some years ago. Silas is drunk on Pimm's and ginger ale with slices of cucumber. I am drunk on decaf Irish coffee. Jonah is drunk on port. Kit is dreaming on the sofa in the living room, his half-an-ear covered with Javier. Javier's sewn-up sternum mirrors his own.

Silas lost his virginity in his father's store, on a chaise longue display not far from where we met him. One day, he told his old-world father of his son's new-world ways, and his father banished him from his house and from the gallery the boy loved more than any other place in the Local Group of galaxies in the Virgo Supercluster. Missing his brothers and sisters, he has projected all his love onto Kit and us. A powerful, pitiful, almost painful love. We have taken him in, half-joking that we seem to recall a room full of antique firearms in his father's store. At home, we all wear nametags, all the time. Kit's title is "House Manager;" Silas's, "Cruise Director;" then there is "Chef J," and finally me—Rory 'Mike Brady' Dane: Hostess."

Silas sleeps in the cabana I built out back, takes impossibly handsome young gentlemen callers there – mostly white men traveling through – but not so often. He reads a lot—books on "theory" and "semantics," whatever those are ("aesthetics," at least, I get). We took a trip to the mountains of late, steaming in hot springs under a freezing rain, sensing on our naked skin that renowned convergence. These kids, they keep us young. Their bodies, their minds, the things they say that make us laugh. When they get the sniffles or don't look both ways before crossing the street, it feels like we are Mother Earth and Pangaea's wrenching apart in our arms.

★★★

Kit's father ships him a homemade violin, which looks beautifully crafted, and sounds exquisite. He's carved Kit's initials on the scroll. You can actually smell the parts that are maple, and the parts that are spruce, but you have to get close. It's a far cry from the blunted ducks of yore. Stunned, Kit holds the instrument in his lap. We visit it when he's at school, and when we see the place of honor he's given it on a shelf in his room, we weep.

His father's violins.
His father's violence.

★★★

Christmas Memorial Stadium is finally done, though they never retrieved all the bodies from the mine over which it's built. Story of America.

I will never undertake another commercial project again. I have recently seen two grand villas completed per my designs—one for an alcoholic Aussie actor, and one for a secretly gay football quarterback. Both overlooking the Hudson. We double our income. Silas alone received $45,000 for decorating the gay athlete's manse. Now we are spending the summer by the pool. We installed an inground pool, the only one within 10 square miles, certainly the only one on the Rez outside the New Yorker Hotel and the community center. Which is weird, given the stocks of mined diatoms piled hereabouts. It could filter a million pools for a hundred summers. Silas is snoozing on the patio, one bronze leg in the water like an "actor" in a Cadinot. Not to be outdone by his little brother or Javier, he has a dark, angry hook of a scar two inches left of his navel, the only blemish on an otherwise perfect expanse of hairless skin. To the right, a spindly, wispy, scrolled design—but it's not a design.

Tenth grade at Arctadia High: He crushed on a fellow soccer player. Silas slipped a note in the boy's locker, asking for a sign. "If you're gay, Wallace, wear a blue shirt tomorrow," he wrote in his note, "and I will show you who I am." It seemed like a good idea at the time.

Silas couldn't sleep.

The bus ride was a horror show of bowel complaints.

Wallace wore the bluest shirt in the history of shirts.

Silas with a rabbit heart got Wallace alone in the locker room at the end of the fuzzy day. And Wallace had lingered as Silas did, after their last period gym. He didn't have to confess it was he who'd written the note. He just sidled into the kid's row and sat near him on the bench, palpitating and woozy.

They didn't speak, but Silas was certain he saw Wallace smile. That was just before the boy's older brothers, two of them, leapt from another row making Indian noises, and chased Silas toward the showers with metal rulers they'd made in shop class. Their plan was to carve the word "fag" on their brother's wooer, but they only half-finished the "f" before his caterwauling garnered the attention of coach Silver. They rushed the rest. And if you look real close, you can see to this day, it says, "fog."

I wonder where my Luc is. I wonder if he ever healed from the awful barbs. He might be some state senator somewhere, traveling by Learjet and much praised for his wisdom and generosity. He might sit at the head of a table, with girls and boys and a wife around pork chops and broccolini. Or he might have found his playful, tender soul inconsistent with the self-image evolved by the barrage of blame, and become a monster lurking in the art supply closet.

We are lucky. We are four scarred survivors under hot tub jets, faces up to the cool air and the constellations, making stupid noises to crack each other up. We are a family.

★★★

Nothing says "sexy" like surgical tubing. First, we were inmates of medicine. Then we were recovering, holding vigils for Kit. We had staples and stitches and drains and catheters, shunts and cannulas, bedpans and weeping sores. We went through all of Dr. Mahler's predicted stages, including eventual acceptance, though that one is squirrely to be sure. We ached for a long time, literally. We suffered dope-induced constipation. Migraines. Flashbacks. Piles. Unsettling dreams. Torn stitches. Bedsores. Stents. Night terrors, all. Once Jonah flung himself out of bed from a nightmare, impaling his leg on a cactus someone had brought as a gift. He said it hurt worse than getting shot. There's some kind of venom, supposedly. It hurts him still now, years later, but he refuses to let the doctors take out the tine.

When Kit came home, it was all anxiety and arguing about what was best for the boy. Every iota of energy devoted to patience and hope, diverted from the phallus. *That's not a banana, Kit; it's called a "grape." Remember? Grape? Can you say it? Sure, you can. Graaape.* This for months will drive a man to Internet pornography.

The Medicine Sisters suggested much succor into all our lives. We spent many an afternoon hosted at their clinic on the pond, variously stinking or stuffed with one or another of their naturopathic remedies. Kit hung out with their nephew, Bon, whom everyone called Puppy Dog, and they got on, mostly without speaking. It was almost comical watching those two peas in their pod, one earless, one eyeless; it was almost unbearable.

There were teleconferences, videos, visits to university libraries. Bookmarks by the dozen, conventions, and consultations requiring flights with layovers, motel stays, greasy diner omelets. Hourly rates to experts. Copies of scans and scans of copies. Several seasons of leaf-peepers descending on the Rez.

But less wounded couples can fuck through equivalent challenges. I know for a fact. The death knell for us was the antidepressants. Jonah couldn't sleep and couldn't work and couldn't stand to be around me after the shooting. The drugs were miraculous, bringing him back in a matter of months. The drugs cleared a fog, revealing a man who could laugh and launch into song without provocation. But they killed the sex completely. This was, of course, ironic, considering this new problem caused me to become severely depressed even while Jonah felt so much better. He baked cookies into the night while I lay upstairs, pining and plotting.

Under the circumstances – they think – some men might think a thousand times about sex with the gorgeous young man in the pool house. They think some might fantasize about fucking Silas on every mahogany antique in his father's gallery. One might imagine himself gentle in some fantasies, gliding his hands over every inch of (near) pristine skin. Another might break the kid's nose, smash his glasses against his face, flatten him onto the mission table. They assume some men might feel free to fantasize, I'm saying, to allow themselves the luxury, just to populate the yawning void. They err who would assert this. Because ... not this man.

Dragging Jonah back upstairs that night would have precluded such fantasies anyway. And titrating off those drugs changed everything. Neither of us needs to drag the other anymore, and this knowledge blankets me in relief. "It's always better on the other side of tragedy," I once heard my foster mother tell a friend over the

Two Spirits 157

phone. The caption under the photo in the *Banner: A firefighter attempts rescue-breathing on a dog, Alaska, after a fire on Elier Street. The animal died. Two residents also died, according to police.*

★★★

He might be only 22, but Silas A. Locklear is the quintessential "furniture-queen" of Northeast legend and lore. At least among Arts and Crafts pieces, he can spot a reproduction at 50 paces. An unexposed tenon will fracture his sense of wellbeing for the day, and he will turn away offers of food. A corbel that doesn't taper can make his Kittakwa blood boil.

And Silas L. will sit on a friend's or a neighbor's machine-manufactured – say Ashley Furniture Outlet – loveseat, the way one might sit on a heap of warm diapers.

"I don't understand," he will say, sincerely. "Some factory in the Carolinas mass-produces this drivel—and people actually pay for it? And put it in their house?"

He does not vote, nor will he sign the most worthy petitions—gay marriage, for example. He does not contribute to any political cause. He doesn't even read the paper or watch the news if he can help it. He does read *Architectural Digest*, though, and some funky, postmodern design and ad mags, too, that cost 20 bucks a pop. He is the best-looking, classiest, most intriguing biped I have ever known. He's the most careful, loving brother to Kit. And somehow we brought those boys together. We and Kit's father, whose actions obliged us to procure a new dining room table.

Style-wise, Silas prefers to surround himself with the soft, pleasing hues and patinas of the pre-1920s Americas. Upon checking into a metropolitan hotel whose lobby designer did not appreciate the symbiosis of textile, metalware, lighting, and fixtures, he will cling to his Vuitton bags.

"No," he will say, reminiscent of Oscar Wilde. "We cannot stay."

He has even got Kit commanding notions on decor. The boy can recognize proper flaking already, can spot a Stickley school desk or boat hull without even checking for the company mark.

Jonah calls it "gay school." An awful joke, considering.

Kit despises ornamentation of any kind, though he can't quite express this yet. He asks why the old Impala requires a spoiler. Jonah says, "Because it looks cool."

Kit says, "But what does it do?"

"What does it do?" says Jonah. "I just told you. It looks freakin' badass."

Kit is pushing 14. He has a nearly invisible web of hair covering his arms and legs. He has one and seven-eighths ears of late. He folds his own laundry. Javier still takes a tumble once a month, along with his underwear, extra Downy, *por favor*.

So Silas and Kit are pals, thick as Snoopy and Woodstock, and just as contentious. If truth be told, they are half like brothers and half like sisters, though this would surely offend their absurd pretentions toward masculinity. They make fun of me and Jonah, and they keep many vital secrets from us. They have similar dress sense (meaning Kit has adopted Silas's style). Neither will consider wearing shoes from a catalogue nor – heaven-forfend – a chain store. Both like turtlenecks now. Even I don't wear a turtleneck, and I could be forgiven, having been shot in the fucking neck. Kit will wear Silas's hand-me-downs, but never ours.

Silas and Kit see shows in the City, artsy, obscure. Silas doesn't drive at night, so a black and silver Town Car comes to pick them up. Yes, Silas has a driver. His name is Max. Kit knows the differences between a French horn and a flugelhorn, between Berlin and Hammerstein. Silas and Kit critique City and Westchester restaurants by ordering the same meal as the other and discussing each dish. "They call this a mélange?"

"Honey, it's a hot mess."

"And how about that frappé?"

"The chef should be beaten out back and left to bleed in the moonlight."

Jonah claps.

Two Spirits

Regularly, Jonah and I discuss whether Kit might emerge homosexual. We're of two minds – for a total of four – about whether we'd prefer this or not.

"Happy."

"Well-adjusted."

"Two-eared."

"Affianced."

"To a warm—"

"A patient—"

"Anyone."

Kit intends to become a novelist of worldwide renown, he informs us. You have to start by writing something, I suggest. No, you have to start by living, says Silas. And Silas's word is gold.

"Don't dash his dreams."

"How am I dashing?"

Jonah says you need all the ingredients before you make a matzo ball.

For some unaccountable reason, the boys are obsessed with a white rapper who goes by the name, "Dirty Jew."

"He's giving me life," says Silas.

"He's our generation's ... whoever," Kit pipes in.

Whether the *shtick* is ironic or not, we do not know—and that's part of the art.

And yet, alarmingly, the boys have also taken to studying German big band music from the Republic era. They go to German heritage festivals out of state, and they're learning German, too. It's like having horses talking to each other in the living room. They've even cut each other's hair in a style super-reminiscent of the *Hitler Jugend*.

"Sexy," says our hairdresser, Berto.

"Scary," says I.

They are helping me design our next house, off the Rez and up a hill overlooking the old Kittatinn Bridge. It will be, as Silas puts it, "unadorned by any element not functional."

"*Ja*," says Kit.

***

Naked under a towel in dark, Silas sleeps in the pool house. Faint flickering of moonlight from choppy water in the pool plays on his skin. In the stone fire pit he built with Kit, I hear sap crackling in the logs. In the fire pit and in the amaranthine scar on his belly, I understand the art and lovingkindness in the mission of our great Maker, some philosophy of simple splendor. And I wake him up, just to talk. He lights a cigarette, a new affectation that makes me grit my teeth like the firetruck factory gal.

He requires my advice about a man who's been wooing him relentlessly, a rich man, of course, some pinkie-ringed tribal council president from Niagara-ways, who sends a helicopter to fetch him monthly, when he stays in the Queen's Suite at a swanky casino, and has learned how to beat the odds at three-card poker. He snaps his thumbnail over one of his incisors. I watch his eyes, and find the depth of ages there, all the possibilities, a world beyond my limited mission. He's going to leave us, soon enough, and evolve into the man he's meant to be, the man his father feared, the man we helped him to become. And the other one will follow not so long after, and we'll be alone again, and happy for them, and lost.

***

Jonah operates his own European bakery now in Nyack. It's hard work, being a baker, not to mention the 90-minute Thruway commute. While I am still curled in the California king in the new house I built, he hauls giant sacks of flour on his bare shoulder, kneading out great slabs of dough in the dark. In the center of the kitchen cooled by fans, a colossal butcher block I built him from cherrywood and chrome commands the room. A huge ceiling fan spins slowly from the rafters overhead. The ceilings are 20 feet high. This is Jonah's dream—but he's not here except on Wednesdays, when he sleeps till afternoon.

Silas is studying in Stuttgart. He sends us handcrafted postcards. He has fallen in love with a German boy named Lothar, the 19-year-old heir to an estate built on insuring satellites and rockets. They intend to buy a vineyard, Silas writes. Riesling, I think. Lothar will finance the whole "*Spiel.*" We will visit in the fall. Kit cannot wait. They speak endlessly on the phone, slipping from Spanish to English to German to French. If Kit had a tail to wag, he'd wag it while they speak. Once, while we drove up to see a specialist in Boston, we saw a Benetton billboard featuring an Asian woman and a black woman, with children in rugby shirts. The slogan read, "*Love makes a family. Nothing more. Nothing less.*" Kit made us stop and take a picture. We hugged him.

Kit goes to work with Jonah most days this summer, and sits at a desk off the kitchen, where he writes with preternatural focus interrupted only by plates of marzipan. He's 16, beautiful (ear is ideal), and nearly done with his first novel, which he has dubbed *Things Unattempted Yet in Prose or Rhyme.* Allegedly (I come to understand from a reading he does at Lou's Bookstore [and part time headshop] in Arctadia), it's a bildungsroman of first love between a German boy and a Jewish girl, set during the War. Hot air balloons figure prominently, we hear. And there is a beloved duck named Ermaline, belonging to the chancellor. He will not let us read a single line, the stinker.

Kit plays his father's violins like a virtuoso, and he's been offered spots at music schools in New York, Boston, and Bern. He's captain of the diving team, too, an all-state forensics champ, and the lead – George Gibbs – in the (weird) school summer play, *Our Town.* A neighbor-dad-thingie could explode with pride.

Jonah makes Kit a sandwich with a fresh roll, then leaves the bakery with one of his apprentices so he can drive our son to rehearsals. They talk: Apparently, there are two boys and three girls in Kit's grade who call themselves "bisexual." It seems to carry some cachet. "Bi now, gay later," Jonah tells me in bed that night. "But I thought I could hear him using the feminine pronoun on the phone before. It bodes ... something."

"Oh, who knows what he and Silas mutter about in that language of servants and megalomaniacs? They could be planning the burning of the *Reichstag* for all we know."

"Cupcake? They're red velvet. Yummy."

★★★

There were six total tragic defects of human existence revealed to Silas in the momentous dream he had when he was Kit's age. They are all narrative devices in Kit's novel (which now features stolen Nazi dirigibles instead of balloons. Oh—and a golem). Jonah and I sit in our new truck in the driveway, listening to an interview with Kit and another young author named Gray on NPR. Kit, who wrecked the old Impala, his right knee, and his diving career.

"And six existential flaws are tragic not just because they limit us, but because we remain indefinitely ... deluded ... as a race, I mean, believing that such inadequacies either don't exist, or don't trouble us. Do you see?"

Terry Gross sees. Gray Cooper sees. Gross reads first from Gray's book, then from Kit's, which the publisher convinced Kit to rename *Mission*, arguing his draft title was pretentious: "'*We are like ragged kids pretending to be royal*,' Kit Dane writes, '*like mamas promising insufficient sons they can be king. Or fathers assuring themselves that queer boys can change their proverbial spots to squares if only you play enough rugby with them ...*'"

More than scars, the words that bind us now together make us family. The words in the dedication of Kit's book. The words on Silas's home page, on Jonah's menu. The words I wrote on the cornerstone of the symphony hall I just built – I know, but the money – and the words in Silas's father's quote-unquote apology. The words, occasioned by time and pharmacology, of Kit's father's confession, finally penetrated a shiny new ear. They took a picture together, and Kit's father wrote, "Love Your Dad" on the bottom, the absent comma turning his intended kindness into a command. We are writing words now for Kit and Renata's wedding toast, and I know I will lose my shit as I recite them.

I sit at the dining room table and trace the ring Kit left with a mug of hot chocolate some years ago, despite our infinite pleas for coasters. One day, I dropped an olive on the dining room floor and crawled to fetch it. When I looked up at the label on the table Silas sold us, I saw for the first time that he had written something there, in tiny block letters: BREAK BREAD HERE AND NEVER BREAK UP. – S.A.L.

The pictures of my boys on the credenza now remind me: *Missions accomplished*. But I know now that this sort of self-satisfaction goeth before every plunge, and, in my life, at least, this sense of security precedes the gun's report. So I open my copy of *Mission* for the umpteenth time, for further reminders of our six seminal limitations:

1. We cannot ever really know whether God exists.
2. We can't get into someone else's head.
3. We cannot fly.
4. We can't travel backward or forward (but slowly) in time.
5. We don't know what happens after we die …

I close the book, and look at the jacket photo of Silas with his loving brother. We all know the sixth shortcoming of human existence—and it's a fucking doozie.

—Wrong—

Friday Sept. 14. Day 11 of the shoot – afternoon.

New Mexico mountains

[NEW FLASHBACK]

EXT. KITTAKWA REZ. LIGHTNING HOUSE - DAWN (9 YEARS AGO)

SUPERIMPOSE: SASSAFRAS: GONORRHEA, SYPHILIS

The cabin's a rickety spectacle of shoddy engineering on Kittatinn Pond. A few KITTAKWAs and a WHITE LADY sit on the porch, waiting for something and chewing the fat.

Six-year-old PD escapes out the porch door. His Aunties, the MEDICINE SISTERS, MAY and JUNE, 40s, try to snatch him as he hops off the porch, and beelines naked past the swampy shoreline and into the woods, Meat Puppet at his heels, all power and grace. Nimble and sinewy, PD's flesh is variously scraped and etched and soiled in American boyhood.

He seems to know every little dip and dive, like he's been running these woods since time before time. Lickety-split, he slides down muddy hills, pivots over creek beds, ducks under thistle branches, weaves through pussy willows.

He crosses a disused trestle - the High Damien - then on the old railroad bed lined with ferns and bittersweet, he stops, squats, balanced on the balls of his bare feet, and marvels at a bunch of tiny, white flowers hanging down in bunches like umbrellas for frogs.

                        PD
            Queen Anne's Lace ...

SUPERIMPOSE: WRONG

His thigh just brushes the wide bottom leaves when he sniffs those dangling umbrels. He instantly recoils at the alien smell: He knows he's just made a terrible mistake.

Zoom up to bird's-eye view. The distinctive white bunches of the giant hogweed bush bloom through the canopy. They extend down the old railroad, choking out native species. Superfast continuous shot of a long line of them, more or less contiguous, for scores of miles from their stronghold far to the west in Pennsylvania: The relentless march of a toxic, invasive species. This is exactly how "those white cunts" conquered the once-mighty Kittakwa.

EXT. KITTAKWA RESERVATION. WOODS - MOMENTS LATER

Zoom down to an Extreme CU of the hogweed leaf. Its sap, sensing an enemy, bolts up to the surface in defense of its territory. It's not malevolence, *per se,* just a lesson in weals about the effects of noxious plant species on naked human boys.

ON THE THIGH

The advent of the sun into the meadow where the Rail Trail empties births painful, purple welts everywhere on little PD. They scar his groin and buttocks worse than thermal burns.

EMERGING INTO A CLEARING

PD weeps and screams like a skinned-alive pig. He picks his way through the long grass, and commits to his physical history the second great mistake of the day: He wipes his right eye with the heel of his hand.

ON PD'S EYE

The poison sizzles through the lens and cornea.

The boy drops, unconscious from pain.

Fuzzy coming-to.

Blinking. Pink.

SERIES OF IMAGES, PD'S POV:

—Canopy.

—Clouds: Mouse. Moose, High-collared elders, huddled, whispering.

—Max's concerned eyes above as he runs slow-mo with PD in his arms.

—Gauzy red blindness.

—Hospital white.

—A Jell-O cup in FG, with a KITSKILL CARITAS HOSPITAL "Soiled Linens" sign in BG, both blurry. The world's all shadows now.

BLINK.

      MAX (V.O.)
  Not so "bon."

      NURSE MOOSE (V.O.)
  Non.

BLINK.

[END FLASHBACK]

*—... like the ditch at Wounded Knee,
& the origin of Augie's middle name—*

Wednesday Sept. 19. Day 3 of the trial.

Hinterland, New Mexico

Is love immortal? Is love immortal. Well. Ya. I don't know what that has to do with my middle name. But ... oh. I see. OK.

His mother intended to call him "Ben," after her hero, Ben Nighthorse Campbell, who she thought was the first Indian senator. The first Native American senator, right? ... But ...

Life. Stuff happened. Shit happened.

And instead they named him Puppy Dog, after his "other mother," this shepherd-mix bitch named Meat Puppet.

So it happened like this—

As it was meant to happen.

Ya. I guess. His mother, April, had a father, Max, another drunk, who forbade her two sisters, May and June, from being there at the birth of the child. Max was dishonored – no good – because April was "barely in bloom when seeded," and because her suitor, which is putting it really nicely, was a lawman who "zephyred in from the West," some under-sheriff from out Cayuga-way with "no hair yet on his pecker." I'm quoting Max here. See, I have the honor of ghosting his blog. He's in hiding. I'm his voice. There's an editor, a professor at Vaughn. she looks over the blogs, cleans them up, fancies them up.

So: Three girls. "Medicine Sisters." Their mother, March Lightning, used to be March Blinkey-Bluesky, secretary for the tribal council, died in a car wreck. Terrible wreck.

Two Spirits

Ya. Which was the story of Max Lightning's shitty life on and off the Rez, until the Thanksgiving Day he became a hero to our people on the level of Washington, Kittadoga, and our own Akt'adia and Ghosh'eyo—the same day his grandson's "white twin," Noah, met his fate under an ATV.

You with me? May I have a drink of water, please? I've answered— Thank you. That's good. Hey. Hey, you're quizzing me here, but how do you know what the right answers are? There are right answers, right?

We've read your script. In the backpack.
Monday's "sides."

We followed the story. That's how we know you. How we know the story. We just don't know whether you can tell it right. Whether you should be the one to tell it.

Well. Ya. About how every time someone on the Rez called his grandson "Puppy Dog," that old man Max drank a Bud after Coors, and plotted great and terrible things against his own people. But it didn't quash the shame.

We shall ask about shame.

Right. "PD" was only marginally more tolerable. His eldest daughter, June, I think, the senior Medicine Sister, took the boy to her house, which my mam always described as "a rickety spectacle of shoddy engineering" out on Kittatinn Pond that Max had always intended for his whattyacall it. Not retirement. He hadn't really worked as a driver, or a trapper, or in the mines, or …

His dotage.

His dotage. Ya. So they put salves of comfrey on the wounds of this baby Bon's scruff. They took him to the funeral of his mother at our firehouse in Arctadia, you know, the community room. Where Sully and I, we … And rubbed deer fat on his lips. Which we—you know. They cooed and wooed him, and wrapped him in blankets.

And?

"And, ya. They made him very fucking soft indeed."

And?

And. Is love immortal? You want to know next.

Two Spirits

Is love immortal? Answer the question and we will seal Sullivan's tunnel of blood.

can't
hold
a
candle

Can't Hold a Candle

For Lenny & Bob, Keepers of the Flame

The Infinite Light is everywhere.

—Lurianic *Kabbalah*, 16th Century

What if whoever or whatever was in charge of the route on the morning of November 22, 1963 had simply chosen *A Different Path* than the one that took the motorcade through Dealey Plaza past the Book Depository and the grassy knoll toward the triple underpass? Let's say five more potholes or some such had rendered that route too bumpy for FLOTUS? Wouldn't the entire world be different now, nearly every individual—at least in the West? Maybe not.

On the 24th, on their first date, Ambrose had only just surfaced from the murk his mother cast, straight into the pall that hung over the world. And straight into the thrall of Emory's arms. The light of the blue candle flickered on their faces. *The Light of Love.*

What if Ambrose hadn't ever lit that first candle to commemorate the occasion? What if all their meals going forward went forward unacknowledged by (an albeit tiny) fire ceremony? Can uncelebrated unions survive the tests of time? Is love itself immortal?

It wasn't Emory's first gift to Ambrose, but blue-tapered dinner candles were the first thing he bought for them together. It remained the most meaningful, even over the decades. They would burn through the first five of those candles within a month. But Ambrose would save the last from that first box. He would save it for always.

Almost.

★★★

He'd light it. Eventually. But not on the August afternoon when he sat on a stool at the counter under the ceiling fan and wrote out all the Thank You notes. Not that early evening, all throughout the roasting of the local lamb he thought he might fashion for kebabs. No. Ambrose vacillated then. And even as he fussed unnecessarily at the oven door, he could see out the corner of his eye the wide empty table in the dining room, which he hadn't set, and here it was, nearly seven. Here it was, nearly 2021.

He might solve the whole conundrum by eating at the counter, maybe with Gray's latest novel, *The Expectation of a Flame*. As of yet, he hadn't gotten past the dedication to "My Fathers, Keepers of Fire," for weeping like some granny past her market days.

He coveted the counter's marble coolness after so many strangers had traipsed through the house these past few days—their garlic breath yet lingered, and he could still see their footprints and party stains in the pile. In retrospect, hummus was not the ideal funeral food.

He'd always enjoyed the view from the counter stools, of the shambling cottage out back behind the avocado trees – "The Gardner's Shack," as Emory liked to call it, like some Victorian novel – where, indeed, the gardener and his wife, the maid, and their brood of kids and cousins and some of *their* children lived, and served in various capacities the clutch of homes in the "*Naranja E*" subdivision of the compound. This evening, one of the women, a stunning young raven with babe on hip, picked veggies from the garden they kept, and took them in a basket into the cottage, where the door was always open, even at night, which had astounded Emory beyond all mysteries of this enigmatic nation: "My God, Ambrose, I saw a winged insect the other day bigger than my spleen."

Tonight, as Ambrose had hoped, "Superdog," the scruffy lab that belonged to the gardener's youngest son, sat in their dirt drive, staring straight at Ambrose through the kitchen window. The men had heard everyone else over there call the animal only by "*Chucho*," which translated best as "mutt" or "mongrel." But the little boy not only called him "Superdog," in English, he sometimes even dressed him in a long, blue cape, and set up feats for him to undertake, which the dog, whether or not he could leap such bounds, seemed to relish attempting, to either please the boy or to be the dog, or both. This ilk of escapade had not been forthcoming anywhere near their former homes in Ft. Myers and Mission Viejo. Not even on the reservation in upstate New York where Ambrose grew up – or got stunted, depending on your perspective – where many a mutt meandered, ownerless.

The table or the counter. Or—he could dust off the melamine TV tray in the kitchen cupboard, and sit with his lamb, rice, and broccoli in front of the television—though that struck him as a bit too native for the circumstances. Besides, Wednesday was the absolute most vacuous evening of entertainment they had scheduled down here in the adopted land of Ambrose and Emory—now only Ambrose. Outside, Superdog barked once. That settled it. Eating dinner in front of the TV! What would Emory have said? As though vapid variety shows and incomprehensible telenovelas would decompose the grey matter any faster than whacking a little white ball around all day, as Emory fancied, and many of their compatriots embarked on thrice a week.

Four days now. Four dinners missed; four unlit candles.

★★★

He considered the volume of un-melted wax. With overawing trepidation, he considered the implications of having halted the sacrament. The first night, skipped entirely. That was the worst, *The Night of the Black Blood Issuance.* (Ambrose was beginning to think in the style of Gray's book titles: *The Incubi of Alien Bonehouse Babble. The Handholding Hearts.* And then, *The Dawn of the Deceased*, though perhaps that one had already been taken by a B-movie writer of the 1950s. Anyway, a guy could be forgiven for forgetting to – or consciously forgoing – the rite, given the circumstances.

The second night, it was *Sissy's Insistence*—another one for Gray's expanding catalogue, though Gray never left out the definite/indefinite article in any of his titles—*A Sister's Insistence*. Gray's Aunt Sissy, Ambrose's elder sister, had flown down right away, and mercifully taken over operations as Ambrose had expected, as she'd always done, since even before the first time he had to choose a tie for *The Reflection in a Casket Lid*. "Where's Gray, Ambie? Oh, Ambie, I'm so sorry. But where's Gray? Where's your son?" But Gray was on his book tour. His tour with his co-writer (a first), Kit Dane, he who fucked up Gray's marriage, and his own with the supermodel, Renata (hot enough for just one name) when they partnered in ways beyond the page. "He has a private jet, you know," she said. Yes, but why knock it out of the sky?

"The big award's in four days, Sissy."

"Big, *shmig*. Are you insane? I'm calling him right now. Oh, he'll be furious. I'll take the blame. Have you eaten? You look gaunt."

The third dinner candle stayed unlit owing to the first of all the dishes delivered for *The Tropical Shiva*, and by then Gray and Jemma, Kit and Renata had arrived in said jet, *The Exclamation Point*, without the girls, who were in Geneva (or Genoa) with something called a "Manny," which made Ambrose laugh out loud for the first time in four days, which you're not supposed to do during *Shiva*, makeshift or not. And there was the Man. Him. Kit Dane. Wunderkind. It was immediately obvious to all and sundry, human and flora, that those two were an item. It shivered the timbers. It shook the bricks.

It was a cold cut sandwich on a seeded bun, the local salami and five slices of cheese, shitty, with a gob of mayonnaise. "Another gross violation," Ambrose whispered to Sissy, adroitly eyeing the hired Rabbi (imported from the Capital) across the sunken living room, standard in the *Campanario (Dos)* model condo, ubiquitous in *Naranja E y F*. "Ambie, I'm sure the anal penetration trumps the mixing of meat and dairy," she said, and he would have laughed again, but for a pang that jabbed him in the "undercarriage," as

Emory had always called the region running roughly from the sternum to the groin.

"Sissy, it was years ago that smiles and companionable silence took the place of any *sexo, per se*."

The Sexo Per Se.

"Well, you sure did make one glorious baby anyway," his sister said, biting her long pinkie nail and motioning with her chin across that low, crowded room to the bar. "And anyway, I'm talking about those two lovebirds." There they were. Gray was mixing a drink in a large copper shaker for an older couple, obvious golfers, whom Ambrose didn't recognize. His son caught his surviving father's eyes, and grinned almost exactly as he had the day he'd been left for dead in his toddlerhood, and Ambrose and Emory had stumbled upon him, thank whatever banana spider god deigned it that day.

Kit's famous wife – who, also, by the way was an accomplished flamenco dancer and modern artist or some shit – eyed the gardener's son as he passed the bay window. She and Kit had no kids because Kit had (also famously) demanded of several doctors a vasectomy at age 21, finally finding a taker. He passed behind Gray and clearly, *clearly* patted his ass. What the fuck were those two thinking?

Later, Ambrose discovered himself holding a fat, half-eaten chocolate chip "blondie" – his second – that one of their expat British neighbors had bought/baked, and the second he recognized it was delicious, ridiculously, a surge of something bilious and inky filled his undercarriage. A horror must have overcome his face because in seconds both Sissy and Gray fell upon him like bats on a bug, and the next thing he remembered, he was sitting on his marriage bed and the door was closed and the central air was way too cool and there was Gray on his knees in front of him, intoning, "*Papi*," intending to console him. But then his face contorted as it had when he was a little boy, and suddenly he'd grabbed around his *Papi's* neck – the only father he had left now – having lost two already, two too many.

And Sissy stood in the corner by the *en suite* (standard, with Corian Jacuzzi in both *Campanario* models), a wad of tissues jammed up to her nose and mouth, and said, "You people are fucking up a lady's makeup."

"You be quiet, Nurse Ratched," said Gray to his aunt, with the delectable, nearly undetectable accent one acquires shuttled from country to country while learning to speak, playing on a world-champion Kids League Baseball squad, attending boarding school in Bern, then bumming on the beach where the Aztecs originated, before breaking through with a wildly popular, barely disguised autobiographical novel of tragicomic virtuosity.

Sissy dispensed two blue capsules to her brother from an elegant canister of many and multi-colored splendor. And it was asked by someone knocking gently at the door whether *The Capital Rabbi* should be let into the bedroom suite, and Sissy said no last rites would be necessary yet, but bring us a bottle of your best local red, and God allowed the three survivors a little bit of laughter once again. It was easier here. Down here. "Imagine Mommy?" Sissy said.

"The gay funeral?"

"Please. The Jewish funeral."

"*This Savage Land.*"

"*Cette Terre sauvage?*"

"Forget it. Head: *Boom*! Bouffant: everywhere."

The fourth night Ambrose failed – and now it was a record, including all past vacations, of which there were many in 51 years, yet during which he had never flagged in his candles – they went not to their favorite bistro in the village, because it would have been too reminiscent of Emory, and some of his golf associates who ate there, Ambrose realized, hadn't yet been notified, and he preferred to avoid such revelations over grouper and mushroom risotto. So Gray suggested they taxi-convoy instead to the old roadhouse where he'd worked as a teenager, a more raucous establishment, popular with tourists and the local (read: lower-rent, expat American) "beach bums," the surfers and dive instructors, the collectors of shells, God help us all, and those who circulated through the busy sands selling bathers "sensations" to augment the sea.

Ambrose could tell by Gray's eyeballs and whole carriage below that this pilgrimage was important to him. Perhaps he wished only to introduce the place to this Kit. So he acquiesced, though he could tell from Sissy's raised eyebrow that she, too, would have rather stayed in the funereal fortress of the *Campanario (Dos)*, and continued to pick at the endless containers of foodstuffs and pastries that "everyone and their thirty-seven cousins" (as Sissy had put it, semi-racist, rather like their mother might have) had delivered, bowing and *Making That Face*.

At his old haunt, Gray got recognized by *Those Who'd Known Him When*, who jumped and slapped his back and hugged him, and triple-kissed him in the style of their country, then genuinely wept with him for the loss of one of his fathers, a man they had come to know and eventually venerate for his tranquility and linguistic acumen. And those who'd never known him, but recognized him from his latter fame (as *One Who Did His Countrymen Proud*), after politely awaiting their turns like so many kids for shopping mall Santas, some scraping, some bowing, some shaking his hand, all said how terribly sorry they were, once they were in his lap. Then a few from either camp attempted to venture onto topics more literary/cultural, and Gray smiled whitely, and they shuffled their feet and made apologies for remembering just then they had critical business they had to attend to immediately elsewhere, which, in fact, nobody, even those at the centers of the crime syndicates and illicit trade hierarchies, ever had in either this part of the country or its immediate sisters after 8 o'clock at night. That was the entire point of the place.

This Kit picked up the literary slack.

The next morning, the morning of Emory's funeral proper, they took brunch out—but that didn't count as a lapse *per se* as far as the candles went. Ambrose had never been to the place before—had never seen or heard of it – it didn't actually have a sign or even a name – nor known there was anything but local flora up that long winding hill overlooking the cove, and behind not one (as most

Two Spirits 179

were) but two sets of guarded gates. He found himself for the first time in days extraordinarily hungry, and, indeed, fruits of the sea and trees, the tartar, and the gelato struck him as exquisitely fresh and delicious.

He was looking forward to finally thanking Gray and Sissy somehow, thanking everyone (there were 20 people at the table if there was one) but he never had a chance to pay the bill. In fact, no bill ever came for signature—it must have all been "taken care of"—one of Gray's favorite expressions since his first great commercial success when he was only 26 and barely out of his Invisaligns. Ambrose realized this was one of the old, elite country clubs at which Gray must have maintained his membership, despite having decamped out of the country years ago. It was far more exclusive than the one in which he and Emory had lived since Gray bought them their place "downhill—a modest little getaway on the green. You can come and go whenever. Or settle back there when you're ready. I know how much you love it. I know that place is—special to you."

As though his presumed birthplace wasn't important to Gray. They'd tried so hard to keep him connected to his homeland; they brought him back yearly, at least; they made sure he learned the lexicon; they spent summers there where his ancestors tended their nets, put coral necklaces on him. It was no use. He was all-American. He played baseball exceedingly well, but much preferred hockey, of all sports. His favorite authors were Twain, Steinbeck, and Vonnegut. His favorite food, macaroni and cheese.

"*Papis*," he'd say, whenever our attempts at cultural infusion became too bulldozery. "One of you was born on an Indian Reservation and renounced—"

"Not renounced."

"And all-but buried all native ways. The other one of you is a super-lapsed Jew. Right?"

"Super? I don't know if I'd go that far."

"You look in our laps and find no lapse."

★★★

"But this is absurd. A whole house?"

"Obscene," said Emory. "How—?"

Several bestsellers. That's how.

They were in a London lobby, sublimely appointed. A car (Bentley) had picked them up to hear their son read, after another car (Lincoln) had picked them up from their home in New York and Gray had "taken care" of their first first-class flight and their hotel, formerly occupied by the Royal Horseguards. The small woman who introduced their son at University College was not only a Dame, but among the top three most celebrated actresses of the past half-century. It was her honor and her privilege, she said, to portray the character of Mrs. Rountree in *You Made Your Bed, Now Die in It*, the British television miniseries adaptation of Gray's third novel, *The Other Undertaker*. It was already the proudest day and evening of their lives.

And now, with no ceremony more elaborate than a smile and a subtle wink to a maître d' for the topping off of their Hendrick's and a splash, Gray slid across the low table their set of keys, along with a brochure for their "Manse Model," "The *Campanario (Dos),*" in the now expanded *Naranja E* subdivision of a property that had been a colossal banana plantation not a decade before, until the multinational fruit conglomerate that had owned and operated it for a hundred years lost an epic lawsuit regarding the financing of death squads. Or something.

"There's a car down there for you, too, of course; nothing fancy. The key's on the key ring, so all you have to do is pick it up from the airport garage whenever you go, and drop it back. There's an annual fee, but it's—"

"*Taken care of,* yes, yes. But—"

"One more thing."

"He's going to tell us now that – what? – he's installed bronze statues of his fathers in the yard?"

"No. This'll probably make you just as uncomfortable, though."

"Oh, no."

Two Spirits 181

"Look—*Papi's* wrist, and your feet."

"Gray, you didn't."

"I didn't have a choice. It comes with the development. Every couple of houses, you have to share the—"

"Slaves? Those are your people, Gray. Where I come from, there was—"

"My people. It's a gardener. A maid. A boy who—It's no different than if you were in an over-55 place in Florida, where they take care of the lawn and everything else for you. It's just the way down there, *Papis.*"

"They're live-ins?"

"A cottage in the yard."

"A cottage?"

"A *shack,* you're saying, *Papi?* It's not the kind of compound with shanties built out of tin and tarps. Give me some credit."

The Best Little Boy in the World.

★★★

A congenial chime and verbal declaration of the oven informed Ambrose that his first widower's lamb would be done in five minutes. He fingered the brass fixtures on the drawer where he kept the candles. Someone – he couldn't remember who now, perhaps the wife of one of Emory's golf cronies – told him that the brand of oven in the *Campanario (Dos)* – was German – cost four grand—and their "upgrade" Sub-Zero fridge started at 10 thousand. Should the Germans be in the oven business?

Ambrose and Sissy's mother, notwithstanding some of her later stiff pretentions, was nevertheless the straight-up Native American daughter of a firetruck factory welder in Foggy Bumfuck, New York: She would have chided them all for *The Talking in Telephone Numbers.* Ambrose found the appliances aesthetically pleasant but technically too intricate and overlarge. In fact, the refrigerator was oriented rather inconveniently with the freezer on the bottom, and the top portion's accordion-style unfolding condiment shelves were simply not workshopped with septuagenarians. The dishwasher, too – God knows what that had set Gray back; it had several silent letters and lots of incompatible consonants in its Scandinavian name – was eerily too quiet; more than once he'd attempted to open it because he didn't know it was running—there wasn't even a tiny light, except on the wafer-sized remote control. And he found the water inside inexplicably, volcanically hot. Dutch?

Oh, two of those three appliances spoke. For all Ambrose knew, the dishwasher did, too, but was merely sullen of late, or just waiting for him to dangle something more nutritive over its angular, selachian jaws. But both the oven and the fridge had been programmed upon installation for complex and satisfying communication on a number of fronts, from reporting on inventory and internal states, to socially intelligent chatter and mere palaver. Emory had found this amusing. So seconds after the *ding!* indicating the five-minute countdown, the stove said, "Sir, your dinner is nearly done!" Ambrose did not wish to feel intimate with his oven. He pictured that when he was sleeping, or out at the market, all the kitchen gadgets conferenced about matters of grave import – the dishwasher suddenly talky, perhaps even the Che Guevara of the lot, rousing the toaster oven and coffeepot to revolutionary action – in their clipped, affected English: *We Must Rout Our Human Overlords.*

He imagined, too, that "their people" – that's how everyone in the community referred to the cottage-dwelling help – considered such extravagances the height of white devilry. It all made him wish to hang a Kit Nation flag somewhere, or grow out his hair and put it in a ponytail. But who was he kidding? White was not a measure of melanin, but a mindset. One he'd inherited from his mother, who'd climb in her coffin with her renouncement pinned as a brooch.

He had insisted on switching all those features off before Gray left yesterday, but nobody could figure out how to sever the appliances' analogous vocal cords, and the manuals were far too convoluted as to anatomy and physiology. Gray promised to Google it and send *His Last Papi* simplified instructions as soon as he was settled back in Seattle. In the foyer, and waiting for the car, he spoke to his "writing partner," That Kit, in Japanese and German in addition to his native language and English, perfected at Oxford. This Kit laughed long and lugubriously. He was preternaturally handsome. The two of them together multiplied their impishness; no wonder they had become the dual darlings of the literary circuit and larger intelligentsia on three continents and counting.

Sissy, Ambrose had been glad to see go back to Boston—he loved her, but her gravity, her solidity, and her resultant seismic anxiety exhausted him, though lately all the weight she'd carried her whole life – including her younger brother's – had begun to slide off her back and splash into the space around her. He wasn't sure how he felt about Gray's departure, though. There were things he wished he had said to his son. Things about his father, Emory, how only once he awoke throwing up – this was after the war – all over their bed, and he was crying, and he said, "Oh God, Ambie so many too fucking many." And how not to catch a bobcat in Kittatinn County: *The Illustrated History of How to Know When to Let a Wild Thing Go*, to roam and multiply and so grow strong again after all the slaughter. And little things about that day, *The Day* – the day they found him as an undomesticated child, his color covered up by dust – haunting, taunting things that Emory never wanted their "Kiddo" to know. Details. Like the shit. And the snails.

But instead they talked of far less theatrical things, more quotidian things. The girls. Jemma's promotion at the WHO. The eighth hole and the ocean spray visible from the bay window. The weather—yep, still tropical. The new book, "The Flame Book," that Ambrose hadn't read yet, but would. The award – *the* award – and how awards don't mean jack squat, but of course they do, of course, Kiddo, we're talking world recognition.

"Shared. I'm honored to share it—" and he looked toward Kit. This Kit.

"You earned it."

"Well, I owe it all—"

***

The Dusty Path. It was their seventh time down here. Those heady days, a world away. All those friends, only a few of whom would survive the pending plague. All those fabulous friends, yet only one still worthy of that term. Who would have predicted that? How much they shared. It was *Their Boy's Week,* they always called it, which meant, for most of the boys (all those fine-feathered friends from home and abroad), hunting after the few brave/opportunistic local lads, or other young men on their own weeks, concurrently prowling. So.

But no such lucky lurk for the Kit Boy. And none for Emory anymore. Not since Ambrose took them both off the market, and certainly not since the war. But they were no less horny, of course, no less relatively young. They had staked a spot they fancied was a secret, in the shady dunes up and down a hill off the "friendly" stretch of beaches on the compound, in between a cove and a village a few miles away, to which they were told never to venture without a machete-toting local guide and a wad of dollars for bribery, to boot.

On their virgin visit here, 1968, Emory's first R&R, soon after the country first opened up to *"Janks"* (they pronounced it; and only that tiny corner of it to their kind), a new friend advised them about *The Path* and its numerous avenues of action-without-consequence. Ha. So after clearing the wandering spiders, and shooing howler monkeys, and shimmying a bit up trees on the lookout for potential human passersby – in other words, once mollified they were alone – they had passed some time there on a woolen blanket, and come to consecrate that land. And come to love it.

Which is why now, on their seventh trip, they'd intended a tender reunion. The others half-joked that they must have been searching for a "third" after all, and they found no need to disabuse those boys—no harm in allowing others to perceive you as more interesting than you are.

In order to reach *The Spot,* though, they had to cross that well-worn path from the village to the beach. In all the time they had "hiked" thereon (that was the code, ironic, given the hammer toes of Ambrose), they'd encountered occasional lovers in the dunes and copses, but never once met a soul on *The Path* proper. But they had seen intermittent trash there – a mango peel, a beer bottle, a dirty diaper, etc. – and the tracks of sandals and bare feet in both directions. It seemed a route mostly traveled in the early morning – say, on the way to hawk wares to *gringos* or cook for them or wipe snot off one's toddler – and late at night, traipsed under various influences, licit and otherwise.

But on this, their seventh jaunt to their trysting spot – '77 already – as they emerged from the thickets with no blades to save their shins, relieved at last to come to this crossing, which meant they were now halfway to the dunes of upcoming tumescence, Emory was the first to put his hand out and arrest an eager Ambrose by the chest. "Hang on," he said. Assuming that Emory had spotted a couple or triple or quad worthy of a peep, Ambrose craned around his lover.

And there was the child, maybe four years old, maybe less, plopped on his bum in filthy underwear, right there in the middle of *The Path*, scooping sand with his hand, and smiling. Buddha-like serenity. It happened to be almost the only spot where the sun was blazing through the canopy of fronds. "What the hell?" said Ambrose.

"Someone's taking a piss nearby, I would guess. We're cool. We're just hikers."

"Do we—what do we do?"

"We do nothing. We have business to attend to. This little guy is minding his own."

The Business To Attend To.

But Ambrose would have none of it. He squatted there dumbly for several moments, eyeing the little chap like some exotic wildlife, and hearkening to any sound from the jungle, which might have been its mama. At some point, he began to shout, "Hullo?" in every direction, and then he tried shouting in the native language, as

Two Spirits

though any parent waiting nearby would have ignored the first appeals for lack of translation. He refused to leave the boy. They tried to speak with him. No English. He didn't seem to respond to their attempts at using his language, either, which, frankly, were just about at the level of a retarded four-year-old—what words do you really need to know beyond those relating to the tummy and the Thomas? "We should go," reiterated Emory.

"You're joking," said Ambrose.

"It's the way around here. We should meddle in the local customs? His mother's probably working the beach or it's his father, selling shit to the Hawaiian-shirts."

"It's wrong. Dumping him here. No bottle of milk or a Coke. No hat, even."

"It's a cultural thing. It's not our—"

"It's barbaric, Em. Look at him. He's grey. There are spiders. I'm not—It's wrong."

"By our standards, Ambrose," Emory said, way too patronizingly to a kid of the Kittakwa clan.

"By human standards. Why don't you go ahead. Go back to the beach. I'll deal with this."

To which Emory Zingel of the New Rochelle Zingels (via the Zingels of Montréal, whose ancestors hailed from Austria-Hungary with the suffix "-stein," later linguacircumcised) said nothing in reply, because what could he say?

Ambrose suspected there were similar circumstances, dusty local boys, in that other jungle Lieutenant Zingel had come to know so well. How many like this had he passed on his way to—?

The Palimpsest in the Package Sent Back from the Front.

★★★

Four minutes. "Dinner is nearly done now. I hope you're hungry!" The oven knew that it was dinnertime because of the pre-programmed 24-hour clock. Grey called this "The Internet of Things," which he had then tried to explain to his father. Ambrose interrupted: "It's what's known as *The Simulated Intelligence Factor*, according to the manual. They had comprehended this much during their tour on the day they moved down. In the same way, when Ambrose opens the refrigerator, it smartly says, "Good morning, Sir. I hope you slept well. Looks like there's still a little juice left on the second shelf. Remember the eggs are expiring soon." If you didn't like the anonymous intonations preselected for you, you could choose from a thousand celebrity voices (#488. Morgan Fairchild / #489. Morgan Freeman / #490. Morgan Spurlock / #491. Piers Morgan / #492. Tracy Morgan …).

But Ambrose did not wish to confab with the ice box while his dingle was bare, so he had to don a kimono every time he wanted a snack. This made life in his own home too formal, even as the Sub-Zero's default voice spoke in contractions and the occasional colloquialism—"Dang it—all out of almond milk. I'll put it on the list!"

He also considered it rude to shut the door on any of the longer greetings before they were complete, as Emory often had, saying, "*Jódete mucho, Máquina!*" And "Lucky for us," he'd say, "it isn't programmed with the Artificial Emotion chip like maybe the ones they're planning to install in the *Campanario (Tres)* models, or it would have slit my Achilles tendon by now."

Emory had laughed, but Ambrose, as he lit the candle that night, found this concept deeply unsettling. Like one of the recent magic realism turns Gray's plots were taking, as in *The Wrinkle God*.

Unaccountable that their boy Gray credits his success – publicly, frequently, eloquently, on the likes of PBS and NPR, no less – to his fathers, when surely it's a product of culture, native creativity—"*genius*" as they called it in the old days. But, of course, nowadays, it was all about That Kit. That Kit was his fucking "muse," if you could hear that without puking up your tilapia wrapped in banana leaf.

It hadn't been the original spark, nor the motivation *per se* for continuance of the ritual, but as an ancillary benefit of lighting a candle every night for more than half a century of dinners (and the occasional lunch/brunch) with Emory, Ambrose offered a little silent benediction for *The Accidents of Passage. That Path*, at exactly that location, that afternoon, all because they were, in fact, randy (just because they weren't taking offers to fuck and be fucked by the other guests of the aptly named hotel/bar/hookup joint, The Swinging Dock) in a land Ambrose first picked more or less randomly to meet Emory during his leave because the latter had asked him to find them a place where they could maximize their short time to catch up as far away from Jew Rochelle and fucking apple-knocking Kittatinn as one could get, as well as, of course, as distant from the war in Southeast Asia as geographically practicable. So owing to a day occurring two years before because they happened to come upon a particular dune on which they came upon each other; in turn, owing to another specific set of circumstances, and so on, all of which led to a blessing that he, at least, had done his best to attempt to deserve since then. *The Path*: If no one blocks it, you find there what you're meant to find, because God or whatever Higher Mind that runs these things will stick some imperative shit there right in front of you.

This is how tradition will morph into superstition and thence into sympathetic magic, no matter what side you're on: *The Stories We Tell Ourselves, and Their Origins*. So he was his mother's son. What if I fail to say a prayer as the flame first kindles over dark blue, even as we're fighting about the college fund, about *The Waning of Libido* this evening? Perhaps then time will suck it all, everything, backward like the tide prior to a mega-tsunami, and take away all the slow-growing gains, inch by inch, book by book, and leave only shit and snails, not even the fleeting impression of the skeleton of a nameless dusty toddler, not even on an untrodden path. Yes, this line of thinking is the same as his mother's, and Ambrose couldn't tell if that pissed him off, or offered comfort after all.

Down here in this country, the cottage-dwellers – whose people started as "Indians" far in the forested mountains – think of fate as *The Swing of the Monkey*: Sometimes he makes it to the next tree, hooray. And sometimes—Well. Maybe it's one iota variance in that vine's veer some 40 years ago, and fate erases from existence Gray's two gorgeous girls today: The bright-eyed and self-possessed, the black-belt in Tae Kwon Do, who grappled with her gender and once broke one poor boy's arm, then held his other hand (her grandpas watched this from the stands) and leaned down as he lay writhing on his back, and whispered a long time in his ear as a tear ran down the side of his face, and finally stood when the paramedics came, and pressed her palms together and bowed to him out of respect. And the other, who emerged dark-eyed and brooding, and remained that way, gravitating more toward Ambrose's gallows humor and her father's cool, dark library, even as her older sister preferred her grandpa Emory's links and swings, or driving in that godawful fast convertible outside the gates, where there was technically a speed limit, but no police force to speak of, and anyway, given a Constitutional unrestraint knitted into the fabric of the culture, it was bound sometimes to trip into outright lawlessness, considered from, say, a Northwest American Indian's perspective.

More than once on their visits "down home," Ambrose had seen Gray's baby girl tentatively talking in the opaque sun with the gardener's son outside the cottage while his parents were polishing tables, mowing lawns, and scraping duck shit off the pathways in the *Naranja E* cluster. He showed her Superdog, and from the distance of the counter through the window, seemed at first to Ambrose to wish to impress her with a brand of machismo common among young males here, but as soon as he received no encouragement for this tack, appeared relieved, and never tried again. And so they sat together on either side of Superdog, and sometimes on their backs looked up at high wispy clouds, and talked, or didn't talk. As much as he loved his younger granddaughter, loved *schmoozing* with her about her favorite books and movies, and recently, boy actors – though never boy bands – and "Emo" boys, and "Manga" boys, sometimes Ambrose considered inviting the whole family down just so she could go over and keep the gardener's boy company for 20 minutes twice a year, and vice versa. It was agonizing to watch the boy there six days a week in the blazing sun speaking to no one but

Superdog, though that dog did obviously talk back in manifold ways. "Why can't I?" Ambrose asked Emory once a month.

"Bring him over? Because it's weird and creepy, and they'll run us off the compound with pitchforks."

"He's so lonely."

"He is? Lurky Uncle Gringo cannot have a play date. You're seventy-four. He's ten. One exotic adoption per lifetime, please."

Emory was obscenely right. Yet every night when Ambrose lit the candle, for the millisecond that the human eye must shut upon the initial flicker of a fledgling flame, he had begun to pray not only for himself and Emory, and for Gray and Jemma and the girls, and for Sissy and the souls of his parents, and, secretly, one Landon laughing on *The Path*, and about whom, more later. But now he prayed also for the dark and lonely cottage boy who talked to Superdog, and the dog who often talked back. It was official. Ambrose had turned into one of those "sensitive" and sentimental old gay men who teared up at melodrama, he told his sister over the phone, and Sissy said, "Ambie, you were a supersensitive and sentimental old gay man when you were twelve."

★★★

After the assassination of JFK, the alopecic, ectrodactyl date of a potentially romantic variety, occasioned by a favor for Sissy, who rarely asked, and never really needed. Afterward, a quick trip to the post office for an overnight package, insured for $500. He didn't want to do it: It was his mother's address, her silver cross, which she'd worn since her Confirmation at the Arctadia Catholic Church, and which Sissy had recently gotten repaired. And it was on the way out of the post office where he first met Emory, who was picking up a package of medicine for an elderly neighbor, sent from a pharmacy in Canada.

First week of December, 1963, as soon as he was fairly certain he could, indeed, tolerate another "date," this time with Emory Zingel (and he was able to ensure that Sissy would stay away all evening with the other nurses), Ambrose polished the kitchen table. Then he polished the cabinets above the sink, and then the long, dark, beat-up banister on the stairs up to the door. He chilled the Moscato in the freezer (where he'd forget it and it would explode, which crisis necessitated an hourlong cleanup), then set the table while the pasta water boiled.

"Your eyes have begun to dazzle again, Little Brother, but this old place really doesn't—won't you let me give you a few bucks and go out for a proper meal?"

Sissy meant he must impress this one (assuming it was true this one was put together better than the last one, or at least kept together, digitally). As he fished around for *The Finishing Touches*, Ambrose came upon a drawer in which Sissy kept a box of long, blue tapered candles. Though the wicks indicated they had been lit before, if briefly, she had restored them back into their box, and taped it shut. He had perhaps the vainest thought he'd ever had: *This blue might match my eyes.* But that ephemeral ideation faded fast, and what remained was a motif: He planned for the candles to send not so much a message of elegance as of gravitas. Surprisingly, given the catastrophe of his last date, he felt serious about this guy since the moment they met. Their conversation under the flag outside the post office was serious. Ambrose had, as Sissy had noted the night before while he fidgeted in his sheets on the sofa, *A Serious Case.* "I've never seen you like this before, Ambie."

"Yes, you have."

"You were ten."

"Twelve. And if you call it 'Puppy Love,' I swear I'll scream. I will break all your things with extreme prejudice. Every fucking Hummel on that ledge. Dead."

"Oh, Ambie," she said. "The sharecropper's boy. That's what bothered Mommy the most, you know. Loudon?"

"Landon."

"And didn't his father—a tractor?"

"Thresher."

"That's right. They say the city hospital's gruesome, but really the worst we get on a regular basis is the ubiquitous GSW."

"GSW?"

"Gunshot wound. Oh, that poor boy. His poor mother, more like it. Twelve years old."

"Yeah. Everyone always bleeds for the poor mothers. Yet somehow they truck on. So you see a lot of dead kids?"

"There are some … I've noticed …"

"Spit it out, Sissy."

"I don't mean to sound so terrible, but I see it all the time, some … kids, who are just too delicate, fragile—too fine, I suppose, for …"

"For this world? To live? You mean … destined for angels' wings?"

"I suppose that is what I mean."

"And Landon Lightning was one of those kids, you propose?"

"I suppose. This new person. Eldred?"

"Emory."

"Is he …?"

"Delicate? Would it reveal too much if I told you that your brother's always been the 'delicate' one in these arrangements?"

She cocked her head.

"And Individual Number Two is generally the more—"

"Yes. It would reveal too much. Give me a minute to poke out my mind's eye." And she blushed when she fully comprehended, then she laughed snortingly until he had to throw a sofa cushion at her.

★★★

"Your dinner will be ready in three minutes. I hope you're hungry!" said the oven, with rising excitement.

How long would it take to get used to eating alone? Never? Contrary to popular "wisdom," it does not take a mere 21 days to form a habit. Rather, it takes more like 66, they (social scientists) say. But surely shit solidifies sooner. Consider the candles: Sixty-six dinners? Sixty-six flicks of the Bic? No. The second time Ambrose invited Emory over to Sissy's apartment, he lit a candle again. He'd bought another whole box – a six pack – to replace the one they'd let melt down to nothing talking seriously about their surprisingly not-so-divergent childhoods as sons of mothers who'd started poor and hopeless and aspired to piety and wealth without ever summiting that Shangri-La, and feeling confident that there would be more dinners, and soon (one hoped) ham and breakfast biscuits or (the other imagined) bagels and cream cheese. There were. By their third dinner, the candles were, if not a habit, a tradition.

He was all of 23 and had waited so long for this, so many nights twisting in his afghan, wondering whether he would ever free that foot from his mother's snare, *The Kittakwa Trap*, not knowing whether such bliss would ever overcome his bones again, whether he might ever look across a short board once more and know that this person, this man, could understand him on the inside, yet still want to bore ever deeper, not cast him off like some disgusting thing such as a slug. Some adult simulacrum of Landon, *The Forever Young*, though he'd allow for reasonable divergences—pubic hair and wisdom teeth, and so forth.

This time he needed *The Key to Keep the Guy*. This time they had to hold fast on *The Same Path*. So it was imperative that it got going quick, and lasted long—and why not forever? Why not until one of them died? It ain't unheard of. So why postpone the kicking-off of ritual? On night four, a week or so later, they had homemade pizza, and Sissy stayed, and it was the first and last time Ambrose noticed Emory looking askance – just for a second – at the lighting of the candle, as though it was too Romantic, somehow too much too soon, or too serious, too gay—or something. But Ambrose persisted. *A Keeping to the Good Red Road*.

Once, about five years later, on the night before Emory would debark their apartment for a stint in that bad place where boys dumped sticky fire from the sky onto other people's sons, Ambrose considered unwrapping that last leftover candle. Then he thought better of it: Emory's healthy return would mark a far more significant special occasion. Right? He wouldn't have been called so soon had the lads been married like husband and wife. Or so Sissy said, even offering to take him off the market.

"Not on your life."

Nor would he have been called so soon had he not refused to recuse himself from the draft on "fellatial" grounds (again, the linguistically indomitable Sissy). Which admission would have prevented him from getting a professorship upon his return – although what famous professor in history did not suck a lot of cock? – or so Em lectured across the candle flame for a month before his exodus. For his part, Ambrose, slathered in a kind of pre-survivor's guilt, got to stay home, not because he was teaching at a poor school, which he was – The Flag of the Torah, just off the Rez, which job Em had recommended him for through an Orthodox brother-in-law (Em's sister, Reba Roth, was a doula affiliated with Kitskill) – but because of his extreme bee allergy, which once nearly killed him as a kid. Could he work as a clerk? A messenger? They didn't need those things. How about Emory's valet?

"What can I say, Sissy?"

"Makes sense. Sure, anaphylactic shock's no picnic on the battlefield."

"But neither is a bullet in the eyeball."

Thus Ambrose fought his fight at home: He lit the candle – well, a candle – with every dinner, and at the corresponding time that Emory, according to his early accounts, would likely be popping open his C-rations of Beans w/. Frankfurter Chunks in Tomato Sauce or Beef Slices w/. Potatoes in Gravy suppers while relentless rain pissed onto his helmet and into the tins. Ambrose wrote effusive letters replete with rainbows he spun in direct and opposite proportion to the lines he read nightly from Brooke, Graves, and, especially, Rosenberg, to try to join Emory psychically in *That Dead Man's Dump* over there:

A man's brains splattered on
A stretcher-bearer's face;
His shook shoulders slipped their load,

*But when they bent to look again
The drowning soul was sunk too deep
For human tenderness.*

Fuck.

For every five letters from Ambrose, Emory sent one, in which he sketched out merely a numerical circle of hell: *"Not good. Four more. Three days since anyone's slept."*

"Remember Garcia from College Point I wrote you about? Yesterday—not fast. Wrote to his father. Difficult."

Finally, *"Leave through Hanoi then Germany in 204 hours! Cannot wait. A friend of Dorothy says this place you picked is bliss. Couldn't you have suggested somewhere not so hot and lush, though?"*

And then some 54 years passed with nary a need for a postcard. Sometimes they diverged, or enervated each other's ids most disagreeably, but only temporarily, and then it seemed even more vital for Ambrose to keep *The Feast of Little Fire* as he had every evening Emory was over there, as if not lighting the long blue candle one night – the night he hadn't cared enough to prepare for his partner, his brother in the trenches – would hasten some whistling missile over *Their No Man's Land*—and why risk that shit? That could be the night the one who loves you is humping through the woods on his way to you, and instead steps into a trap. Hadn't he attended this miserable seminar before with poor young farm boy Landon? You must keep him in your mind at all times if you can't hold your arms around him. It is almost as good. Almost.

★★★

In all that time, though, they never actually spoke outright of the candles, neither joked nor sentimentalized. And didn't brag. Except once, at a Fire Island party, sometime in the late '70s ("I Will Survive," "In the Navy," "Heart of Glass"), during a discussion on the bamboo / brushed concrete deck of good friends (who did not remain good friends for long), the conversation turned to the subject of romantic gestures. A young couple, of whom Emory and Ambrose had become fond, had struggled of late to appreciate each other, one said. All the men at the party took different tones and tacks, offered suggestions poles apart, according to their stripe and either *The Paths of Their Parents*, or *The Map of Dirt Roads*, presumably.

But when the general tenor seemed to turn away from commitment, monogamy, inseparability – when several of even their closest encoupled cohorts suggested men are simply not suited to stay faithful to a single partner for life – "like breeding geese" – Ambrose saw his young protégés slump, slide away from each other slightly on the deck chair they shared, and a little ripple of disappointment seemed to wash over their faces, even as they laughed out loud about their prospects for conquest, for they were both preposterously handsome youths, fresh faced, charming, and disarming, and people at this party were barely dressed, if that. One kid was from Kansas, which might as well have been Kit County, New York, and the other came from northern Minnesota, which could have been Canada, from which Emory's people hailed. Yes, they were sewing their oats still, those two—but surely something had compelled them toward each other once the revolution of the disco ball froze, and they found each other's eyes: Ambrose could see it, see something so familiar in the way those boys looked at each other, into each other. It was not the look of the beach or the bathhouses, not *The Alley Gape* but *The Cathedral Stare*.

Oh, if only he were a photographer or poet or simply not a pussy, he might have asked them to pose for him, just so he could spend the early evening etching them into eternity. At 36 and 37, though, Ambrose and Emory were already twice the age of these innocents, and perhaps Ambrose suffered a bit of smugness and pride over their longevity after all—but hadn't they earned some right to gloat, with their own kid, half the age again of those boys, just then probably at his Aunt Sissy's condo scarfing ice cream and grinning at some inane

Krofft spectacle on television, featuring anthropomorphic dune buggies, sea monsters, or forest apes?

So Ambrose finally ventured upon the topic of the candles, and numerous ears pricked up. He intended to make the point that if you feel yourself falter, that's a feeling, but one could always act as if. We all spend so much time spitting in the face of our parents, of conventional ideas of marriage and society, he said, but how do you suppose they all got through it – most of them, anyway – and "How do you suppose we all got here?" What's the fucking bedrock if not love and the comfort of knowing that the one to whom you offer yourself is the only one? (But did Landon absolutely know that fact in the meaty core of his bones that night before he fell into Oblivion? Know that Ambrose knew no Other—in some ways, never would, once he sealed up the cave they'd inhabited alone around a campfire, in delicious nondisclosure?). Sure, everyone on the deck that afternoon assumed that Emory and Ambrose, *The Sergeant and the Farmer*, had committed only since inheriting *The Kiddo*, had settled out of necessity like some suburban idiots who perfunctorily forewent the prophylactic out of respect for the Pope. He was about to disabuse them.

He even nearly mentioned the lone, lingering, candle.

But he was shocked when Emory stopped him from divulging *Their Observance of a Daily Blaze*, even among the amiable company after all that wine and weed and sun on skin, with the sound of the waves lapping in between the tracks of the host couple's Concept stereo, a pride and joy they considered comparable to their friends' acquisition of baby Gray. Even though their young, beloved Midwest friends were faltering, were sweltering amid temptations of The Pines, the parties, the Meat Rack medley, the Christopher Street "stroll" at home. Emory dropped his chin and glared, and even pressed his partner's knee, so that all Ambrose could do was stop mid-sentence and smirk like a Des Moines dullard.

Later on, when the subject had changed to who-in-Hollywood-was-homo – Sure, Raymond Burr eschewed the "tuna" in honor of his dead wives and a little cancer kid who croaked, sure – and the pool lights were turned on; and the bathing suits came off – ya! – *Among the Young* and lithe who hopped from house to house and pool to bed, and the coke and meth and Librium flowed; and some of the couples were coupling; and others uncoupling for the evening; and those young men were talking close and quiet on a chaise longue, Ambrose cocked his head, about to ask, *Wherefore the Solemn Secret?* But Emory was smiling wide, winking, and not only because he was stoned and appreciating the view, all the hills and hollows—still astounded to see *live* young men in the altogether, all their limbs and digits accounted for. Ambrose understood, mostly— This thing, the candles, was theirs, and others would have to come up with their own.

★★★

After the war, Emory still stretched his good hand to the center of the table and spun the candles sometimes, absentmindedly, and that sufficed for long existential discussions of a Rosenbergian bent. In fact, sometimes (and exponentially so later into their twilight), they went many nights without saying anything, but Ambrose knew that Emory would eventually come back to him someday, though perhaps always absent that part of his young self he'd left naked and scared in that rain forest, in those rice paddies, *All the Way Over There*. In the meantime, some infinitesimal quark of Em returned to Ambie every night, illumined by the blue candles' flame, bit by bit rebuilding the man he once was. And because it sufficed for Adam to intend to restore the divine sparks to God through the mystical isometrics he bent out of inclination to sin, it was enough for Ambrose Cooper, the man who loved the man who once was Emory Zingel.

Who at least was here. Now. Now seeing those boys like that by the poolside, naked, perfectly intact, arms entwined as they slipped into the shimmering blue pool like a Hockney portrait, and kissed— yes, it must have seemed miraculous to him, impossible, and whether their love would survive our brand of minor minefields on this side of the sea didn't matter a whit. *Amor vincit Omnia*, at least for tonight. All we have to do is hold this hill tonight, hold this ground until tomorrow's home fire warms our hands again. Immortality's a function of endurance—and patience.

As it was, their young friends did stay together, pretty much. And three or four years later, one of them joined *The First to Die*, the fodder for Nancy Reagan's cannon. The other took a much longer, much louder route, à la Landon. But neither was alone. This war, though—it was worse than anyone might have predicted, even imagined, that afternoon and evening on an island so far from that Oriental slaughter Emory Zingel had somehow escaped.

★★★

"I mean it. We should just go."

Was it in that other jungle over there where Emory had become inured to the sight of a child suffering alone? What must he have seen, endured, but, since those scraps in his letters, never spoken of—never? After 17 minutes – felt like an hour – first spying on the boy from the forest, then emerging to attempt to communicate linguistically, then playing peekaboo, then coconut catch and release, Ambrose reluctantly agreed to go back to The Swinging Dock without *El Chico*. Not before moving him to the shade, though, onto a towel, with all their (child-friendly) provisions, such as they were. The idea was that if they removed the kid from this spot and his parent(s) did return, surely they'd panic, and where would they go to find him? Ambrose said they should take the boy to the police, of course, and Emory cocked his head and pursed his lips, which was one of the only things about Emory that Ambrose truly despised, and looked at him with upturned eyes. That look meant this: Two American men who list their visiting address as a known homosexual labyrinth deliver a half-naked toddler they say they came upon in the jungle in a known homosexual trysting spot after having spent three homosexual hours with him there ... *Stop saying that!*

"I haven't said a goddamn thing."

But fuck him—he was right.

At the tea dance that night on the beach, Ambrose couldn't boogie down to Blondie. Didn't want to drink those signature "Azure Balls" – flaming cobalt and amber cocktails the bartenders (hunky young New York boys imported by the bar manager, a bull dyke [nick]named Crunt, almost certainly lamming after some fiasco *del Norte*) served, shirtless in kilts colored like the nation's flag – famously thought to be aphrodisiacal. There intermingled under the flapping canvas with the idyllic local, "liberal" lads (read: rent boys), he refused the Curacao-based concoctions for fear he wouldn't be sober enough ... in case. That night, Emory didn't dare venture upon amorousness, despite that he'd been denied in the dunes. "He's OK, Ambie. As we speak, there are probably a thousand kids right now in the sand here, under the palms and they're all fine."

Well.

Maybe.

But Ambrose wasn't, and that comment didn't help. He told himself, looking up at the maddeningly slow-turning ceiling fan, the maddeningly lazy, half dead fly, listening to their friends (who wouldn't, barring a few, remain friends for long) in the next room laughing as they attempted to liquidate their Azure Balls on each other's expanses, that it was not about Landon. Not because of how the kid had shivered, all alone out there in the Kit County snow, his thigh crushed in a bobcat foothold trap one whole night and day, another night and half a day, howling for Ambie (punished and banished to his bedroom for manifold crimes and only one, *The Only One*), yowling for his father, long dead, for anyone, but no one ever came, not even Max and his Kit-trained trappers to capture their delicate, sensitive prey.

So they both had maimed boys in their past, dead boys for whom to light the *Yahrzeit*.

Crunt's Swinging Dock hotel was hot. Which was putting it mildly. You had to sleep naked. Ambrose slipped out from under Emory's arm, stepped into his shorts, then took them off again and put underwear on and redressed—Emory was right about police suspicions down here regarding their kind—*las mariquitas*. He put on his least flamboyant shirt, the one he would have worn had his mother been coming (i.e. one without ladybug icons). He put socks and shoes on. He slipped out, and when he passed the gate, the young – *The Truly Too Young* –attendant, possibly dotted and winged himself, winked at him, assuming he intended an assignation with one other than the man with whom he came to The Swinging Dock; he gave a thumbs up – this trick was common and tricks there ubiquitous – and hit the button to swing the iron gates ajar. But then he looked at his mammoth watch and offered in the local dialogue a colloquialism Ambrose had heard before – from The Crunt herself – and which amounted to "Watch your back" (*"When leading with your cock, don't un-blink the eye behind"*). Indeed. Who knew what snares lay in wait for little boys in fruited woods?

By the time he returned to the hotel compound in the middle of the night with that grey, snoring babe in arms, Ambrose had steeled himself for any consequence, any reaction from Sergeant Zingel, from the livid to the hysterical. He hadn't expected disconsolate. The lamp now on, Emory pulled the sheet up over his lap, and held his face in his palms, perpetually calloused since the war. "I knew he'd still be there, Em. I told you. That's at least twelve hours. What did I fucking say?"

"And he's still not a skeleton, I see."

"Oh my God. Listen to yourself. There were snails in his underpants. Snails."

"What the fuck were you doing looking in his underpants?"

"Christ, Emory. I had to change him. He shat himself. OK? He's a—I had to wring 'em out in a muddy fucking stream. I'm taking care of him. So. That's that." The grey boy had been fast asleep and purring, but now his big eyes were open as he stretched and twitched a bit, enquiring at the foot of the bed. The two of them looked at him a moment.

"He's not a puppy."

"That's my point exactly."

"We're in the shit now, Ambrose. We're muddling in fucking bullshit jungle justice, prejudice, and medieval 'law.' Not to mention whatever machete-wielding mob might stumble out of their drunk and storm the fucking rainbow gates and burn our hut down in the morning. You—you kidnapped him. That's right. You took him—you—"

"I don't care. Listen carefully. Sergeant Zingel. You can let me deal with it, and march on to more ... festive environs if you like. The dunes were crawling with—"

"All right, get me my Hanes. I'm not gonna let the poor kid—Has he eaten? I could eat a brick without a fucking drink."

"*Shhh*. Em. Little pitchers."

★★★

It was first a dumbstriking shock, then an incredibility, and finally a heartbreak that brought our Ambie C. back nearly a decade later to the echo of Landon's wailing in that trap—and afterward a horror for months on Sissy's sofa while she worked the nightshift and brought home soup (potato, leek, tomato) in Styrofoam cups, and literally dragged her little brother nightly to the shower, turned it on, and would have stripped him to his skivvies but for the shred of Indian Catholic dignity left somewhere in the crescent of his pinkie toe nail: Yes, pick a cliché representing depression, and Ambrose Cooper underwent it after his family's abandonment. *The Unexpected Orphanage*.

With hindsight, he could tell that his father had been behaving cagily at his grad school commencement. His parents had driven dutifully out to Chicago in the wagon, posed for pictures, but then requested afternoon tea with him alone at the Palm Court, whereas he'd hoped to include some friends, and go for a heartier lunch, maybe steak somewhere more fun. He knew something was radically wrong when his mother *Then Declined the Darjeeling* and allowed his father to order her a martini instead. The last time he'd seen her drink was the night they walked into his room and she sat

Two Spirits 203

at his desk chair and his father sat on his bed (!) and they told him that his friend Landon had not gotten far in his runaway bid as originally feared; that Max, Landon's brother, had found him far out in their woods; that he'd "had an accident" cutting through the Lightning land toward the State Road; but that God was *The Great Redirector*, *The Righter of Roads*, and thank God for that. Young Ambrose ought to be grateful that his parents had put a stop to the nonsense, *The Wrong Path*, and arrested him, Ambrose, in his own injudicious tracks; had kept him there upstairs, close to home, "to their hearts," they said, and not let him fall, not allow to go astray as Landon and his family had tried so hard to tempt him, and nearly succeeded from the looks of that business in the barn that day your father—but it is hard to blame them; "We're not placing blame," not with that boy's father gone; it's over. He can't lead you down ...

She never said a single word, though. The entire time, his father said the words, rehearsed, but he was merely a mouthpiece, *Just a Puppet*. He looked back at her for confirmation – approval, rather – lest he be relegated to the doghouse, a cold homelessness in the Kit County winter, colder than a spider in the snow.

So it was the same again at the Drake nearly 10 years later. They had earlier that day settled all accounts with the University, the bookstore, and Marshall Field, his father said, taking a big gulp of whisky. Big. They no longer intended to see him again, he said, except when exigencies of ceremony compelled them. At first, he thought his father was joking, but who—?

"What are you talking about?"

The question was rather too loud. Other graduates were dining there with their families. A few he knew. And some turned, out of concern. His mother would have said to gossip. And there was Norbert Wiener, the commencement speaker, entertained by the Provost and the Chair of the Math Department a couple of tables away. That faction toasting with teacups.

"But this isn't—We're not closing the door, Ambrose. Not forever, no. That's—Well, that's up to you, right?" And he turned to look at his wife. "To your ... decisions, here on out."

But this was their decision. His educational maintenance – all that time since his father had caught him and Landon on the barn loft and was obliged to tell his wife (though would that he could eat his own mind's eye), until now – well, that was a given, that was supportable. But now the taps were shut. But *This Insistent Path.* We are afraid that we—well, birthdays and such. You have to look at it from your mother's. Christmas can't. You're an adult and so. But for us to. Sissy. You can't expect. Gosh'eyo and Aric Hatch? Your mother, where she grew up. And I. You know that we. And so we simply.

Ambrose stood, removed a five from his front pocket, and slapped it on the table to cover his half-drunk White Russian. Divine Righter of Roads? Shame us, ban us bodily from each other's ambit, and then tell yourself and the world that it was God evening the score that night by snapping steel on the body of the boy who "ran away?" Sure, the Lightning land, its rolling, foggy, forested hills, ran between the fields where Max and Landon's father had labored before the bottle took him and the highway to Cutchin and Kettering one way, Arctadia the other—but the way the buzzard flies, that was also the fastest way to get back to Ambrose. Did anybody even think of that? Or was that why she was drinking that night for the first time, and still? It was the final, rational thought he would entertain about his mother for many months. *I'm a foundling now,* he considered, staggering a long way back to his apartment by foot, openly weeping all the way. Or is that only after you're found?

The whole time. Sissy said nothing. What the fuck? At least she cried. She blubbered.

Even a decade later, some of the dreams full of mist and screaming he still suffered about Landon were so entirely terrible that Sissy stooped to flirting with a doctor – the least unctuous of them – to procure her brother sleeping pills. When she got home in the mornings, that's when her real nursing started. She became *An Emotional Cardiologist* for her younger brother. She sat on the floor with the TV volume down and her hand on his belly as she had for weeks after Landon died and he wouldn't leave his room. When her mother's engine first derailed, and dragged her family behind.

"Look how the one got stuck, got trapped, destroyed on *That Irredeemable Road.* Landon bloody devil."

Sissy was a candy striper at the time; she'd seen them bring the boy in. She knew the trap had snapped so tightly that the paramedics had to amputate his leg at the scene. He came on a gurney to the coroner's downstairs, and the leg came in a separate bag, and she thought to herself how her brother had probably seen that leg not just in gym class, or on the raft on Kit Pond, and traipsing over the rail trail in shorts. He had held that leg, maybe kissed behind that knee, probably, probably, in a way she'd never done before, with any boy, with anyone, and likely never would—it hadn't ever crossed her mind to.

She couldn't think of anything to say to Ambie. She wanted to comfort her little brother, to stop *The Inconsolable Pining*, punctuated by wailing on unfortunate occasions. So she settled on his stomach. The tummy she could satisfy with pancakes and soup and frozen pizzas. Abdominal stand-in for his soul now starved. It seemed to help. She held his hand, too, like making a circuit in Science class. She thought to herself, *This is right; we're connected. We've always been connected.*" But now her little brother had become somewhat of an alien thing. Against her will. With the advent of the sexual element. Imagine. Her brother and another boy. Her friend Barney delivered pictures of those two, pictures he'd taken of them on the lake, and in the fields. Innocent poses, all. But. Behind those eyes. Under their bathing trunks. The flashes, the disquisitions in her 15-year-old consciousness so utterly confounded her, disquieted, discombobulated her brain.

She considered any manner of fanatical actions to take on his behalf, once Ambie fell asleep in the post meridian. She took none. Except frantically picking at the back of her neck. The scandal that ensued – the inquest that divulged *All The Many Lurid Particulars* – broke her mother into shards of pure humiliation. And Sissy's few friends (barring Barney, who she cut off) stopped calling, stopped sitting with her in their French Club meetings – *C'est mon crayon jaune* – stopped razzing her about her hair and silly Christmas sweaters, which she wore in all seasons. She rode up as close to a psychic break as one can come without requiring institutional intervention by the Sculton thugs in white coats and beards. But snapping was never an option. Not for *The Rock of a Brother's Gibraltar*.

She told her brother all these things a long time later, decades, one night when they were all drunk, and Emory talked of *his* Landon, his great love in childhood, occasioned by that gentleman's recent expiration—age 54 in a bowling alley, "*A Post-Strike Stroke*," he joked, and then he cried just a little, and it was the first and only time she'd ever experienced her soldier brother-in-law displaying that depth of emotion—of human vulnerability. It touched her deeply. She told him she loved him, for *The First but not the Only Time*.

He said, "Ah, thanks, Babe."

★★★

So Ambrose moved in with his sister at age 22, a homeless, jobless, manless, orphan with a paid-up degree. She opened a card he got from his father soon after, but refused to read himself. It said, "*Ambrose, this is killing me. Literally. You know your mother. I hope this family can come back together again someday.*"

But that was up to her. And for years thereafter, his mother refused to offer Emory or her own, only, son any more than a token (and even then quite curt) hello at the dozen or so confirmations, funerals, baptisms, and such at which they found themselves occupying the same structure or landmass. She later pretended that even Gray simply didn't exist on *Orbis Tertius*, doubly unfortunate for her given that Sissy would never sire grandchildren, not since the rape; and Gray, so bubbly, brilliant, interesting, warm. And triply so, as Gray would never know his biological ancestors.

Even sadder still, Ambrose's dad. She could always detect by that man's glances and *A Definite Micro-Grimace*, the dejected look he had whenever he saw his son and his son's partner dancing at these events, or holding up their sunshine boy for pictures—how much he longed to rejoin the joy of their lives. He walked his wife out of those churches or catering halls, carefully cradling her elbow, seating her on the nearest bench, and driving the Cadillac around, a new lease every 39 months. Did Ambrose respect his dad for standing by the girl he took to junior prom and the only one he ever loved—or ought he to have slapped her across the chops from the start for everyone's sake including her own? That's a tough one. To know his father secretly suffered and feared his own wife? So who wound up walking alone the way to dusty death?

Ambrose made himself a no-show at her funeral, though Emory attended. The latter returned with a letter from his father-in-law to his lover:

Your Mother is gone. She loved you very much and always did. She had her stubborn ways (mulish maybe) and they were hard to understand. I hope you will come to forgive her. And I me. Enclosed is something she wanted you to have, in case you don't come.

Love, Your Loving Father

He had long before stopped loving her. He had to. He put the silver cross he inherited through that envelope immediately in the junk drawer. It belonged with the rubber bands and chip clips. Not beside his heart or any of his other vital organs. But when he lit the candle that first night after the funeral, lit it with their paella dinner, silently he said a prayer that she would find *The Path to Peace*. Her mouth at all those weddings and christenings and such, her lips—constantly tight. Was it the cancer now absent its leaf? Or her dire need to believe she'd done the right thing in the face of obvious uncertainty? In the end, whatever it was literally ate her insides out like bookworms can consume a tragic novel as sure as a farce in a hot, wet clime.

That Sunday night after he failed her a final time, he had a dream in which Landon ran out of a black dirt onion field covered in bright fog to greet her joyfully, and he motioned her, smiling, laughing, and she was confused and wanted to go back, but he kept calling, laughing, *C'mon, C'mon,* This is The Way, *It's this way, With me,* and Shelter Rock was there in the field, and he looked so happy and his legs were strong and his hair was flopping in the breeze and she opened her lips and couldn't help but gasp a little one-syllable laugh. She had one hand on her chest as she did whenever she felt distress, palm pressed on the cross, but she reached the other hand out, just a tiny bit toward him, toward the misty onion plot, the boulder's mica-dotted flanks shimmering in moonlight—

And, as often happened in his dreams of Landon, he heard the trap snap shut, and he woke up, not at all knowing how he should feel.

***

"You've just emerged from *The Well of Decrepitude.* You're twenty-three. And that's what you drag in? Niagara Falls bald and wearing sandals? Sandals, Ambie. On the day we bury our President? Not to mention he's missing a toe. Are you kidding me?"

"At least he's not self-conscious. But forget about him. There's a new one. We met in front of *The Post Orifice.*"

"Just tell me this—Is everything still attached on this one?"

"Funny you should ask that. All but one wee thing," Ambrose said, instantly blushing and covering his face with two slices of Wonder bread. They were making sandwiches for Sissy's shift.

"Oh, you have to tell me."

He slid the bread slowly from his face as though being born. "Well, he doesn't wear a *yarmulke* or anything. And he's not *kosher,* but—"

"Mommy will shit a brick."

"Snip-snip!"

Imagine—a "Hebrew," as she liked to call them.

The following night, during their first official date, at one point, Emory touched the base of the blue candle, held it between his thumb and forefinger, and turned it 45 degrees either way while he spoke, at Ambrose's urging, about the merits of his Math degree. Then he looked up, asked Ambrose about Comparative Lit: "Not so much into numbers?"

"No, I love numbers."

They clinked glasses. "What's your favorite number?"

"Pi! What's your favorite letter?"

"Schwa." And Ambrose served the dessert – pie – that Sissy had baked for him before her shift, on the express promise that he would not pretend that he had made it himself.

★★★

Two-minute warning to lamb. It took 13 months to sort out all the legal mumbo-jumbo to adopt Gray. All that time, Ambrose lived down here. Crunt hired him at The Swinging Dock, and let him stay for free as compensation. He learned the language, more or less, met many fine people, and a fair share of bigots and illywhackers. He came to love the culture. He legitimately sought the child's parents – any family – though he got the impression the local and national "authorities" were not quite as thoroughgoing: Where was the gain? But Ambrose was persistent: Perhaps something awful had befallen the kid's progenitors. In those days, crime ran rampant, and the police force, such as it was—utterly corrupt. If the boy's parents were involved in the drug trade, they could have easily "disappeared," and anyone tasked with that dispensation might have spared the baby— honor among thieves and all. It was also a Catholic country, though perhaps the most passionate papists were already on the wane.

They did not allow *The Baby Gray* to stay at that hostelry of iniquitous repute, but a Christian mission ran an orphanage nearby, where Gray got good care and the companionship of a kindle of similarly inconvenienced mop-headed fellows and gals. Ambrose visited daily, and volunteered on weekends. After the initial suspicions abated and numerous references were tendered by various consular officials who checked into the Yankee professor's past and present, Ambrose became a candidate – as miracles occur more often in such a country – to adopt the boy, but this would have been out of the question for a single male. Of course they kept his penis-packing companion out of the proceedings, at first. They'd hatched a clever scheme, and imported Sissy, who shared the Cooper surname. They showed a passport, and this seemed to suffice, with all parties assuming they were man and wife, and no one ever asking for a certificate of marriage. Yes, they lied on the application, but this was not strictly "illegal," *per se*, and anyway, better for the boy.

"Uncle" Emory descended once a month, and the tenor and agenda of their visits had changed dramatically. They became an oddball little family. A number of bureaucratic processes slid more smoothly when greased, their lawyer told them, so Emory wired more and more of *The Lubrication Lucre*, until one afternoon with a final flourish of ink and stamp, they were possessed of a human heir. A year before, they were butt-fucking in the forest above a private beach, stoned out of their gourds; and now, unfathomably, they had a son in tow. And they were deliriously cheery. As soon as they found themselves back on northern soil, their lawyer fought for Emory's right to adopt Gray, too, and the case stopped the presses. They won, when Gray was already nine. All three of them won.

★★★

Ding! "Your dinner is done!" said the oven, "Enjoy!" and the interior light automatically phased on *Like an Alien Dawn*. He peeked. Indeed, the lamb looked perfect. A huge portion, though. It would take him a while to learn how to cook for one. To shop for one. To think. His father had told him that after his mother's withdrawal, as they slowly returned to each other's orbit.

He turned to the table, then the counter again. What would he do? Continue lighting the candle in Emory's honor—or not, or don't, either way marking his passage?

He thought of his father again. Every night after he put his pajamas on and got under the sheets, Bud Cooper opened his wife's Bible to the gold ribbon bookmark. An old family Bible, supposedly owned at one point by Akt'adia Kit herself, gift of the minister who conducted Ghosh'eyo's funeral in the field. He read exactly one chapter, just as she'd done since the day they were married – since long before – no matter how tired she was, no matter where they were. So he carried on that custom after she died, not for her, but for him, to remember her by, to continue her in him. And in doing so, he came to grow closer to her, he said, and "to feel her there next to me in a way I sometimes maybe didn't even while she lived and breathed." He confessed this over cappuccino on the lanai in front of Gray and the girls, and even the young one – *Miss Morose*, he called her, not unlovingly – smiled.

So of course Ambrose lit the candle. *The* candle. Even before he opened the oven, he closed the drawer, for he drew not the latest blue candle out of its most recent box, but ventured to the top of the linen closet and fished around for that old, old almost empty box. The box Em had given him as their first gift. He removed the remaining candle. He twisted it lightly into the silver holder, and lit it at the kitchen table with the butane trigger lighter he kept for that purpose (there was a rad one for the grill outside).

No, he wasn't ready for the dining room alone. Then he set his place on a placemat. The oven continued to chime politely, elatedly, to remind him of his ready meal. It was something of a perpetually giddy, overeager nag. Returning to the table, he put the plate down, poured a glass of Malbec, raised it, tapped the base of the glass to the tip of the candle, and sipped.

He was just about to cut the meat when, with his knife and fork raised on either side of the plate, the wind shifted outside in just such a way as it did sometimes to block the sound of the ocean, and carry instead a faint strain from the other direction, from the gardener's cottage behind him. It was music.

He put down his utensils. Pushed his chair back. He got up and turned from the flickering flame. He walked to the counter and looked out the window over the high-arching "waterfall faucet," another costly add-on in the *Campanario* (*Dos*) model kitchen. He could see the back garden gate and beyond that, Superdog, the good shepherd, sitting, facing him, panting in the evening sun, his tongue blue-black and long, eyes happy, tail slowly sweeping the dust.

He leaned way over, popped the complicated locks, and shoved both casements open—Emory hated the bugs down here; said they were worse than in the war. And just then, the gardener's son – how had he never learned the kid's name in all this time? – came bounding shirtless, barefoot, from behind some bushes, laughing, and tackled the dog by the neck. Superdog yelped and tumbled head over tail, and got up and shook off and barked and happily scrapped with the boy, who kept running, in through the ever-wide-open door of the shack. The dog sat back down in the same spot, no worse for wear, and resumed his watch.

Ambrose walked over the tiles to the back kitchen door hardly anyone but *Their People* ever used (and usually when *The Misters* weren't home), unlocked it, and stepped onto the patio. He left their hurricane door flung open for the first time since they moved in. As he walked the flagstone path to the back gate, Superdog woofed once, chirpily, at him, stood on all fours, and wagged his whole ass wildly.

Ambrose realized the music was not the same insipid shit always playing on the radio down here. Someone was strumming a guitar inside the cottage, someone slapping the table as a drum, and others, many others, men and women, singing, semi-*Cumbia* style. He looked straight into the black of that door and the music got louder as he drew near. Then that boy's face dawned out of the dark.

Two Spirits

—Gimme 10 inches and make it hurt—

Saturday July 1. Screentest for PD (Sullivan Winter's replacement). Actor No. 4

Outside Colorado Springs, Colorado

ON PD'S DEAD EYE

EXT. KITTATINN POND. NIGHT (PRESENT DAY)

SUPERIMPOSE: RASPBERRY LEAF: CHILDBIRTH, MENSTRUAL PAIN

Max and PD squat over Noah's dead body at the end of the Kittatinn Pond dock. A stack of three cinder blocks and nylon rope awaits. Meat Puppet rests her head between her paws, her eyebrows dancing to the booms and bombs in the near distance.

                MAX
    I'm thinking about Jung.

                PD
    What?

                MAX
    <u>Who</u>. Carl Jung. He said introduce a man
    to his own shadow and you introduce him
    to his own light. You get it?

                PD
    Not really.

                MAX
    He doesn't get it. I'm talking about
    yer shadows, Bon.

Max looks over Noah, the lake like black lacquer.

                PD
    I wish you'd stop calling me that.

                MAX
    That's your name. Ankles or neck?

                    PD
          One ankle.

Max starts wrapping the rope around Noah's foot.

                    MAX
          That sorry-ass bitch intended to call
          you Ben. Wanted her to do "Landon," for
          my brother. No. "Ben," it was gonna be.
          Then a whole chain of fuck-ups and foi-
          bles followed. "Ben" was for her hero,
          Ben Nighthorse Campbell. Heard of him?
          Of course not. Well, she erroneously
          believed he was the first Native Ameri-
          can senator. He was, as a matter of
          public record, the second, after a
          feller name of Charles Curtis, a Kaw
          from Kansas who'd preceded Campbell by
          90-odd years. And she fucked up his
          lineage, anyway. See, she'd always as-
          sumed that Campbell was Crow, because
          he went to the same Crow boarding
          school where her grandmother had gone.
          That's my mam. One block or two?

                    PD
          Two to be sure.

Max nods, starts looping the rope through the holes in two cinder blocks.

                    MAX
          One to get ready ... Yeah. Turns out Old
          Ben is predominantly Northern Cheyenne,
          on his papa's side. Fuckin' Cheyenne.
          His mother was Portuguese of all
          things. His father was a drunk.

                    PD
          Like mine.

                    MAX
          Yep. And mine. And hers.

                    PD
          You.

                    MAX
          Heh. Welcome to the Kittakwa Rez, Bon.
          Get to know us. Anyway. Guess she fig-
          ured maybe this kid could someday be
          the second (actually, third) Indian

Two Spirits   215

                    senator, Senior Senator Ben Ohkawdara
                    Lightning, of New York, a prevailing
                    man of the Bear Clan. Heh.

                              PD
                    Just because we both had—The Kit have
                    as much to do with the Cheyenne as—

                              MAX
                    Ain't that some shit? In the confusion,
                    though, one of them temporary nurses,
                    real moose from Montreal environs, got
                    yer name wrong on the birth certifi-
                    cate, put "Bon" down. No one bothered
                    to correct it. Same whore - not a
                    nurse, a *whattyacallit* midwife - who
                    looked after yer blind ass, night
                    shift, when you were six. What's the
                    third cinder block for?

                              PD
                    Me.

                              MAX
                    Gotcha. Under.

                              PD
                    Under.

                              MAX
                    Yeah. Mademoiselle Nightingale's name
                    was Yvette. Maybe. A Jewess, I believe
                    she was. Bent her over a dialysis ma-
                    chine, I did. She said, "Gimme 10
                    inches and make it hurt, Chief." Heh.
                    So I fucked her twice and broke her
                    nose.

                              PD
                    Goodbye, Grandpa.

Max slowly nods. He lights a cigarette. He looks off in the
other direction.

A PLOP and SPLASH, O.S. Rope friction against the side of the
dock. Then a YANK and another SPLASH, O.S. A mournful HOWL.

                              MAX
                    Goodbye, Puppy Dog.

All righty. Cut. Wow. Wrap this one. I think we got it. We got him. He's the one. What's his name?

—Said no one ever—

*Monday Sept. 17. Day 3 of the ordeal /
Day 1 of the trial.*

Lost in New Mexico mountains

The problem with caves is that [grunt] in the winter, unless they possess geothermal/supernatural properties like Shelter Rock [grunt], they get pretty fucking cold.
The walls are stone, after all.
Ya.
What are we gonna do? We're gonna die.
Sully, I guarantee you we're not gonna die. We're gonna build a fire. Over here, by the way out, so we don't get smoked like pork chops. And if we have to later on, we'll wall off a room back there.
There are wolves or whatever.
Whatever. We'll survive. We'll get you home to Diablo.
This is all my—I'm the survivalist.
Ah, but I did research for the movie. And all that stuff we learned in the Frogs. Remember? No, all you remember is "Put the wet stuff on the hot stuff" and "de-ass the area when it's life or death conditions." All you remember is the macho fireman shit. Well, some of us [grunt] weren't so—some of us loved the lessons.
Who the fuck were those guys? Augie? Were those … guys? Were they—were they—
They were just guys. Guys dressed up. To scare us.
It fucking worked.
Ya.
That one guy. With the feathers and the face—
Ya. But look. Just a costume. Like on <u>Scooby Doo</u>. Just trying to scare us.

It worked.
So these walls, the stone walls, are good reflectors, heat reflectors, remember. And we don't have to worry about starting a wildfire, 'cause there's no vegetation to speak of in here. But—
We're gonna die, Augie. Let's burn it all down.
We're not gonna die. But it's gonna still be, like, super cold. Super-duper cold. And you're in shock because of the—
Don't.
I have to.
You fucking don't.
I do. I have to look. All right. Curl up. Fine. I'm gonna build the fire—but then I'm gonna have to look.
And do what? What can you do?
I don't know. But I have to look. Take it out?
Gone. That's the point, I think. Ha, ha. Now cauterize it, as all you can do. And you're not doing that shit. You're not.
OK. But I have to look. Your nose is broken, too. That'll heal."
They—
Pretty resourceful using blood for lube, right? Too soon? Ya. Too soon. I'm sorry. Your nose'll heal. We'll get a doctor to knock it back into joint. But you're bleeding from the ... And that's a—
Death sentence. Just let me fucking die here. I'm not going home. I can't go home.
I won't let you die. I'm taking your ass ... sorry.
We both took EMT training. You get whattyacallit, fecal matter in the bloodstream. Sepsis. Shock. Death.
I'm building a fire. And then we have to get undressed and huddle for warmth. That's the only [grunt] way. Preparing the ground. A high, tight platform. So the updraft of [grunt] ... Thank the good gods for Frogs and 4H.
"I pledge my ass to death."
You're not gonna die. Not from that. It was an icicle. They did it with an icicle. They put an—
Said no one. Ever. They—
You can deal with it later.

They—
The psychological stuff. Fallout and whatnot. Let's deal with the immediate—let's triage. Ya. You don't have to say it.
I don't have to say it.
No. I think the fact it was an icicle means ... it's gonna be OK. It was sterile and ... ice. That's what you put on a wound. And your own blood, from your nose.
Yeah, but you don't put it in—
Ya. I'm gonna make this fire my bitch. One match, Baby. Remember? We learned everything there is to know about "The Spirit," they called it at the Academy. "The Spirit is a shapeshifting beast that can be called forth, can be fed, can be starved, etc. ..." Think I got the voice right. Once it's good and going, it's trying, like us, to stay alive. You remember.
We respect it.
We respect it.
They put—
You're in shock. You're right about that. That one step. Stay still. Don't expend any energy. I've gotta go out there and look for more—
No.
—Fuel. We're up so high it's gotta be superdry to work. Feather wood, remember? Heartwood. Pinecones. Duct tape. Lint. I'll be right back.
Don't leave me, Augie. Please. Don't go.
I'll be right back, Sullivan Aric Winter. Wise man of the Coyote Clan. I'm going to save us.
I'm gonna die. I wanna die. Let me die.
Listen, the only thing that's gonna kill you is straight-up shame.
That's what I'm saying.
You have nothing to—
They shoved a—Oh, God, Augie.
I know. C'mere.
Augie. Augie. Is shame a good thing? Isn't shame a good thing?

LOSERS WEEPERS

Losers Weepers

For Jason & Jayson

No matter how bad things get,
you've got to go on living,
even if it kills you.

—attributed to Sholem Aleichem

The rabbi sang. Not for show, but as an act of devotion. It wasn't unusual – I've since been told – for a rabbi to sing in the *Bet Midrash*, the place for prayer. It started long before we boys arrived at school; some said maybe even the night before. We heard him as we filtered in from our various buses, carpools, and chilly hikes from the "Slope"—the half-Jewish / half-black section of town.

We were forced to pile in through the damp back corridor since a snow pile had collapsed the roof above the main entrance a year earlier. Before the Old Rabbi bought the building, it had been a slaughterhouse—non-kosher, in fact. It was only half-converted by the time I began attending in the seventh grade. The back entrance was wide enough for a convoy of cows, but still we all bumped and shoved each other, stepped on each other's toes. It still reeked of cold blood. Snails clung to the cinder block walls, even as we hung our coats there on pegs arranged in class-order. We could see our breath there in the morning, and this made it obvious that I was inhaling the same air others had exhaled.

First the words rubbed the skin of our eardrums. Quick and clear in ancient Hebrew. Soon they spilled over each other as the Young Rabbi worked himself into a condition of pure pain. Then the melody evolved into mourning, the words elongated, tones stretched. The Rabbi's voice stuck to our bones and chilled them. Walking while he sang was like moving underwater.

Two Spirits

Janusch, the young Polish janitor and bus driver, supervised the morning routine. With his one good hand, he helped us yank our shoes – wrapped by our mothers in Baggies – out of our snow boots. We threw our lunch boxes on the floor, and some boys' coats never made it to their pegs. We jostled each other and told the younger boys to shush; the Young Rabbi was singing. With cold toes we went to the *Bet Midrash*, the former meat storage locker, and pushed open the scratched plastic doors.

The Young Rabbi's voice was the single thing on Earth or in heaven that could shut us up. The dirge had somehow passed the risk of degenerating into sobs; it was all agony, yet he kept it up. Even those of us with only rusty Hebrew understood in our marrow the ancient meaning. We were Jews, and tears were said to flow through our veins.

As our eyes adjusted to the murky dark we saw Young Rabbi Roth hunkered at one of the sticky cafeteria tables, swaying with the words, as is the custom. At some point, one brave older boy cast the fluorescent lights over the figure of the Rabbi, yet it failed to rouse him from his reverie. As the bulbs above him flickered, we saw his eyes wide open, but like a blind man's, startled, resigned.

We filtered in, and Janusch, leaning away from his bad leg, handed each of us a prayer book from the ping pong tables that lined the room's perimeter. We made our way solemnly to the benches before the velvet-hooded *Torah* ark. As he sang, I felt disembodied as I did the day I was given codeine tablets after Dr. Nova yanked a tooth.

The Rabbi's voice is how we measured time. In school another day as friends; as study partners; as enemies, some, at our small *yeshiva*, *Degel Hatorah*, Flag of the *Torah*, on the distressed end of Pine Street just below the Slope, in the cold, upstate winter of 1980. Experiencing the Rabbi's voice was the most religious experience I'd ever had, and remains so now, 17 years later. Sometimes I lay awake in the early morning and remember how those prayers embraced me like a blanket, then never again.

***

I was at the *yeshiva* for only one reason, and not for an Orthodox Jewish education. My parents simply didn't want me in the public schools because I'd likely encounter the "wrong sort" there. Although they never said it outright, they were afraid of the "Indian overspill" and the black kids who loomed below us in ranch houses on the low end of the Slope. My mother politely smiled at the black and Indian boys who dared knock on a Jew's door on behalf of the Urban League, St. August's School, or the Kit Community Center up the road a piece on the Rez, though she forever declined to donate. When we passed them playing ball in the park that crowns the Slope, my mother gripped her steering wheel and *tsk-tsk*'d. She made the same tongue-clucking sound when a newscaster reported another teenager's botched abortion in the City, the high incidence of child neglect and abuse among the neighboring Kittakwa, or East African rebel boys marauding through the jungle with guns. Somehow, little Israeli boys hurling stones at Arabs on *Shabbos* was justifiable defense.

Soon after we moved to the Slope, the subject of my schooling began to dominate. It was decided (not by me) that the lesser of two evils was to surround me with "Super Jews," as my mother called our more fervent neighbors. My father struggled over the decision to let the zealots get a hold of my soul.

"Better he should get *shivved* by one of those monkeys after his lunch money?" my mother asked my father as they ate BLTs on the back patio.

My mother referred to that summer before my first year at the Flag as my "heathen season." I let my hair grow, and watched them discussing me at dusk on the patio from my bedroom window.

"Sandy, it's the seventh grade. No one gets iced until freshman year at the earliest." My father making light. My mother used to say to me that he made a mess, he made us crazy, he made a terrible wage, and he made light. Of course the one thing he didn't make –

Two Spirits

in my mother's eyes – was any kind of sense when it came to raising a child.

"Laugh, Morris. Go ahead. Our only son is all we're talking about."

"We're not even religious. The last time the kid saw a rabbi, he was getting a foreskin alteration. And that supposedly ended our obligation to the man upstairs."

My father always referred to *HaShem*, God, as "the man upstairs." Until I was seven, I always assumed he was talking about Mr. Reebus, the old man on Canadian crutches who rented the attic in our first house.

My mother said, "He has no *Yiddishkeit*, that kid. He doesn't know where he comes from."

"Long Island?"

"No, you *putz*—Mt. Sinai. Noah's Ark. The twelve tribes, the forty days and nights, the Four Questions, *yadda yadda*."

"Sandy. Sweetheart. You know they'll teach him we're sinners."

She considered this, and wiped Hellmann's mayonnaise from the corner of her mouth. "Morris," she said, "It's either that or Happy God Damn Martin Luther King Day every week and a half."

End of discussion. With her pinkie finger, my mother stirred the ice cubes in her Arnold Palmer, then lit a Kent 100. I became a Jew.

★★★

As soon as my parents fell asleep after dinner that August evening, I went out into the cool air. I wondered how I'd tell Adam that we wouldn't be in the same class come September, not even the same school. I could have taken the sleek BMX bike for which I'd saved three years of birthday and *Chanukah gelt* to buy, but instead I plodded up my road the two miles to the top of the Slope. The ice cream truck didn't stop for me, even though the *schmuck* inside (a black guy) saw me wave.

As usual, Adam was catching for the Black Boys, who were down by two to the Jew Boys. Adam flipped up his mask when he saw me sulking by the park gate, and sent me a smile which nearly cost him all his teeth. He signaled me to wait, and made sure to score a double as soon as the BBs were up. He strutted from third to home – what my mother for some reason called "shuckin' and jivin'" – knowing I watched his every move.

After the game, he came tear-assing toward me, and knocked me down before I could turn and run. "Hey, hooknose."

"Hey, jigaboo."

The other guys knew that Adam and I were pals since the May we'd met on the BMX track. But still, you had to be careful in our line of "bidnezz," as Adam called it. I often found myself afraid other kids could see my insides leaping like fish in a bucket whenever Adam touched me. Or touched himself in front of me. He had me pinned, hands clasped around my wrists, my legs immobilized, his nose to my nose. He surveyed the gang in the dugout, but never found a moment to give me his tongue. He managed to grind his hips enough to get me going, though.

He let me up, insisting we head to the woods. Down the side of the hill opposite the Slope, the woods inclined steeply for nearly a mile. Somewhere down there, you crossed onto Kit land. The whole thing ended at a cliff high above the river (technically "creek"). A disused railroad bridge crossed the water far below, wind whistling through holes rusted into the steel. They called it the High Damien.

Before you reached that bridge, where drug addicted mothers and lonely widowers regularly leapt to their great reward, you could find our tree fort. But you had to be looking up—way up. The fort was so deep in the woods, so high above the canopy of Fraser firs and spruces that no one but some woodpeckers and us had ever seen it.

As soon as we were perched in the fort, Adam unlaced his high tops. "Let's do sumpin' sordid," he said.

"Don't feel like it much."

"I'll do the feeling around here," he said.

I didn't respond, and he kept staring. "Well, I'm takin' my pants off. Feels good in the breeze, if you please."

For a second I felt I might cry. The summer even smelled like it was dying. The prospect of not seeing Adam every day, not breathing in his skin or tasting him all over was unbearable. I scooted backward, settling my spine against the sappy trunk. He didn't say anything stupid then. He didn't make light as my father would have. He didn't have to ask me what was wrong.

Instead, he climbed over his rumpled jeans and crawled toward me like a wildcat. Wearing nothing but a grass-stained jersey, he lay in my lap and hugged around me. We stayed that way nearly an hour until dusk crept down the hill. Then we got to "bidnezz."

Afterward, Adam said, "Why you gotta go there, Man?"

"Eat lunch with you Alabama porch monkeys every day? As if. They don't even want me down your side of the Slope."

"Not to mention up my—"

"Nobody gets it, do they?" I said.

He squinted at me, and I saw his black pupils like the slits of some night creature from The Midnight Picture Show. "Nope, nobody gets it."

Licking my belly button, he paused to say, "Ever told them about me? Even that you're friends with a nigger at all?"

I nodded no, head hangdog. He laughed without making noise, then looked up at my face. "My mom says you offed Jesus."

"Me?"

"*Those people*, she says. You know. 'They live like animals.' This morning she goes, 'I swear I think those people are eating out of our garbage.' I almost pissed in my pajamas. Hey, maybe we oughta try that sometime."

"Eating garbage?"

"The other thing. Reminds me of being a little kid."

"You are a little kid."

"Bigger than you, ya' cracker." He pulled his jeans on over bare skin. "You liked that?"

"Chocolatey delicious," I said.

"You racist kike."

I followed him down the ladder of rotten planks.

Two Spirits

"You coon."
"Goldberg."
"Darkie."
At the bottom, he cupped my cheeks in his hands, as my grandfather always did, saying, "Such a *punim*!" He looked deeply into my eyes, studying. It terrified me, melted me. His hands were so warm. It was as if I would never see him again, as if he was trying to imprint himself on me before heading off to war.

"Hebe," he said, and kissed me. We were 12.

★★★

Now I'm 29 somehow. The millennium's about to change. I've traveled, sometimes by choice, and often not. And I've allegedly learned. I run a bookstore now, the only game in town. Subsidized by the Council or I'd be way out of "bidnezz." I coach boy's baseball since the former (far more beloved) coach tried to kill himself and nearly succeeded. But still I don't possess the language to talk about music or love. I can't explain how boys, when they are 12, 11, 10, are capable of what I've seen. I can't describe now how our lives were intertwined, as though we knotted our souls by swallowing each other's essence over and over. But I do know ties unbind. The boy who was your twin becomes a stranger. And even the boy you were, slips his hand from yours when you're looking ahead, and time abducts him. You can never roll over in bed again and know his body, his grace, his hope. It's too late to be thankful for him, to love him. It's over.

He's gone.

Each morning, without a bell to warn us, we seated ourselves on the wooden benches in class order, youngest boys up front. A thousand nights I've wondered since, if it really could have happened this way. The singing ceased, and miraculously, without precedent or antecedent in any school I've known since, silence of a monkish kind filled the room. Every boy prepared for the morning prayers, as though physically unable then to chat, swat, sneeze, or pick at skin.

Two Spirits

Perhaps to atone for such impossible precocity in the a.m., the very bowels of hell were vomited up each afternoon in the secular classrooms and on the concrete playground, once God broke for the day. We drowned each poor teacher (bar the Young Rabbi) in chaos until their eye muscles twitched, the insides of their cheeks bled from chewing, and all their quaint notions contra corporal punishment were no match against the will to whack us in the ears. It was, without a shred of the exaggeration of which boys are fond, entirely within our power to bring our afternoon teachers literally to their knees. This still makes me proud, though I can't put my finger on exactly why it should.

Those joys are over now, of course. A week goes by now and "every morning's waking up's as bad as birth all over again," as Adam once wrote me on an unsigned postcard from some Spanish-speaking island where he nearly died of something awful years ago. Now coldly facing the facts – as my father would no doubt recommend when under duress – ain't no comfort to me, Kids. The facts are rarely in my favor, Dad. I'm not a good boy anymore. So hints of long ago rapture in tiny things, like the memory of the Rabbi's voice, make matters even worse.

When I was a child, I used to pull a shred of errant cuticle skin all the way down my finger. It was agonizing, even before I squeezed all the blood from the digit until it was yellow and weak. "You can't leave well enough alone, Louis," my father always said. But finishing a job (the Young Rabbi's credo)—I guess there's a certain satisfaction in that.

So what did I get out of my *yeshiva* education? What did I get for the thousands my parents shelled out? Fucked up beyond recovery is what I got. Since leaving that school, I've lost both my folks to organisms more ravenous to have them than I ever was. I've been dumped by one great love and widowed by another. I've gotten drunk and gotten sober, several times. A college professor – English, of course – once masturbated on me when I passed out stoned, awaiting him in his basement office, but that's for another chapter.

During my brief stint as a commercial real estate appraiser (don't ask), I was even shot in the abdomen once by a teenager I startled in the laundry room of an abandoned motel in Houston. He left me crying, to die, and I babbled, begging for him (Adam, I guess) to forgive me. But I have never been hurt as bad as Young Rabbi Moshe Eliyahu Roth hurt me when I was just 13. Not even Adam was able to break my heart and spirit both.

★★★

Young Rabbi Roth was the son of the school's principal, Old Rabbi Roth. He was not a run-of-the-mill *yeshiva* rabbi. Except during his morning chants, he wasn't pious like his father, a wizened, studious man. He seemed young to us, even then. Different. And not just because he refused to don the standard white shirt, black coat, and rabbi(t) fur hat. Something inside him seemed different, as though he were closer to who we were, able to understand what was happening inside us. He could look right through you and even said, on rare occasions, "There's nothing in your head, your heart, your soul, or your puny body I don't know about firsthand, like the back of my hand. Believe you me."

Young Rabbi Roth had been to a regular ivy league college. This was meant to be a secret, as higher education was not an option open to good *yeshiva* boys. We were warned that college, with its co-ed living and liberal arts, represented everything dangerous and damnable about the secular world. Hearing your kid wanted into Harvard was as feared by devout Jewish parents as hearing he wanted to pimp black junky whores in Times Square.

And travelling? Forget it.

"Wanderlust," as my mother and thousands of Jewish mothers beside her called it, was for the *trumbaniks*—the bums. And for Christian missionaries. Apparently no place besides the Holy Land was worth a Jew's bus fare.

Yet Young Rabbi Roth had stomped on four continents since graduating college. He'd once hunted a lion with the Masai tribe in Africa. He'd parachuted from a balloon over Patagonia, and witnessed a killer whale fling sea lions high in the air before gulping them down like popovers. He played jazz on the streets of New Orleans in the summer. He kicked a soccer ball around with Laotian boys who wore only dirty cloths around their waists, and straw hats. And now he volunteered for – he lived with – the Kittakwa, up the highway on their reservation. He tutored them in English and History. He built roads. He built actual roads for them. And helped restore the rail trail and the Kittatinn, the original Hudson River bridge.

The Young Rabbi had shattered every rule and proved something – something – if only we could figure it out.

Needless to say, we hardly ever had to endure a boring American History lecture in the Young Rabbi's class, so often were we able to coax him into reminiscing about one or another of his exploits. And then we were like wheelchair-bound children hearing a mountaineer tell of conquering the K4—thrilled and heartsick.

He'd stalk around the room waving his arms, yanking loose his colorful ties as he told us truths to wake us up and fibs to keep us dreaming. Our ears leaned into his voice. Our eyes remained alert. If he suspected attention wandering, he'd grab a boy by his hair and pull hard, not a mere tug. He'd just as soon pelt you in the Adam's apple with an eraser if you started to nod off, or throw candy corn across the room into your open mouth when you answered a deep question deeply. On a roll, we would begin to clap and chant "*orr orr orr*" like trained seals while chewing the candy.

"Orenstein, you're a genius," he'd shout. "Kleiner—genius. You guys are about to make me weep openly at the depth of brilliance here, shimmering, living—get me a glass of water."

The Young Rabbi always managed to sneak in a proper history lesson, of course.

"Slipped it in sideways," he'd confess at the last bell, proudly—else his father would have fired him. We'd been mesmerized by the raucous tale of his stint playing soprano sax in a street troupe in Baton

Rouge—"with a bunch of mothers straight out of the state pen, some of them with eyes missing, but stand-up fellas in a pinch." Later, as Janusch drove us up and down the Slope on the rickety bus, we realized that somehow we knew all there was to know about the free slave movement, and the French and Spanish settling of the bayou.

Young Rabbi Roth was the best teacher I ever had. And he was our hero to the last boy.

For the first time the other day, I looked at our class picture in what passed for *yeshiva* yearbook. The photo's too tiny to see what's in his eyes, but now I know. "Right back at you," I said to him. "There's nothing in your head or heart or soul or grown man's body I don't know about firsthand, like the back of my hand. Believe you me." I realized I'm even older now than he was when he held my four-chambered heart with two strong hands that year. I wish I could go back and hold him, too, beg his forgiveness, thank him.

★★★

One morning when the bus broke down, Janusch led us on a hike up the Slope toward school. We all limped behind him the way he limped, with one lame hand in our pocket. And black guys in the backs of pickups, dusty from the mine like those pictures of the dust-bowl, stared at the spectacle, bug-eyed. Janusch found it hilarious. He rarely spoke to us students – some said the Old Rabbi had forbidden it – but that morning he wouldn't shut up.

He told us he'd hurt his leg and his hand when he was five, escaping with his parents from Poland after the War was supposed to be over. He told us that Catholics, like his family, were just as hated then as Jews, but we didn't believe it. His parents somehow wound up working for the Roths—his mother as a maid and his father as a custodian at the Old Rabbi's first school. The first Flag had burned down before we were born, killing Janusch's father and some Kit fireman (the rented school was on their land). Janusch told us the

Old Rabbi was like a father to him since, still scolding him, in fact, although he wasn't a kid anymore. His mother died when he was a young teenager, and the Roths all but adopted him. That was the way of the Kits. Few managed to keep their own parents, but fewer still kept only their own kids for 18 years.

We pressed him the whole way for details of the Young Rabbi as a boy, but he wouldn't budge. "All I say is, you're lucky you've got him."

The designation "rabbi" means teacher, and was used as a sign of respect before all our teachers' names, even the *goys* who taught math and English. Young Rabbi Roth was not ordained, and certainly no longer *frum* – Orthodox – though he had grown up that way. We learned this by relentlessly testing his knowledge of simple Jewish law and custom. To some extent he tried to avoid detection – probably at his father's urging – by not answering on the grounds that he was not our *Rebbe*, our spiritual and *Talmud* teacher, or claiming the answers were "top secret." He never *davened* – prayed – with us, choosing instead to "prepare for class" during prayer times, although none of us had ever spied a lecture note or lesson plan anywhere near his person. One of the boys had claimed to have seen a Taco Bell bag once in his car—a beat up, 10-year-old convertible Mustang no real Jew would ever sit in, no less drive. He called it "Mussy." He called it a "her."

All this made him even cooler in our eyes, different, daring, and not a little – but just enough – dangerous. At the same time, most of us fretted over his soul. Did he never pray like a regular Jew? Did he never kiss the *mezuzah* when entering a room, or put on *tefillin* first thing in the morning? Did he really, as one boy once reported, doff his size eight blue velveteen *yarmulke* and crank up his stereo as soon as Mussy barreled out of our sight? Did he dance at night with those Indians, smoking and circling their fire?

Yet all these puzzles paled in contrast to the one great mystery surrounding Young Rabbi Roth. Why was he at our school – why would he choose to spend his days with us when he could have been anywhere else in the world, including his beloved Indian reservation? When he had been nearly everywhere else, why come back to the Slope? Was it true his father had begged him to return because he'd gotten divorced from a *shiksa*? Was it true he was in love with someone here in his hometown—someone who for some reason he couldn't marry? A Kit girl? Gossiping over these juicy riddles filled many a rainy day's recess period, playing table tennis and knockhockey in the steamy *Bet Midrash*.

"I heard he was an assassin for the IDF, and killed, like, a hundred Arabs."

"I think he's a spy for the *meshugena* Reform movement, to see what we're up to. He's only pretending not to know his *Aleph Beys*."

"Bull."

However unorthodox his methods and behavior were in the afternoon, though, each morning over, they were annulled by the sheer devotion evinced in his ritual chanting. It was not mere recitation – not rational, somehow – but rather intuitive, inspired. I believe in God to this day because no man could sing such professions of Jewish faith were it not a gift from Him directly. So said the great teachers, and so proclaimed one of the Young Rabbi's favorite prayers:

"Elohai n'shama
Shenata'ta bee t'hora hee."

My God, the soul that You have placed in me is pure.
You it was who created it. You formed it.
You breathed it into me and You kept it within me.
You will take it from me, and give it back to me in time to be.
All that time the soul is within me, I'll give thanks unto Thee,
Oh Lord, King of the Universe, Master of All Made Souls.

Even the Old Rabbi closed his eyes and smiled, swaying, as his son intoned that prayer. This mitigated the prior afternoon's ranting in the Old Rabbi's smoky office, when the father chewed out his son for "pushing the envelope too far, too far, Moshe. They're only boys."

I overheard this conversation in the Spring of that seventh grade year.

"There's no such thing as 'only boys,' *Abba*," the Young Rabbi said, "only great souls in boys' bodies."

Wow. I pretended that the brand new copying contraption in the secretary's cubby was jammed, so I could continue to eavesdrop through the closed door. The Old Rabbi was furious with the Young Rabbi for reading us a newspaper clipping about an abused Kittakwa boy whose parents had denied him even a toothbrush. The boy was our age and lived not four or five miles from the Flag, but in a different universe entirely. That was the Young Rabbi's lesson—even I got that.

"You wanted me here, *Abba*. You invited me."

"Your own life you can toy with like a *dreidel*, Moshe, but not with my boys you don't."

"*Abba*, they're not babies."

"They're babies."

"There's a whole world out there—you can't just—"

"I can. That's the whole idea, Moshe. To keep them from all that *dreck*."

"When I was thirteen I was already—"

"*Ach*. That's exactly what I'm afraid of."

Already what? I was desperate to know. What was the Young Rabbi up to at my age? Was it possible that he knew even my most sacred of secrets firsthand? Like the back of his hand?

"I'm just saying times have changed," he suggested. *Oh, no.* I cringed. Everyone knew you should never say that to the Old Rabbi.

First he banged a book on his desk again and again. Then, "For us," the Old Rabbi shouted, "Never. You talk like a *goy*. Or worse—like the Reform. Is the next thing we get a 'lady rabbi' or maybe we go straight to handing out communion wafers and drinking the blood of—"

I felt my lunch – tuna fish and potato chips – coming up, and swallowed acid. I knew I should get back to my class with the dittos I was supposed to copy, but I was glued on the spot.

Janusch startled me with the broom he maneuvered with one hand and a bottle of Windex hooked on his belt. "Little pictures have big ears," he said, having misheard or misinterpreted the American idiom. I couldn't speak. "We be nice to him later. It's a hard day, looks like." He smiled, and walked off.

Back in the office the biting tones made the skin on my neck creep.

"You can't pick and choose the tenets you believe in. Is that the line, *Abba*?"

"Sure you can, Moshe. Go ahead if you want. But you're not a Jew anymore if you do."

"So God hands Moshe the rules on the mountain, right? We've proven they've been transmitted without a glitch through hundreds of generations since."

"We have."

"So how the hell can I argue with that?"

"I don't know, Moshe. How can you?"

"*Abba*. You know, don't you? Why I came back? So why make this so hard for us?"

A pause.

"This we don't discuss."

"But I need you to—I have to know you understand who I am."

"We don't discuss it."

"This is the craziest place we could possibly be," the Young Rabbi said.

"Out! Out already with this talk."

Then the secretary sneaked up behind me and pressed the stop button on the Xerox machine. To my left, we stared at a stack of a hundred copies of my open hand.

Us. We.

★★★

Two Spirits 237

"Hey, *shvartzer.*"

"Hey, sheeny. What up?"

In the back of his brother's van, I told Adam the whole conversation I'd heard, and other hints I'd been reviewing all afternoon, such as that the Young Rabbi wasn't married, yet wore a silver ring on his pinkie; he played an instrument; and he always talked about his best friend growing up, a boy named John.

The first revelation was that these feelings Adam and I shared could conceivably be carried past childhood without necessarily transforming us into the likes of the swishy, frock-wearing fairy that Benny Hill played on TV. We had never thought about the prospect of not marrying, of loving men in adulthood, and frankly, it was as much a horror as a relief.

Once we started picking apart the Young Rabbi, our imaginations carried us away.

After shagging on the cold floor of the derelict Xmascrete plant: "You know he kicks serious ass on the diamond, though? His fastball's a wicked pisser?"

"What did you expect?" Adam said, in a mock-Yiddish accent. "He should throw like a *goi*?"

We laughed.

The second surprise came when Adam started grilling me about the Young Rabbi's looks. Until then, I had never considered any grownup guy (or anyone besides Adam, in fact) a potential turn-on. But as I catalogued my teacher's every feature for Adam – his olive skin (no beard, thank God), his blue eyes, the way on the playground playing hoops you could see dark nipples under his T-shirt – my body formed its own opinion. Adam was already working on me, and after I ruined a new shirt from Marshall's with the Young Rabbi in my mind, I felt both frightened and strangely hopeful. Adam slept like a baby in my lap, and I stared at his face, imagining what it would look like five, 10, 15, 50 years down the line.

When he awoke with a whimper, he said, "Had the dream again."

I stroked his temple. "Heaven's gate?"

"Yeah. This time Saint Pete – white – says to me, looking down and nodding no, he says, '*You're kidding, right?*' Hey, you know, there's only one way to prove it for sure."

"What?"

"Mister Mystery. Rabbi Cocksucker Kike. I got two words for you."

He started again on some bidnezz, so I smacked his ear and said, "What?"

"The Garden Bar," he mumbled.

"Oh, shit."

The Garden Bar was the only gay bar within 20 miles of the Slope, Adam said. He'd been trying to get me to check it out with him for months. He said his brother used to go there to make 10 or 20 bucks in the alley off some queer—and get his rocks off, to boot. It was there Adam's brother had learned the thing he taught Adam, and Adam taught me—though I couldn't imagine ever doing that in an alley.

"Spring Break we strike," he said. "Now let me finish."

***

"My nose hit the steering wheel. *Whapp!* You know? Which was the first I knew an accident was underway. I was just sitting there waiting for the light at the turnoff for school."

Young Rabbi Roth was recounting the accident, which had caused us to suffer a droning substitute with crusty eyelids for nearly a week while he recuperated. The school fell to pieces because Janusch was employed by the Old Rabbi to stay at home and cook soup for the Young Rabbi, and help him to and from the bathroom.

We gathered around the Young Rabbi's desk as he whispered conspiratorially, a bandage still over the bridge of his nose, and crutches leaning on the desk:

"I wasn't worried, you know, because I wasn't prepared. Which I guess is good on the one hand. How do you prepare anyway? This guy was going about forty—"

"A *goy*?"
"Yup."
"Drunk?"
"Don't know. But you've all seen the *shmata* car I drive. She's held together with duct tape. Mussy dents in the rain."

We nodded, but that was far from true. We all loved his car. We craved a ride in that 302 V-8 Cruise-O-Matic. Fuck.

He always talked to us as though we were adults. The subject matter, certainly, but more importantly, the casual tone, the expectation that we could *schmooze* just like grownups. It made us feel special.

"You know that whole 'You-don't-feel-pain-when-you're-in-shock contingent? No? All right, there are these people. You always see them on *Rescue 911*. Oops. It's a TV show, never mind. They show real life emergencies. Anyway, on this show these people relive whatever horrifying catastrophes they miraculously survived. Teens trapped in icy floodwater. Arms hacked off by farm implements. Hot pots of chili spilled on twin toddlers, and so on. And these knuckle-dragging *yokels* always say the same thing. They didn't feel any pain, you know, because of the shock. Who are these people? I want to know. 'Cause in a about a millisecond I was unconscious and I still had plenty of time to feel it hurt like ... All right, show of hands: broken nose?"

No one raised his hand.

The Rabbi nodded. "Good. Let's keep it that way. You don't want to know what it's like to get your *schnoz* bashed in. Once in Spokane or Seattle I was coming home from a gig and—never mind. I've been going to the railroad bridge lately, you know, like I did when I was your age. You sit there, just you on the High Damien, but you don't want to be alone. You think about your life, the decisions you've made, secrets ..."

He started drifting, looking off into space, which he did sometimes.

"Rabbi?" one boy asked, trying to get him back on track.

"Right. Sorry. So those guys. They remind me of those even sillier guys. Like my friend, John ..."

Now, normally, we all groaned when the Young Rabbi brought up John, because it usually meant he was about to foist some moral on us. But for some reason, we didn't moan this time. It was the look on the Young Rabbi's face. He seemed on the verge of revealing to us some great secret we weren't slated to hear for many years, such as what the hell a G-spot was, or exactly what lobster tasted like.

"See, John and I are different. For example, he was always convinced that if you fell off a cliff, you'd die of shock before you ever hit the ground. You know, if you go soaring off the Sears Tower, you wouldn't even be scared because you'd die of a heart attack in mid-air. You gotta wonder about guys who believe that. You wonder whether they're playing with a full deck, whether they're dreamers. I used to say to John, oh yeah, if it's true, how come guys who jump out of airplanes don't die of shock? *Aha*.

"Then once, about ten years later, he read a Physics book. John never went to college, but he read a lot. Dreamers do that. So he called me up in the middle of the night—he had to track me down, I wasn't even in the country—to tell me his theory was right all along."

The Young Rabbi leaned back in his chair and surveyed our faces. He called this "pausing for effect." You could hear a *yarmulke* clip drop.

"It's true, John told me, you shouldn't be afraid because you'd definitely die before you hit the ground. But it had something to do with your neck breaking from the pressure, not shock. I still think it's bunk, personally. Again—skydivers. Let's take a vote ..."

***

There was a boy in our class named Dovid, who pretended to have been born an old man long before, and to have lived and gotten progressively younger. He was sad, mostly, knowing he had only 12 years left to live. The Young Rabbi never tried to stop this foolishness. Instead, he asked us to find what we could learn from Dovid's plight. After all, he was still in school, still 12 no matter which way he'd arrived there, still subject to the same rules we all were.

Funny thing. Dovid's eyes did seem the eyes of an old man. The body was young, fast, fierce in a scuffle. The eyes, though: He was always removing his glasses, rubbing his grey eyes, pinching the bridge of his nose between his fingers. Dovid voted no. It's never shock that kills you, instantly, but exhaustion after a much-protracted misery.

There was a boy, Isaac, son of one of the other lay teachers, who wowed us with a different kind of music. He could do the rap from Sugarhill's "Rapper's Delight" and Blondie's "Rapture" word perfect.

There was a boy, Yosef, who was always blaming the world's problems on the *shvartzers*. When Young Rabbi Roth assigned an essay about time travel, this fine-looking, delicate, otherwise kindly boy named Yosef wrote a long, articulate treatise on why he'd go back in time to advise Lincoln not to free the slaves. He got an ovation from most of the class.

The Young Rabbi gave him a C, and asked him whether he thought it might be possible that there was some similarity between the Jews' enslavement in Egypt and the blacks' enslavement in the New World. "Nope," said Yosef.

And the Old Rabbi agreed. "It's apples and oranges, Moshe. And besides, the boy's too young to understand."

"He's old enough to be intolerant," said the Young Rabbi, right in front of everyone in the hallway, "so he's old enough to be tolerant."

Yosef voted yes, he hoped it was true that he wouldn't have to hurt when he hit the ground. I hope so, too, for Yosef's sake.

There was a boy, Akiba – "a great, gurgling brain" the Old Rabbi called him – who'd taught us all a trick his parents, followers of the aging Schneerson, taught him. Ask a question of any book you might be holding, in other words, not only the *Torah*. Ask it any dire, consequential question and say, solemnly, "Book, please tell me the answer. I place my trust in you to offer up the truth." Open the book. Read the first thing you see. Stop when you're done. That's your answer, and it will be true:

I am staying at home for the time being.
Running a ranch is a man's job.
Jews are news.
A child whose birth predicted a gloomy melon harvest.
10:00 p.m.: Harts are targets for murder.

Akiba blindly grabbed a thin pamphlet from a shelf and asked for the answer to the Young Rabbi's question. "If I fell from a big height, would I die of shock before I hit the ground?" He opened the pamphlet.

The answer: "Please contact your local synagogue for more details."

"Aha!" said the Young Rabbi, smiling.

It is in fact the case that after laughing, after learning how to really trust in the divination, that every single question can be answered by any single string of words from any source at any time by anyone. Try it. There's comfort in the concept, and some trepidation, especially among the Orthodox. The Young Rabbi, after watching Akiba work this oracle said, "A game not recommended to the clown, the cynic, the guilty, or the godless," and answered a clicking at the door from Janusch, bearing a glass of water and some Tylenol for his stepbrother. How did he knock with that one hand in his pocket?

Now, of course, I know the reason this art, called "stichomancy" ("Bibliomancy" if you use that particular book) works. Adam told me after I taught him how to play. "Ain't nothin' nobody can ask you haven't already answered in your own thick head," he said.

"Sometimes you gotta ask though, ay?" I said.

"Oh, baby. Yeah you do."

★★★

It was a Sunday at the end of *Pesach* break. The Young Rabbi spotted us crouched behind a Ford pickup truck, just as we spied him leaving the neon-lit Garden Bar with another man. Within an hour, he would be gone from our lives.

These are the things I see now. I see his face collapse from a beaming smile into a mask of death as we lock eyes across the gravel lot. I see his hand slip from Janusch's hand – it's the hand he always keeps in his pocket – and the matching silver ring on the janitor's pinkie glinting in the streetlight. Janusch doesn't see us, tries to hold on and fails as we all did. The Young Rabbi turns to Janusch, says, "John— Oh, God," and drops a bottle of Christmas Maple Ale, which shatters.

I see me, too, somehow. What I must have looked like to him crouched with Adam, mouths agape and eyes rolling over his face. I see myself now most often this way, frozen as a child, doomed to live out eternity drowned in guilt and shame, sorry forever for asking such a question. I try to apologize to him with my eyes, to explain how I never thought about what he'd go through, what it might mean to him to be caught. How I'd thought for some reason it would be exciting, how I thought it would make us special to each other. How I didn't think.

I see the Old Rabbi hunched over the *bima* the morning after, a brave face in a room without a song. With tears in his eyes, he never mentions his son, our beloved, but tells us for the first time about another son we never knew he had:

"On a cattle car, I squeezed him out between some slats. He was five years old. It cut him everywhere, stem to stern. He was screaming at me to let him stay with me on the trip we were taking from our village. Instead, I threw him from the death train going fast, into the grass of a field in Poland somewhere where I'd never been before, and of course I never saw him again."

The Old Rabbi can talk of his father, too; his father who died nobly, praying in a queue of Jews, all shot in the head and heaped into a pit. He has the choice to speak of his son, Moshe, who might or might not have died sinfully, maybe stumbled drunkenly off the edge of the High Damien, or tested his lover's theory. The Old Rabbi goes to the place and wonders (I know; I see him from the tree fort) and still – for now – chooses not to mention his son's great name.

I see the truth to wake me up and lies to keep me dreaming. I see the Young Rabbi fly from the railroad trestle. The truth. Down below the spinning rocks of the gorge and the black water of the Christos dizzies him. I see me and Adam shivering in the tree fort, and the rabbi creeping past below in blue jeans and a polo shirt. Lies. It's the Young Rabbi I wish we really saw that night, called out to him, asked him up and begged him for forgiveness, for assurances we'd survive and maybe find happiness one day. Instead we cowered, pretended we could still be boys just a while longer.

I see the Young Rabbi at the Garden Bar, refusing a ride in Janusch's pickup, Janusch crying as he must have the night his mother, the Old Rabbi's maid, died of an aneurysm in the room they shared at the Roth's house. I see Janusch/John afraid. I imagine a different night for them, when they go home and unbutton each other's shirts in bluish light and, without talking, make love on a blanket on the hardwood floor of the Young Rabbi's study with their Great Dane watching, his head cocked. I wish this night for all of us, just once, as a gift from a loving God.

I see a nerdy boy; a shy and awkward Polish boy named Janusch who only his best friend, Moshe, calls John. He thinks about Moshe all the time, wishes and tells his mother his wishes, that he wants more than anything to be Jewish, to be like Moshe. He wishes he could go to school with Moshe Eliyahu, not the public school where everyone makes fun of his accent, his limp, and his lame hand. His worst fear, which sometimes even wakes him, is that Moshe will really see inside him one day, and hate him for the very thing Janusch prays to his God is lurking under Moshe's skin, compliments of his God.

I try – in my mind, my mind, my mind – to see them giggling one afternoon ditching school, their bare feet dangling toward the river from where they sit nearly touching thighs on the High Damien. I see Moshe swearing to John that a body dashed against the rocks below would writhe even after the skull and spine were snapped. And John, with words in broken English, a smile, and an arm around his best friend's shoulder, trying to transmit into Moshe the solace of believing that we will all die mercifully of shock before we ever hit the ground.

I see me in the old *Bet Midrash*. A murderous mute, under the eye of the clock. I see my former classmates, mouths open, screaming, Indian-dancing, pouncing through the chalk dust cloud in front of the board, through papers flying and the hot paint smell of that room, which never quite covers the stench of death. But they're silent. Not a sound to caress an eardrum. Not a palpable song such as the Young Rabbi's lamentations to hug around me in the corner, to hold me through the mania of sucking cock and putting on *tefillin* in the same day, to stop my joints from buckling, my body from collapse.

—The missing letter—

November 1782

Dear Mr. and Mrs. Frumie and Jake O'Ryan,

It has exacted five long Years to get this letter to you. First to discover your Identity, which, given the locale I call Home was no small feat. Then to locate my Sentiments, varicolored, about your Son and our brief but seminal experience together. And finally to find my Courage to contact you at last.

We met the night I died perhaps. The night of my Re-birth. And I was with him in his last moments on this Plane. I found him dauntless still, and handling his impending departure with great good Humour. He showed excessive compassion for me. Which says a lot about the Boy, no? He didn't shoot me, for one. For, yay, I was on "the other Side." With the Oppressors, the Lobsters, and only then learning so.

He gifted me a Totem important to him. He was concerned I should return to my drumming Duties, for I, like your Son, drummed. Filled with Shame and Loathing I am to have drummed to animate the Hearts of Hate.

He told me you would like me.

I found you because he wore a SC insignia and someone – you, Mrs. O'Ryan? – had stitched your surname on his Cap. He did not share with me his Christian Name, but said you named him for a Saint. Well, imagine my surprise when I, at length, discovered his Name was Adam, and they call you Frumie.

In South Carolina! Jewish settlements in America for a century, I learned on several sojourns to the Library in the environs of my new Stake (the closest Library consists of the oral mythos of Men and Women alone, and one need not enter a dwelling to "read" from its bounty).

How you happened upon the surname "O'Ryan" remains a Mystery shrouded in Fog. I live now in a place with a lot of Fog.

I confess I never associated Saints with the Hebrews. My own father, the Doctor, was an admirer, though, and left me a Book, which explained to me the most pious ones among you, the Hasids and the Zaddiqs, approach a certain Sainthood. Good. Saints belong with the Living, no? I live now among Many, though your kind might likely take umbrage with that assertion.

Adam was made of clay, and soon after your Son departed I must inform you another Boy appeared. He entified out of Nowhere – Oblivion – naked, befuddled, as though newborn. He pointed to the Sky, and perhaps because I still had your Son's name in my consciousness (but he really was pointing to the constellation) I named him "Orion."

Ma'am, Sir, I am not saying I believe for certain that I met again your son Adam *in* Orion.

But any essay into Kabbalistic reincarnation and resurrection will reveal the distinct leeway for such an occurrence.

My wife, Akt'adia – a Saint if ever one walked the Earth – instead believes Orion was the reincarnation of her Brother, purloined by other oppressors you might know better than my Kind. He might have been the reincarnation of my cousin Dez. Or maybe my brother, Thomas Henry. Or the Doctor himself—my Father. Else I don't know.

I know this for certain. He sainted me the Night I died. That Night I was re-born. He – in both Forms – and Others schooled me in the Certainty that we are not many People—only One.

I wish you great Peace and great Understanding.

Yours,

Aric Hatch
Lately of the Kittakwa

—We cowed him—

Thursday Sept. 20. Day 4 of the trial.

Not Nice New Mexico

We tamed him.
You punched him in the nose and you—what the fuck?—with a—
We cowed him.
Who the—?
We are the Shards.
You keep saying that!
We are the Eleven Shards awaiting our Twelfth and we are the answer. We will be, when we are complete. Will you complete us?
The answer to fucking what? How to rape kids?
What we did to your friend is a thousands-of-years-old tradition.
So is, ya, I don't know, cannibalism.
Funny you should—
Fuck! No. Just stop. I'm doing what you asked. I'm answering. I'll do anything.
Not anything, Influencer Talbot. Hardly.
Kenneth. Please. Guys. Women. Just let us please—
It's all in your power. The People have the power. But the question is,
Are we many people—or one? That's the seventh of eight questions you must answer. Tell us a story from the Kittakwa that answers that question, and we can move on to the final.
You have to help him. Sully. Please help him. He'll die.
We won't let him die. We will keep him alive. He will be a constant sacrificial—
That's worse. Fine. Fine. I've got one. I know the answer. Are we many people—or one?

Two Spirits 249

LOOKING BACKWARD TO SEEING YOU

Looking Backward
To Seeing You

For D.R.E.W. Grauerholz

The past was safe in its cage. Why not have a look?

—Vladimir Nabokov, *Laugher in the Dark*, 1932

I. Griffin A. Bond

They would say that he had cheated on his Chaucer test for her—so as not to disappoint her. She had such a tight body—preternaturally tight. And those razor-thin glasses, and that Japanese nose with the spattering of freckles. They would say it was a travesty (expulsion, double homicide) because he was by far the smartest fucking kid in Medieval Lit. He didn't need to plagiarize. Not him.

And yet. They would say it was the course, and it was absolutely par. There was his mother in the motel after all, the New Yorker on the Rez, the burning waffles in their toaster, all those sloe gin fizzes, and that one hard-done-by dog the neighbors found had caught a case of death. The doe-eyed daughter of the weekday maid—there was also that, you can't forget. All her flaps and folds undone.

And that phase-in period of imperceptivity when he wore the pale retainer, forced to stare at all those chalky molds of jaws and teeth in cases made of glass. All those jaws that rimmed the waiting room of Dr. Nova's office: the orangutan, the lemur, and the *Mongoloid human male (11), victim of a surgical malfeasance* in the Lesser Antilles or someplace akin. There was that thumping in the fourth grade at Aric Hatch Grammar. In between the garbage pails awash with milk and tater tots, when they kicked him in the balls so hard

Two Spirits 253

he puked, and cried, and shit himself a little after all his musculature failed.

There was the instant he decided he would swipe the awesome poster of the Blue Angels jets in a diamond formation, from the shop at the Air and Space Museum on the National Mall – even though he had the cash to pony up, his mother's Kent 100s kitty, adeptly purloined – and all the yards of bowels this crime unspooled through the subsequent days, through the consequent ages, which he never could re-tuck the way they came.

But they would say that all that paled, juxtaposed to the "influence" (that fucking word) of the pin-dick instructor, Mr. Glass—that excuse for a teacher, Alan Glass. They'd have to disinter that man and then expose him, strip the corpse and nail the blame through his grubby dark sternum. Mr. Glass, that terrible tutor, that nonperson, that minus of a man, who kept an overeager kid on the bus for his own bitterness, who kept a boy for jumping over the fuzzy rope on the visitor's waiting line at the FBI, who made him taste his shame on the back of the bus as all the other kids ambled over the Sturbridge Village cobblestone, eating old-fashioned peppermint sticks and watching those booby-girls in bonnets churn the butter, spin the motherfucking flax. On Mr. Glass's frontal bone, a *matzo* ball, dripping into the sockets of the eyes. A "hate crime" they neologized. Well, hell to the J.E.W., be it known by a gentlemen's agreement—it was hate, indeed. The white-hot hate of a million burning hexagramoid stars.

They would argue over Chaucer, sure—but never over Glass. They would argue over Chaucer as it might have been Marlowe. It could have been the Hunchback Warty Toad or the Lady of Cambridge or even Christine de Pizan in the third trimester. All their prose had imprinted on his dermis like a Pillow Book, their secrets throbbing in the adenoids his baby doc had always found inflamed and crimson in an otherworldly way. You see, he didn't need to copy. He knew all their work by heart. Isn't zero motive the best defense?

They would say he cheated in her name, the name of Tachibana-Walker, and didn't do it for himself. And they'd be *on the right track*, at least *barking up the right tree*. She'd made her frumpy husband, Charley – that browbeaten Anglo androgyne – ship from home those cartons of Lance brand peanut butter cheese crackers and cases of Jolt Cola – just caramel-colored water, caffeine, and corn syrup – so she wouldn't miss the flavors of the land that had adopted her. And a *chef*, no less, her Charley.

There was a pastel little elbow of a vein behind the Tachibana kneecap he had twice witnessed twitch before she scratched it on a summer night after class in Hyde Park. *Oh*. They would say he lost his shit behind that knee of his professor, Judie Tachibana-Walker, on the Summer English Lit Programme, the so-called SELP. They would talk, not unromantic-ally, of a modern "Kensington Horror." His symphony of evisceration. A tympanum of pain.

And they would rightly assert that Dr. William Rensselaer, Exec-Director of the SELP, bore no blame at all for the fall. But careful scholars would conclude that the excess of response (summarily sending the boy back to Drummond, in Kit County) had sealed the major players' doom. Dr. Old-Bill-Ren-Fair had launched a ship from Dover, albeit well-meaningly, with incendiary cargo, far from Tachibana-Walker, and toward an old colleague of his, August Richter, not the foil of Griffin's tale, but the paradoxical *finis*.

They would say that Dr. Richter had to end a life of service, noble teaching, and long tenure once that anchor was aweigh.

Yes, that's what they would say, after careful peer review.

For his part, the boy, in sound(ish) mind, Griffin Aric Bond, was aware – just remotely, as he catapulted forward, left his body and his circumstance to hearken to those phantoms, those slavering future biographers decrying Alan Glass (that nonentity); to glorify that Joan, that Helen, that Queen of Egypt, Our Judie T-to-the-Dubs; validating for the global literati and assorted aficionados of forensic psych all the depths and the direction of his soul (inclining East) – that they would *not say a thing*. That there would never be a "they" to say. He wasn't absolutely crazy, notwithstanding what he'd been through, what he'd done, and what he planned to do. No one would ever know.

Notwithstanding a facility for disassociation, on some fuzzy plateau along the way, you evolve through the imperceptive stage into heightened discernment. You begin to see things as they really are. You change. More like you *evolve*.

Maybe they'd remember him? It was no small affair after all. It was an affair about which it would be worth saying a little something or other. It wasn't a fucking shepherd dog in a Dumpster behind the Sinclair station shitter, in the shadow of a decrepit trestle in the Kitskills, that's for sure.

So he cheated. He paid a patron who was a lesser person a higher amount for the final paper than his father had ever held in his hands at one time, or so he surmised from one Polaroid (blue Barracuda, wife-beater, dog of dull extraction, sucking up for a pat on the head).

They would picture Griff with a bloody nose and his hand below the belt like some perverted anime kid, spying from behind some ancient oak on Lady Tachibana-Walker while she picnicked on Pop Tarts and Kool-Aid from a torn-open cardboard box in the abbey garden. She was an animal for American snacks. She should have been a sibyl. He couldn't think about her husband, the *chef*, the lepton, without picturing one of those sharpened grapefruit spoons doing terrible things to his soft parts, which most of them surely were.

Let's get it over with: They would say, wouldn't they, that Griffin was a latent homosexual, that he cut his nails that time in the ninth grade because he dreamt or hoped or wished he would somehow find his fingers swimming warm inside his friend, Cal McAutrey, on that camping trip up The Black Diamond Trail on West Kittatinn Hill—but they'd be fucking *maniacs* asserting that. Really, who did they think they were ascribing *hopes* and *dreams* and *wishes* when they'd never even *met* him, when he had in his left ball alone twice the brains that they possessed? Not that he hadn't imagined the inside of Cal McAutrey in a range of permutations, but ... Well—it was incongruous, the very thought. It was different with Cal. And he himself, Griffin Bond, was so far advanced beyond categorization, beyond the *designation*. Who could pin a pinkish pyramidal amulet on such a specimen as he?

And wouldn't they discover how much he liked our Jelly back then? Some fungus from her favorite, Kittatinn Pond, had claimed her toenails (seven) but an otherwise idyllic mien encompassed Jelly Greene. She was Boudicca with braided hair and knees covered in filth and rashes. They spent hours together, the three of them, on the shore of the sump, sunning themselves and massacring toads in novel ways. They spent *crucial years*. On the railroad bridge. The jungled Christos banks. They learned. They learned.

They would say he must have fumbled with Jelly like those nonpersons said Adolf Hitler tried to fuck one Stefanie Isak, that walking *schnoz* for whom the *Meister* supposedly suffered, after their seminal stroll on the *Landstraße* in Linz, circa 1905. But they would have to concede as well that no such consummation occurred between Griffin Bond and Calvin Bon McAutrey, either. Only Griffin would know how unnecessary consummation *as such* had become. How he once turned after dropping a dumbbell in the gym at AHS and saw in the mirror the back of Cal through a door as he padded down the hall in his tiny black Speedo, the top of the crevice of his buttocks exposed, the *crevasse*, and the black hair at the back of his neck pulled and pointed straight down with the pool water draining there, like Christos Creek weeds coursing toward the sea—like those rats at length streaming out our neighborhoods in Vilna and Minsk like pus from an abscess.

Griffin followed Cal into the locker room. He smelled much less like chlorine than like the hand-rolled cigarettes he smoked, which permeated his hair, and didn't wash clean in the water. His lips were cold and shrunken, turning blue. He held his arms up to his chest and shivered from the shoulders. Like a little boy. Griffin summoned something ancient, something alien, from a tiny gland behind his eyes, and said: "You need to get warm, Cal." The air hummed. It was different with Cal. They should say. They should say. Cal understood him. Cal forgave.

They would woo the world with their depiction of the swimmer who would move the stars to pity, yes, but how would they paint poor Konrad Papasophocles, the other "man" in Griffin's life that year? In a perfunctory paragraph, if that (more likely a footnote), as a mere trifling former "roommate," any influences accidental, otiose, frankly quite a stretch. In any case, no one would think the world worse-off for the loss of that lad:

"Someone came and took the furniture." Breathless.

"Did Cal call? Wait—what the fuck? What happened to my stuff?"

"Some women."

"Konnie—who? Turn this off. How can you call this music?"

"Some women who said Old Bill's booting you off the SELP, and they were giving the futon and the bookcase to some new kid; that's what they said. From Swaziland. Gonna be Dickler's roommate now on the second floor. No. Wait."

"From *Switz*erland?"

"Oh, yeah."

"Some women? I abominate this man's so-called music. How can you stand to listen to this fucking *non-song*?"

"Yeah, with, like, a clipboard and a hand truck, all official and shit. This is a tower of a song."

"*Shit*. Was there a message from Cal? Where were they from, these women?"

"England, I guess."

"Konrad. You're an idiot with no *savant. Of course* they're from fucking *England.*"

"I guess. Right. We're on the Goddamn Summer Lit in England Program,"

"Right," said Griffin, surreptitiously lifting and pocketing the sock Konnie had recently used to clean up his afternoon dance with himself. He sat in front of Konrad. He got directly in his face. He talked sweetly: "So, what I mean, Konnie (friend, flatmate), is what c*ategory* of women came to take my furniture and said Old Bill was booting me back to Drummond on the next troop ship or whatever for allegedly cheating on Chaucer while you were listening to the worst rap song written by the (*wigger*) hand of man while your own hand or both played the skin flute?"

Konrad gaped, his too-wide nostrils flaring. He screwed up his lip, really wanting to get this one right. He turned down the stereo with the remote – Boots-brand petroleum jelly still shone on his palm – in order to hearken to his answer, which he seemed to hope would arrive on the air.

"What *category* of women?" he asked the air and motes of dust occasioned by the shanghai of Griffin's kit and caboodle. "I don't know ... I guess ... *cunts*?"

***

PASSWORD PROTECTED CORRESPONDENCE

Subject: Re: Diatoms and Kindred Spirits
From: Dr. August Richter arichter@vaughn.edu
Date: Sun, Jun 02, 2000 7:26 am
To: Griffin A. Bond griffbond@studentwire.com

Dear Master Bond,

If you're reading this, you've deciphered out of the tendrils in ether the password. Good lad. I hope this finds you in the relative pink. I hope, too, you'll tolerate my replying via e-mail, which I find so much more opportune, given my to-do-list re: The Rebel Angels' *"semiquequindecennial" (I think it's called!), my nine rheumatic knuckles that object to the graphite grip, and the fact your generation demands a level of expedience and urgency that would have left the younger me and my comrades rather breathless in the proverbial malt shop. Not to say I wasn't happily surprised to find your real old-fashioned letter in my in-box last week (down in the Salt Mines that are my offices). So unusual that I'm sure the mailroom clerk – the young fellow fourth-in-command there whom they call "Johnny Duh," because he's a bit "touched" as they used*

to say – was as taken aback as I, perhaps even more so by the postmark (while not "exotic," per se, it does smack of some noir intrigue). But then I noticed shimmering in the margins of your missive that you're a young man quite extraordinary in the strict sense of the word, on several, perhaps forgotten and certainly underappreciated, fronts. It's funny that you found me.
Funny.

You're right, it's not that I don't receive a rather leonine share of fawning fan-letters every year from beaver kits, especially around spring, when my "C-list" students come scratching out of every dam for a recommendation to graduate school (and the occasional enterprising high school senior, such as yourself, fails [unlike yourself] to more subtly inquire after a free pass into Vaughn by impressing me. Note to America's Youth: Paraphrasing my errant entries on poorly-researched websites will not impress me. For one thing, I was never "as a young man persecuted by the Nazis"—far bloody from it!).

Mr. Bond, you might remain a Drummond High School senior, but you're already on the fast track to Vaughn if you're a student of Dr. Rensselaer's competitive SELP. But your adviser or "Old Bill" himself must have told you that they wheel me out now for only two public lectures a year, and I teach only the one class, such as it is. You know you needn't glad-hand me to get a seat: Since the Mesozoic, it works by lottery. I am told one must allot one's whole shebang, though, 100 percent of the Fall chits, then some frostily detached automaton selects from among the hopefuls, and you get a call from the English secretary (who's actually human, and Scottish), Mrs. Balflour. Of course the small matter awaits you, to officially apply to Vaughn, and find acceptance, as I'm sure you will.

Nevertheless, I will make a call to Admissions to put a word in for you. A young man thereabouts owes me a "solid," so I hear the kids say. It is rather late in the season, though, no? In any case, I would find myself glad indeed for you to join me next semester, should Fortune's Wheel spin in that direction. Surely an adventure or two awaits us in convergence.

I'm happy you enjoyed The Rebel Angels. *Can't say many younger readers dig that deep a well in pursuit of "glimpses in [my] juvenilia of later genius" (the very phrase makes something gurgle in my guts, even 65+ years on).*

Griffin, before I get to your queries, I want to express to you a potent and quite literal empathy for the agony I can tell you've undergone since the advent of your awakening. I appreciate your humor, though I see through its membrane, like looking at water weeds suspended below the ice on our local pond. One wouldn't expect sincere self-deprecation—it's unseemly for our kind. I'm glad you'll be back at your studies, though there might be greater dons than I about, and into, whom you should inquire for the mastery you must achieve.

Tell me a little about your experiences at Drummond—all I know of it is the Honors program seems to spew forth ultrabright and eager students, several of whom I can remember found spots at Vaughn. A Travis, I recall, a Frazier, and a something-or-other Scandinavian, who arrived at an unfortunate denouement in only his Chapter Two, compliments, as I recall, of an overturned Chevrolet Lumina, no? A young lady called Lopez, too (which, like "Wolf," I note, means "wolf"), who swept forensics some years back. Maybe that was a long time ago; I can't quite remember. I'm like Faulkner's old soldiers now, who look back at all the past as a great meadow full of dancers, seen through the narrow bottleneck of the most recent decade of years.

And what of Old Bill? He's one of the finest, and you're blessed to have him as your tutor over there. He has forgiven me many a trespass. Remember me to him, if you'd be so kind.

Well, under the terms you propose re: confidentiality (and in return for your thoughtful, albeit cryptic, confessions; smart lad), allow me to dispense with some cursory answers to your seven (!) lengthy queries, viz.:

1. Yes, I was your age when I wrote it. Younger, maybe. It won an un-prestigious novella contest at my even less prestigious college; I believe it was $30 or thereabouts, a weighty sum, and I bought brandy with the booty, got drunk with a friend after a long shift in the commissary, and vomited on a waistcoat that my "grandmother," Ilsa, had sacrificed to buy me. I recall a contentious conversation with the editor of the campus magazine – "The Disparaging Eye" is my best translation (not too pretentious, and no Dial, that rag!) – that was to publish the story. He said it read like Thomas Gray's love letters to Horace Walpole, or James Joyce's to his Nora, and I was "encouraged" by the board to consider revising. I looked up the references, and spent another few hours trying to chuck up the one or two kernels remaining in my digestive tract. These were far different times, I'm sure you understand. Anyway, it was impossible to celebrate a book about "him," when he no longer occupied space on this mortal plane. That's not quite right. But you know what I mean.

2. Yes, indeed, I based the character Bem on my first cousin, Felix Wolf, and, yes, we were very much under the spell in those days before the curtain dropped after our hour. You say you've read "all the interviews." Have you archived them? This might prove fruitful, given the statistical improbability of winning a spot in your first foray. I might find some funds to support it, or perhaps some internship credit, which the aforementioned Mrs. Balflour can arrange. In any case, you will recognize this is the first time I've ever acknowledged the fact of my beloved Felix since he closed his (yes, to question 2a) green eyes, I hope thinking of me, because you are the first one ever to uncover – somehow – the genesis of the love story under the bildungsroman. No, I think the line, "Still with uncircumcised taste in my mouth ..." is a dead-end: As I recall, I intended to refer to that irony, xeric tang one wakes up

with in the high desert when there is little water to be had. Though perhaps my subconscious had the quill. It makes my cheeks burn now to read that line. In binary code, it is easier to write than I might have thought over these past sevenish decades. Perhaps it's that I'm not looking at you as I admit it. I would prefer to look at you. Or maybe you just jangled the right nerve by sharing what you did about your own recent "kindred tremors," as you called them. Lovely.

3. No, I have no idea how you put it all together. Or, as a better critic might say, how you took it apart. Have I ever been "sussed?" you inquire. What do you take me for? You ask me if I can deduce the way in which you puzzled out my two most fractured secrets. I confess I'm at a complete loss, and I confess I reached overnight the height of romantic absurdity in imagining scenarios in answer to your question. As you seem to know my enigmas and still find facets of me to admire, I suppose it's safe to render more: Since your missive, I've had trouble sleeping for feeling vulnerable. Hilde thinks I've got prostate grievances, and I haven't disabused her. I spoke with a young colleague, Dr. Mahler, para in our Psych. Department, who offers me ad hoc "therapy," for lack of a less humiliating term, from time to time, over sandwiches on a nice bench. If she only knew! Her head would explode, as you say your young friend underwent as of late. I had a dream that you were somehow Bem or Felix, or a changeling of one or the other, or some such nonsense like that (the green eyes opening, splashes over the cheeks, and where was I? Keeping in mind, there was no blood. It was all dry as an ancient bone that last afternoon. That's sort of the whole idea). But there's no other way you could know. Perhaps I don't want to know. I am, in any case, much intrigued. I cannot say I necessarily relish rekindling the emotions occasioned by reminiscing over those days with

Felix, nor reconsidering his end. I imagine it's rather like the phantom pains reported by amputees: For a moment, it's good to feel the twitching of your old leg, even if the feeling hurts. But then you reach down for a healing touch, and find there's only fetid air south of the stump.

4. Yes, Professor Emeritus conveys a comfortable sinecure for my continuing efforts in research and writing, and allows me access to young persons such as yourself, with open hearts and minds. At 82¼, I'm afraid I can't handle the load I've carried in the past, though, in more ways than one. Academically, just one class, just once a week, which my assistant, Jamilla, manages virtually without my interference. She grades the papers and proctors the tests and offers the lectures, and she advises the students, all rather swimmingly. I'm embarrassed to admit, she even ties my shoes, as my poor Hilde can no longer bend the ways she intends to bend, but rather toward some curled-up, question-mark end. The course, "Canonization in World Literature," to address your sub-question 4b, attempts to answer the riddle, "What makes a classic a classic?" There are days I feel I can barely fathom an answer to that imperative anymore. I can think of a "classic" or two from my younger days, one of which I believe you hit upon marvelously with an allusion so esoteric as to be nearly absent, but nonetheless apparent to me, as I'm certain you intended. Your calling my first book a "classic," by the way, makes me blush and causes great digestive distress, as I think I already mentioned. Or perhaps that's the sardines. Hilde used to beg me not to eat the heads. Yet I have always eaten the heads. I must ask Jamilla to correct the errors I find in all the unauthorized "cyberspace" versions of said classic. I understand there's a protocol for that. 4c. Extracurricular activities, you ask? It's been many years. I have my memories on cold nights.

5. Yes, I can steel myself for this. We had survived that perilous expedition to Aconcagua, so we tackled Kilimanjaro with a less-than respectful fear. His name was Ludovicus – "Dov" – and we had met in the climbing club at Tübingen. After what God made me endure in the loss of Felix, I expected a life lease, a permanency with Dov. It ended in an ice cave after only a year. I married Dov's sister instead, my Hildegard. Funny old world. 5b. Does she know? She knows. She doesn't know.

6. Yes, in fact, I'm afraid I am aware, and more than peripherally, of the "artist" about whom you protest since your former flatmate chose his work for an anthem. Not principally because I see on my students' T-shirts images of him with those sharpened swords overlapping into a Star of David, and I hear his "rhymes" from their dorms (neither of which the Vaughn administration can seem to find a good rationale to ban), nor because he appears in endless diatribes from the manifold not-for-profits that send their variously Zionist and post-JDL paper airplanes into my apolitical hangar. No, Dirty Jew, the rapper ("hip-hopper?") first frog-marched into my consciousness right behind the tanks of technology that steadily invade all our space, tearing up a thousand Benny Goodmans, Barry Manilows, Neil Diamonds, and Barbra Streisands in their tracks. "First, they come for the trade unionists ..." But I don't share the zealotry of your complaint. In fact, as a former subversive myself, I understand, at least I like to imagine, what Dirty Jew is "up to," as we used to say. I don't understand the music per se. Is it music? Is that the correct term? I have heard several of his hits, some of which feature on Jamilla's personal jukebox, emblematic of the musico-cultural miscegenation in the global era: I have heard "If You Prick Me" and "The Final Solution," and one that I think must be called, "Über-Judenrat." Perhaps the less said about that one, the better. You mention

Two Spirits 265

the work of my soon-to-be-ex-colleague, Emory Zingel, an old stallion from our Math Department, who, indeed, my Google-y informant just reported, recently published a paper on Dirty Jew, though for the life of me, I cannot guess Em's interest. I have asked Jamilla to procure me a hard copy, and I will attempt to get to the bottom of the conundrum. Watch this space.

7. No. Its principal utility is that it's heat-resistant, so they use it as an insulator in plumbing and electronics. Its alveolation (hollowness) makes it ideal as a filter for clarifying candy syrups, which is ironic, considering Felix's sweet tooth. If you look in your medicine chest, you'll find it's also employed as a filling component in toothpaste, soap, and detergent. They were going to use ours as an abrasive in metal polishes, and that had all of us worried. In the long run, it's the sharp edges of the crystals that carve into your lungs. The kind of thing you see lots of daytime TV lawyers hawking about. But it's also absorbent – they use it to dry up industrial spills, and even in kitty litter, speaking of industrial spills (Hilde's little tiger, Tigger) – so in the course of a few minutes, should a surfeit be introduced, it's a simple matter of choking / drowning in the dryness. Not a simple matter, really. Did you know – of course you know – that right around the corner from both of us lies the richest cache of the stuff on the East Coast? Coincidence? It called to me. From the other side. And did you know your school was built over a former yeshiva, which, before those days, was a (non-kosher) slaughterhouse? Marvelous.

By the way, why are you returning to Drummond mid-term? I trust you're not in a jam. In any case, I think I should greatly enjoy a visit from you while you find yourself stateside. Come and see me in the mines. Bring me some of the photos you hint at: Those shall get my old tail wagging, I imagine!

I hope you didn't assume this old codger had any kind of psalming sagacity to drip on you and take away your pain. Let me just send you a handclasp and a (chaste! I don't want to be fired for sexual harassment, which everyone at Vaughn's panicked about since that incident last term, to which you alluded, speaking of the Math Department) embrace across the miles, and I remain,

—*August W. Richter, Professor (Emeritus) of Literature*

II. August Richter

Ilsa had labored in the mines – the Jew's lot, she would say with some pride – since long before the boys' parents had walked on legs. Somehow the bosses let her keep a large and lazy dog, Lambert, ever-slaked in the white powder—barring its wet, black nose, from which it sneezed reflexively about once a minute. She enlisted this poor dog's suffrage like a crystal ball prior to all quandaries of any import, such as, "When shall I join my Sender?" To which he responded by looking up at her, imploringly, as if to say, "I just don't know, Old Bird." Then sneezed.

Ilsa stooped, and something in her spine cracked when she shuffled; it sounded like a bag of pretzels. Nevertheless, she could swing a pick like a strong man half her age, and sometimes proved it. But mainly now, with the help of her one-legged granddaughter, Stef, she ran the signals for the rail cars to cart out the *kieselguhr*. Between the runs, she sat on a stool some of the time, when she could, when the bosses were gabbing or playing *Schnapsen*, both of which appeared to require the utmost concentration. And when in her estimation a man or her granddaughter required the stool more than she, she offered it—and leaned on Lambert with both hands while he shook off, and then in vain attempted to look regal while he sneezed.

Two Spirits 267

Ilsa was an improvisatory nurse, and a font of legal and marital counsel for the older miners. For miners old and young – and notwithstanding her hunch and her powder-crammed crow's feet – she became the downy Eve in the otherwise sharp gardens of their various inductions. She mothered the boys whenever she could, and they found need of her mothering daily. She shared her cheese sandwiches with them when they looked hungry. She chipped away the ice between them when they railed and rowed. She mended their tools when the handles snapped, and she sewed their socks when they fell apart. When they gashed themselves, she unbelted the cotton pad she kept beneath her dress – the boys assumed to keep it free of the *kieselguhr* – and pressed it, warm and slightly damp, to their wounds full of dusty blood. She gave them all Schrafft's candies – the opiate of the mining masses – dispensed from a creepy grey, Corn Man figurine made of mothball boxes. In Ilsa's kingdom, every man, woman, and child was equal and worthy. August Richter almost believed it.

Twice a day, Ilsa licked the ball of her thumb, and wiped their lips and their eyes of the dust, and smiled wanly when she could finally see them. She said she felt like she was making Golems out of clay, filling them with fearsome spirits. She kissed them on the lips, and said she was breathing new souls into them. If that were the case, then our souls stink like onions.

More than anything else, though, Ilsa was a poet, the most talented one the boys believed had ever walked the earth or under. As they toiled in her orbit, or stumbled toward her, holding up torn fingernails (and holding-in their tears until she touched them); as they huddled around her stool at lunch or supper, she made them cajole her to embark. They had to beg. Then elegiac anecdotes would flow, often moving the boys to the brink of becoming undone.

She had been born under the Kaiser as he unified Germany. But in her stories, she mentioned her girlhood only obliquely—it maddened them. Her poems were steeped in such stuff of her youth, though, at least according to the boys' imaginations. There was an icy Alpine lake recurrent. There were a couple of arch crows that a young girl (she?) finally cowed into submission, later puppets for the children's Punch and Judy shows. There were lightning strikes on the peaks in summer. And there was a boy.

They keened to hear of him, and clawed for the smallest detail. She said it hurt too much, and shook her head. They understood. She knew they understood.

August understood. He also had a boy.

Their fathers were brothers. And both fathers had died within days of each other at the second battle of the Marne, August's by a French bayonet, and Felix's under the tracks of a British tank. Their mother, the boys' shared grandmother, discovered twin telegrams on her table, next to a plucked fowl, and pressed the tip of a carving knife behind her ear, then shoved. The mine had rendered the boys' grandfather lung-lame some years before, and when he lost his wife, he lost his will as well as his nursemaid, and decided, too, despite the utility and kindness of his daughters-in-law (one Jew and one Christian), to die. So their mothers worked double- and triple-shifts at the munitions plant, and required their boys to "go under," as they put it in Schwindebeck in those days, though they'd have rather dispatched the new men in their lives to the same crimson moorland where their husbands had met the Green One.

Professor Richter was ashamed to admit that all these decades later, he had learned nearly nothing new about the organism that took his first great love from him in boyhood. Over months in the mines, Ilsa had told the boys some basics, which of course he still remembered. The diatoms they mined were unicellular but anything but plain. They made intricate geometric forms, which Ilsa and Stef sketched into the mine wall with the purple pencil she used to record the train loads. They were hollow now millions of years on, like microscopic coffins, she said. "They'll be my casket, too. You'll see. I will somehow fit inside." They were mostly non-motile, though a few had flagella – like sperm, she said, interrupting her marine biology lesson for a far more intriguing turn – with which they could glide themselves blindly through brine. They were as vital in the oceans' food chain as sperm for the brothers who created the cousins who formed a bond far under the Lüneburg Heath. Without the diatoms, she said, through a perilous game of dominoes, every human on Earth would die within days.

"The same stuff that slimes the rocks in a stream?" August asked.

"The same."

Since his boyhood, of course August Richter had always had access through books and colleagues to the details of diatomaceous anatomy, life-cycle, and recently, even genetic sequencing. On occasion, at the beach, or when sailing, and sometimes when looking at rocks that might contain some fossils of their ancestors, he thought he might look into them further. They intrigued him. They terrified him still, on some almost inaccessible level. Well, that really wasn't so strange. There were so many, and so many kinds. They enjoyed an endurance and vitality he envied. They had power. His avoidance of their study felt conspicuous to him. He sometimes fancied that people would notice it, and somehow know.

So, as these things go, he sublimated his terrible passion for the creatures into all manner of otherwise "healthy" human intrigues. Therefore, naturally, they consumed his dreams, in which he became one of them, part of a huge, collective, invincible ribbon:

There is only one sensation, one comfort, one truth: carriage. *Every tendril thrums with the waves' caress, the eternal certainty of quite involuntary motion. We are neither aware nor unaware that We're never delivered, but always on Our way. And as We roll ceaselessly where the winds and currents will Us, We are One, We are wonderful, and all made things know it is We who are the pith and essence of the world.*

His wife would wake to find him in a sweat. She would put her teeth in and her glasses on. She would pad to the kitchen to bring him cold milk and potato chips. He watched her watch her bony hand on his pajama leg. Did she long for him to take her?

In some remoter quarters of the mine, the labyrinths opened to immense vaults, like cathedrals of the underlord, spiderwebbed with catwalks slung with iron candelabra. In other places, chambers narrowed into niches where the miners had explored for more *kieselguhr* to no avail, and had thence abandoned them for greyer pastures. Some of these latter recesses had become places for "making lemonade," as Ilsa and the other oldsters euphemized. Boys younger than August and Felix were made to stoop and dig troughs around the perimeter; now "lemonade" pooled in them and formed a strange, cool skin. You had to hold your breath and close your eyes to enter. For those few who hadn't trained their bowels to wait to surface after 12-hour shifts, there were facilities, too, for the expulsion and containment of "fudge," located in an alcove called "Hookworm Hall." The very breath of Satan permeated that space.

Yet more importantly, there was one tiny nook, an inmost antechamber off a suite of long-forsaken spaces accessible only through a dangerous, chained-off stope, a refuge the boys called "Our Room," and which, for some geothermal reason they could not comprehend, remained as warm and dry as Morocco amid the damp chill of the rest of the mine. It was in their room that August and Felix first fell asleep in each other's arms, first swore to protect each other no matter what, and despite the ostensible impediments, so that neither bayonet nor tank would sever them from each other as it had the brothers who were their fathers. To solemnize this oath, they took turns with a limestone arrowhead they'd found in the mines, and carved into each other a small, imprecise asterisk on the cleft of the left buttock, where no one but they and their Maker would see it. Accomplishing this operation necessitated cinnamon schnapps and a torch held between the teeth. It was both a birth and death.

But it was in Our Room that such a severance would indeed eventually occur. Another birth and death. So that boy preferred a one-legged girl to all the boyish appendages August had to offer. Which was untenable, of course. Of course. Right? A pickax to the proper arteries. A massive cleft of *kieselguhr* dumped on Felix and Stef. It happens. Force Majeure. And funny thing about the survival instinct: They had to open their mouths eventually.

Two Spirits

III. Judith Tachibana-Walker

Her fifth book won a prestigious prize. Her father said, "Now you've made a sum total of five hundred dollars on poetry. I make that in a day at the store." The Tachibana family owned a chain of low rent party stores, and required her to work 30 hours a week from the time she was nine. But they paid her, smartly, and she spent much of her time reading books she borrowed from the older man at the bookshop next door, who liked the crisp pleats of her skirt, he said. One earns an opportunity for uninterrupted study by poorly organizing shelves of pastry bags and cake toppers, Wolfman masks and balloons. By the time she was ready for college, she could pay in cash the sum due after sizable scholarship gains.

A PhD in Poetry unlocks some unanticipated doors, her father would find before dying while stocking fangs and fake blood. Running the poetry program at Drummond was pleasantly remunerative and rewarding. She liked the SELP. And she especially valued her female students, the insecure ones, and the quiet. Nothing thrilled her more than unearthing an inkling of brilliance in their otherwise muddy stuff. Not that it happened often. At the condo in Fall and Spring, she graded quotidian prose and attempted to edit pedestrian poetry for *Omnibus*, the dreadful student lit mag she advised. She drank limoncello and vodka on the couch, and complained to Charley. Charley nearly always said the right thing. He wore a blue apron with a yellow insignia depicting a happy-face spoon. He made dumplings with tiny cubes of firm tofu and chopped bok choy, and said just the right thing while swaddling them in lettuce. He made hamburgers with mashed bread interwoven, apricot pie, and homemade ice cream with real cacao. There were times she wanted to drive into her husband's eyes those ice picks they kept wrapped in silk ribbon in the sideboard, he was so attentive and kind.

She could call Charley now – he might still be awake, baking something – but it wouldn't be the same. There's that lag in the international cell service. There's the natural disconnection caused by the difference in their time zones. Charley usually came to London at the end of the SELP, dovetailed a few days with the closing activities, then took over, and swept her to Italy or to Greece, places he'd backpacked and camped and climbed and ate in college and thereafter. Granted, their lovemaking was borderline sublime during the first week of seeing each other after those months apart. It was epic sex. But she saw Charley as one of those brief, brilliant poems that Williams fit on prescription pads between patients, as the American version of haiku. You read them because they are crisp and clean like linens drying on the line. You don't dive in for the depth or complexity of an Eliot.

She could leave the hotel room, walk past the museums and the sculpture garden. She could sit in the back room of the kebab house across the road, and read Dante and suffer small bites of *kofta* curry. She could take the tube to Charing Cross and wander that bookstore that had fluttered her heart since she first found it 20 years ago when she was making inquiries into lesbianism with a dark Turkish girl she'd met at a Cure concert, stoned out of her gourd.

She could fuck the kid. Griffin Aric Bond.

She could work on the third of the swan poems, the difficult one. It was all about the scansion and enjambment. He *defended Grendel* and empathized with Beelzebub, and not just to be clever. She could forgive his youthful misjudgments about Blake's mental health. He wrote stunning prose. Ridiculous. He had those ... eyes.

If she were to make a connection somehow between the lake and, not *heaven*, exactly, the way Brooke had, but some sort of ... He *just* lost his mother. Imagine that. God knows what happened to his father. She could watch TV. The British made such better television than the Yanks. He was unusually attractive, the kid. He was mercurial in class. Some days he jumped right in, and other days he moped. She had seen him in Hyde Park without his shirt, reading while some locals threw a Frisbee. He was rugged in a scrum (Rugby,

Crew: She had lurked through his yearbook page the prior semester). This despite quite delicate facial features. He wrote in his final paper, in a footnote: "I understand viscerally the synaesthesia in Wordsworth's 'Lines Composed a Few Miles above Tintern Abbey,' but I don't see it as the mere apex in the dawn of Romantic felicity, as you implied in the seminar—as critics have hailed since the Preface to the *Lyrical Ballads*. Rather, what I see evinced is the poet's incipient madness, *viz.* ..." A *high school* student—the cheek! No, he was a different kind of poem altogether. He would require not a little deconstruction. The plagiarism incident was just another "meaning" to uncover.

She could fuck the kid before they sent him back to New York ...

IV.   *Calvin Hatch McAutrey*

Dude, it's über-freaky how careful he always was. You remember, from way back. Just look at how he "handled" poor Konnie Papawhatshisface. Not a fingerprint, I'm saying, either literal or ...that other thing, from English class—*figurative*. Nothing to bond him to the body. Not even a body, well—not for a while. Yeah, that's what he always called it, you know: "handling." "I *handled* so-and-so last night, and boy do I have blue balls now." And what did Konnie ever do? He fuckin' fawned over Griff. He brokered that midterm exam paper somehow, trading some toady for Dirty Jew tickets. He loved Griff, didn't he, in his half-retarded way? Shit, he could have been a *disciple*. How do you figure ...? Griff must have let him get under his skin somehow. Maybe that *poet*, Professor Yellow—maybe she wasn't the only "chink" in his armor after all. Ha!

No, that's impossible. He was too good. No, I was Griff's only "mistake," wasn't I? The only sloppy fuck-up. Is it un-cool that I'm vaguely proud of this? Totally proud. It's probably uncool. Look, nobody said I'm well-adjusted, either. After all, *I know.* I mean, he *told* my ass everything in that soggy orange tent on Kittattin Hill. Why do they call it a "hill?" And *I told you* this shit, too. Why do you pretend you never heard this? You fucking remember. It all started with that teacher. Holy shit on a toasted bagel, he was only 10 years old at the time. Can you imagine? I mean, how does a *child* manage the fuckin' logistics? Where does he get the *strength*? The mental / spiritual stuff, I understand. But the sheer strength. You know what it takes to break a human bone? Well—look who we're talking about. Hey, you want some of this? It ain't bad for the money.

Yeah. Then there was that toddler in Beacon, you know. Taken apart. The teenager, I think two years older than us, where the whole idea was, like, to turn him inside-out, and he half-succeeded. You shoulda seen it. Shit, maybe even his own mother. But there'd be a kind of justice in that. Right? Remember he told us about that nozzle, and the smoke? Can you fucking *imagine*?

His eyes, man. Right? You remember he's got those eyes that, like, shine, that weird, metallic blue. Like airplane model paint blue. You called them "starry" when we were little. Remember that shit? *Ahhh*—you remember! You were smitten. Admit it. I could see them reflecting the fire. That night in Mountain Dale. I didn't believe him at first, because of those eyes. And because I didn't want it to be true, I'm such a pussy. No, I'm just *normal*. Am I? Anyway, anything's normal contrasted to the way *you've* ... Why are you such a twat to me lately? Huh, Jelly?

I'm sorry. You know I don't mean it. Look. Look at this one.

I thought that might get your attention. I'm sorry. I know we said "no secrets," but who are *you* kidding? Anyway, this one's obviously different. There was all that fucked-up shit when we were little, but this one's ... It was in the Greyhound station in Monticello after one of our trips. Yeah. Some random kid who was waiting for his stepmother. Not random. That's the thing. Griff could spot 'em, like, a mile off. You remember we followed that kid once at the 4H fair, the kid from the bunny thing? And Griff freaked him out in the goat barn? We were seven, maybe eight. You remember he shit himself, that kid? Remember the smell? Shat himself?

So Griff tells the kid that same joke:

A bear and a rabbit are both taking a shit in the forest. The bear says to the rabbit, "Hey, does the shit stick to your fur?" The rabbit says, "Yeah." So the bear wipes his ass with the rabbit!

Then ... then what? Then he rubs the kid's neck and sweet-talks him. You know? Like a horse or whatever. He calls him "pretty," which makes the kid screw up his face. He tells me to block the door with one of those "Wet Floor / *Piso Mojado*" signs, and plug the big janitor's thing into the socket. He calls it "an experiment in suction." His hypothesis turns out to be *correct-a-mundo*. He was always a smart guy, Griff. That's one of the scary things.

I'm sorry. It's not *our* fault, you know? Hey, I *love* that crinkle in your nose. You never do that anymore. You never put lip gloss on anymore.

It's about Scotty and Duke, isn't it? You think it was totally uncool I let him blow me all those times? Jelly? We *discussed* this. Don't pretend. Lookit, I'm not supposed to be OK with two High School baseball star *brothers* – from Cali – who want to suck me off and worship everything that comes out of me for a long weekend? You think it makes me "that way" or whatever? You fucking *know* it doesn't. If anyone's a certain way, Jelly ... Well, I'm just saying take a look at yourself in the mirror if you think that where we, whatever, shove our parts, *makes* us one thing or another. I'm just saying you can *overcome* shit. Jelly? Hello?! Are you in there? Did they not snap you out of this shit at Sculton? They didn't.

I've been thinking, ever since that institute or institution, whatever it's called, you can't be crazy, because you asked me, didn't you, you asked me straight-up the other day, when you were out there wandering by the pond, "Am I crazy?" Which you *can't* ask if you're full-on crazy, right? That's what they say. What does Mahler say?

There are some legitimate questions left. For example, it's hard to get a grip on why I'm still above the ground. You know? I mean, I know it's not because I'm clever or particularly precious or whatever. What makes me a bona fide person instead of an amoeba in Griff's system of *whatyacallit*—taxonomic classification? It's gotta be my excellent cock. Right? Everyone says so. *You* say so. You used to. All the time. It got fucking boring already. Not that it does me any good with you. It's like Fort Knox down there. It should be Fort *Dix*! You get it? Jelly?

Fine.

It does make me wonder, though. He only kills the ones he loves? Sounds so stupid. He spares us 'cause he thinks we're somehow pure and innocent? You and I have both had our ankles in the air too many times for "good" to have saved us. I sit in the den when it's late and your dad's asleep and you're baking those chocolate chip cookies with the Oreos inside—*Inception* cookies. Or I go outside when your mom is blathering on with you about the surgery. And when you take that shot up the nose and it knocks you out, I go on the porch and I wonder: Exactly what about Calvin McAutrey makes him so … *unworthy* of the goddamn graves Griff digs?

And where do *you* get off? Do you even know what "amoral" means? Did you learn that word from some Yoda-gook at the nail salon? Was it printed on that hanger they used at that fucking clinic? *Amoral.* Like your father making us fix that fence with him all night after that Lightning kid died on Shelter Rock, then telling the cops it was fixed all along and the little hellion must have jumped it? *Mrs. Lightning, little Diablo is dead and bloated—and fucking* stupid *to boot.*

All right. I'm sorry. You know how I feel. Jelly? Please. *Pleeease* go down on me. It'll take two seconds. You have no idea. You'll be back doing whatever you do. Wherever you go inside that head. You want me humiliated and hard? You got it.

Fine.

So you're saying I'm supposed to call this old Dumbledore at Vaughn College, out of the blue, and warn him some kid called Griffin Bond's about to swoop into his life and—what? They'd have me committed for sure.

Oh—sorry.

Shit. Do you remember how he liked to balance shit on his head? That was some weird-ass shit. That Patti the Platypus Beanie Baby, with its yellow *whatyacallit* flippers on Griff's forehead while he napped. Or just sitting watching *Ghostwriter* and that one girl with the titties you could see through her shirt, and you look over and Griff's got the remote on the top of his head, smiling like some blissful idiot who just ate a pound of Peeps. The calculator, too. When he did his homework, remember that? You'd see him, like, intently staring at the problem on the page, his tongue out, Old School, and this ridiculous old calculator an *accountant* would use – a fucking *adding machine* – perched perfectly on his head, and him still as stone so it wouldn't slip off. It was the only time he didn't rock his ankles. You gotta wonder where *that* shit came from. You wonder if we're gonna be OK, you know, when we get older.

There's no way.

Look at this one. *Loook.* See? That's a first edition "surrealist" poetry book on her forehead. That's the slanty-eyed cooze professor he was sweet on over there. And her face is all *smeared with semen*, speaking of surreal, but that book's all perfectly balanced, right, and *open to a certain page*, all portentous-like. That's how you know it's him.

Here, gimme back the Polaroid. I never read the guy. The book, I mean. Tarzan? Something like that. Hold on. He put the quote on the back of the picture. But I don't get it:

Agates ... spots ... worms ... equilibrium ... barriers ... interdictions provoked by movement itself ...

Whatever the fuck. Seems like it needs more commas. Maybe that would help. You know it's hard to get Polaroid film anymore, at least around here? Did he order it online? Did he have a bunch of it stored up and shit? That alone is fucked up. Do you know how many of those pictures he's sent me? Yeah. That's what's in that thing over there. Oh, yeah. And in every one, he's got something balanced on their fuckin' head. Deeply, deeply fucked.

There was a crumpled packet of Virginia Slims on his mother's head, I swear to God – No, *Kent 100s!* – but her top half had slid off the couch, and all this shit spilled off the coffee table onto her, so it might have happened accidentally. On Konnie, it was deliberate, though. A jar Griff must have taken from some science lab or wherever at the school over there. It looks like it's got a pig brain in it. Or maybe it's human, I don't know. They've got all kinds of crap at those labs. Can you imagine, though? Do you think he shows it to them first – the thing he balances on their head – before he ... you know? Do you remember that pigeon? Dove? I can't tell where the picture was taken, but it looks like maybe a train tunnel, I think, or underneath some kind of flyover. Konnie's naked. Not too shabby, either. His mother's gonna think all kinds of terrible things about him if they ever ...

I was thinking about the three of us playing pirates in the bat cave behind your house. Shelter Rock. We had so much fun together, didn't we? It was fun. Using the loft we built in there as a shuttle cockpit? You on the railroad tracks and we wouldn't let you up until the train was bearing down so close the wind of it blew back your hair? Didn't we discover, like, *everything important* about ourselves in those days? Does that sound ... whatever? Didn't we truly, like, *love* each other, and wasn't it completely, I don't know ...? Remember that dachshund we found in the woods? That was awful.

When you're folding laundry, Jell, when you go into those weird trances you do ... I worry about you. Really, Baby. You are so not OK. I wonder, what would Griffin Bond balance on *my* head once I was dead and he was through with me? Probably my cock.

    V.   *Dr. William W. Rensselaer*

His old friend August objected to "asshole" as an appellation of insult. "It's unlikely you've loosened up enough to consider this, Chum, but an asshole can be quite a lovely thing," he said to Bill, "depending upon the possessor." Then he raised his cane just perceptibly in the direction of the bench beside the statue of the College founder, Raleigh Vaughn, whereon sat a specimen of youthful indignity in a Dirty Jew concert jersey, baseball hat backwards – "forward boys in backward caps" – baggy shorts, and one leg up so he could tie his sneaker. In the hollow thus formed, one so inclined could mine a lifetime.

"Oh, August. And all without Viagra at a hundred-and-two. What would that long-suffering wife of yours say?"

"Imprimis, I have two decades till I get to a hundred and two. And Hilde, I imagine, would giggle girlishly, and open a package of MoonPies, and pour a glass of milk for me, full fat."

"That's sad, really. But I would kill for a wife so secure in herself."

"But I have."

"So you've intimated over the years. Anyway, look, I'm sticking to it. *Asshole.* I grant his kid just disappeared on my watch. You're on edge the whole time you're over there, you know. You remember from back in the day. It doesn't matter that they're seniors. You constantly fear you'll have to make that call to the parents. *Your daughter got trampled by a polo horse. A cab on Bond Street cleaved your son in twain.* Whatever you'd have to intone for such an occasion."

"I remember."

"Yeah, but this time, I actually had to make the call. They're immigrants right off the boat from Athens, and I have to tell them that I literally *lost their son* in London in the year 2000. And Papa really rubs it in, I can assure you. Tells me I'm not 'fit' to supervise his child. You know, I wanted to say, this is not easy on me, either, Bub."

"Pity the poor director of the SELP. But it's difficult to imagine a parent not reacting just that way, Old Bill."

"Indeed. But, here's the rub. Later, it turns out – and I'm not saying I'm glad to be able to laud this horror show over the father – his kid went on the lam because (get this) it looks like he raped and straight-up murdered one of our teachers."

"No."

"Yes."

"Whom? Not Dickler? For God's sake, his son was—"

"No, no. A new one. A poetess. Asian. Beautiful. Kid's DNA was strewn all over the place. All over her face. Smeared."

"Good gravy, Bill."

"Nice. The paperwork. The husband."

"I believe his flatmate sent me a missive, you know."

"Funny. Griffin Bond?"

"The same. A bright prospect."

"I couldn't agree with you more. But, you know. I had to send that prospect packing."

"I gathered something along those lines. But the little something-or-other didn't say. Nothing to do with that awful business, I assume."

"Oh, no. Just some quotidian plagiarism."

"The devil, you say. He didn't seem the sort."

"They're all the sort. But what the hell does Griffin Bond want with you? I'll put an end to this, August."

"The hell you will, Old Bill. Frankly, I'm quite flattered."

"I bet."

"He even read one of my books."

"That's intriguing. He reads like he's famished and novels are Twinkies. Which one?"

"See, that's where it gets interesting. The first one. From back during the Punic Wars."

"But that's been out of print since Eisenhower, no?"

"Or thereabouts."

"He wants into Vaughn? Let me just say I won't be able to recommend him."

"He recommends himself."

To which Old Bill harrumphed. "I suppose all the ones who aren't homicidal maniacs tend to get the nod these days."

"Well, those with parents who can pay."

"Pip-pip."

"You said 'beautiful.'"

"Hmm?"

"The exquisite corpse. She of the besmirched visage?"

Two Spirits

"Oh. Undeniably. I identified the body and all. *Mister* Walker – a CIA chef – was fit for Sculton Asylum, and could not perform the obligation."

"So I see your loins are still in working order, too, despite your heinous wife's efforts at dampening all arousal on the oblate spheroid."

"Judith Tachibana-Walker. Yes. That woman was ... Well, it sounds beastly to say it, but she was one rather worth murdering, I reckon."

"I know just what you mean."

VI.   Mitchell Allen Gorevich

Master Race. Animal Grace. "Nose Without a Face."
By Marilucia Mago for *Newsworld Sunday*

The afternoon I met ALLEN GOREVICH at a garden party behind Gracie Mansion, he was joking over Arnold Palmers with the mayor and some celebrities: "The biggest hip-hop artist of the decade is a stone-cold Hebrew," he said, "but his agent, manager, and producer are blacker than eggplants."

The mayor laughed at the irony. It's OK to laugh, or Gorevich wouldn't have written lines like this one, from his song, "The Merchant of Venom:"

My matzo balls
tempt all the girls
and I unfurl
like Milton Berle ...

Laughing is the whole idea—or half the idea, at least.

The music business has come a long way since our parents jived to Little Stevie Wonder, the mayor said, shaking his head.

Sure, said Robert De Niro, lanky temptresses on his arm. "But some things always stay the same."

Bob's right. Firstly, the on- and-off stage antics of Gorevich's rap persona, "Dirty Jew," garnered the same kind of controversy as Elvis's hip-sway in the '50s and Iggy Pop's full-frontals two decades later.

Here's the formula:

Start with the same kind of hyperbolic sexual swagger that defined rock and roll, punk, and hip-hop, albeit with a decidedly Judaic twist:

My cut c*ck
hard as a rock
cut through the schlock
with awe and shock ...

Pepper with some whip-smart allusions à la Eminem, again, certified for *Pesach*:

Beat you with my kosher pickle
insult your ass like Donnie Rickles ...

In the chorus, ensure the rhymes are novel, tight, and evocative, like Snoop Dogg's (if he wore a *yarmulke*):

I ain't posin'
I am chosen
End the Third Reich
with my kike spike ...

And for the turn, when you can get away with it, spoon on some Public Enemy-esque social consciousness:

Night raids and lampshades
Burning tires

Nazi fires
Blazing blue irises ...

Which is where the other half of Gorevich's idea came to fruition—the half that's obviously all about stirring Jews and Gentiles out of complacency. In his anthem, "Too Soon?" he meditates on the defining moment in modern Jewish history, just as black rappers have plumbed the depths of slavery to get a grip on the *zeitgeist*:

Chowing at Boa
Shadow of Shoah,
Do we think it's over?
Marry their daughters?
No, that's when they prep the Zyklon B—
That's when the drums beat to quarters, see ...

A greater lightning rod I've never seen installed in my City on the Plain. To call Allen Gorevich "controversial" would be like calling the Easter Bunny furry. His debut album, *Nose Without a Face*, was banned or censored in 13 countries. It's true, by the way, that for the album cover and TV interviews, Gorevich's makeup artists were charged with accentuating his "Hebraic Nasal Appurtenance." He told me so himself, after a few of the aforementioned cocktails.

Gorevich was born on April 20, 1969—Hitler's birthday. His mother, Harriet Gorevich, was a librarian in Monsey, New York. His father, Alan Glass, a lay *yeshiva* teacher in the Slope neighborhood farther northwest, populated by an uneasy mélange of blacks, Jews, and Kittakwa Native Americans, whose large reservation abuts Kittatinn County. Alan Glass was killed in a presumed anti-Semitic attack in 1993, the body mutilated. The school, *Yeshiva Degel Hatorah*, had 13 years before lost a teacher and staff member to suicide. It closed down. The murder remains unsolved, but police say they believe the elder Gorevich was the victim of a serial killer. The killer apparently left a "calling card," but the cops won't say what it was, fearing it might inspire copycats.

Glass's father had long ago Americanized the family name, and Gorevich reverted back to the original to call attention to his Eastern European ancestry.

Young Allen attended Brooklyn Tech, followed by Columbia Teachers College. He excelled in math, and wrote his thesis on a mathematical puzzle known as Zeno's Paradox. He maintained a lifelong fascination with a mathematical equation called a Taylor series, which my editor, Nancy Kint, a very smart lady, assures me looks like this:

$$e^x = 1 + \frac{x}{1!} + \frac{x^2}{2!} + \frac{x^3}{3!} + \cdots, \quad -\infty < x < \infty$$

It turns out, and I am not making this up, Gorevich infused many of his songs with musical equivalents of (or, as he preferred it, "homages to") the Taylor series. Apparently, math teachers everywhere play his music in their classes to demonstrate "a representation of a function as an infinite sum of terms calculated from the values of its derivatives at a single point."

Perhaps this is a far cry from the musical bacon-and-marshmallow sandwiches of an Elvis Presley, or the spit-and semen-soaked pandemonium of a Johnny Rotten. I'm not even capable of pretending to understand complex mathematical equations, no less articulating to you what this egghead stuff is all about—what it means and why this particular musician was so obsessed with this specific formulation.

My sister's husband, Brian Rammel, who's a math mastermind at Wake Forest, tells me that if you (somehow) "graph" the dueling synth melody lines of the Dirty Jew song, "Tay-Sachs Day Parade," it looks like this:

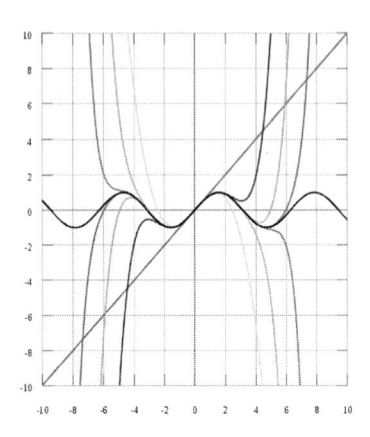

... Which is, apparently, "awesome" and even, on some level, "eerily impossible" to express musically, according to math geek bloggers. It's all Greek to me, but were I still in some Freshman intro to Calcunometry course, I would certainly prefer to study such a concept – and work off the weekend's buzz – by listening to the *New Yid on the Block* CD, than, say, whipping out my slide rule, and listening to some old greybeard blather on.

"It's very simple," says Gorevich's sister, Maddie Glass, of Yonkers: "Our father was a teacher who loved math, and Allen loved our father, tough as he was, and math. It's no surprise he would explore this love within his songs in the complex, pure, and lyrical language of numbers."

And speaking of love and mathematical equations ...

In 1996, Gorevich married MARIS GRACE, who performs under the moniker, "Animal Grace." Maris is the daughter of famed hip-hop producer, CASEY GRACE. Her father introduced them after meeting Gorevich at a private concert on the Caribbean island of

Mustique, where the rapper bought some 600 acres in 1991. The couple had three children: Plato, 3; Dana, 2; and Groucho, 1.

Mitchell Allen Gorevich was 31 years old. He was my friend, and he was a genius.

RELATED
Controversial Rapper 'Dirty Jew' Found Dead; Presumed Killed
Police Explore Links in Rapper's, Father's Violent Deaths
Listen to Dirty Jew's Last Interview with *Newsworld*

VII. *Jamilla Eccleson*

June 1, 2000. 3:30 p.m. I'm not used to writing in longhand, and I'm concerned that my parents' lawyer hasn't called me yet. But seeing as how I have nothing to fear or hide – and subject to thorough review by said attorney – THIS IS MY OFFICIAL STATEMENT, AND I HEREBY WARRANT THAT MY RIGHTS HAVE NOT BEEN IMPEDED BY THE OFFICERS OR DETECTIVES WHO QUESTIONED ME.

First and foremost, I HAD NOTHING TO DO WITH THE DEATH OCASIONED BY THE VISIT OF THE KID, ~~GRYPHON~~ GRIFFIN BOND TO THE OFFICE OF MY ~~EMPLOYER~~ BOSS, AUGUST RICHTER.

The Blood
The blood on my clothes you found in Professor Richter's office is NOT THE KID'S BLOOD. It's not MY blood, either. It belongs to Professor Richter—BUT NOT FROM TODAY. What had happened was: He was incontinent once. It was "Number Two." This was about two years ago. Sometime early in the Fall semester. ~~It was a bloody mess~~. It was soon after the second or third colon surgery. Mrs. Richter (Hildegard) hadn't wanted him to go back to work so early. He made me pick him up early, and I could tell he was moving slower than usual, and squirming in the car seat. We'd been pretty "intimate" before, yes, but what I meant when I said

that was intimate CONVERSATIONALLY, and to some extent, emotionally. But physically, there was always a distance. From both sides, but mostly from his. ~~It's not just that he came from a generation of "non-huggers." And~~ I don't think it was because of whatever he went through during the War, which he had shared a few times, but not in any detail. He was just "decorous" (Mrs. Richter's word).

He always wore one of his four suits, and always wore a tie, even to the doctor when I took him. He was a perfect gentleman. So it was very uncomfortable that day when I had to help clean him up. He'd been on the stepstool he climbed to knock books off the high shelves with his cane. So there was "issue" everywhere. On the floor, the stepstool, and all over his pants, socks, and shoes.

I took him into the little bathroom down in what we call the "Salt Mines," our suite in the Yaffe Hall basement. I cleaned him up. ~~I could tell he was humiliated.~~ I changed into my gym stuff from my locker, and left him alone in the bathroom to put on MY extra sweats, which had a LITTLE of his blood on them, but were nowhere near as bad as his clothes. I stuffed his messed clothes in a bag, and brought it to the Dumpster behind the boilers.

~~My stuff, though, I put in a separate Heft bag and left with Mrs. Richter to I didn't want to throw them out I was worried, especially because of where the blood the circumstances that brought the blood.~~ It wasn't just blood. You could take it to a lab. You probably will.

I called Professor Richter's doctor, who told me not to worry, that he had probably just burst a clot. I drove him home. ~~Mrs. Richter must not have cleaned my jeans very well.~~ I DON'T UNDERSTAND what the jeans were doing BACK at the office. I assumed they'd thrown them out ages ago. ~~I never got them back—clean or other~~

~~I thought I'd seen a lot of blood that day. That was nothing.~~

The CDs

Two Spirits

Yes, the rap CDs in the silver Hyundai Excel (Plate No. ENP 347) belong to ME. ~~Freedom of Speech much?~~ What do those albums have to do with anything, anyway? Violence? ~~I don't even know where to begin in debunking the myth that the music I listen to for FUN could somehow make me an accomplice to murder.~~ Please check the Internet to find that since his killing, two of Dirty Jew's albums are in the Top 10. That means MILLIONS of people have his music in their car. ~~He's won multiple Grammy awards.~~ And if you're thinking about anti-Semitism, you have to understand that the name of the artist is meant to be IRONIC, like "Niggaz With Attitude," etc. ~~I think I'm supposed to just answer the question, and not "volunteer" anything extra.~~

The Kid
I review all of Dr. Richter's incoming e-mails before he gets them, but I think the kid had corresponded via snail mail. I'd never met him before this morning. I'd never heard of him. We had no contact, and no relationship. ~~Unequivocally.~~

In the morning, I found a Post-It note from Dr. Richter informing me that a prospective student – I think he told me a "Drummond student," but that didn't mean anything special to me, because we get a lot of those – was coming to visit. He wanted me to avoid making any appointments for the rest of the day. If the janitor hasn't come yet, you can find that note in the recycle bin below my desk. For the record, I make approximately one appointment for him every six or seven days only. I'm sorry this is out-of-order. This is why I prefer computers. Couldn't you install one? This would allow ~~confessors~~ witnesses to edit their ~~confessions~~ accounts for maximum clarity, especially as it relates to timelines, etc. And you could save, sort, and file all your statements better. ~~Off topic.~~

~~Sorry.~~ I met the kid, offered him a Coke. ~~He had very blue eyes.~~ He didn't want the Coke, and asked for coffee instead. ~~You'd think that's weird—a very adult affectation. But lots of kids.~~ I introduced

Two Spirits 289

him to Dr. Richter, and went to the machine for the kid's coffee. This was about 10:15 a.m.

I talked briefly with Mrs. Balflour ("Dee"), and I got back to the ~~Salt Mines~~ suite at about 10:18. The door to the inner office was closed. I knocked. It looked to me like Dr. Richter was annoyed that I was interrupting them. ~~I can't explain, but I just know him very well. They were whispering, almost conspiratorially.~~ I gave the kid and Dr. Richter each a cup of coffee, I left, and shut the door. I could be mistaken, but I thought I heard the kid say, "Nice," and I got the impression he was talking about me. ~~I know this sounds weird, but the tone was distinctly lascivious and gave me a chill like it was a line from a Stephen Kin.~~ I didn't hear Dr. Richter's reply.

For about an hour, until approximately 11:20 or 11:30, I worked on my dissertation. This will be RELEVANT later: My dissertation focuses on the poetry, prose, epistles, and "ephemera" occasioned by the Mogen Dovid Saber, a little-known but seminal armed resistance at Bergen-Belsen in May 1943, in which Jews killed three senior SS officers. (I know it was 11:20 because the Salt Mines are right next to the boiler room, and the big Yaffe boiler kicks in at 11:20 every morning in the Spring and Summer.) ~~You can confirm with the~~

The Noise

I heard a ~~weird~~ sound a little after 11:30. Dr. Richter had fallen off the stool once and fractured a rib. I heard it – ~~a soft "oof!"~~ – and this sounded like that again. I rushed over, but couldn't open the door. The handle turned, but something heavy was blocking the door~~, which was highly unusual~~. I called his name. The sound got louder. It sounded like kids whipping towels in the locker room ~~or like when fish flip around at the fish ma~~. I was worried Dr. R. had fallen against the door, so I called the kid – I was panicky and couldn't remember his name – but HE didn't answer, either. There was something about the sound. ~~It was very disconcerting.~~

~~My sister suffers from a mental illness. She's up at Sculton. Anyway, in one of her bad breaks when she was younger, she beat our Great Pyrenees with an iron table lamp. I think at some point, I recognized that the sound coming from Dr. Richter's office was A LOT like that sound.~~

I thought about running up the stairs to Dee's. I don't know how much time passed. ~~I don't think a lot.~~ Not a lot, I don't think. I thought about trying to clear out the book-storage closet between the outer office where I sat, and Dr. R's office—there's a door in there, but I'd never used it, and I had no idea whether it was locked. I always assumed it was locked.

I called Public Safety. They can tell you what time. I told them I thought a student was attacking Dr. Richter. I told them to send one of the officers – one of the guys recently "deputized" I think you call it – by you guys, I assume – to carry guns. ~~They can tell you exactly what time I called.~~

I kept trying my best to shove open the door, but I couldn't. Eventually, the sound stopped. And then I heard ~~someone playing~~ that Dirty Jew song playing somewhere from inside.

The Security Response
When the campus police came, they couldn't open the door, either. Remember, I was OUTSIDE the inner office door when they arrived. ~~I couldn't have~~ They shouted, and they dialed Dr. R's number. They called you at the same time, I think. We decided together we would get some tool from the boiler room and bash open the door. One of the guys went down there and came back with a ~~sledge-hammer-kind of thing~~ large implement. They busted down the top of the door and climbed over the old credenza that someone – it COULDN'T have been R., so that leaves the kid – had shoved up against the door.

The music was still playing. Loud.

That's when I saw HIS FACE through that hole as they climbed in and ordered him to get on the floor. ~~I'll never forget it.~~ His nose and his cheek were spattered with blood and I couldn't figure out

Two Spirits

what else – ~~I thought it was cottage cheese at first – Dr. R. ate cottage cheese for lunch sometimes, from little cups that Mrs. R. packed for him with little ice packs~~ – but now I know it was brain matter. But his breathing was so calm. They kept shouting at him. He didn't drop to the ground. ~~It was like looking at Hannibal Lecter in *The Silence of the*.~~ I could see there was blood up in arcs across the ceiling and on the bookcase~~, as though someone had swung~~. They were screaming, "Put it down, put the weapon DOWN!"

I said, "IT'S NOT A *WEAPON*. That's the professor's CANE!" ~~But was it a weapo? Now I~~ I couldn't see the body at that point, but I heard one of the security guys say, "Oh, God," when he came upon it. "Oh, God," the next one said, too.

The "Journals"
R. had asked me NOT to organize the files in that storage closet. He said they were "personal," and you know they actually say "Personal and Confidential" right on the boxes. So I NEVER SAW any of those diaries ~~you read to me from~~ from which you read ~~those random~~

All he told me was that he didn't take any crap during the War. ~~I HAD NO IDEA HE~~ I don't believe what you told me. ~~There's a~~ There used to be a picture of Dr. R and Felix Wolf together on the credenza. Also, he wrote a semiautobiographical novel about that kid (out of print now, but they're about to bring it back for its anniversary). ~~Them together.~~ I always assumed – from the way R. reminisced – that FW was killed by the Nazis. Dr. R's NEVER talked about it. ~~Not specifically.~~ Shoveling some crap they were mining into his best friend's mouth? ~~Watching him die in some hidey-hole in the mines?~~ I don't get it. Why?

And as for the "SPREE," that sounds even more ridiculous to me. He's an old man. He was just a kid back then. A wholesale slaughter of the Gentiles in the mines? ~~A scraggly teenage Je Up till then, they're all comrades, then all of a sudden, like some "sleeper," he goes all apey-Jew on them?~~ YOU DON'T KNOW

292   Two Spirits

THIS MAN! I have to make sure he gets his nitroglycerine pills ~~if~~ when he complains of angina. ~~His wife's going~~
   ~~Plus, I'm sitting out there for three years, and I'm in all his classes, and he knows exactly what I'm writing my thesis about, and he just FORGETS TO TELL ME HE'S A NAZI-KILLER from way back?~~
   BUT, ~~yes,~~ NO, I don't get what happened today. ~~I understand there's a dead, that Dr. R somehow~~ There must have been some reason, is what I'm saying. I don't know. But this is so FAR-FETCHED.
   [WITNESS ALLOWED TO SPEAK WITH HER ATTORNEY 7:11 p.m. —HDP]
   [WITNESS ALLOWED TO RESUME HER STATEMENT 8:59 p.m. —HDP]

The Diatomaceous (sp?) Earth
On the counsel of my attorney, I am not prepared to comment on this subject at this time. I will say that the KID had a BACKPACK on – I'm sure you "recovered" said backpack – so I didn't see whatever "sack" you told me about. I have no way of knowing what the kid was planning to do with a little bag of pool chemicals. ~~If he was the one who If the bag didn't come fr~~

The "Homosexuality"
It wasn't the same back then—especially in that era in Germany. ~~"Homosexuality" is a clinical state, which we can presume existed among humans in every period of history, not to mention in every animal species studi. They say that penguins and~~
   ~~But "gayness" is a modern social con~~
   If you do a close reading of the novels, and if you just hang around him long enough, you just know. He never made a pass at ~~any boy student, any colleague~~ anyone to my knowledge. Of course not. Like I said—"decorum." ~~I don't want Mrs. R. to find out about any of this. That's moot at this point, I'm sure.~~ The other guy you mentioned, whose name I don't remember, but I think

Two Spirits   293

it's the same name as one of the Teenage Mutant Ninja Turtles, was a friend from college in Germany. I don't know if that's the right word, "friend." They were SUPPOSEDLY caught in a freak storm on Mt. Kenya or someplace like that. Africa. A bunch of people died. ~~Kilimanjaro?~~ The guy wouldn't have to be MURDERED to die there. You could look this up. The mine thing and the mountain thing: ACCIDENTS. ~~After 82 years, it would be statistically improbable for~~ ~~We had our mine accident here, outside Arc~~

~~I'm serious about the g.d. computer—my hand is killing me. You could search for key words if you had an e-copy of all the statements.~~

For your thesis to work, you're assuming he's spent 80-odd years targeting non-Jews and gaining their trust, then savagely killing them. Why? He wasn't remotely Orthodox. He didn't eat kosher. He worked on Saturdays. ~~And as for the kid it doesn't matter he was supposedly~~ You do know there's a major difference between "homosexual" and "homicidal." ~~It's all too pat. That he would … But with his cane, no less?~~ ~~I'm telling you, the only thing that makes sense is that I have to beli~~ I have no idea why.

THIS IS THE END OF MY STATEMENT.

—Jamilla Q. Eccleson, PhD (ABD)

VIII.   Angelica Greene, 28

January 8, 5 p.m. Session 7. Sculton, NY. DID patient, "Jelly," continues to describe acute dissociative symptoms, *i.e.*, long "blackouts," inability to recall important life events and data, unexplained bodily trauma, severe headaches (Imitrex, Topamax, Tramadol), and a vague awareness that she "sometimes goes outside her body." Tried hypnosis to address (in her terms) her "pathological fear" of sex with her boyfriend, Calvin, her "childhood sweetheart," now a train conductor absent for long periods, whom she suspects of near constant and serial cheating.

Hypnosis brought on a bad headache and disorientation. Suddenly, pt began speaking with a German accent, sounding distinctly younger than her 28 years.

The host personality was born and raised in rural New York (Kit Rez), the daughter of lower-class Unitarians. But questioning revealed that the alter that emerged for 30 minutes was "Greta," an Anne Frank-like figure who told me she escaped from an Austrian concentration camp, circa 1942. I engaged with this main alter, whose whole mien became waiflike, scrappy, and apprehensive. She shared disturbing details of her life in the camps, including rape and other sexual depravity at the hands of "sadistic" guards. She described being put in a "hole," which was dark and cold. She particularly feared the camp doctor, a person named "Link" who "forced [her] to do bad things" in the hole. At one point, I thought Dr. Link was emerging, too, as another alter. But it turned out that Greta was just quoting him – practically channeling him, his words seemed so ingrained in her consciousness/subconscious: "Farther!" "Eat it!" "Leave that off!" etc.

She said that she had run away from Dr. Link, and took with her a little brother, whose name she didn't specify. She believed her brother to be in grave and imminent danger from Dr. Link, whom she insisted was pursuing her still, though she conceded, "The war is over."

The whole time Greta manifested, the pt covered her head, first with her arm, then with her whole shirt pulled up from the back, and finally with a tube of lipstick with which the host, Jelly, had earlier been fiddling. I have not seen this behavior in any pt before, but I once heard Dev Mahler say it was a thing she'd seen. Must ask for more details.

When Jelly reemerged, she thought she'd blacked out from migraine. The lipstick fell from her head into her lap, and she looked at me, half-laughing, as though I had played some trick on her.

I told her that I didn't agree with her prior diagnosis of BPD – she's not borderline – and she seemed relieved. I told her I thought I could help with the headaches, but it might take a while. I asked her whether she'd ever heard of DID, and she at first feigned not understanding. I asked her whether she knew what "disturbance of identity" means, and she said no, but seemed to dissemble, squirming and stopping eye-contact. When I asked her about "multiple personalities," she responded energetically, and said she'd seen several recent movies, three of which she named.

I explained that the DSM-IV locates the root cause of a number of serious mental conditions – I didn't mention DID *per se* again – in serious childhood trauma, often sexual, during the impressionable formation of "self." She responded, "bat cave," while incongruously shaking her head, but would not elaborate when I encouraged her. When I asked her later about the bat cave, she smiled and asked me how I knew that's where she used to play as a girl with Calvin. "Shelter Rock," she called it then. That's a well-known but not well understood geological feature on the Kit Rez, the ownership of which has been contested for a few hundred years. Some other pts of Kit extraction have expressed beliefs about the boulder's various supernatural properties.

I asked Jelly whether she'd be willing to do some homework, to which she excitedly consented. I suggested she read the Charlotte Perkins Gilman short story, "The Yellow Wallpaper," and keep a journal of her initial responses. She said she had a gift for me, too, because the music in my waiting room was "depressing" (Cher? Neil Diamond? Depressing?) and because I had said something last session about celebrating Hanukkah. She gave me an MP3 of songs by Dirty Jew. I told her it's not customary to accept gifts from pts, but I would give it a listen, then return it next session. It might offer a window into some shuttered room.

January 9 [update] Consulted Dr. D. Mahler, Dir. (Ret.) who insists I'm not necessarily out of my league. Treatment strategy is cooperation and alliance-formation of alters, with the ultimate goal of unifying them into one whole based on primary personality. Mahler reminded me that alters don't typically "age" relative to the time of their genesis, and are generally unaware of the progression of time on the plane of the host. "Greta," who is 11, lives in constant terror for her person and for her "brother," with no conception that whatever abuse she suffered occurred 20 years ago. It's critical to bring Greta into the present. M suggested I videotape next session with Jelly, who seems unaware she has alters—though Greta is aware of Jelly, and another personality I don't dare yet summon again, apparently an older male named "Sammy" – also Jewish? – whom Greta is worried about because "he's planning on hurting himself again." Why all these Jews, and what connection to the Jewish rapper whose music she shared with me?

Summary. The advent of a suicidal alter obviously raises the stakes. Also, I'm struck by the congruence of the "cave" in which Jelly played as a child *with* her boyfriend, Calvin, and the "hole" into which "the Nazis" put her. If there was abuse in this cave, could Calvin have been a victim, too? And who is the enigmatic Dr. Link?

Personal diary [Darla, do not transcribe]. I went home after sessions yesterday, and ate my usual pint of Cherry Garcia, and watched a satisfyingly formulaic episode of *House* with Pesky on my lap. I might or might not have napped, but I suddenly became aware that the CD my patient Jelly had given me, which I had been absentmindedly worrying in my hands for a while, intending to pop into the player, was now poised on the top of my head! I was surprised to find it there, shocked I had no recollection of placing it there, and dumbstruck that somehow I had unconsciously mirrored Greta's coping mechanism. As soon as I became aware of it, it slipped off my head, and I caught it in my hands: A good-looking youngish man with a prominent nose. He's the one who was killed some years back. A heinous attack, I recall. I asked Lisa whether she remembered anything about that case—it happened near here. She never talks about her cases. This was before she made Detective, but she was on the scene (Amazing, that woman. Did she just come home that night, wash off the gore, and make me a chicken pot pie?). She said that the killer had placed something *on the rapper's head!* She can't remember what it was, but she recalls the cops assuming it was meant to be read as a distinctly anti-Semitic message. So what was it? A macaroon? A knish? I Googled it—but nothing came up. Do my assumptions make ME an anti-Semite? Foreskin?

So strange. After I drove home last night, I realized I had been thinking loosely about what comfort that "balancing" behavior might have offered my disordered and unbalanced patient. Now I retroactively realized – now that the disk was conspicuously off my head – that the feeling of it up there, balanced, a tangible reminder that my skull still sat atop my spine, had indeed offered me some intoxicating sense of calm and steadiness that I had not experienced in some time. So much so that I was compelled to put the CD back on top of my cranium—and damned if I cared whether Lisa encountered me in such a posture. I sat for several minutes in my study clutching the disk, vaguely aware that mist was rising outside my windows, as it often does at night this time of year, finding this compulsion exceedingly difficult to resist.

—A turd-eating grin—

Friday Sept. 21st. Script. Recovered from Vic's backpack.

Santa Fe Police Dept. Case #8994033

[FLASHBACK]

INT. LIGHTNING HOUSE. (15 YEARS AGO)

SUPERIMPOSE: HORSEMINT: BACK PAIN, CHILLS

A dark back room, all the shades drawn. Gameshow playing on an antique TV in BG.

Young Meat Puppet warns about something with a series of low growls. She's pregnant. Her water breaks on the old linoleum, and she collapses there, spread-eagled. She keeps looking at something, O.S., whimpering, even as the first puppy slips out of her.

She's looking at—

PD's mother, APRIL LIGHTNING, 18. She's sweating, panting on the floor nearby, her bloody panties around her ankles, nails scrabbling the tile like a horror movie. She SHRIEKS. She's giving birth. She reaches for Meat Puppet, who struggles to slide herself closer.

[END FLASHBACK]

INT. KITTAKWA REZ. BIA SECURITY HUT - NIGHT (PRESENT DAY)

Max, way worse for wear, pats a bloody nose with a BIA sweatshirt, handcuffs dangling from the hand.

                        MAX
        That's why they — not I — call him
        "Puppy Dog." After his "other mam,"
        who you better fucking hope you
        don't find out there somewhere.
        She's a crusty old cunt, but she
        will tear a tomorrow into all your
        fuckin' yesterdays.

Two Spirits   299

He looks at the bloodstained jersey, tosses it on the floor. He holds one nostril and blows hard. Pink-tinged snot sprays the table.

                    MAX (CONT'D)
        My sorry-ass daughter, April, I was
        fixin' to take her to Kitskill Caritas
        myself, my grandson wasn't so goddamn
        eager to come.

                    GREYWELL (O.S.)
        What's a "Two-Spirit," Mister Light-
        ning?

                    MAX
        Well, now.

Sitting across from Max is a creepily neat-as-a-pin bureaucrat, a USG-certified dickhole in a flak-jacket over a pink Oxford shirt. He's HUNTER W. GREYWELL, "Hunt" to his friends, except he has no friends. He wears old-fashioned Nazi specks, which hang off one ear. Grey eyes, soulless. Looks like the kind of guy who as a kid pulled the legs off spiders just to watch them hobble. He consults a binder, purses his super-thin lips. Sniffs once and daintily wipes his nose on a herringbone hankie.

Two Underlings, anonymous SPOOKS in suits, flank the door. One chomps gum until Greywell ties the man's bowels in a knot with a look.

                    GREYWELL
        Let's get back to that. It's 2003.
        Thanksgiving. Lovely day for an Indian
        to be born. Or is it ironic? You were
        on a bender with a young Caucasian
        hoochie, mid-haul. Stolen toasters from
        Syracuse to Newburgh, is that about the
        size of it?

                    MAX
        Blenders. High-end. Her name was Pearl.
        No—<u>Amber</u>.

                    GREYWELL
        I promise that tomorrow, I will person-
        ally sever the glans of whatever simp
        intern faggot faultily recorded the
        wrong appliance in this report. I can
        promise you that.

He blots his nostril again with the hankie.

>   GREYWELL (CONT'D)
>   Tonight, I would ask you to just nod,
>   please, if I get it more than, say, 86
>   percent on the nose. Now: We were dis-
>   cussing Bon's paternity.
>
>   MAX
>   Oh, you'll appreciate this, G-Man Joe.
>   Her "suitor" was a lawman, some state
>   under-cunt with no hair yet on his
>   pecker and a net worth of—What?

He looks to the Underlings.

>   MAX (CONT'D)
> $16K? Sixteen-five?

Greywell smirks, genuinely impressed with this adversary.

>   GREYWELL
>   Whereas it was the fruits of a proud
>   criminality that had fed your three
>   girls—
>
>   MAX
>   Ungrateful wenches.
>
>   GREYWELL
>   ... that had fed your Lear-like triad
>   of ingratitude all those years since
>   their mother ... let's see ...

He flips.

>   GREYWELL (CONT'D)
>   ... Ah ... a secretary, was it? Yes.
>   For the tribal council. Part time medi-
>   cine woman. Oh, yes. Treated many a
>   man. She ... expired rather ... Oh, my.
>   When her Volkswagen bug, purple and
>   black, flipped over 11 times on the no-
>   torious Cutchin Mountain in dense fog—
>
>   MAX
>   13 times. They said. Car's still there.
>
>   GREYWELL
>   Noted. ... coming home from a "party"
>   after work. I take it she was the fa-
>   vor, as she was wont to be.
>
>   MAX
>   Probably.

Greywell uses the hankie to dig into his nose.

Two Spirits

                    GREYWELL
          Sorry. Must have caught a touch of
          something. Kit Revenge, perhaps?

                    MAX
          I don't follow.

                    GREYWELL
          The pox and whatnot. Syphilis. All that
          nasty business. Nothing personal.

                    MAX
          Yer good.

Greywell smirks, goes back to the binder.

                    GREYWELL
          Blah, blah, blah. Your teenaged ser-
          pent's tooth, April, finds herself with
          Indian bread in her oven. Hairless dep-
          uty, not wealthy. You kept her at home.

                    MAX
          That's right.

                    GREYWELL
          You disallowed her sisters — says here
          they were well trained by aforemen-
          tioned mother in matters medical —from
          attending the poor girl.

                    MAX
          Right.

                    GREYWELL
          You intended to take her to the hospi-
          tal your damn self.

                    MAX
          You BIA?

                    GREYWELL
          C.

                    MAX
          Ah. Then you can be excused for lexical
          lapses. See, in Kittakwa, which I
          learned at the end of a cattle prod
          from a feller could be your grandpappy,
          when I was a kid back in Old George's
          War - and which my daughters now barely
          comprehend - to "mean to" and to "in-
          tend" are synonymous with "to reach for

                    or stretch toward," just as they are in
                    English.

                                GREYWELL
                    Boned up on your cultural history all
                    those years at Monterey Shock?

                                MAX
                    On yer dime. Literally. Got certified
                    to teach the pups and all when their
                    ankles weren't up in the air. See, take
                    that .45 you got strapped to yer calf
                    all snug as a bug in a rug like some
                    pussy cowboy. Often, when you reach for
                    something, even when you stretch, you
                    still fall short.

                                GREYWELL
                    That could be the title of your autobi-
                    ography, Mister Lightning. Literally.

                                MAX
                    Sure. I getcha. Story of Max Light-
                    ning's shit-ass life on and off the
                    Rez. Until tonight.

Greywell leans back, thoroughly enjoying the entertainment.

                                GREYWELL
                    What happened tonight so different from
                    the aptly self-described "shit-ass"
                    script your Great Goat-in-the-Sky God
                    wrote for you?

                                MAX
                    Not what happened. What's gonna happen.

A turd-eating grin blooms over Greywell's puss.

                                GREYWELL
                    Enlighten me, Scout.

                                MAX
                    Well, now. Cowboy.

If it hadn't been for that smile, that particular sobriquet,
Greywell might yet have retained his right to head home this
evening. But he did. He said. He gone.

The tension in the room snaps from slack to tight like a wolf's
just popped up in a sheepfold with a chainsaw and raging hard-
on.

Two Spirits

                    MAX (CONT'D)
          Tonight, Mister C.I.A-hole. Well, to-
          night, I get to be a hero to my people.
          Sure. Washington-level. Hiawatha. Hand-
          some Lake. Heard of him? Akt'adia her-
          self up in here.

                    GREYWELL
          And how do you figure on perpetrating
          this glory of yours tonight?

                    MAX
          Well. Tonight this "scout's" gonna tear
          out yer tongue with his teeth like his
          ancestors would. Gonna gulp yer blood,
          assuming I'm immune to that little bug
          you got. Sure. Then I'm gonna tuck that
          sucker all neat up yer pink, puckered
          shithole where these boys here can
          felch it out like their mams taught
          'em. I'm'a hock yer piece down there
          for a glass pipe and a dime bag. And
          whatever discarded sex doll wife of
          yers in Westchester or wherever, well,
          she's gonna find herself an Indian in
          her cupboard, Sir. A well-endowed In-
          dian. To-night.

Seconds pass. Smiles fade.

The two men bore holes through each other's skulls with their eyes. Old-School standoff.

The SPOOKS get twitchy, make like they're going for their guns. The Boss raises a hand to still them. Damned if any $16K toadie's gonna settle this score for Hunter W. Greywell, "Hunt" to his friends, except—

[FLASHBACK]

INT. LIGHTNING HOUSE. (15 YEARS AGO)

Meat Puppet GROWLS.

Max stands back.

In BG, April, bloody and dead. Her mouth frozen open in a silent scream, government fillings glinting in a stream of sun that sneaks under the shade. Her eyes open, too, sunken, and the lino looking like the ditch at Wounded Knee.

The dog lays in FG with her litter beside the washing machine in the kitchen-cum-cupboard. She's still lapping up the placenta.

Tucked among her brood is Max's grandson. She's cleaned him off, and carried him over. Now he's nursing beside his littermates. The kid is fat and happy, healthy as a just-fucked horse. Meat Puppet shows her teeth. Max will never get close to her little pink "pup."

[END FLASHBACK]

BACK IN THE SECURITY HUT (CONTINUOUS)

The stare-down intensifies like a spaghetti Western.

Then—

The sound of Meat Puppet SAVAGING someone O.S. SCREAMS. The bitch is back.

Max, arthritic joints and soused liver notwithstanding, leaps onto the table with a single spring. He WOOPS like a banshee— like one of his fearsome warrior ancestors.

                    END ACT 1

—Cultural appropriation—

Thursday Sept. 20. Last day of trial.

Nowhere in New Mexico

You're not real Indians. Oh My God. Not real Native—you're as much Native American as the average fucking terrorist strapped with a bomb vest is a goddamn Muslim. It's a corruption. A *whattyacall* it, a perversion. You're trying to—Right? I see it right here. You. You have that tattoo. That – what is that – it's a fucking Jonas Brothers tattoo. And you. Over there. Yeah, you. Fucking cunt. You got that satchel at fucking Whole Foods. It's hemp. I've seen it. Take the label off, at least. You're not real Indians. Oh my God. This is a—you've taken—I don't know which is worse. But how fucking dare you? You think this is – what? – you're stealing … You're judging us? Are you absolutely fucking kidding me? So you wanna know what happens after we die? After you die? I die. I'll tell you. I'll show you. *Sharts.*

two spirits

Two Spirits

Finally, for Nora and Amy

... the youngest one, a tall, blond, sleepy boy ...

—Roberto Bolaño, *2666*, 2004

Rhubarb: trauma, infection

Noah lies crumpled just above the ditch on Pine Tree Junction Road. It's dark, and the peepers are noisy again after the choppers with their searchlights pass over. The firefight in town has subsided, PD hears. His watch beeps: 11 p.m.

Noah's breathing sounds exactly like the rock tumbler PD's Grandpa Max left on throughout the winter atop sawhorses in the shed to polish the stones from Christos Creek into dazzling blue-brown swirls and blacks with white specks, which he called, "dinosaur eggs," and which whatever random skank he was banging sold to tourists for him, on the side of Route 30 for beer money.

Noah's T-shirt is shredded, and a red rash blooms on his chest and stomach, punctuated by gravel and dirt. The skin of his left shin is flayed open like the anatomy doll PD's aunts, the Medicine Sisters, kept in a cedar box in the cupboard behind the kitchen table. His legs are broken. His face, too, has been nearly torn off. A large flap containing his ear is folded halfway over those lips PD has kissed, that have kissed him, and the skull and muscles of his neck are showing, red and white and purple. His long hair and some gnats and leaves stick in the blood and motor oil. There isn't much blood, though. PD pulls the hair off and folds the skin back down, and pats it, wants to touch it with his lips. "You fucking promised, No-No ..."

In the far distance, PD can hear the men calling on bullhorns. The sirens in Arctadia sing. More motorcycles. Meat Puppet whimpers—she can hear it all, too. She trots around the body, sniffing, licking. One of

Noah's black sneakers is missing—nowhere in sight. The sneakers cost his moms $239.99 (a birthday and Christmas gift combined, he told PD). His ankle is bent the wrong way as in *Family Guy*. Puppet noses tentatively at one of Noah's molars with its root on the gravel, beside a brown seed pod the Medicine Sisters taught PD to call a "polynose," but which his Grandpa Max had always called a "helicopter."

"You're dying, Noah." But he's already dead. The universe up here knows it.

Now he does almost kiss the boy. He leans down and whispers to Noah's lips, "You know what I'm gonna do, No-No."

The boy is weightless. Ether. PD carries him – his head loose on the neck – down the ditch and into the woods toward the pond, with Meat Puppet trying to lead, dragging her old bones and attempting to keep her tail straight. PD talks to Noah as they pass through the ferns: "Nice and easy, White Boy."

Under the High Damien Trestle there's a crumbling stone bridge over the Christos Creek that his people have used for 300 years. PD seldom considers his ancestors. The young men and women who hunted and loved on this land have been strangers to him, completely: His Grandpa Max was right to be righteous about it. But now PD sees Noah like one of so many of his warrior forebears, mortally wounded while fighting for the right to call Kittakwa home. No, in the "grand sweep of time" that his aunts invoke over glasses of homemade port at night, it's not unusual for a 15-year-old boy to lie broken, torn-open in these woods, nor for a bit of lilac-tinged organ meat to peep from a gash beside a young warrior's navel. It just doesn't happen all that much lately.

Noah. His twin. If he dies—PD will die. Thing is, though—there's another option.

★★★

Rose leaves: bee stings, impotence

In this place, a shady glen where the birds slalom-race for the evening insect feast, they first saw each other naked, three weeks ago. Can you fall in love in three weeks? Can you fall in love in the three seconds it takes to glimpse a shady glen of utopia? Of course you can.

It was Indian summer. PD blindfolded Noah there with his own underwear, made him wait, sitting with his knees up on a boulder, cocking his head when he heard a stick break or a late toad *kerplunk* into the Christos. He was afraid, but he smiled. Oh, Lord, the way he sat. The way he was sitting. PD watched him from behind a sugar maple, having to consciously breathe. This must be how Aric Hatch and Akt'adia felt upon first seeing the Great Ghost, Ghosh'eyo.

★★★

Thyme: infections, fungus

Lark Nixon Obermeyer III had worked for the Bureau of Indian Affairs for three years and three months, having been hired right out of Reed College after a distinguished spell as an intern on the Upper Umpqua. He was born a Quaker in Whittier, California, just like Richard Nixon, who had been his grandparents' patron saint. His girlfriend, Danica, was a Quaker, too; they had met, not at the meetinghouse, but at a church-sponsored volunteer event on Cannon Beach. Now they planned to get married, but not until they had saved the $10,000 they decided they needed for their wedding and subsequent honeymoon on Lamu Island, Kenya. They chose Lamu because, yes, it was a World Heritage Site, but mainly because they had read it was in dire need of beach-cleaning—the detritus of Mombasa clung to the mangroves and choked the dhow channel, they'd read in a newsletter to which they subscribed. Shore-rehab is how they had met, and how they intended to spend each summer—and their honeymoon summer should be no exception. They would clean a small stretch of beach together, and take before-and-after pictures, and post them on their website. Imagine showing that to the children and grandchildren, Lark said as they held hands, sharing a peanut butter and agave syrup sandwich.

In service of ferreting away his 60 percent portion of that $10,000, Lark made $27,990 per annum (plus excellent benefits) working for the BIA. His double major in folklore anthropology and ecology had earned him a coveted role as a Natural Resource Specialist. But his eagerness in that position, his Quaker mien, and his open, trustworthy face, had recently merited him Tribal Liaison status, with far more direct interaction with the people. They gave him a Lincoln Town Car and a kick-ass ATV to traverse the dirt roads in search of illegal traps and marijuana in the hillside firebreaks. They gave him a cell phone. They didn't give him a gun. He'd spent the past year and a half in Kyle, South Dakota, on the Pine Ridge Reservation, where Danica visited three times a year (He got one long weekend off to visit her). But four days ago, he was called to upstate New York to assist with a Critical Operation on the Kittakwa Rez. The FBI sent a plane to Rapid City for him and some sinister-looking black-ops colleagues. They told him to pack one bag—the plane was small.

He dialed Danica. "I think I just got called up to the Big Show," he said. "This has to mean they're considering me for the Supervisory NRS. Know what that means? Sixty-eight-thousand-nine-hundred-and-something bucks. We're golden."

"I'm proud of you, Lark. Maybe we could donate a used Bobcat for the Rockaway project? I saw one on eBay for, like, a grand."

"Your wish is my command."

***

Angelica: high blood pressure, irritable bowel

Now PD is nearing 16, the age of consent for Kittakwa boys. Estranged, to say the least, from his Grandpa Max, who suffered a spate at Monterey Shock (having just made it under the age limit of 50), and still unfamiliar with the details of his patronage, despite some pleading when he was eight and nine and 10. The most important thing is that PD's a Two-Spirit now, although only the Medicine Sisters know this for certain. They know that his mother, their little sister, April, would have loved him still. So they love him still. They know their father, his grandfather, Max, would cut him open from tip to toe and barbecue his innards if he knew, sending the smoke to the Four Directions. They have perfected subtle warnings, e.g. "PD, you keep your *self* to yourself,"

Two Spirits

and so on. Still, they see how he stares at the firemen when they come to the edge of the Lightning land to train for dousing wildfires. They see how he looks at occasional sons of leaf-peepers from Brooklyn, from Jersey. They know he knows something when he stares at the framed photograph of his Great-Great Grandpa Randy, Max's grandfather, the one that hangs in the hallway. Randy Lightning, aide-de-camp – and more – to Chief Kittadoga, in his crisp Union uniform, over the patina-stained plate on the frame that reads, "Civil War Hero, Proud Kittakwa Son." Randy was a Two-Spirit, too. That's the way it goes.

His aunts are busy all day with their art. They trained the boy since he was small to identify the healers and the balms, astringents, laxatives, and anti-diarrheals. All day Kittakwas and some liberal whites from Kit County come through their kitchen and exam room in the sprawling ranch on the pond with the broken-down dock. Sometimes so many folks come with PMS and gout, with the shakes and sleeplessness and "jimmy legs," that they gather on the porch and chew over their pains and talk politics while they wait. PD manages triage. He serves them cans of V8 and pink and orange Gatorade, extremely watered-down, which they call "bug juice."

Inside, one patient at a time. This morning it is Diablo Talbot again, which thrills PD in a weird, secret place. The boy is mostly nonverbal now, having lost his words to an aggressive glioma on the language expression center of his left frontal lobe. They have it in check.

Thrilled because once Diablo, though he was already 15, messed himself while waiting for the Medicine Sisters, and it fell to PD to clean him up with a sponge in the shower. Diablo for some reason (PD's aunts said simply that "the brain's a strange place") was also constantly cold. He shivered, though the water that day was almost too hot to PD's touch.

"Talk to him," they'd counseled. "Tell him everything you're doing. Remember there's a human in there. He can process. He just can't express."

So PD said, "OK, let's turn around now so the water—OK, now for the booty ..."

The women take a history, which PD has heard so many times he could conduct it in his sleep. They palpate Diablo's glands. They study his feet. They smell his breath. They swirl a cup of the patient's urine, and hold it up to the sun when there's sun, and the light of the oven when it grows dark outside from clouds.

They fish for words long locked in the boy's addled white matter.

Then they send their little healer's apprentice, their beloved orphan Puppy Dog, into the larder under the house out back, which they have stuffed over decades with natural remedies. In the dispensary, he gathers from the jars and hooks the various cures for Diablo and the other people's ills. He has learned to measure by the eye (you need only one), by the hand, and by the nose. He has learned to mix by fist and finger, and by intuition.

And twice a week, this morning included, for the secondary constituents of Diablo's special remedy, they send Puppy Dog off to the woods and meadows of the Kittakwa Mountains to pick the various leaves and nettles, the petals and acorns, the roots and vines their people have employed for at least 12,000 years. They have taught him to scrape the bark, and uncover the nuts without crumpling the skin. In the kitchen, some of this stuff they mash with the mortar and pestle, and some they cook until it concentrates to paste. Some leaves they chew and spit into a jar. Some twigs they heat on a fire outside, then scrape the char into rosewater or lemon juice. A complicated still of Max's early devising decocts the essence of certain flowers and berries, using pressure, steam, and time.

The Medicine Sisters have always been able to lower the blood sugar of diabetics. They can reduce blood pressure, too. They can stave off strokes, and take away the pain from teething and old age. They can make a man ready for love, and a woman set to stop loving when it's her time. For jaundice and rheumatism, chicory. Sassafras for syphilis and gonorrhea. And, with one special, tiny, unprepossessing leaf they call the "Lazarus" – a leaf, it's worth noting, that no tourist has yet come to peep – they could perform a feat worthy of the White Warrior of Nazareth, he with the beard and shroud, hung on cedar, hung around Diablo Talbot's neck.

But this leaf does not come easy.

This leaf does not come cheap.

After the Lazarus leaf, the Medicine Sisters dispatch their beloved nephew nearly naked to the ramshackle raft that bobs in the center of Kittatinn Pond, only three or four times a year, unless the need arises for more, always at dawn when the tribe is asleep or sleeping it off. Years ago, his youngest aunt, June, trained him to take the ride "Under," down below the raft to collect the tenderest baby leaves of Lazarus, to ferret it into a canvas bag around his chest like a sash, and to return, and never to confess, on pain of dishonor and possibly death, where it grows, and from what microscopic interaction with planktonic fossils might galvanize its powers.

For this leaf, they always intone, *"Some must suffer, so many will be saved."*

PD had not yet experienced – hadn't truly understood – such suffering as occasioned the need for the Lazarus leaf. Sure, he learned in school of both of his nations' histories, the one drowned in tears, and the other a heavy pourer. He hadn't known real pain. Not until Noah's people came.

***

Verbena: depression, anxiety

Kittatinn Pond is not pristine. PD once looked at a drop of it under a microscope for a school project, and shrank back at the teeming life and the army of death he saw. But why should he have been so surprised? He holds Noah there now with both hands under the boy's back. His blond hair floats out all around, and he looks like an angel—they're always white, blue-eyed, and blond, aren't they? When the water gets under the skin at the side of Noah's face, it opens up again, and suddenly his face is half-wider, as though this whole time the face were only a mask over some mute ugliness. PD turns away and simultaneously presses the skin back down. He scoops water over the eye sockets, and wipes them with his thumb. He rubs his thumb over the teeth that are broken, presses the tongue. Noah stopped breathing some minutes ago on the dock. He's not hurting anymore. He's not No-No anymore. Not yet.

Two Spirits   315

The clavicles. The sternum. The bottom ribs. The belly.

Some say this pond is where the British drummer boy Aric Hatch first encountered the Kit legend Ghosh'eyo. Some say a lot of things.

Meat Puppet rests her head on her paws on shore, picks up her head, whines, and puts it down again.

Two years ago, PD brought that microscope home one night. The teacher told him he could. And in between two pieces of glass, he put a drop that came from his thinking hard about the firemen when the EMTs and Junior Fire Frogs pull their gear down to the boots and pour water over their bodies while they try to catch their breath. What he saw there through the lens with his good eye – the powerful tails attempting to propel his bloodline forward – made him so sad and frightened that he curled up and bit his pillow. He dreamt, he always dreamt, that he crawled in the window of his grandmother's VW as it rested on its back like an insect, and she reached out for him, and she said, "Where is your brother?" Even though he was an only child. He would bring him to her.

★★★

Clover: scrofula, constipation

The leaf-peepers sidle off Route 30 in dribs and drabs in mid-October, but come November 1st, a comical clan in minivans and Avalons descend onto the Rez. The only motel, The New Yorker, filled by 3 o'clock, despite not having been redecorated since the Rockefeller administration. The ice from its ice machine tasted like mold and Lysol. But the pool – one of two on the Rez (the other was at the Community/Cultural Center) – was, owing to virgin diatomaceous earth hauled out from the nearby Christmas claim before the collapse, and stacked in sacks in the old concrete factory warehouse, so crystal clear it hardly looked like water at all.

The two local "Rez-tauranteurs," Tommy "Tomahawk" and Tony "Squash," competed for the tourist green with autumnal "Indian" specials, and both cashed in. And always on the first weekend day of November, the Arctadia Volunteer Fire Department and Ambulance

Corps held its annual fundraising pancake breakfast/bingo, hosting hundreds of peepers from Long Island and parts south, at $8 a pop, all-you-care-to-eat, attracted every year by pamphleteering that featured the artwork and person-to-person salesmanship of the cutest reservation children, of whom there were several hardened vets now, cynical as homicide cops.

Since he was seven, it's been PD's job at the pancake breakfast to serve the little cups of orange or cranberry juice, "*YOU'RE CHOICE.*" It's in this capacity on November 2nd, 7:45 a.m., that PD notices the white boy for the first time—a tall, blond, sleepy boy. He's wearing headphones, the old-fashioned, bulbous kind, lately back in style. He smiles, but barely, when he gets to the juice station at the buffet, but seems to be off in his own world. PD, on the other hand, finds his bones rattled like the skeleton – "The Chief" – the Medicine Sisters keep festooned behind the kitchen cupboard door to show their patients where the hip bone is connected to the thigh bone, and so on.

The white boy is with two women in their 40s. One is Asian and the other, Caucasian. They look like a Benetton billboard PD once saw outside Montreal when he went with his Aunt May to fetch his Grandpa Max from the Canadian clink one winter weekend (expired prostitute). The white woman, gaunt and pale, wears a blue wool cap that seems handmade. She asks PD where the ladies' room is, and soon after, PD, in search of a mop bucket, sees her in the truck bay, puking up her pancakes in the slop sink. She's holding her wool cap in one hand. She's completely bald.

"Colon," she tells him, wiping her mouth on her sleeve. "A real pain in the ass."

PD blinks.

"*A pain in the ass?*" she says. "You get it?"

"Oh."

"I'm sorry. That's so not right. Could you ... I'm sorry ..."

PD helps her clean out the sink with the broken faucet hose. "You're a good boy," she says. "I bet your mother is proud as hell."

PD doesn't tell this woman that his mother is dead, and he never met her, and because of that, they accidentally named him Bon instead of

Two Spirits 317

Ben, and that once, some Kit County kids came and painted "*Squaw Hore*" on her tombstone.

The white woman puts the cap back on, and looks at herself in the funhouse mirror that is the side of the industrial washer used to clean the turnout gear (another of PD's firehouse duties). She puts lipstick on, and sprays her mouth with something.

"So we're here for a month. What would you recommend?"

"Here? On the Rez? Why?"

"Lara – that's my partner – is doing a paper about your tribe—Oh, I'm sorry; is that the term?"

"Sure. Tribe."

"Good. She's doing her PhD at Columbia. No-No – Noah – and I are making a vacation out of it. We're staying at the New Yorker – ha! – That's an establishment I won't soon forget. I say 'Tribe,' but it seems as though you guys are pretty fully … how can I say? Assimilated? Is that politically correct?"

"Noah?"

"Our son. With the headphones. I mean, I'm not saying I expected, whatever …"

"Bows and arrows, feathers, peace pipes …"

"Yeah."

"But you did."

"But I did. 'Cause I'm a certain kind of idiot."

"So. Noah."

"Yeah. The one that looks like he'd rather be anywhere else? But he loves it here. I can tell. I'm one of his mothers."

Two mothers. One for each spirit?

★★★

Wild cherry: upset stomach, insomnia

They walk up to a ridge where they can survey the whole Kittakwa reservation and much of Kit County. Noah's heart's at the back of his throat, though he can't fathom exactly why.

They share a Baggie full of Reese's Pieces and salty peanuts. PD takes off his shirt, and tucks it in the back pocket of his jeans. "Vitamin D," he says.

"Cold."

"Pussy."

Noah takes his shirt off, too, reluctantly. He thinks he's too skinny, too pale, too … or not enough something is more like how he feels.

"Funny how you're the one with the long hair, ay?"

"It's stupid."

"No."

Noah can feel goose bumps flowering over his chest. "My dad. Supposedly. He had long hair. I never met him."

"So it wasn't like a turkey baster or something?"

"Everyone always asks that. No, it was the usual thing." He motions with a finger through the OK symbol. "They were students together. I never even saw a picture. He killed himself."

"Fuck. Pills?"

"An eighty-storey building in Thailand."

"Eighty. That'll do it."

"Yeah."

"Around here we have a giant railroad bridge."

"That'll do it, too."

"It's so …" PD reaches out. "Does it get all knotted and shit?"

"No. Look, see, it's pretty smooth."

"I like it."

"Yours is good. In the sun, it's, like, a little lighter."

The November sun is strong here. It's burned away most of the fog, dried the drippy leaves his moms for some inane reason marvel at.

They settle in a small meadow partially shaded in birch. PD says, "C'mere; it's warmer over here." Noah shifts closer. PD talks about fire trucks, "tankers," "tenders," "rigs," and something called a "Big Bertha." They're all built at the firetruck factory, Kit County's second-biggest employer, maybe biggest now the Christmas mine and concrete plant were going under. "Literally once a month, we have a school trip there. It's pathetic to see people you know. You know? Like they'll never get out of this place."

Two Spirits 319

"You want out?"
"Fuck, yes."
"Me, too."
"Out of the City? Why?"
"I don't know. Maybe it's different when you live there."

PD plays with his AFD Fire Frog pin. Next year they will graduate him from Junior Fire Frog and let him go on calls as a junior firefighter. For now, he tells Noah, he cleans the trucks. He drills with the men. He rolls hoses. He studies the way they speak and the way they move. Sometimes he does the "rehab," and gets to pull down all their gear and pour water over them with the EMTs.

PD falls asleep with a tiny piece of grass stuck to his lip. Noah can hardly look at the kid without hurting in some warm, wet cave inside him that he never knew existed until now. He wants to run and fling himself off the ridge into the jagged rocks below where the Christos winds through a sun-starved glen. Or he could find that railroad bridge. It might not be 80 storeys but it's fucking high. He wants to take out one of his eyes and put it where PD's dead eye is. He wants to smother them both, to poison them both with some deadly mushroom, to advance to the next world together, where for some reason he's always imagined his dad is, playing guitar in a meadow, flipping his long hair. He wants to shake the kid, wake him and tell him that he—

It is, as his moms would say, a "classic conundrum." He considers what his Chinamom, Lara, the PhD-to-be, would do. She'd think it out. Fine. So, the problem is one of impossibility; the way he wants to ... what's the word? ... *possess* the boy, is just not a thing that can happen in this universe. To *incorporate* the boy. To *be* the boy. No, the problem is one of degrees. The problem is those lips and their indentation. That wide nose. The muscles of his arms, from rolling hoses, from swimming, from climbing Concord grape vines in the woods. From DNA. The problem is time. He's leaving in two and a half weeks. The problem is birth and biology. The problem is you have to make a choice. The world is black and white. You can't survive in grey for long. The problem is God.

★★★

Chamomile: scrapes, noisy babies

"Don't call me a pussy, because not jumping into a lake in upstate New York in November is perfectly goddamn rational. It snowed once already, didn't it? Around Halloween?"

Noah and PD sit, bobbing on the rotting raft. A little rowboat docked. The sky is grey. The tops of the trees rustle in the wind, and down below, the mist eddies again. There's a faint chop on the surface of the water. Noah has left his iPod and enormous Sennheisers on the porch, and it's the first time since the blindfold experiment that PD has seen the boy without them. There's a dark hollow up Noah's pant leg past the ankle. He wants to put his hand there—or take up residence. There's a greenness to Noah's eyes that makes PD taste the Sourball candies the Medicine Sisters keep stuck together in a bumpy bowl on the porch for patients.

PD motions to Noah's jeans. "You can't go in the water in those. They'll drag you down. You won't be able to move down there."

Noah gives PD a look. *Down there?*

"Boxers or briefs?" PD asks. "Hopefully not boxers, because you need something tighter or—"

"What the fuck? I'm not taking my pants off. It's like the fucking Arctic out here. Arc-tadia. Hey, what are you doing? You gotta be kidding me."

PD stands, takes off his sneakers, shirt, and jeans. "I go first, and you hold my ankle. OK?"

"You're insane."

"Noah. Trust me." He does his best routine now: "I am the wise Indian, at one with nature. All that shit."

Noah, hugging his knees, looks up. He finally smiles.

"*Whut?*" says PD.

"Nothing. It's just, the way you look ... I wish my phone wasn't—I'd take a picture."

"C'mon." But Noah's looking, too. No one's ever looked at PD the way Noah's looking. He's glad he put on clean underwear, one of the pairs his Aunt June bleached to hell.

Two Spirits   321

"Shit, I'm gonna fucking die out here like the Trail of Tears or whatever," Noah says.

"Take 'em off. Cowboy."

"Damn it. Fine." Noah unbuttons his jeans. He holds his thumbs below the waistband, and looks around. "Oh, wait." He carefully removes his wet, black canvas high tops – "Old School" – and places them beside each other in the center of the raft. He pats them like a pair of beloved bunnies. Then he takes off his jeans without standing, by hitching himself up on his elbows and raising his—ah, boxer briefs, striped horizontally, blue and grey. He holds his arms and hands awkwardly. "My sneakers'll be …?"

"It's cool."

Noah folds his jeans, and places them on top of his shoes. "Swimming in the winter. Jeez, what do you guys do in July? Go skiing?"

"No, July is scalping season. OK, now come over here." Noah scoots over to the side of the raft. "How long can you hold your breath?"

"Umm, I don't know, but for some reason, that's, like, the scariest fucking question anyone's ever asked me."

"Thing is, it's going to seem like a long time, but I swear you'll be OK. Just don't panic."

"Great," says Noah. "And we're going … down there? All the way to the bottom?"

"Sort of."

"Sort of. Awesome. Why?"

"Under."

"And why are we doing this again? Going under?"

"I told you to trust me. Just hold onto my ankle. Seriously. Don't let go."

While PD straps a canvas bag around his chest – like a mailman – Noah talks under his breath, doing his Chinamom's voice, a spot-on impersonation: "Yay, I used to have a son; his name was No-No. I don't know; he just disappear one day in the water; so, so sad for mommies, no No-No no mo'…"

PD checks the coiled chain on the corner of the raft. It's threaded through three donut-shaped dumbbell weights. One holds the chain to the raft with an old railroad spike. One, knotted at the free end, acts as an anchor, so once PD drops it, it pulls the chain off the raft in loud rings, rushing toward the bottom. Noah can see by the length of chain that drops into the water, the old glacial lake is even deeper than he imagined. It's going to be ice down there. And black. Now he notices that the chain passes through the hole in the center of a final weight, the largest and heaviest weight, so that it can slide up and down the whole length. PD positions that weight at the far corner of the raft. Noah can't quite fathom what it's for, but the thought of it causes a certain vein a certain pain with which he's become achingly familiar of late.

"I read that pretty close to hear, over on the Hudson, there used to be a riverboat elephant, and these two boys—"

"Freezing."

"Hold my ankle."

"Now?"

"Now hold my ankle and hold your breath. Let's go."

With considerable strain, PD holds the weight on his lap, then plunges into the water.

Noah gets it now. He holds PD's slippery ankle with both hands as they fly straight down, carried by the weight through which the chain is strung. It couldn't possibly be colder. But the sense of speed outpaces the cold. It's like a winter amusement park ride, but so terrifying that Noah's afraid he'll lose his bowels. He can feel his stomach descending a second or two slower than the rest of him. His eardrums undergo unpleasant pressure as they dive down deep and fast—too fast. Shit. The sound of the weight scraping on the chain is ethereal, and they're moving so fast and going so deep that the sound changes constantly, becoming higher-pitched. The Doppler effect? No. What the hell is that called? Pockets of terrible cold. His ears are pinging. The chain is scraping his shoulder blade.

Holding PD's foot makes Noah feel like part of PD, and for a split second he remembers some old Bible story his Americamom told him: Someone held onto someone in the womb, or fought his twin, or something. Was it Cain and Abel? Jacob and Esau?

Will they ever hit bottom? The descent is so rapid and shocking that Noah forgets he's holding his breath. But below him now, PD is doing something with the weight and the chain – Noah can hear the sound change, like a train braking – that slows them down quickly, and suddenly Noah remembers it's been a while since he's had oxygen. He can feel the weight gently thud onto the bottom. He can't remember whether his eyes have been open or closed this whole time, but now he makes it a point to open them. Not completely black. A dusky grey-green. A few tiny bubbles. Water weeds—menacingly undulating. Some grotesquely overlarge and ugly fish in the distance. He looks up, but can't see the surface. Now what? It'll take forever to swim back up. Can he hold his breath that long? No. So he's gonna die down here. Or he could bolt up. But isn't it bad to go up too fast? You get that thing – the bends! – and they have to put you in an iron chamber for a year.

He lets go of PD's ankle, and PD raises it, points violently toward it. Noah takes the foot again. *Trust me.* PD turns back down and begins to burrow in the mud, like he's digging for treasure. He kicks up a cloud of sediment, and it's so much warmer than the water around them. It feels good. Noah is staring at the large, grey, dumb-looking fish. He lets out a little laugh – a little air – and when he looks down to see whether PD has seen it, he literally can't believe his eyes.

★★★

Mint: teething, nervous headache

"Hunt Greywell."
"Lark Obermeyer."
"*Mucho gusto.*"
Lark never believed in fate. If you wait for destiny, diapers and syringes come sweeping onto the beach—not off. His father, Lark Jr., always told him you make your own way in the world. That made sense to him. But on the jet to Stewart Air Force Base, the guy sitting next to him, some assassin-looking dude wearing a black baseball cap with no logo whatsoever, turns to him and says, "We're gonna be part of history, soldier. Think Neil Armstrong, right? Think Jonas Salk. How cool is that shit? We were made for this shit." And he punches the ceiling of

the plane. For just a moment, Lark can feel himself swept up in something that feels like fate—and it's comforting, exhilarating, not a little bit terrifying, too. It staves off the nap he was planning to take after the Scotch the guy made him drink. To play a part in something important seems for the moment worth more than the $40,000 differential between "Supervisor" and "Specialist." Wouldn't it make Danica proud? Lincoln! Brockovich! Bloody Obermeyer III! That's how they getcha'.

But. Important ... how? What would he have to do to earn that place?

★★★

Milk thistle: hepatitis, cirrhosis

"What the fuck just happened?" Noah's gasping for breath, dragging himself onto a slippery perch in a green-glowing cave. "How did we—?"

"We went Under."

"*Un*—?"

Noah had felt them pushing through the mud somehow. He held onto that ankle for dear life, and it – PD – pulled him through the dirt, through the ground, writhing and struggling like a mudskipper or a Biblical twin. He was flailing with his other arm the whole time, and gulping down the little air that remained in his mouth. He had a vague memory of PD kissing him, breathing for him, halfway through, and his lungs straining. Now he's dizzy. A feeling of warm oblivion and a whole-body torpor overwhelms him, and he has to lie back on the warm stone. "Where the fuck are we?"

Hot stone.

PD places his palm on Noah's stomach, and Noah finds this soothing—and more. He opens his eyes. He leans up on his elbows. They are overlooking an underground lake, lit bright green somehow from below, with a black stone ceiling just above their heads. There's no room to stand—it's breathtaking. "It doesn't make sense, because ..."

"We never went back up," says PD.

"Yeah, we were going ... We only went down."

"And through."

"It's like … It's like we came out … the bottom of the—or something."
"Something like that. You ready now? Can you follow me?"
"Wait."
"What?"
"Dude."
"What?"
"Your eye."
"Oh, yeah."
"It's …"
"It works here. Under, it works."
"It's …" Noah smiles wide.
"Ain't you sweet."
They crawl a few yards – the vertical space narrows alarmingly, and PD pauses at a small opening in the stone at the terminus. "It's a long haul, and you have to—"
"I ain't going through that shit. No way," says Noah, still panting. It's exceedingly warm. "Where the fuck are we?"
"OK, then … pussy."
PD scrambles through the hole. Noah watches him wriggle until his feet disappear. He stays still a moment, catching his breath. He can hear the water lapping at the cave walls behind him. Where is PD? Why is it so fucking warm down here? Geothermal whatever? Could he just dive back down and swim to the "bottom," and somehow get back up to the raft? *Oh my God.* He can hear his pulse pounding in his ears. He shakes his head, and sweat goes flying everywhere. He got a lot of water up his nose. He holds one nostril, and blows through the other. Mud from the bottom of the pond, cooler than the ambient air. He peeks in the hole. Just black. No sign of him.
"PD?" Noah puts his palms up on the floor of the hole. "PD? Goddammit." He sticks his head in a little. He pulls himself up, and slithers onto his belly on the smooth stone, which is shockingly, unsettlingly warm. He can hear the echo of his coughing. His feet are still somewhat cooler—he's not all the way in yet, and this gives him enormous comfort.

"Are you there? I'm serious. This is fucking—" Echo. Hollowness. Nothing up ahead. It's a pizza oven. The passageway is so tight, he has to scrunch his shoulders and shimmy his hips to get all the way in. Now he knows why he couldn't go in with loose boxers—he'd have lost them already. He drags himself forward a bit, reminding himself of the worm experiments his Bio class had done the year before. It hurts his neck to keep his head up and looking forward. But he has to look forward. My God—what if he has to go back? Could he back himself out? He doesn't dare attempt an inch. What a horrible way to die. "Puppy!?"

Still no answer.

When he breathes, he can feel his belly and chest tight against the cave walls on every side. It's the worst way to go. Where the fuck is he? What's going on? He imagines his skeleton in there, like some stupid story from Americamom's Poe book next to the toilet back home. He has to continue on. How long is a "long haul?" A mile? What if it's 10? What if he shits himself? What if water comes rushing through this tunnel? What if PD is dead ahead, and the two of them are stuck there forever? On top of that, his ball was already hurting—and now it excruciates the snakelike journey. Could he turn over? He cannot. It's a tandoor oven. It's like when one of those bubble-lumps of undissolved shake powder gets stuck in the straw at Burgeropolis.

Thank God for his own sweat, which lubricates that journey. And that's like—

Well. He wouldn't exactly know.

After many minutes of dragging himself, exhausted, he sees an orange dot, which at first he assumes is a flashlight from the canvas bag that PD is shining to show him the way. But PD couldn't have turned around to light the way. He realizes with equal parts relief and fear that the tiny orange dot is the end of the tunnel—it's light. Which means PD must have passed through already. But it's so far away. Knowing he can see the way out, though, he relaxes a moment and rests his cheek on the hot stone. He tries to slow his breathing. What is this fucked-up place? How far "Under" are they? Are they surrounded by *whattyacallit* … magma? Is this a lava tunnel and can it—

His heart is pounding. His left nut is aching like someone just dropped a bowling ball on it. What if something comes through the other side behind him? What if some creature creeps up out of the green-glowing water, and slinks through the cave on talons? How would he fight it off? He couldn't. It would just eat his feet, then his calves ... He shimmies again, double-time on his forearms. His hips scrape. His elbows. Soreness. Tenderness. Tightness.

Is it possible it's getting even narrower in here? What if that hole at the end is only six inches wide? And hotter? What if it's a fire? *This is a coffin. A long, long coffin. That thing they burn the coffin in when you're cremated. I'm about to die. But it's going to take a long, long time.*

But the tiny orange dot begins to bloom like a starburst until finally he can tell it's definitely the "light at the end of the tunnel," and this becomes a mantra that motivates his body forward, lizard-like, snake-like, worm—

When he gets there, spent, chest aching, heart pounding, heavy breathing, nearly in tears, he's staring right at PD's smiling face eclips-ing the light behind him. PD grabs Noah by the shoulders, and pulls him through the last bit, slick with sweat, as though taking him out of one of those drawers at the coroner's office. He carefully lowers him down onto warm, wet grass. "It's like being born, ain't it?"

"Please tell me there's another way out. Please tell me that. Please. I can't go back that way. I can't do that—ever again. Please. We either stay forever or—"

"Sorry."

Noah can't stand. His legs are shaking. His neck is cricked. On all fours above him, PD whispers in his ear to soothe him. He tells him this is a good place, a safe place, the best place there is. And the worst is over. The only bad thing. A long time passes. Finally on his feet, Noah checks himself. There are scrapes on his hip bones, and one long scratch on his chest. One of his palms is bleeding a little.

"I'll get you something for that."

"I fucking hate you. Where is this place? I don't understand. I wanna go home, but—"

"I'll show you."

PD pulls Noah's underwear up to cover his hips and rump, and takes Noah's hand, and the two scrabble up a mossy rise. Now they overlook a thick forest of ferns and pine trees down a slope below them, and a wide mountain range in the distance, with the sun above. *The* sun. Above. It looks like – a lot like – but – no, it's more green. There's a green tinge to everything like that laser Pink Floyd show his moms took him to, but—

"Welcome to Kittakwa." PD starts picking through the ferns in his bare feet. "C'mon!"

"Am I supposed to get what's going on?" Noah follows, his toes feeling clover below. A host of insect noises variously drone and chirp. Noah has the organ-expanding sensation of hearing what it must have sounded like in prehistoric times. "'Cause I totally don't. Are we— are we back …?"

"Kittakwa. The real one. The *Under* one. Well—another one. No one besides maybe one or two of us each generation has ever been here. My Great-Great Grandpa Randy. My Aunt May. All the way back to – well, we have this legend, never mind – but all the way back. You have to be special, they say."

"Special?"

"A Two-Spirit. It's complicated."

"No shit."

A large, tuft-eared owl stares at Noah from a tree branch, pivoting its head to follow them. "We're in fucking Narnia."

"Kittakwa."

"Right."

They walk silently through a copse of trees—pretty normal-looking trees, although their colors are excessively bright. They cross an emerald brook. Noah studies the water. "Could I drink it?"

"It's water."

"Yeah. In the Upside-Down World, where we're hiking in our underwear."

PD plucks a giant leaf off a bush, folds it into a bowl from his satchel. He scoops some water for Noah, and holds it up for him to drink. "It's something about magnetism or something – polarity – that makes it seem like you're not—and then there's these fossils, these hollow, microscopic guys … You just have to go with it."

"So thirsty …"

"It's hot. Yeah, that's one of the things."
"It's November."
"Up there."
"Go with it."
"Like, you don't have to understand how an internal combustion engine works to use a car."
"Uh-huh."
"Or, it's like a trip. Magic mushrooms?"
"Never done anything like that."
"We have a few things here. In fact, they come from Under. And, you know, you have to go with it. You ride it. You fight it, it's confusing. It can get ugly. There's this one guy, at Sculton, when he was a kid, he—never mind."
"A 'bad trip,' my America mom says."
"Right."
"This is a trip."
"Yes. Except it's real."
They start walking again. "My Chinamom would shit a fucking cinder block. Her dissertation—"
PD stops short, and Noah bumps into him. PD puts both his hot hands on Noah's chest. "You can't tell her. You can't tell anyone. Ever. Noah. You can't."
"Are you fucking kidding me right now?"
"I'm serious as … *There*!"
PD leaps up a moss-covered berm on all fours, then proceeds to shinny up a wide tree, holding tight by his thighs. It's like looking at a million years ago, except for the Fruit of the Loom label on PD's underwear. Around the tree, a pale, spotty ivy winds. "Look." Within the ivy are knots of a darker plant, with a white-speckled lavender flower. PD plucks a few of its tender leaves. He swings the canvas bag on his shoulder, and puts a bunch of them in. A screech, a gravelly screech – "otherworldly" is the wordless word that comes to Noah's mind as he hears it – splits the drone, and for a moment, all the invisible bugs and birds and toads cease their sympony, before starting up again, double-fold.
"Never mind that. That's a—they're harmless—relatively. Unless—"
"Can we get the fucking fuck out of here?"

PD laughs. He holds one leaf in his teeth. He's gripping the trunk now only with his legs, like some Rikki-Tikki-Tavi boy Noah remembers from a storybook his moms read him when he was small and sick and feverish with something he can barely remember. He feels a little like that now. Is this—

A croak. "One of those freaky frogs you lick? Is that what's going on?"

PD climbs down a bit, then jumps to the ground from at least six feet. "Lazarus," he says. He holds up a tiny leaf. It's shaped like a mitten, with a small thumb next to a wider section where a child's fingers would go to keep warm

"This is why we're here?"

"Sit down on that rock. Yes, this," says PD, holding up a leaf, "is why your moms came here."

"They know? About this place?"

PD shakes his head. "No, of course not. I mean that's why they came here, even though they don't know that's why they came here. It's why we met, too. Sure it is."

"Dude, I am so fucking confused it's not even funny. I don't feel—"

"It's a little funny."

Noah puts his head in his hands. "So confused ..." Then his hands move to his lap.

"The rocks down here are really warm."

He looks up. "Dude—Don't you know? What you're doing to me?"

PD takes Noah's hands. He puts the little mitten-shaped leaf in one of them. "I know. I'm sorry. It can be—down here. But listen. We're here for a reason. Your Americamom needs this leaf. Taste it."

With one hand he squeezes himself – the warmth was helping abate the pain below – and with the other he sniffs the leaf. "PD, I just wanna—I don't wanna play this game."

"Go on. Trust me."

He breathes deeply. Smells sweet and pungent and otherwise tropical "Under." Fresh. Misty. Smells *green*. He places the Lazarus leaf on his tongue, then begins to chew. "Sweet. Tastes like ... what is that? Root beer."

"Right? Or Sarsaparilla. That's what I say. But it depends on who's tasting. Some people get chocolate. This one kid, Diablo, says caramel. Well, he doesn't say, exactly."

"Do I swallow?"

"That's what she said."

"Ha, ha." He swallows. "She needs it? Annalisa? Why?"

"She needs it," PD says, taking over the operations on PD's lap. "Don't tell her what it is or where you got it. Just put it on her salad or something. Or in her tea."

"And? What's it supposed to do?"

"The Lazarus leaf? Oh, this little fucker cures cancer."

★★★

Meadowsweet: inflammation, pain

The day that Noah found out about his Americamom's disease, he had disappointed her in the morning. The shower head: Lara and Noah liked it on the massage-blast mode, but Annalisa preferred it to be kept on "Gentle Rain." It was not a matter of sensory preference. Rather, she argued it leaked all day when set to that massage mode, and no amount of pipe tape seemed to stanch the drip. She had asked them several times to remember. Lara remembered. Noah remembered, too, at least in general. But that day, he was distracted in the shower, worried about a vein in the bundle at the top of his left testicle, which seemed to be twisted slightly, and constricting blood-flow. He could feel a dull, sickening ache. This was not a good thing. Not good on several fronts. Not to say his moms hadn't proven perfectly adept at handling all infirmities boyish since he was born. They didn't blanch. They didn't judge. But he was past the age when it was comfortable for him to broach such subjects, no less show them something twisted or otherwise under the belt.

His father, Annalisa's ex-husband, Carson, was in a blue aluminum coffin underground in Tamarac, Florida. Annalisa had a brother, though: Noah's Americuncle Doc. He was adroit at these kinds of things. He went to medical school. But now he worked as some sort of honcho for a scary big drug company on Park Avenue, where helicopters landed on the roof, and limos dropped off execs in front of where Noah met Doc for lunch about three times a year. Doc had explained what he did for the company, and he was often in the *Times* or on *60 Minutes* – not always in an ideal light – but Noah didn't pay much attention to the particulars. He did understand that Doc's job paid for Noah's ski camp and Noah's orthodontics. Noah's DJ equipment, his Lego Death Star: Things were tight since Lara left her job and went back to school. Then Annalisa got sick.

And he knew, too, that Doc's job was good enough to pay for a yacht moored in New Haven, and a classic car collection, including the awesome Maybach and the orange-and-black Bugatti Veyron Super Sport, which practically made you cum when you sat in it. Noah decided to call Doc at work. He toweled off gently. He forgot to switch the shower head back to its approved setting.

Blame it on the left ball.

On his way out to school, the doorman, Rigoberto, asked Noah how Annalisa was.

"Americamom? She's fine. Why?"

"Oh, I had to clean up the Technicolor yawn last night."

"Huh?"

"She vomited. Right there on the ficus between the elevators."

At school, Noah got razzed for limping—his buddies assumed it was the wrestling match the day before, in which he'd been humiliated by a "homo" from a private school, an archrival. Jesus—maybe he did pull something in that match. It had been all he could do to keep from getting a hard-on. If you try too hard, could it …? No. That was impossible.

After lunch, he got his hair caught in his locker. Then, walking home, the pain in his ball intensified. He had to stop and sit on a stoop a moment. Doc hadn't returned his calls. He dialed Tigereye Biodynamics for a third time, and again went through all three gatekeepers.

"Darren Christianson's office."

"Hi, Bee. Is Doc in, please?"

"Noah? Is that you again? You poor booby. He's a bad man. I'm gonna go interrupt him. Some stupid *blah-blah-blah* in the conference room since nine. Please hold."

Two Spirits 333

An ancient band singing the *Glee* song, "Don't Stop Believin'."
"Noah. How much does she need this time?"
"No. I gotta talk to you. Can I come by?"
"Meet me on the north side of the Pocahontas statue in the Skyway Lobby. Six-forty-three." Doc scheduled his time in three-minute blocks. It was his thing. It was in all the interviews. And he didn't let you set an appointment unless you called the morning of—between 5 and 7 a.m. Flying in from Sweden or Marrakesh next month? Gotta wait. Call in the morning. He'd guarantee you a meet.

He arrived at Tigereye at 4:39, and waited until the appointed time, when Doc, in a silvery suit, sailed down the escalator Trumplike, talking to what looked like the king of some African country, in full regalia. At 6:42 and 39 seconds (Noah checked his cell phone), the two appeared in front of him. The black man, in a flowing robe and austere headdress, looked up at the Pocahontas statue, which, at some point, Doc had told Noah cost a million dollars, and took 11 years for some recluse to sculpt.

"Noah London, may I introduce his eminence, Mamadou Mansour, the Senegalese Minister of Health."

" *'Right in the ghetto, oooh of Senegal!'* "

"Noah!"

"Pardon?"

"No—it's Akon. Senegal ..." Blank stares, ebony and ivory. "That's where Akon's from. *Akon*? The singer? Shit."

"I do not know this Acorn of whom you speak."

"A-*kon*. Here. Wait. On my—"

"Noah."

Noah handed the minister his '70s style headphones, handmade in Germany at a cost of $1,500 (a gift of his uncle Doc, of course). The minister put them on with ease, and made a facial gesture indicating he was listening intently. "Hold on ..." Noah forwarded to Akon's song, "Senegal."

Within seconds, the minister was smiling widely, swaying his hips, and nodding his head up and down. He parroted the lyrics: " *We own that land / We own those diamonds!'*

"That's badass, Uncle Doc. This dude is rockin' the fuck out."

The minister took off the headphones. "I find this fellow both talented and amusing," he said.

"I know—right?"

"And you say he is from Senegal?"

"Senegal, West Africa, Man. He's proud of it. I think he sends, like, millions back and everything."

"I shall return and tell my people of the success of this Acorn in your country."

The minister hugged Noah, a proper shoulder-to-shoulder bro-hug. Noah laughed.

At 6:54, he was back upstairs in Doc's office, mesmerized by the view of midtown out three walls of pure glass. His pants and A&F box briefs were around his ankles, and his uncle was on his knees in front of him, leaning in as close as possible and mumbling something about an "idiopathic varicocele."

That's when the minister breezed back through the door in search of his briefcase. The minister froze.

"He's my nephew!" Doc shouted. "No—*wait*!"

The minister bowed slightly, backed away slowly, turned, and left the room, closing the double-doors behind him.

"Nephew!" Doc chased him out into the secretary's suite. "His balls!"

Relieved by Doc's diagnosis – "testicle's overtaxed; go easy for a week" – Noah texted his Chinamom that he'd be late, and he and Doc went to a ridiculously expensive restaurant where Doc ordered him some kind of pigeon-looking bird on a bed of weird noodles. Doc told him he was working on a deal with the Senegalese – and, off the record, their rivals, the Cape Verdeans – for some kind of mineral "elixir, diatomaceous."

"Yeah, but he thinks you're a dirty old freak now."

"Nah, he's probably picking up some skater in Washington Square right now. You know. When in Rome ..."

"Some skater listening to 'Acorn' on his iTunes."

Doc gave Noah two crisp hundred dollar bills, and called the Tigereye car service to take him back uptown.

He walked in the door at 10:09. Both his moms were sitting in the living room, and neither had a book in her hand. "No-No, we talk now,"

Two Spirits 335

said his Chinamom in her "serious" voice. That's when Noah remembered the shower head, and started to apologize. They both smiled. They asked him to sit between them, which made him uncomfortable for some reason. The evening would end with his holding his Americamom's hand as she threw up blood in the kitchen sink, then his staring up at the ceiling, wondering how long it would be until she died.

★★★

Marshmallow root: bronchitis, peptic ulcers

"Don't fuck with me like that."
"I wouldn't."
"You did. You are."
"This'll cure her. Wham-Bam. Fucking cured. We've been doing it here for, like, I don't know, a long time. Eons. Epochs. I don't know which is longer."
"You're telling me the Indians—"
"Kittakwas."
"… have the cure. For cancer."
"Nobody here's had cancer since the last Ice Age. Unless they, like, want it."
"And it's down there—*up* here? Under. Wherever. In the forest outside a cave with, like, shimmering green water. You gave me peyote or something. We went down the water, through the mud and—"
"Don't overthink it."
"Go with it."
"Just put it in her food. The tumors'll find someone else to kill. It takes about a week. And don't let her eat any apricot seeds."
"Of course not."
"Now: Aare you going to tell me where we are?"
"Shelter Rock."
"Shelter Rock. So. Not Kit Pond."
"No, that's back that way. You come out here. We have to walk."
"We have to walk."
"No one's noticed that—"

"That no one gets cancer here? Not yet. No one gives a shit."

In the following days, as his Chinamom sojourns to various tribal authorities for her study, Noah watches Americamom get better, incrementally. On the first day, she stops puking. On the second day, she says her stomach doesn't hurt. On the third day, she eats two hamburgers at Tony Squash's. On the fourth day, she says she wants to go for a walk (and when she gets back to the New Yorker, she tells Noah she actually jogged). On the fifth day, she sings – John Denver (she's a huge John Denver fan), and later, slow dances with Lara at Tommy Tomahawk's after dinner (Styx's "Come Sail Away"), inspiring a few tribal ladies to dance with each other, too, though none too seriously. And that night at the New Yorker, Noah and PD can hear them laughing and then making love in the next room. "*Eew.*"

"I told you so."

"It's like—"

"A secret."

"A miracle," says Noah. "Don't you see? What would happen if you—?"

"Yeah, I see exactly what would happen. Don't you?"

Noah's crestfallen. Guilty. PD turns away on their sleeping bag, and when Noah puts his arm around him, the kid feels cold and stiff. He remembers his history, all right. He knows. "OK," he says. "I get it."

"You don't."

"OK, I don't."

PD turns onto his back. Noah curls into him, plays with the few black hairs in the trail leading down from his belly-button. He cries.

"*Whatsamatter?*"

"Just ... Thank you. You have no idea how much I love them both."

"I have an idea. But you got two mothers. I got none."

"You got three aunts."

"It's not the same."

"And you got a tribe. I wish I had a fucking tribe."

"I'll be your tribe."

Then, über-early in the morning (at 5:56, after PD's fire pager went off and he flew out the door), Noah puts on his sneakers and shirt, and walks through the dark woods to Kittatinn Pond. He sits on the shore,

Two Spirits 337

chilly, with Meat Puppet's grey muzzle on his lap, and he looks out at the raft bobbing in the chop. Was it possible? Did it really happen? He and Meat Puppet circle the whole lake. They look for any sign of ... anything. Noah squints, trying to segregate the green tones from the rest of the spectrum. No dice.

They traipse all the way to Shelter Rock, but the fog there is so thick and creepy that Noah doesn't venture into its cave.

Around 7:30, Noah can see clusters of people coming up to PD's porch to consult with the Medicine Sisters. He goes back into town, and sits alone in the shitty little "café" (muffins and coffee) behind the motel. Every once in a while since that April, he's had to put his hand down his pants and untwist his left nut veins. This is one of those times.

"Another muffin, Sugar?" says the waitress, who's toothless and 102 if she's a day. Was she on the leaf? Noah goes back to check on PD, but the room is still empty. He feels a pang that he'll be leaving soon. "Pang" is way too weak a word. How will they manage to see each other? He pulls his hair back into a ponytail and ties it with a blue rubber band. He stares in the mirror. At 8:13 a.m., he texts his Uncle Doc on the Verizon Friends & Family Plan: "Mom's CA gone." He isn't sure why he does it, but he tells himself it's to keep them together. He isn't sure what will happen next. But by 10:30, he and PD are awakened by the sound of Darren Christianson banging on Annalisa's door the next room over. His limousine is parked in the crescent of the New Yorker, and several tribal children are assembling, ogling, entreating to see inside.

"Who's the G-man?" PD asks, looking through the blinds from where he stands in his underwear.

Noah feels his nut veins twist again.

Someone takes a photograph. On behalf of Tigereye Biodynamics, Darren Christianson arrives on Indian land with a half-smile, with all due reverence and honest awe for the Indians, just as Captain John Smith came to the Powhatan. And out the door comes Annalisa, also smiling, and takes her brother in her arms, and spins him around, laughing the whole time.

★★★

Maple bark: sore eyes, cataracts

Choppers, dogs, and scientists. Goons with satellite phones. An alphabet soup of agencies. Lark always knew that the BIA supervised 55 million acres—it was on the test. But what he'd forgotten until the briefing at the Kittakwa Long House – a museum up until this morning – is that those are the mere "surface acres." The Bureau's real mission was managing the 57 million acres of subsurface "mineral estates." These resources are held in trust by the US government, they said, on behalf of American Indians. "Trust" is the operative word.

Trust me.

From hour one, Lark didn't like that the man who appeared to be running the show, a corporate civilian named Christianson, kept referring to the Kittakwas as "natives." What's next—a treatise on the "noble savage?" Tigereye Biodynamics is a government contractor, he's given to understand. But it seems like it's the other way around. There's another one – Hunt from the plane – who's menacingly quiet so far. Seems like the real honcho here.

He doesn't like the subterfuge. They're pretending it's a virus. On the basis of that pretense, they can "legally" violate the sovereignty of the Kittakwa Nation, granted by Andrew Jackson in 1831 (and contravened more or less constantly since, whenever it advantages the good ol' "*US of A-holes*," as one of the protestors' signs proclaims. Yes, there are already protestors, as though these signs were made up in advance. And why not?).

They tent the tribal Long House. They box the displays. They fill it with Army cots.

They blame a couple of middle-aged women, "the Medicine Sisters," for spreading a novel, deadly bug, "Arctadia Flu." They send Lark and a team of NRS, DEA, ATF, and FBI assets to pick through all their potions, tag and catalog everything. A plane at Stewart awaits their collection, and will take it to Quantico or Langley or someplace like that. They arrest the two women, May and June Lightning, and take away all the patients on their porch, for extensive questioning and "involuntary medical sequestration" on aforementioned cots. They land a Tigereye chopper on the shore of the women's pond to the barking of a mad, old dog. They send motorboats through all the kills. Men photograph each flower, shrub, and tree. They spray-paint red "X's" and cyan "O's" on rocks and tree trunks. No one tells Lark what they're looking for.

A hundred of so arrive at Shelter Rock in unmarked, black Mercedes Sprinters. Geiger counters. Hazmat suits and masks. They tent the whole shebang. It's like that scene from *ET.*

They have the right to seize Kittakwa land outright, they say. A crusty elder named Max Lightning – the father of the Medicine Sisters – informs them they have the right to toss his Indian salad. Tigereye Security deploys a Taser on him and the others who protest. They say Lightning is a dangerous ex-con, a rabble-rouser with a history of violence and anti-government action. They are planning to fly him somewhere, but he disappears like the wind into the glen.

Lark sees them putting up posters declaring "Eminent Domain." He sees them taking blood from all the children screaming in the Long House. He sees them raiding the tribal records. He sees them sending scouts to Monticello, Kettering, and Liberty in search of the medical records of all Kittakwas. He sees them surround the local hospital with guards toting M-16s, Why? Paradoxically, no one here is sick—not really. There's no evidence of a virus. And if there were, where are all the NGOs? The National Institutes of Health? The World Health Organization. Why hadn't they issued protective gear for the troops and the agents? Why are they literally keeping volunteer doctors and nurses at the border, but letting in a horde of National Guardsmen dispatched from upstate New York, from New Jersey, and Vermont?

They've cordoned off all the exits and entrances to the Rez. The Army puts manned Humvees at every intersection. They order all personnel – including the NSRs – to patrol at night on ATVs and dirt bikes. He watches CNN reporters sneak in, and sees them arrested for interfering with officials in a health emergency. It's exciting, but it's not what Lark signed on for. It's not the way he wants to earn his wedding money. These people are not the enemy. But these people obviously possess some secret – the "Resource," they keep intoning behind closed doors – that might just get them all killed, just like the old days.

At 7:54 p.m., Lark calls Danica in Salem. "I love you," he says.

"Me, too. What the shit is going on there, Lark? It's all over the news, Baby."

"It's a cluster-fuck. They're using 'neuromuscular incapacitation,' they call it. I saw a memo authorizing deadly force."

"Lark. What does this have to do with you? With trees and rivers and bear cubs?"

"I have no idea. Something. I hope—I'll be OK. I think."

"I'm watching MSNBC. Those frog-looking divers are combing a stream there."

"The Christo—"

The sound makes him drop the phone and hit the planks on the pier where he's been standing, to avoid anyone hearing him. The reports will show the shooting starts in earnest at 8:01 p.m. on November 22th, the day before Thanksgiving. In the first five minutes, 41 people will die. It's a tiny fraction of what's to come.

For this leaf, many must suffer for some to survive.

★★★

Dogwood: fever, diarrhea

Meat Puppet is exhausted. She's aware she's one of a thousand sentries born to guard the shore whenever the Two-Spirit takes the plunge under the raft. Her ancestors have done so since Kittatinn Pond was just a drop in the ocean of lakes the Kittakwas called home. She's always uneasy behind her ribcage until the boy breaks the surface—she's supposed to be. And when he returns to shore with that bag around his shoulder, he always smells funny, and good, and warm, and green, like the Under world. But where is he now? Now divers with toad faces surface with machines that blink and beep, and she barks at them until it hurts her throat, and then one of them points something at her hocks, and all her muscles – including her heart – seize up, and she slumps to the side and cannot take in air, and joins her pedigree in the other world below.

The radios crackle. The divers jump onto their boats and head back to town for reinforcement.

***

Dogbane: dropsy, heart complaints

At an old card table in the basement of Tony Squash's place, Uncle Doc disabuses Noah of his accusation. It's not that Tigereye Bio wants the cure simply to extend the lives of its shareholders and other white brethren. It's that they wish to control the distribution (duh) of the cure throughout the world, as "the environment" – the one, of course, that they created – now threatens to escalate cancer exponentially. But of course they want to control the profits that such a treasure would eventuate.

"You'll never find it," Noah says, and bolts up, thrusting his hand down his pants.

"That still hurts? Stressful—"

"I fucking hate you."

And the shooting outside begins.

Doc locks eyes for a moment with his sister, then Lara, and it becomes real to him that he'll never recover from what's about to happen, although maybe – maybe – it'll be worth it in the end.

Busy at the windows, none of the guards sees Noah run up the stairs to find PD – To what? To apologize? – to show him whose side he's on.

***

Hops: toothache, stomach trouble

On the back dash of Max Lightning's pristine Caddy ('79), a row of crisp old baseball caps with various union and POW emblems looks like a bunch of stern men's heads to Lark, facing the headlights from where his ATV is stopped, straight-on, in the pocked center of Pine Tree Junction Road. He'd been hightailing it into the woods to flee the shooting in town. He wasn't sure whether he'd keep riding, whether he'd hide, or whether he'd play dead somewhere until it was over. He was sure he would not start shooting Kittakwas for some *resource*.

In front of the car now, a young man stands in silhouette, eclipsed by the big car's headlights, and at the same time, shielding his eyes with his left hand from the ATV's light. All Lark can see is that the kid's hair is long—he must be an Indian boy. And when he reaches into the waistband of his jeans with his right hand, reaches all the way down, Lark is certain it's a weapon the boy's after, and all the men in the big car will pile out in a second and shoot him to ribbons, and take him from Danica and his parents and his $10,000 wedding on the beach in East Africa, where all the wedding party will get to cleaning up the dunes with the village children.

So he guns it. The boy tries to dodge the quad, but the left front wheel catches his leg, and drags him under in a flash. Lark can feel the kid's head get run over. He throws up a little acid in his mouth. The engine seizes. Another boy comes out of the Caddy. Just one boy. The rest of the car is empty. The boy wears a cap that says, "AFD."

Lark is stupefied as the boy moves toward him and the body below. He felt this way once before. At the meetinghouse, when he was nine. He was polishing the pews one Sunday evening as penance for using the Lord's name in vain. A woman walked in. He'd never seen her before. She wasn't a Friend. She had long, red, painted nails. She put a cigarette out with her shoe on the high-polished floor of the knave. Without speaking, she started to smack him, again and again, on both sides of his face. He didn't know what he'd done. He tried to weasel away, but she held his belt loop. She tore off his Wrangler corduroys, and started to spank him, holding his neck against the back of the bench. She hit him so hard that he couldn't even scream. She dug her nails up inside him. He bit his bottom lip, and it bled now down his chin and onto the hymnal. Then she stopped. She dropped him in a heap between the pews, and lit another cigarette. And then she left. He never told anyone, and then he told Danica one night – steak night – in their favorite corner of the dining hall. She said it might have been the devil. He suspected as much. He'd never said "God Damn" again, although he used all manner of other curses. She cut her nails that night, and never grew them back again.

Two Spirits

Now he sits on the ATV, inhaling, exhaling, as the boy from the car comes closer. He kneels and checks on his friend below. The friend with the long hair is blond—a white boy. He looks like he's sleeping. Maybe he's sleeping. The Indian boy stands up. In the diffusion of the headlights, Lark can see that one of the kid's eyes is glaucous, like a frozen snow globe, like that serpentine cat's eye gemstone he bought for Danica in Arizona. He's seen this before in the region: giant hogweed often blinds children. And just as he did in the meetinghouse when he was nine, he takes the beating without complaint. A motorcycle helmet might be hard enough to protect the head when the head is in it. But by the same token, the outside shell can shatter a skull in three or four blows at most once the head is out.

★★★

Geranium: eczema, hemorrhoids

"Your hips are wide."
 "Good for skateboarding."
 "My people aren't shaped that way."
 "Are they too wide?"
 "Are you kidding? Perfect. Even covered in mud. Especially covered in mud."
 "Did we fall asleep? I'm sore. But this doesn't hurt anymore."
 "That's good. You were asleep. Not anymore."
 "I like this on you, Puppy. This over here. *Bon.* Mine's not like that."
 "I don't like that on me."
 "I dream about that. How long can we stay Under here? It's so warm. What happened? Something happened, right?"
 "Long as you want. We have everything we need in Kittakwa."
 "But won't I miss my mothers?"
 "I don't know. We have to be each other's tribe like we said. That has to be enough now. Do you think we can be enough for each other now, No-No?"

Author's Note: Who – and *Why* – are the Kittakwa?

Maybe you're wondering how and why a white Jew became obsessed with the POV of a fictional Native American tribe? Maybe you're bothered by my "cultural appropriation;" I hope not "triggered." Perhaps, I pray, you're satisfied that I handled the sensitive nature of another's culture with maximum dignity and not a little élan; that was my mission.

First, this book is about the Hudson Valley of upstate New York, where I grew up, and where my soul roams, though I've flung myself, as people do, far from my Empire State moorings. And N.Y. – both up- and downstate – is all about its ancient genesis. From the names of towns and counties, rivers and lakes where I've lived and played – Hauppauge, Nyack, Cayuga, Seneca, Manhattan – to the roads I've traveled, my home state is tied to its "Indian" ancestry. It is imperative we don't forget, especially as politically a majority of us seem to seek exclusion (not inclusion) in our vision of a Great America. We were not here first. This is borrowed land—at best.

In 1989, as a student at The Colorado College, I first traveled to the Pine Ridge Reservation in South Dakota for a Folklore Anthropology project. How this came to be I'm not embarrassed to confess: I closed my eyes and pointed to a map of the greater Rocky Mountain region. I opened them on Wounded Knee. Had vaguely heard of it. Set off for the long drive. Instantly made friends there. Helped build a road. Helped raise a kid. Had mystical experiences in the sweat lodge. Interviewed extensively an elderly resident whose mother had known Sitting Bull and Standing Elk, and the infamous Massacre. Eventually accepted an offer of "adoption," and the rest is history.

A year later, I got a grant to study and write about the Oglala Sioux. Two of those stories got published and won awards.

Two Spirits 345

Ultimately, I, too, would bury my massacred heart there at Wounded Knee. A reverend named Tom – Anglo, of course – had stomped on it—and the loss of a child and a dog (occurrences so frequent on the Rez you might assume they could be taken in stride: They cannot). Christian missionaries have done more to subdivide and conquer, rape and pillage ("colonize") native peoples than any government, devil's brew, and poverty combined. It is from those hateful religious influences that most modern homophobia on the Rez derives. It is not directly from indigenous beliefs, where various *berdaches* and two-spirits were traditionally revered. Gender fluidity, which has ground-rushed Western culture of late, is much in evidence in many tribes and has been since time before time.

So, having left my vital organ there on Pine Ridge, it continued to accrete story ideas and characters, coalescing with my earlier experiences in the hills and hamlets of New York, slowly building a book – maybe three books – and becoming the Kittakwa Tales. It wasn't until I undertook the A Million Words Away project that I fully understood the extent to which my stories simply *belong* there. It is their home. That's all there is to it.

Sojourns through other locales in Africa, North- and Central America solidified my intrigue over aboriginal peoples. Those ideas melded and became the Kittakwa.

A stray comment by a former colleague, the math professor Bill McGregor, provided the impetus for the Prosper Kit plotline, the bonesetter boys on the steppes of Canada. I originally intended it for the novel *Healing Star*, but I decided, I think rightly, to extract it. It remained homeless until I realized it offered the key – the "solution" – to the loosely-gathered novellas here collected. It's a nice companion to the novel this way, and interleaves the two books.

I haven't quite liquidated the Kittakwa narratives in my still-operating neocortex. I hope you haven't seen the last of them. Or me.

—Ian Blake Newhem
West Hollywood, Calif.
February 2020

Acknowledgments

The author expresses his heartfelt appreciation to the following:
Firstly, to my father, Stephen Jon Newman, may the Flying Matzo Ball Monster rest his soul, for taking me through the trails of Putnam and Duchess Counties, N.Y. when I was young, & for slaking my lust for the outdoors, for all things rural and rustic. We talked of myths and mist and mysteries galore there. I miss you.

Moreover for my mother, Maris Barbara Newman, RIP, who died just eight days after her beloved Steve, still telling stories to herself and to me.

The Oglala Sioux People and the population of the *Wazí Aháŋhaŋ Oyáŋke* (the Pine Ridge Indian Reservation), especially the Twiss family of Rapid City and Kyle, S.D., for their generosity in welcoming me into their family way back when.

The Colorado College for awarding me the grant to study and write about the Oglala Sioux and the greater Native America, also way back when. I couldn't possibly have gotten a better education than at CC.

Jared Joseph Jobe and Dana Nossaman Keilman for accompanying me on my first forays to "the Rez."

The Mountaindale N.Y. Fire Department & First Aid Squad, and the Sullivan County N.Y. Fire Training Center: Thank you, Sirs, may I (please *not*) have another?

Walt Winchenbach III for providing ample cranberry-pumpkin bread, emotional succor, entree to "the Park," and etc. during the whole AMWA project.

Treza Mirakhor for she knows what.

Jacob Glover and Alex Sorondo for their editorial prowess in reviewing these hastily-prepared stories for accuracy, consistency, and style, such as it is, on such short notice.

Benjamin Templeton Cooke for all his backing, personal, professional, and public. Likewise, Matt Pritchard for providing a backbone from my brain.

Norman Mallard for interpreting me in his special language of collage—more on Norman next.

HH Leonards and Ted Spero, proprietors of the O Museum in the Mansion, Washington, D.C., for their generosity in providing me an arts residency and way more than that—For their respect and devotion to "All things counter, original, spare, strange." They've created a monument to creativity in Dupont Circle. Please, please, give it a visit. You won't be disappointed.

Lastly, but no way leastly, my partner Ángel Ramon Valenzuela Diaz – 56 percent Native American! – for his great good love & empathy, and his love of good books.

—*Norman Mallard: A wee bit about the ar-teest*—

Juiced and jazzed and generally jiggy that the great collage/assemblage artist Norman Mallard agreed to create eight original art pieces herein.

I worked with Mallard once before, when he provided supercool mood boards for *IRL*, a TV series I developed (which you'll probably see more of soon). And I'm honored to own a Mallard collage, mixed media on wood, which hangs in my home in WeHo.

Mallard hails from Akron, Ohio where he works as a fulltime graphic designer and occasional fine artist. He's an avid reader (reading at least one avid a week), and we've spent scores of hours discussing (dissing, digressing) literature and art in all its forms.

He grew up in Norfolk, Va., trained in Atlanta, Ga., spent a few formative years in Richmond, Va. (a town he adores), and settled in Washington, D.C., where he thought he'd stay forever. But a twist of fate led him to Ohio, where he'd never even visited. He finds he loves it there, too. Far from a tortured artiste, he's more a happy little seedling who grows wherever he's planted.

Professionally, Mallard has worked with many clients over his long career, ranging from shipping companies to banks to nonprofits to small business to universities to governmental- (and non-governmental) agencies. He's created ad campaigns, flyers/brochures, websites, postcards, annual (and non-annual) reports, and logos. He likes logos best. For 95 percent of his career he worked at agencies and design firms, but is now on his own—and has surprised himself by loving it.

Mallard is self-taught as an artist, but brings his strong design training to the table when he creates. His preferred medium is Collage/Assemblage (He likes sticking things together.) His work often employs juxtaposition and humor to make sense of an ever-changing world, and his reliance on images and graphics from the past speak to this.

Humble to an extreme, he only occasionally shows his work publicly – National Collage Society's annual juried show (twice); Summit Artspace's juried competitions (thrice) – mostly showing in his basement studio to family and friends.

Until now.

I sought out Mallard not only because of the strong narrative bent in his work but because I think he's the living artist I know who best exemplifies a certain imperative occasioned by the insane barrage of media (images, icons, idioms) heaped on us daily by technology and the always "on" world. Mallard's art seems to me to seek to reassemble in small, more digestible bytes his ideas of an ostensibly confusing but perfectly sensibly put-together world. How does everything connect? Each of his pieces represents one mashed-up, mixed-media mélange *re*-presenting some aspect, some angle, some view of the whole of our modern existence. But interfused through its constituents. As though his brain's a machine that can dissect the universe slice by slice. Animalia, technology, time, humanity, gender, geography, language, etc., all exist, jumbled, interpenetrating, comfy, juxtaposed, on a single plane.

Wow.

A MILLION WORDS AWAY
12 BOOKS VS. 1 BRAIN TUMOR ™

Ian Blake Newhem is a 50-year-old writer who was diagnosed with an oligodendroglioma (nicknamed Ollie), a brain tumor sitting on the language expression center of his left frontal lobe. Before he loses his language ability, he will write 12 books of fiction, one a month, in multiple genres and formats, with multiple collaborators. One million words—all in a year.

For more about A Million Words Away, more books, the AMWA podcast/blog, and to subscribe:

Patreon.com/AMillionWordsAway

AMillionWordsAway.com

And now, listen to "Professor Blake" live on *The Operative Word*, Sun nights at 7PM Pacific, on KABC talk radio 790.